Dazed, every fiber in her body shrieking with pain and exhaustion, she lurched down the alley, Lance bearing the brunt of her weight. "Leave me behind!" she gasped. Each time she came down on that right leg, pain knifed her bones. She felt sick. "I'm slowing you down!"

"Shut up," Lance grunted. Sweat gleamed on his face and neck. "If we can get out of this alley . . ." He stiffened. "Oh, shit."

Viki followed his gaze. A car—black, tinted windows—skidded to a screeching stop in the mouth of the alley. All four doors popped open. She looked frantically right, left—and there! "Service door, left, *left*!"

Lance kicked once, twice. The door popped. The service corridor was dark and narrow; to their right was a door that led down to a basement. Lance fried the lock and kicked the door as a diversion before taking off down the hall, hauling a limping Viki.

*Not going to make it.* Any second, she expected a bullet to slam into her back or a laser to burn a hole into her spine. Then, just as they reached the connecting door to the lobby, Viki caught movement out of the corner of her left eye. Before she could shout a warning, their attacker launched a fierce turn-kick that hammered Lance's chest. Off balance, Lance reeled as their attacker followed with a crescent kick to Lance's face. The blow connected with a crackling sound like smashing eggshells. Blood spurted from Lance's nose, and he caromed off of Viki. They tumbled to the floor.

Viki came down on her right hip. She screamed, and her pistol spun away. Frantic, fighting against a sudden swell of vertigo, she fumbled for the gun—too late.

Their attacker scooped up the pistol and jammed the weapon so close to her face that Viki smelled burnt metal and spent powder. Her eyes clicked from barrel to hand to face—and then she froze as both she and her assailant gasped.

"*Tai-shu?*" Viki whispered. Then: "*Katana?*"

### MECHWARRIOR™
### DARK AGE

# DRAGON RISING

### A BATTLETECH™ NOVEL

## Ilsa J. Bick

A ROC BOOK

ROC
Published by New American Library, a division of
Penguin Group (USA) Inc., 375 Hudson Street,
New York, New York 10014, USA
Penguin Group (Canada), 90 Eglinton Avenue East, Suite 700, Toronto,
Ontario M4P 2Y3, Canada (a division of Pearson Penguin Canada Inc.)
Penguin Books Ltd., 80 Strand, London WC2R 0RL, England
Penguin Ireland, 25 St. Stephen's Green, Dublin 2,
Ireland (a division of Penguin Books Ltd.)
Penguin Group (Australia), 250 Camberwell Road, Camberwell, Victoria 3124,
Australia (a division of Pearson Australia Group Pty. Ltd.)
Penguin Books India Pvt. Ltd., 11 Community Centre, Panchsheel Park,
New Delhi - 110 017, India
Penguin Group (NZ), cnr Airborne and Rosedale Roads, Albany,
Auckland 1310, New Zealand (a division of Pearson New Zealand Ltd.)
Penguin Books (South Africa) (Pty.) Ltd., 24 Sturdee Avenue,
Rosebank, Johannesburg 2196, South Africa

Penguin Books Ltd, Registered Offices:
80 Strand, London WC2R 0RL, England

First published by Roc, an imprint of New American Library,
a division of Penguin Group (USA) Inc.

First Printing, February 2007
10  9  8  7  6  5  4  3  2  1

## ACKNOWLEDGMENTS

Writing a book, like raising a child, takes a village.

In mine, I am privileged to have the most supportive of editors in Sharon Turner Mulvihill, who blends intuitive insight with good, old-fashioned book sense and a continued willingness to push at the margins. For all her faith, great good humor and diligence, I am supremely grateful.

My deepest thanks also go to:

Kelly Bonilla, for answering more than one panicky e-mail about design specs;

Øystein Tvedten, for always managing to turn over rocks to find answers;

Randall Bills, for combing out all those nits and patiently replying to every inane question;

Ben Rome, who not only suffered through my Starbucks withdrawals but was instrumental in hashing out historical particulars for some of the major characters—and who, after a mind-numbing marathon game at GenCon, also coined the following definition for "pulling an Ilsa" and thus ensured my place in GenCon apocrypha:

> **ilsa** (il-SA) *v* **1:** to consistently roll one under the minimum required to-hit number, followed by selective curse words **2:** to curse every die touched with poor rolls [countered by a phaedra]; i.e., "To pull an **ilsa**." Ex: *The* Cygnus *ilsaed every attack against the* Jupiter, *allowing the enemy forces to approach unmolested.*

*For David, the wind beneath my wings*

# PROLOGUE

## *Aji:* Future Play

**B**rilliant. Just absobloodylutely *brilliant*. Not so bad when the johnny laughed and called her a fat black slag. Her fault, not getting the bling up front. No, what was bad was when he up and bashed her nose.

Sweetie Pie struggled out of the Loading Dock Bar on a balloon of moist air that reeked of cigarette smoke, rancid beer and second-shift dockworkers stewed in grime and oily sweat. The wind snatched the door, clapping it shut with a *boom*. Bone-numbing blades of cold wind cut tears from her eyes, and her ruined nose and split lower lip throbbed to life. Shivering, she huddled in a pool of watery yellow light, her chocolate-brown skin washed to the color of muddy piss.

*Got to get home. Clean up. Do a pinch of dust, buoy the spirits.*

Sweetie Pie set off, wobbling, against the wind. Her stiletto heels ticked and cracked against the icy ferrocrete. She had to think what to do. She couldn't pretend there hadn't been no war what trashed the economy and let loose a flood of refugees besides, Armitage being about the only city the Dracs ain't reduced to rubble. Maybe Halstead Station. Jobs there, with Katana Tormark moving her command kit 'n caboodle to the planet. Chances of getting off the game was better *there* and . . .

Something—a premonition, maybe, a tickle at the back of her brain—spiked her awareness like a nail. Her eyes flicked left, darted right, and then she spied them: two bulky silhouettes in the semidark of a warehouse doorway.

*Oh, sweet buggery Christ.* Her chest squeezed with apprehension. She stopped dead under a streetlamp. Planted her feet wide to get her balance, wished she wasn't in heels because she couldn't run. Hoped the light would save her. Worried it wouldn't.

The men sauntered forward, the darkness peeling away. One was much bluffer and very tall, with broad shoulders and hands wide as shovels. Both wore identical black pea-coats and gray, grease-stained mechanics trousers. As they got close, the shorter one called, "Got a little time, Pie?"

A little of the tension bled from her shoulders. "Oi, Bill, is that you?"

"The very article," Bill said. A black watch cap clamped his scalp, and his rough features were ruddy with cold. He squinted. "Darlin', happened to your mug?"

"Client. Whacked me, said I weren't worth the price. So I'm knackered. Walking back to me flophouse for a cuppa and a kip."

"That so?" Bill's smile bared the smeary orange teeth of a duster. Quick as a whip, he snagged her right forearm and reeled her in. "What say we get nice and comfy right 'ere? What ya say, darlin'?"

Up close, his breath stank of curdled milk and sickly sweet, day-old dust. "Oi, now, Bill," she said, fighting to keep the quaver out of her voice. "Ain't nothing you wants I can't do you, but I'm all banged up, and—"

She gave a short scream as the men moved in fast, so fast she didn't have time to react. Bill had her by the arms, and then the tall one was behind, clapping a horny palm over her mouth and ruined nose. Through a starburst of pain, she bucked as his arm snaked round her neck and squeezed. Panicked, her lungs burning, she writhed, twist-ing, the blood pounding in her ears, her temples.

Then, somehow, she was on the ground. Cold palmed her back. Bill's hands fumbled beneath her skirt, his fingers tearing at her waist, her thighs. The tall one loomed; his right hand squeezed her throat, his left pinned her wrists above her head, and she couldn't breathe, no air. She hurt, please sweet Jesus, she couldn't . . .

"Hey!" A man's voice. An arc of bright light scything the darkness. "HEY!"

"Wuh?" Bill froze, a thin, silvery rope of drool trembling

from his lower lip. Then he was reeling back, his eyes wide. "Christ, what . . . ?"

Suddenly, the vise round her neck was gone. Her hands were free, and she reeled in air on a wheezy shriek. The cold air hacked her throat. Dimly, she heard shouts, the heavy thud of men's boots on ferrocrete, and then a singing whine. Pushing up, she braced herself on wobbly arms. Her mouth tasted brackish, like wet metal, and she spat a foamy gob of bloody saliva.

Then, a light played over her body. She winced, put up a hand to shield her eyes from the glare.

"You all right?" The policeman hooked a hand round her right bicep as she swayed to her feet. He had no mittens, and his fingers were very cold.

"I'm all right," she lied, just wanting to get away. "Ain't-cha going after them?"

"They're tagged. Let's take care of you first," the policeman said. His light swept her neck from side to side—and then something in his voice changed. "Nasty bruises, though they don't show well with your coloring."

His tone sent prickles down the back of her neck. *Smug, like* he *could do it better.*

"It's all right," she said, a little desperate now. "Just need a good bath, a coupla painkillers and I'll be right as rain."

He was silent. Her heart hammered her ribs. *Let me go, just let me go, please let me . . .*

"Well," he said, finally, "if you're sure. I'll give you a lift."

It was only then that she realized he'd never released his hold, and there was something, well, *off.* With his hand. There was just enough light to see it. Her gaze dropped, and, then, she inhaled, short, sharp, horrified, the ball of a scream stuck in her throat—because his hand, what she *saw* . . .

His hand was as white as the belly of a dead eel. His skin *wrinkled*, like the folds of a latex glove several sizes too large. As if his skin had drifted from its moorings of tendon and muscle.

As if his skin was dead.

# PART ONE

*Fuseki:* Let the Games Begin

# 1

**Aomori Mountains, Dieron**
**Former Prefecture II, Republic of the Sphere**
**13 June 3136**

**O**kay, so call her pissy, but when the chance came to kick some serious butt, Katana jumped at it. Who wouldn't? Brand-spanking-new *Hitotsune Kozo*, grab the solid weight of that joystick, and get down and dirty dealing out some fine, old-fashioned destruction and mayhem. What, she's gonna say: *Gosh, no, let's have lunch*?

Only things weren't turning out so well.

High in her *Hitotsune Kozo*'s cockpit, Katana labored up the western wall of a canyon over the equivalent of a moonscape pocked with blast craters and studded with mounds of debris and jumbled trees hacked to kindling. Immediately to her north, a tremendous river thundered in an immense cataract. Three hundred meters below, fast-moving, silver-blue water battered massive boulders with a deep boom, like the roar of autocannons.

Clots of dense black smoke boiled from a phalanx of wildfires all along her western flank. Some of the fires had been ignited by enemy weapons, but most, like the evergreens, had been set deliberately. A damn good tactic: The fires made hash of her sensors and the soot-choked smoke smeared fingers of thick grime over her canopy.

She'd been maneuvering through foothills and mountains for several hours, and although her own legs didn't feel the strain, her 'Mech's temp was inching up, like a hiker working her way to heatstroke. She'd taken hits these past few days, too many too close for comfort on her torso. Enough to shred two-thirds of her armor, most of it dead center over her munitions store, right where it counted most.

A man's voice, deep and weary, on her comm: "Anything?"

"Nope. Where are you, Theodore?"

"Your four o'clock, other side of the canyon," Theodore said. Katana pivoted and then spied a soot-smeared *naginata* blade on its long distal tang ripping a seam in an inky curtain of smoke. Sun glare reflected by the titanium blade winked in fitful bursts, like the frantic semaphore of a ship in distress. A second later, the V-shaped hulk of Theodore Kurita's *Shiro* hove into view on a lip of rock along a scalloped ridge. The sun bounced twinkling stars off the glittery gold and rich oxblood accents of his 'Mech's *kabuto*, with its modified *fukigayeshi* wings, and *do* scarred gray and blackened by ash. The *Shiro*'s armor was scored from missile hits, a ragged gash jagging down the 'Mech's left thigh, exposing bundles of myomer—as if a drunken surgeon had slashed through skin and flayed muscle with a blunt scalpel. Another slash, lumpier at the margins, had chewed away armor perilously close to one of the *Shiro*'s three right-torso missile stores. The *Shiro* raised in a salute the *naginata* blade wedded to its left fist.

"Gotcha," Katana said. She rested the *Kozo*'s left leg on a rocky shelf some hundred and twenty meters above the canyon floor. "Careful. That eastern ridge is kind of rotten, and the wall's steeper."

"You're not exactly in the most defensible position. All it'll take are a couple good punches, and you'll get knocked right off that slope."

*Yeah, yeah, yeah.* She backhanded sweat from her neck. When she shifted, her couch made a wet sucking sound. "I figure a traverse is better than a head-on climb. Otherwise, my autocannon'll be punching rock. What's your status?"

"How many different kinds of bad are there?" Then, without waiting for her reply: "Look, this is between you and me, okay? No one else on this channel, so just listen."

"Listen to what?" Of course, she *knew* what he'd say because she knew Theodore. Their friendship had been forged in battle, and a long JumpShip trip home.

"Katana, my weapons' status has gone from bad to the other side of crappy. I'm out of autocannon. I've got two racks of LRMs left. I know you want to win—"

"It's not just about winning."

"Bull. This is about you being the new kid on the block. I'm on your side, remember? You know I won't interfere, not when the Combine's watching. But a good commander listens. She's flexible. Now, it's just plain suicidal for us to be out front here, with no reinforcements, and I don't like this canyon. We should withdraw."

"No," Katana said. *Oh, don't be an ass. He's right, and you know he's right.* "This is our last chance to take him. It's my op."

"I know. That's what I said." More silence. Katana could picture Theodore in his command couch: his tanned leathery features creased with sweat, his lips thinned to a crack above his square chin and those frosty Kurita-blue eyes set with determination . . .

But there was something . . . *wrong.* Theodore's reflexes were slower, his *Shiro*'s gait more herky-jerky. Yesterday, he'd made a misstep, coming down hard on his left leg before compensating with his right in a wildly exaggerated arc. And then his 'Mech *froze.* Right leg rigid and locked at the knee. Just for a few seconds, but she saw it.

A sudden revelation: *So maybe this is also about* him *saving face, not exposing weakness.*

She had to respect that. He was heir, after all. She exhaled. "Okay, we're gone. I'll just . . ."

She broke off as alarms screamed. Her eyes snapped to her HUD winking to a fiery red. Incoming, but not targeting *her*! Targeting . . .

"Theodore!" she screamed. "Look out!"

Roiling emerald fire punched the *Shiro* so hard Theodore swayed, reeled and nearly toppled.

"Theodore!" Katana jerked left, tracked the source and . . . *there!* A *Zeus*, high above, blasting through curtains of black smoke like a demon released from the maw of Hell.

*But* I'm *the one he wants! Got to get Theodore out of here before . . .*

"Theodore, back off!" Katana shouted, already pivoting left, leaning into the mountain, bringing her pulse lasers to bear. But her aim was awkward, her angle hampered by the mountain, and her shots blasted wide. Throttling up, she banged her 'Mech forward, punishing the rock, desperately wishing she had the claws of a *Shockwave* so she could grab hold and haul ass to the top. Her right leg jackhammered the rock, but then she felt the shifting of rock and scree, and she slipped. Gasping, she threw her body left, a motion that translated to a swooping arc that only shoved her 'Mech off its center of gravity. As she began to fall into the rock, instinct took over. She straightened her left arm, the impact shivering all the way into the cockpit. The arm groaned as seventy-five tons of endosteel drove her pulse lasers straight into the rock, and then her left arm jammed tight.

"*Damn it!*" She yanked back, trying to extricate her lasers, ignoring the warning shriek of her DI as her temp climbed. She could figure out the problem without the help of her diagnostic interpretation computer, thank you very much.

"Katana!" Theodore yelled, his voice hitching. There was a series of dull sonic booms, and Katana spared a quick glance and, horrified, saw a lance of saucer-shaped *Sholagar* fighters scream from the sky. Lasers pricked the *Shiro's* back, needling the cockpit, just as a spread of LRMs bulleted against Theodore's right torso, directly over his store of missiles. A blinding series of explosions blossomed bright and hard as suns gone nova: *BOOM-BOOM-BOOM!* The roars reverberated across the canyon, redoubling as echoes—and then Theodore's armor plating turned to sludge, to molten welts, the edges humping like badly formed scars. The *Sholagars* sped by the *Shiro,* then broke right and left, turning now, rocketing for the 'Mech, lasers slicing away the *Shiro's* twin banners, the ones decorated with the Kurita dragon.

"Katana!" Theodore shouted, his voice broken by bursts of static. "My firing system's frozen, locked out, and my emergency dump's off-line!"

*My God, he's too close to the edge, too* close! "Theodore! You can't do any more good here, just get the *hell* . . . !" She broke off as the air overhead screamed with the passage of LRMs loosed by the *Zeus,* rocketing streamers of death. She gauged their trajectory, and understood their enemy's strategy, too late. "Theodore! The *ridge!* Back up, *back up!*"

But Theodore was already reeling, the *Shiro* lurching left, its leg swinging to broaden its stance—and then the 'Mech froze, right leg locked and still too close to the edge.

Helpless, Katana watched as the missiles plowed into the ridge, shattering rock like fragile glass, the concussive power of the blasts so strong that chunks of the mountain rained over her canopy, bulleting against ferroglass and armor. The ridge splintered, and the rock beneath Theodore's feet disintegrated. The edge crumbled to dust—with Theodore still there, still frozen.

And then the rock face suddenly slid free, like an iceberg calving from a glacier. The *Shiro* rode a wave of pulverized rock and debris that evaporated beneath its feet. Screaming, Theodore was in free fall, pulling an avalanche in his wake, his blade snapping in two as his 'Mech rebounded off a protruding rock shelf, the *Shiro* turning a somersault just before its munitions blew. A series of blasts, each more powerful than the next, billowed fiery orange and bloodred.

And then there was only silence because Theodore was gone.

"*Onore!*" Katana roared, the simmering magma of her fury erupting in an explosion of venomous hate. "*Koro shite yaru!* I'm going to *kill* you, you son of a *bitch*!" She swung round, brought her autocannon to bear. But the *Zeus* was already on the move, disappearing as it retreated from the rim. The *Sholagars* had regrouped but very far away and circling, not initiating another attack run. Waiting. And then, when the *Zeus* maneuvered onto a jutting portion of ridgeline north of her position, she understood at once.

*Long-range missiles, and me trapped like a fly on sticky paper. No way to get free unless I try to break off the arm, but then . . .*

A flash as her adversary's missiles roared from their rack, arrowing right for her but . . . What was going on? She gaped, wondered if her enemy had lost his mind, because she saw that the missiles were going to fall short, not hit her at *all*. . . .

"Oh, my God," she said, a clutch of sickening cold knotting her stomach and then flowing like ice water through her veins.

He wasn't aiming at her at all. Instead, he'd targeted the canyon wall.

The missiles thundered into the canyon wall above and short of where she sprawled, her lasers mired in a trap devised by her folly and petty pride. Beneath her feet, the ground shook with the violence of an earthquake, of the earth splitting in two. Then she wasn't standing on solid ground anymore but hanging for a brief, tenuous two or perhaps three seconds before her laser arm, unable to hold her 'Mech's tonnage, snapped.

The shrieking ululation of alarm klaxons mingled with her screams as she tumbled down amid rocks and debris. Her *Kozo* skidded right and then hit with a tremendous *BOOOM*, the autocannon mounted on its right shoulder shearing and then tearing free as the 'Mech turned head over heels. Trapped in her command couch, her body bounced and strained against her harness, jouncing like the hopeless struggles of an insect stuck in a web. The world dissolved into a gray blur and black smoke, spinning, cartwheeling . . .

Desperate, she wrenched her upper torso, trying to fling her 'Mech flat, and flailed with her right arm. Her 'Mech responded, mirroring her movements: its twin-headed dragon sickle flashed forward, grabbing at rock. The principle was the same as an ice climber using his ax to stop a fatal slide. She felt the sickle snag and leaned into it, grimacing with the effort, the 'Mech's temperatures now so high that the scream of her alarms was one continual, piercing note.

Against all odds, she stopped falling. The sickle caught, and held. It shouldn't have. The sickle should've snapped because a 'Mech was proportionately so much heavier than a human—but it didn't.

Yes, *yes!* Her heart rebounded with a tremendous thump against her ribs. *Not much time, get moving, get moving!* Grunting, she swung her legs, battering the rock, trying to gouge footholds. But then her ax jerked and pulled free with a groan of metal, and her *Kozo* peeled away from the mountain, its limbs splayed like a four-pointed star.

Beyond her canopy, the sky retreated and grew darker as she plunged toward the river. She couldn't eject, couldn't use the jump jets. She hurtled down the abyss and suddenly understood the despair of the damned.

She hit the water, very hard. Hard enough that it was as if the water were solid, an open palm that smacked her in the back. Momentum slammed her body, trying to thrust her out of her command couch. Her harness, strained beyond the breaking point, ruptured, and she barely had time to throw her arms up to shield her face before she smacked face-first into her canopy. Later, the diagnostics would show that the bones of her face shattered with the impact. Water rushed over her canopy, and the sky—so far away now— wavered, shimmered, disappeared.

But not before a final image was forever branded on her brain: the *Zeus*, wreathed by flame, a nightmare demon from an underworld she couldn't imagine.

And then everything fizzled, broke apart into multicolored pixels as the sim terminated and went black.

Silence.

Then a voice she heard even over the roar of her heart in her temples and the bellows of her gasping lungs:

"I believe," said Matsuhari Toranaga, Warlord of New Samarkand, "you are quite, quite dead."

# 2

*Imperial City, Luthien*
*Pesht Military District, Draconis Combine*
*13 June 3136*

Her personal bodyguard, Joji Ashido, had pulled back the easternmost shoji overlooking a kidney-shaped pond ornamented with jade-green saucers of water lilies and the paler hues of a lush silver water grass. The Kuritas' latest treasure perched on a high berm: a weeping cherry crowned with purple-pink blooms so plump and densely packed its branches bowed.

Yet, in the midst of this tranquility, Emi Kurita spied a storm brewing in the distance. Slate-colored, heavy-bellied clouds unfurled, loosing a pillow of air that smelled of ozone and wet metal.

*And so.* Emi Kurita knelt upon a tatami mat and tipped

fragrant, steaming green tea from a *tetsubin* iron teapot into a peacock-blue, crackle-glazed ceramic cup. *Let the games commence.*

Proffering the cup, she said, "Brother, you must not take this so to heart. *Tai-shu* Toranaga had superior forces, positioned to better advantage. You did your best."

Grunting, Theodore accepted the tea with his right hand, something Emi noted with dismay. He'd shaved—nicking his throat several times, judging from the beads of dried blood. There was more silver brushing his temples than she remembered, and he'd lost weight. His cheeks were sharper, his chin a little more square. He was haggard, as if wearied beyond fatigue.

And yet . . . and yet, his attire revealed much about his state of mind: a pair of flowing black *hakama* trousers and matching *keiko-gi* jacket, belted at the waist with a twist of Kurita-red sash. A man ready for *kendo kata*, and other drills aimed at honing a warrior's mind. A man prepared for battle.

*But are you a match for this, the fight of your life, my brother?*

Replacing the pot upon a matching round iron trivet, she peered into her tea, as if to divine its mysteries, or their future. But the tea was just tea.

Theodore said, "A shame my best wasn't good enough. I couldn't hold my own."

"You performed admirably," Emi said, her tone a study in neutrality. *Yes, I will speak to him of our shared disaster, but I must approach this with caution. Bad enough his body betrays him. He doesn't need a sister's sharp tongue to cut him to the bone.* "Besides, you were a tad outnumbered."

"I know," Theodore said. "The hell of it was Katana really didn't have a choice. Toranaga issued a challenge. She couldn't very well refuse, not in front of Father."

"Would you have wanted her to?"

"No. It's just . . . Emi, she brought on this defeat herself, maybe to prove how tough she is. I don't know. If she'd only listened—"

"She did not, and that is her bitter pill, not yours. Brother, you cannot save her from herself. She will either fall, or rise and make Dieron whole."

"With what, exactly? She's got a fractured district, virtually surrounded on all sides by enemies nibbling away at the margins. Even the worlds we thought we'd sewn up—Styx, Saffel—they're still not completely secured. Katana's got to push back *and* forward at the same time, with limited resources and, on some planets, populations that aren't exactly welcoming. The task is nearly impossible: raising troops and matériel, while fending off attacks in her realm." Theodore stared down into his cup, his face set in something just shy of a glower. "Imagine how much more trouble she'll have when Father names the new warlord for the Benjamin District tomorrow. Then she'll have to watch her back, too, and then there's Toranaga."

"I thought we were all part of the same, happy Combine."

Theodore gave her a narrow look. "Don't playact at naïveté, Sister. It's beneath you. Katana was Toranaga's enemy today, but he surely is poised to become *our* enemy tomorrow."

"You mean Yori." Emi sipped from her cup. The slightly sweet green tea was still quite hot and scorched her tongue. Yori Kurita had arrived with her patron, Toranaga, a week ago. There were wheels upon wheels turning in that young head, yet she carried herself with a self-possessed, cautious air that bordered on chilly. "Yori is a threat, even if she does not know or wish it. She may be the granddaughter of a bastard, but she's taken our name. That reveals which way the wind blows, and it hails from New Samarkand, Brother. This may yet be the storm that sinks us."

Theodore gave her an odd look. "You've grown blunt, Sister."

"I am Keeper of the House Honor, but I am my father's daughter, your sister, and a Kurita above all else. Why do you think Father installed the sim in the palace? To broadcast that we still have plenty of teeth." She added, more gently, "Though I do not think we saw yours, Brother."

"Since when have you become a critic?"

She touched his arm to soften the sting. "Since I drilled *kendo* with you, Brother. I know how formidable you can be."

"And *I* remember you ducking under my *shinai* and

thwacking my bottom more times than I care to recall."
Theodore grinned with genuine pleasure at the memory.
"We were happier then."

"You mean before Mother and Ryuhiko," Emi said. It
was not a question, and it hurt her heart when Theodore's
smile dribbled away, like water leaking through a sieve.
But she needed her brother to be realistic and face facts.
"Brother, *kimi o ai shiteru.* You know that."

"I love you, too." Theodore's voice was hoarse. He
blinked and looked away, his gaze drifting to the garden.
"That's a lovely cherry tree."

"Yes, it is. But all flowers fade, Brother. Everything dies,
even the most beautiful, the strongest. Even the best may
die young."

"Die young." And then he did meet her eyes, and what
she saw there dug a talon of grief into her heart. "Don't
you mean *me,* Emi?"

They stared at one another for several seconds, the silence filled by the warble of a distant songbird. Finally, Emi
said, "Chomie hasn't produced an heir. You must continue
the line. Father will die someday, or he will become infirm.
Then you will lead, but you cannot if you have no heir.
You and Chomie have tried for years, and failed, and you
are not getting younger. That is Yori's danger, Brother. She
is young; she is a Kurita; she is wedded to Toranaga by
will or design, and that could not be worse than the devil
himself. Why not take a lover? Perhaps Katana—"

"No." Theodore's tone was flat, final. "Not Katana. Not
because she isn't attractive or strong, she *is.* But I'll not plant
my seed in Katana, or any other woman. I love my *wife.*"

"Your duty is to the Combine."

Theodore flared. "It is no service if I betray my wife. I
can no more contemplate that than . . . well," he made
a vague gesture, "than *you* might entertain compromising
tradition by taking a lover."

"Tradition?" Emi arched an eyebrow. "Omi Kurita's
spinning in her grave."

"Don't be coy. You might break with tradition, but I
suspect you'd do so only for life or death. Anyway, we both
know that this goes beyond having another woman, Emi."
He let out his breath in a long sigh of weariness tinged

with despair. "The curse is in our *blood*. All the wishing in the world won't change that."

Emi waited a beat. "Do you have an alternative, a plan?"

"Yes. But Chomie's against it."

"For heaven's sake, why?"

Mute, he shook his head, shrugged. Stared at his hands, the right covering the ball of his left fist. When he didn't speak, Emi said, "Brother, are you well? Have you seen a physician?" When he shook his head, she pressed, "But you must. You *know* you must. You are not concerned enough already? Despite your defeat today? Despite the fact that I saw your right leg, how it locked? Despite the fact that you drink tea with your right hand? You are left-handed, Brother. Your *Shiro* has been modified, the *naginata* blade wedded to your left hand, not the right. If there is nothing wrong, show me your hand."

"This is absurd." Theodore reached for his tea. "I don't have a problem. This is pure fool—" He broke off as his body betrayed him, as the fingers of his left hand and then the hand itself quaked. Tea sloshed over his fingers.

Emi tried reaching for him. "Theodore, it's all right, it's all—"

"Damn you, *damn* you!" Wrenching free, Theodore sprang to his feet and unleashed his fury in a sudden howl, hurling the cup with all his might. The cup tumbled through the air, end over end, spattering tea and shattering against a far wall with such force that Ashido, standing sentry outside the room, was there in a second, his hand on the butt of a laser pistol.

"Mistress." Ashido was as tall as Theodore, but his black hair was much longer, spilling across his broad shoulders. His deep brown eyes took in Theodore, and then clicked to Emi. "There was a—" he seemed to choose the word with care, "commotion."

"It's fine," Emi said. She didn't even try to smile. "Thank you, Joji. You may go. We'll take care of the mess later." She waited until Ashido bowed and then retreated before going to her brother. "Theodore, we can talk about this, we can . . ."

"There's nothing to talk about," Theodore said. His words were clipped and terse. His hands fisted, released, and fisted again. "I'm fine. There's nothing to worry about."

"Oh, Brother." And then, before he could pull away, Emi cradled her brother's trembling left hand in hers. When she pressed his fingers to her lips, tears wet her cheeks. "Mine own brother, my heart," she said, and then her voice broke. "You know there is."

# 3

## Imperial City, Luthien
## 13 June 3136

**V**incent Kurita dipped an ink stick into water, tapped away a stray drop, and then bent to grind his stick against his *suzuri* stone. This was the magic: transforming this stick of glue and camphor, soot from burnt pinewood and lamp-black, into creamy black ink. His shoji was open to the garden, and he worked on the balcony, his easel a long, low meditation table that normally rested alongside his suit of armor.

He hadn't painted for a very long time. But the urge had come on the heels of his dreams. Nightmares, really: desperate and black. Violent. Those dreams meant something, though. Vincent was not a religious man, or superstitious. His wife—his Ramiko whom he married very young and loved well before she was taken from him—she was always the one for that, chanting her prayers and divining the workings of spirits and demons. Yet he *did* believe in the workings of the unconscious mind, and so he painted, adopting the same kind of restful alertness he brought to the dojo and a good, sweaty session of *kendo kata*.

He painted. His brush scored snowy-white rice paper, the *kami*, with black whorls. Odd, now that he thought of it: The *kami* also were the gods of Shinto, those divine forces of nature that imbued a waterfall or a storm with its power. Vincent paused, bamboo brush in midair, not really seeing what he painted but turning over this new concept. The *kami* were like avatars, crossing over from their spirit world to this physical, tangible world. Yet they were not omnipotent.

*Even Amaterasu, that fiery sun goddess born from the left eye of Izanagi, had to resort to magic to see into the future.*

*Ah.* And now Vincent let go of a small sigh, a tension he didn't even realize he'd held easing from his shoulders. Paint and let the mind roam, and whatever was important would surely surface. "Because there we are again," he murmured. "At Katana, her Amaterasu, and at this crossroads."

All right then, what of Katana Tormark? So, he'd made her warlord of a still-incomplete district and left her to her own devices. Was it fair? No. Was Katana probably, as she would say, pissed off beyond all reason? Probably. Was it the way of the Combine? Absolutely, and much more dangerous for *him* if he helped her more than he already had.

Vincent had known she'd lose the challenge. Oh, she was stubborn and brash and probably brilliant underneath all that insecurity. Yet Toranaga was older, experienced, and calculating to boot. Vincent hadn't wanted his son involved at all, but he couldn't stop Theodore either. To do so would have made Theodore look weak, something his son couldn't afford.

But then Theodore had died in that sim, and a chilly frisson of death had walked the ladder of Vincent's spine. There was evil, dark and patient, waiting its turn. There would be sorrow.

Because, already, there was Yori Kurita.

*Yes, how to turn you to fight for me, Yori Kurita, and not yourself—and, most certainly, not Toranaga.*

If Vincent saw, so very clearly, that Yori was a threat, why was Ramadeep Bhatia playing this down? Spouting absurdities about her usefulness to the Combine, her being the last full-fledged samurai to leave The Republic, blah, blah . . . All that was *true*, but Bhatia was too shrill about it, as if by waving his hands, he would divert Vincent's attention from the man standing behind the curtain.

*Bhatia's got a strategy, some plan, just as Toranaga* must, *else he'd never have brought Yori here. Well, I have eyes, and I am not so dazzled by my finery that I cannot see past the protestations of my spymaster. I, too, have influence where you least expect, plans you will not derail. I may yet pull one or two miracles out of my sleeve.*

Time passed. The light faded. The sky shaded to pewter. And still Vincent painted. He was genuinely surprised when a servant crept in on soundless, stockinged feet to remind him of that evening's reception. Reluctantly, Vincent put aside his brush—and it was only then that he really saw what he'd painted. When he did, his chest turned icy.

The tree, yes. The berm and grasses. Roses in bloom. But that was not all. Because there were vipers: black sinuous forms slithering through the grass, twining round the cherry tree, squeezing the delicate blossoms in a death grip.

Serpents in *his* garden. Vincent stared. What had he been . . . ?

There came a swift, crackling flash, and then a boom of thunder answered with a roar that made the balcony shiver and his legs tremble. By all the gods, *this* was his nightmare come true in the violence of this coming storm, that dark and eerie light that was not light but its absence, the light eaten alive by brooding clouds that were black with foreboding. His answer was in the storm—and, yes, in the painting as well: in the snarling, ravenous *obake* with their gaping mouths and clawed hands. And in those ghastly visages, he spied his enemies. The swarthy skin and slitted black eyes of Ramadeep Bhatia. He saw Matsuhari Toranaga, his samurai's topknot forming from a mushroom. And in the clouds, there were *yurei*, the ghosts and spirits of the dead, and then he saw . . .

"No." He rose, backed away a step but could not tear his eyes from the painting. Because there he was, quite clearly. *His* face, but how changed! Eyes bulging, his mouth wide open in a silent scream of despair.

"No," he said fiercely. "No, I will not *yield*, do you hear me?" He looked from the painting to the cloudless twilight beyond his balcony, and the cherry tree, its boughs twisting in a feverish dance born of an evil wind. "Feast on another man's soul! You'll have *none* of me or mine!"

Brave words. Maybe foolish. Or just futile. He didn't know.

Yet this he *did* see and understand: the weeping cherry ravaged, its blossoms falling to the earth in an early snow.

# 4

The noble was a stultifying boor enamored of his own oily tenor. Yori's mind idled like a 'Mech on standby as she bided her time. She saw her chance when the noble's gaze flicked over her head. At the same time, the general gabble subsided, the way a restaurant suddenly hushed when a waitress dropped a tray.

Goggle-eyed, the noble stage-whispered, "Oh, my word, would you look at Katana Tormark! And, oh, I don't care for that hairstyle. Long hair like yours better suits a woman, don't you think?"

Yori said, "Mmmm," but the noble was already moving off to get a better look. Relieved, Yori snagged a glass of something fizzy and non-alcoholic from a passing tray. (Past experience: Keep a clear head, otherwise disarming an assassin was that much harder.) The buzz of conversation resumed as she drifted upstream through a river of glittery, bejeweled costumes. No one paid her any mind. That suited her fine.

*Now, let's see what all the fuss is about.* Half-turning, she raised her glass, her gaze wandering, very casually, and . . .

*Oh, my* God. She nearly choked on her drink. Well, color *her* amazed. Every single member of the DCMS, including Yori, was in dress uniform—but *not* Tormark, *noooo.*

Instead, Katana Tormark sported a breathtaking *furisode*: a spectacular kimono done on rich orange-and-gold jacquard, festooned with creamy peach and blaze-white blossoms stitched with shimmering gold thread. A *maru obi* encircled her waist, and she wore delicate, teak geta sandals with V-shaped thongs of gold cloth.

Tormark had also cut her jet-black hair. Very. *Very.* Short. Finely spiked and stylishly mussed. This, combined with her height, long neck, oval face, high cheekbones and flawless chocolate-brown skin, lent Tormark a regal bearing, a little like an exotic—if somewhat punk—queen.

*Well, she's got guts—either that or a fatal predisposition to suicide.* A smile crept over her lips that she quickly erased. *Careful, Yori, careful. No allies here, only adversaries.*

Yori watched as both Theodore Kurita and a very, well, *captivating* young man with fine bones, wheat-colored hair, and a full sensitive mouth approached Tormark. She saw the flicker of disapproval on Theodore's face. He was not as . . . *unconventional* as Tormark. Indeed, he was a creature of ceremony and, yet, what was this? Theodore bowing! Offering Tormark a flute of champagne!

*Hmmm.* That Theodore Kurita accepted Tormark was as loud as a proclamation, but with Makoto Shouriki in tow as well? Very interesting. Perhaps her senior by five or six years, Shouriki was a physician and scientist. Rumor had it that he was distantly related to the Kuritas in some way, though she couldn't pin down how. (Perhaps they should have a little talk, bastard offspring to bitch's whelp.) He was quite handsome, and so tall, she'd look like a doll standing alongside him.

*Soooo, choosing up sides. Ah, but what does Shouriki really think?*

She caught herself. Why should she even *care* about Shouriki? Because he looked friendly? Nice? Kind, the way he so easily chatted with Tormark? Envy jabbed her chest, and she quickly quashed the emotion.

*Remember, if you're a Kurita, you have no friends. Only camps and loyalties and your good common sense. Have a care, Yori, have a care.*

Well, whatever friends or allies Tormark might fancy she'd made, she hadn't shown well as a *warrior*. Yori had watched the whole sim. Tormark had more battle experience, but Yori would *never* have been so easily gulled. *She* was not reckless.

Yet what was that little stunt she herself had pulled during that sim on Northwind: leaping over that ridge at full throttle and dropping seven meters straight down? Sure, she'd taken out an *Enforcer*, but then she'd gotten stomped by the second one. On Ronel and in a very real battle, she'd punched her *Grand Dragon* headlong into a contingent of Carter's Corsairs, *and* two klicks beyond any effective cover Julian Davion could provide.

*Yes, but* that *was different.* Frowning, she sipped her drink, barely tasting the tart bubbly citrus. *That was deliberate, fooling the Corsairs into thinking that* I *was mounting a counteroffensive so I could buy Jules some time. As soon as he pushed through, I got out.*

By contrast, Tormark had made fatal errors. She'd outdistanced her support troops and the rest of her lance. And *why*, for heaven's sake, take Theodore Kurita along? His *Shiro* was badly damaged and of little practical benefit. Could Tormark really have been that cowed by protocol? Yori was sure *she* would never . . .

"Well, there you are." A man's voice: coolly disdainful, flat, dismissive. "Sizing up the competition?"

Though her pulse tripped, Yori pivoted with a nonchalant shrug. "Are you implying that I am not content with our esteemed *tai-shu*? That is uncharitable. Whatever can you be thinking, Hatsuwe Mototsune?" She left off the honorific, just for spite. Hatsuwe would never dare challenge her in the palace. For one thing, no swords allowed. For another, killing a Kurita in the Kuritan stronghold . . . well, it just wasn't done.

Hatsuwe's coal-black eyes, a little narrow and his only defect, nearly disappeared as he squinted in anger. Their feud had begun when she'd exited the prestigious Sun Zhang Academy with a performance record good enough to be the envy of any samurai. But she had especially galled Hatsuwe, the son of a high-ranking New Samarkand noble *and Tai-shu* Toranaga's fervent admirer. Toranaga was a cunning crocodile, and Hatsuwe, the slithering slime-eel trailing in Toranaga's wake.

All that made Yori wish that Hatsuwe were  ugly. He was not. In fact, he was an exceedingly handsome man who took very good care of his body. Certainly, she'd seen it often enough. Hatsuwe never seemed to tire of stripping down to a loincloth and prancing around a dojo. His skin was a warm bronze, and when he wrestled, his oiled muscles glistened and rippled in the light. Nevertheless, he *was* a slime-eel, and a *yarichin* besides.

"You are *yariman*," Hatsuwe said carelessly, in an eerie echo of her own assessment of *him*. "Give yourself airs, but you were Sakamoto before you ever were a Kurita, and that only by the skin of your teeth."

"My grandfather would beg to differ," Yori said, silently thanking the gods that Sakamoto was a common name and she was in no way related to the deceased warlord. "I would never be so ungrateful as to contemplate jumping ship for *Tai-shu* Tormark. Our *tono* is ever my lord." *And boku no shiri ni kisu siro.*

As if he'd read her mind—that he should kiss her sweet, pink arse—Hatsuwe's angular features flushed copper. "In that case, you won't mind rejoining his party. Toranaga-*san* wants you."

"Ah." She placed her half-finished drink on a nearby tray. "Well, lead on. I can't imagine our *tono* being so very pleased that you've kept him waiting just so you can think of new ways to insult my honor."

"*You*," Hatsuwe spat the word like a curse, "have no honor worth offending." Then he executed a crisp pivot and stalked off.

She was nothing if not mistress of herself. Yori followed, shoulders squared and eyes forward. Her warlord—her taskmaster who would never allow her to forget, never—waited, and an audience later on with the coordinator, that *fop*, besides.

*No friends here, only adversaries to conquer—and enemies to break.* She eyed Hatsuwe's back. *So beware, Hatsuwe Mototsune. Beware.*

# 5

**Warlord Toranaga's Quarters**
**Imperial Palace, Luthien**
**14 June 3136**
**Early morning**

"**A**nd what do you think, eh?" Matsuhari Toranaga sat cross-legged upon a tatami and leaned against a crimson silk bolster. A low teak table squatted to his right, an *Igo* board speckled with clusters of white and black stones alongside a stone cup within easy reach. The air was close with the earthy scent of the strong potato liquor, *imo-jochu,* Toranaga favored. He'd changed into a comfortable, very simple cobalt-blue kimono, and loosed his topknot so his salt-and-pepper hair fell about his shoulders. The hairstyle was new and seemed to please one very important young man. Otherwise, Toranaga was a bluff man, though the care he took of his body was reflected in a neck thick with corded muscle, a broad chest and sculpted biceps and forearms.

Toranaga sipped loudly, smacked his lips, and said, "The illustrious Katana Tormark, the coordinator's golden girl . . . What did you learn? Come now, speak plainly. I've had my quarters swept for listening devices."

Yori said, "She's courageous. That *furisode* was daring."

"*Daring?*" Toranaga challenged. "How so?"

Yori was calm, though—*honestly*—she felt like a schoolgirl in pigtails being drilled by a dyspeptic professor. On the other hand, keeping her head, figuratively, made it much more likely her neck would never be lonely. "Tormark's tactic was a stroke of dramatic genius. She trumpeted her difference." (Certainly *she'd* never have dared. Attracting attention was the last thing she wanted.) "The *furisode* is an extraordinarily formal kimono that, according to ancient Terran tradition, is given to a daughter when she reaches maturity."

"Mmmm." Toranaga looked over his left shoulder. "And you, Hatsuwe, do you *also* believe Tormark to be bold and daring?"

Yori's eyes slid to the samurai, who held a sweating jug of cold *imo-jochu* at the ready. (Though Hatsuwe was *not* the only other man in the room. *That* person she'd do well to keep clear of, though she knew *he* watched *her*. Oh, yes. *He* didn't miss a trick.) *Doting* was the only word to describe how Hatsuwe waited on Toranaga, and Hatsuwe now met her gaze with both defiance and a malignant, triumphant gleam. She did not waver. *And just because you wait on him, do you think to kill me while I sleep? Come to my bed, pig, and I will show you two* shaku *of steel.*

Bowing, Hatsuwe said, "*Tono*, Tormark is reckless and stubborn. Certainly, wearing a *furisode* was like taking out an ad."

"In what way?"

"Why, the invitation, of course. Doesn't the same ancient tradition also suggest that a woman is . . . available? Everyone knows that she and Theodore Kurita must be lovers. They had such a long time together, and he certainly favored her tonight."

"True." Toranaga eyed Yori. "Do you agree?"

"*Iie*, Toranaga-*sama*," Yori said, bluntly, though she softened it with the slightest of bows, pretending a respect she did not feel. Hai, *I am your tool, but I have a brain and wits, and if you think to favor that idiot over me, you are much mistaken.* "Tormark isn't the type of woman who's gotten as far as she has on her back, or in any other position. Perhaps it has never occurred to Hatsuwe-*san* that not *every* woman is eager to share a man's bed, even if it *is* his."

Now *that* was a gamble, though she'd employed an honorific the slime-eel did not deserve. From the look on Hatsuwe's face, Yori knew she was on dangerous ground. Yet she also had a very nasty premonition of where Toranaga was going with this, and if she could deflect his attention from *that* to Hatsuwe . . .

Hatsuwe's words were barely a hiss. "I demand an apology, Toranaga-*sama*. I would not bloody my blade with one so beneath honor, but a samurai must not let pass the yapping of an insolent cur."

Toranaga surprised her. "Stay," Toranaga said to Hatsuwe—and then he did the most remarkable thing, something Yori had never seen him do, ever. He closed his hand around Hatsuwe's wrist. Not so much a restraint as it was . . . a *caress*. The gesture would've been innocuous to anyone who did not know these two well, who had not spent her time observing, cataloguing, weighing. Yet there was no doubt. With that touch, Toranaga treated Hatsuwe with a familiarity she'd previously not suspected.

*By the gods! All that meticulous care with which Hatsuwe has treated his body . . . is he* besotted? *A prelude to* wakashudo?

She knew about *bi-do*, the beautiful way. Indeed, this had been and continued to be the way of the samurai. Unless she was very wide of the mark, however, Hatsuwe's infatuation hadn't been reciprocated.

Hai, *now that I think of it, Hatsuwe looks hungry. A very good play on Toranaga's part: The things you can't have are the ones you desire.*

Toranaga cut into her thoughts. "Well, then, what do you think Tormark *is* saying?"

She was ready for this. She had not survived this long by being a witless fool. She knew she had very wide, expressive black eyes and now she arranged her features to reflect the utmost sincerity. She even bowed before speaking, so there could be no mistaking her meaning. Then she looked Toranaga square in the face.

"Piss off," she said.

There was a moment's explosive silence. No one breathed. Yori didn't move.

Then Hatsuwe's face twisted with fury. "*Tono*, this cannot *stand*! She *must* . . ." He broke off not because Toranaga restrained him but because of what the warlord was doing, something that Yori thought Hatsuwe had never seen. She knew *she* hadn't.

Toranaga was laughing. Silently, mouth open, shoulders shaking. Like a dog. He managed a sobbing inhalation, thumbed tears from the corners of his eyes and then turned to look at the third man, who'd said absolutely nothing so far—and who terrified Yori right down to her marrow.

"Well, Hamada," he said, still chuckling, "what say you to that, eh?"

Kazuo Hamada, the warlord's spymaster, blinked. He did this slowly, like a drowsy lizard. His eyes were, however, like a cobra's. Flat. Black. A little dead. He was nondescript in every other way: of middling height, neither too fat nor gaunt, with dull pewter hair and a somewhat beaky nose. Except for his eyes, Hamada was unremarkable—something you'd want in a man who'd set up a spy apparatus rivaling the ISF.

"She is correct," Hamada said. "Sleeping her way into Theodore Kurita's good graces is not Tormark's *style*."

"Not *her* style, perhaps," Toranaga said, eyeing Yori the way one did a skinned duck hanging by its neck in a shop window. "Have *you* considered becoming somewhat *closer* to the coordinator's heir?"

Yori waited a beat then said, with great care, "What are you suggesting, *Tono*?"

"Stop that." Toranaga backhanded her question. "You're a clever girl. What do you *think* I mean?"

*Steady.* Yori laced her fingers, the better to appear submissive. *Do not give a millimeter, do not show a gram of weakness.* She chose what seemed safest. "I hadn't considered it, Toranaga-*sama*."

"Well, consider it," Toranaga said curtly. He picked up his mug but didn't drink. "Cultivate an acquaintance. Then, for God's sake, get the man into your bed. If you were to carry the heir's child . . ."

"And *then* what?" The idea was so repulsive, she felt like screaming. "Theodore is married. He's had ample opportunity for dalliances, to spawn a whole clutch of heirs. That he has not speaks of his will and loyalty. Besides, what makes you think he would be interested in me?"

*Or that I would stoop to something so* vile?

"Haven't you been paying attention?" Toranaga rapped, all good humor gone. He took a long swallow of the harsh liquor. His cheeks flamed. "I didn't bring you here just to rub that peacock's nose in shit! Theodore is your top priority. I don't care if you have to twitch your skirts for him to catch the scent. There's not a man alive who can resist an *ian-fu*."

Yori exhaled in stunned surprise. He could not have insulted her more if he'd slapped her in the face. And was that a suggestion of a *smirk* on Hatsuwe's lips? How dare Toranaga suggest that she was *baka no baita!* She had an awful moment when she burned to remark that, certainly, no woman stood a chance with *him*. She wrestled the impulse back. Toranaga would make sure that Hatsuwe didn't kill her so long as she was useful. Yet she didn't doubt that, in a fit of rage, Toranaga would slice off her head himself. Thank the gods, wearing one's swords without the coordinator's express permission while on the palace's grounds was forbidden.

"I think," she said finally, "that I won't be in a position to demonstrate the lack of elastic in my knickers. After all, I'd planned to work with the Sun Zhang Academy masters at revamping their sims to reflect changes in The Republic's defenses and strategies. I trust that was why you left me behind on Terra? To spend time with our enemies and know their minds? I do not see how what you suggest can be accomplished, *Tono*."

"No?" Toranaga grunted. "Well, how fortunate for you that I've plans of my own. I will *graciously* offer your services and troops to Theodore, something he and the coordinator can hardly refuse. After all, you are a relation even if your grandfather was a bastard. Besides, you've spent all that quality time with those young pups—with Campbell and Davion and all the rest. You've had a chance to see the latest Republic technology used in training warriors. You are an invaluable resource."

"I see," Yori said, adopting as neutral a tone as she could. "And I presume you've already felt out *Tai-sho* Kurita? Informally?"

"I knew you were a clever girl." Toranaga looked greatly satisfied. "He wishes to discuss this with that peacock he calls Father. Tomorrow, we warlords meet with the coordinator, and I will make my gift of you official."

"I see." Then she bowed because there was nothing more to be done. She held it a tad longer than she might otherwise in order to hide the burn in her cheeks that she tried—and knew she failed—to control.

*He tasks and taunts yet lauds me to the coordinator and his heir just enough so it's clear that I am* his *creature.*

"And what if he refuses?" She'd come out of her standing *rei* as slowly as decorum dictated, but she caught the way Toranaga's eyes shuttered. *Ah, you are not as clever as you think. What are you plotting, you vile worm? You've got a fallback if this doesn't work out to your satisfaction. I feel it in my bones.*

The moment passed. "He won't," Toranaga said, and gestured for more liquor. As Hatsuwe poured, Toranaga said, "Hamada, any words of wisdom for our young protégée?"

"Only two." Hamada's eyes were viper-flat. "Don't fail."

When she was gone, Toranaga said to his spymaster, "You're sure of your information?" He read Hamada's hesitation, that slide of his eyes to Hatsuwe, who was still in attendance: *You really want to talk about this in front of him?* Toranaga motioned for Hamada to continue. "I have no secrets in front of my most trusted intimates," he said, addressing his spymaster but watching for Hatsuwe's reaction. He was rewarded by the way the samurai's chest actually swelled with the compliment. Excellent. He needed Hatsuwe more than the young man knew. As for secrets? Well, not even his spymaster knew all.

Hamada said, "There is no mistake. Bear in mind, however"—that cautious slither of the eyes toward Hatsuwe then back— "if you proceed down this path, there is no turning back."

Well, that was obvious. Yet Toranaga was betting that if even half of what was rumored about Tormark's true troop strengths were true, she would have no choice but to call in a very particular marker, on a very specific planet with some very specific people she'd worked with before.

*Like a game of* Igo. He studied his board. He was black, and he'd made beautiful shapes, carved out eyes and lungs. He thought he might win, though the game was long from over. *When Tormark makes her move, I'll be there, with my stones, ready to suffocate her and steal her liberties.*

The worry—the Master of Stones who must be carefully watched—was Ramadeep Bhatia. By all indications, the ISF director clearly understood the dire circumstances of a regime led by a prancing puff more interested in his bouffant than a BattleMech. Something up Bhatia's voluminous sleeve, he was certain.

*He took such care to extend me an invitation to speak to the new recruits at the Internal Security College. What's he up to? An alliance?*

Hatsuwe shuffled closer. "More wine, my *tai-shu*?"

"No." Toranaga raised a hand to stop the young man from pouring. "Even *I* have limits," and then he placed his hand on Hatsuwe's. "In some things." He let his hand linger just enough to encourage Hatsuwe, to tease him with the possibility that, yes, the young samurai might well be *very* desirable. He was gratified to see the slight flush that stained Hatsuwe's throat, and that slight hitch in his breathing—a quick intake of desire.

*Perfect.* Yet only a fool believed sex was the only tool. *Because people want power. Power is raw and alive and as tangible as this robe I draw round my waist. I will wield power with the same care I use to place my stones, closing off my adversaries' liberties until I eat them alive.*

What would happen, would happen, and all in good time, and then there would be Katana Tormark and then the Kuritas to take down, all in a row.

*For that which does not destroy you will make you strong, and your seed is* weak, *Peacock. I know your* secret. *Your seed is shot through with disease—but I am here, and I am strong, Peacock.* I *am* strong.

$$=== 6 ===$$

**Imperial City, Luthien**
**14 June 3136**

**W**hen that little bitch of a geisha Katana Tormark took her place at the long table in the Black Room (attended only by an ancient fossil on whom Ramadeep Bhatia hadn't laid eyes in over forty years) and launched into an exhaustive prattle about troop strengths and deals done with Clannish kittens much better off trimming their toenails than fancying themselves conquerors, Ramadeep Bhatia wanted to jump up and down and scream at the top of his lungs: *THIS IS OLD NEWS! YOU IGNORANT SLUT, THIS IS THE ISF YOU'RE TALKING TO!*

He didn't. Oh, it went without saying that he wouldn't have minded if a few enterprising assassins had dropped from the Black Room's ceiling on myomer cables, drawn their blades, and lopped off the little geisha's head. He'd pay good money to watch them carve away her ears, gouge out her eyes, yank out her tongue by the roots and tie it round her neck. *Anything* to still that *yariman*'s voice drilling into his brain until it bled.

Instead, Bhatia did what he always did when he wanted to kill someone and couldn't. He plotted. He sat back, wiped his brain clean, inhaled a very long breath that filled his lungs to capacity, and then let the air go in a silent, drawn-out sigh.

The Black Room didn't smell bad, just sterile, like a laboratory. The room was self-contained in every way— computer, air filtration, water, and even an underground bunker, just in case. No fear of eavesdroppers either: a white-noise generator, boosted by the room's faraday cage and combined with ceramic filaments woven into ultradense ferrocrete walls, created an environment virtually impervious to surveillance. A phalanx of well-trained guards protected against intruders.

Or unruly warlords: Two hours ago, *Tai-shu* Toranaga had appeared, his sheathed katana in his right hand, as was his custom, and his *wakashiri* firmly thrust into his *obi*. Weapons in the coordinator's presence was an affront of the worst kind. (Oh, all *right*. The man was a peacock, but Bhatia *did* have to protect the plumage, at least for show.) Since he'd given no dispensation, Bhatia had informed the warlord, as nicely as possible, that the swords would have to go.

"No." Toranaga had dressed the part to the *hilt*, so to speak: hair done in a traditional topknot; a wide-shouldered, crimson *kataginu* over midnight-black *hakama* and matching *obi*. The warlord's voice was flat and hard, and without turning aside, he held out his left hand. One of Toranaga's aides slid a scroll into Toranaga's palm, and this Toranaga extended to the ISF director. "The coordinator has granted dispensation."

"I see." Bhatia scanned the document, the better to mask the slow simmer in his gut. What the hell was Toranaga up to? Subverting *his* office . . . it was like a challenge. Not unlike Toranaga, but *very* unlike the Vincent Kurita to whom Bhatia was accustomed.

*So, my dear Peacock, in granting Toranaga a dispensation, are we finding a misplaced backbone after all this time? You think to challenge* me? *Is that why you felt impelled to install a sim, to show the world that you still have teeth? Bah! You're an old woman, and I will see you* fall.

As for the geisha, the question was not only how but *when*. Wahab Fusilli, the worm in Tormark's apple, had virtually nothing to report and had gone silent. Not surprising; there was little call for the man to travel into *his* sphere of influence. If only the HPGs were up, if, if, if . . .

So how to kill the little bitch? Anything that happened in proximity to Luthien would immediately be suspect. So, away from Luthien, a little loss of pressure in her DropShip? Perhaps a malfunction in her ship's jump drive? Or simply a stiletto neatly slid between a few ribs as she slept?

"Very well, *Tai-shu* Tormark," Vincent Kurita said, and Bhatia snapped back to himself in a rush. Damn, he'd lost track! The coordinator continued, "When do you expect to launch your attack force?"

Tormark said, "I am hopeful that by year's end, we will strike to retake Dieron. Much will depend on my ability to secure troops."

"We understand," the coordinator said. "But what of this news we hear of unrest on the border worlds . . . Biham, Sadachbia?"

"We've had a few difficulties. Nothing we can't handle, *Tono*."

"Indeed? Is not Sir Reginald Eriksson the primary architect of the Biham resistance?"

Bhatia was a little surprised. The Peacock rarely showed teeth. *Tormark's fault that Eriksson's a thorn in her side: She let him live.*

Tormark spoke with care. "On Biham, yes. I'm hopeful that my personal relationship with him will stifle further resistance."

"On one planet, perhaps," the coordinator said. "But you do not have personal relationships on every border world. Have you considered that these resistance movements might be receiving . . . encouragement?"

"*Hai,* we are studying the problem. *Tai-sa* Crawford has carte blanche to act on this matter in my absence. I am confident of his abilities, *Tono.*"

"Then let us hope your confidence is not misplaced." The coordinator looked to the others. "Is there any order of business we have overlooked?"

"*Hai, Tono.*" Toranaga rose, bowed. "I have a matter of great moment to discuss."

Bhatia's eyebrows flinched for his hairline. What was this?

"Indeed," the coordinator replied, his face as still as a pond.

"*Hai.* I have taken the liberty of speaking to *Tai-sho* Kurita about the matter." Toranaga inclined his head toward Theodore, who sat at his father's right hand—a nod the heir did not return, Bhatia saw. Indeed, Theodore's face was a studied blank. "I wish to make you a gift of great value, *Tono.*"

"Ah," the coordinator said again, and then he spared only the briefest of glances at his son, a glance that Bhatia read instantly.

*Whatever Toranaga has planned these two have undermined* already.

"Yes," the coordinator said mildly. "We *thought* you would."

# 7

## Katana's Journal
## 15 June 3136

**O**kay, I thought I'd never do word one of a journal again. See, last year, somehow, parts of my old journal leaked. Not much, and not very important stuff, but you know newsies. Screaming headlines, and then, of course, they start those frigging forums for people who wouldn't know a joystick if someone jammed one up their ass. So, of *course*, they're qualified to weigh in on me. *She doesn't* sound *like a general.* Or *She needs a psychiatrist.* Or *Who'd follow* her?

You know what I say? Piss off. Really. Get real. We all come from families, and we all got problems. You think a general speaks in declamatory language all day long? *Let us engage the enemy! We will fight with honor! Excuse me while I pick my teeth with my bayonet!*

<Snerk> Hell-*oooo*. Get a grip.

(Let's hope somebody leaks *that*. People'd go nuts. Tempted to do it myself. On the other hand, that's why I decided to use this microrecorder. Hard to break the encryption, and it looks like an ordinary bracelet.)

Anyway . . . this trip. Just all kinds of fun. There's so much going on—with the Nova Cats, the so-called Republic March and that schemer Erik Sandoval-Groell. And me trying to get enough frigging troops to capture one lousy planet while I'm scrambling to pull enough people in to secure the worlds I was already supposed to have taken last year . . . I feel like a gerbil on a wheel running to nowhere.

As for last night? Anyone reads this? Yes, I wore a bright orange *furisode* to the reception. Just wanted to clear that up. And, for the record, here's what the coordinator said: "Next time, perhaps we should distribute sunglasses."

Now, *why* did I do that? Very simple. First of all, it's not a crime. The uniform's just tradition. So long as I don't show up buck naked, I can wear whatever I want. See, after the sim, everyone expected me to come in with my tail between my legs. No way. So I did the *furisode*. Put a whole new complexion on the evening, that's for sure.

One person thought I didn't see her noticing *me*, but I saw *her*. The AMAZING Yori Kurita. Sure, I understand that she had every right to commandeer my troops on Ronel. She saved their butts. But they were *my* troops, and now I get to deal with this little kitten upstaging me with my own people. Worse, watching me *lose* that sim and then having to listen to Toranaga yammer on about how much better their sims are now that the Kitten's worked on their systems, blah, blah, blah.

And then today, Toranaga makes his little gift of the Kitten and her troops—*my* troops—to Theodore. Gee, kind of hard to miss that, gosh, Katana's the one who's got a campaign to wage, remember her?

Worse, I've had desertions . . . and none more puzzling than the Bounty Hunter. Gone for over four months now and not a whisper. Where can he be? Andre got some garbled reports of the Hunter being on Asta, but they couldn't be confirmed, and now the Hunter's dropped out of sight.

I don't know why this bothers me so much. Why I seem to actually, well, *miss* the Hunter. Wonder where he is, and if he thinks about me . . .

Uh-oh. I'm not going there. I don't even want to think about that.

Anyway . . . so, Toranaga did his thing. Then the coordinator did *his*. First, he named *Theodore* as interim overseer for the Benjamin district. Knock me over with a feather, but it's a godsend. Having Theodore in Benjamin means I don't have to watch my back. Whatever Ghost Bear's sending over the border, Theodore will beat them back, freeing me up to concentrate on Dieron. I figure this is as far as the coordinator can go for me in front of the others.

As it was, this still might have been too far. *I* saw the look Toranaga gave Bhatia. Something . . . odd there. (Though Bhatia was so stunned, his jaw actually dropped. That was worth the price of admission.)

But then the real bombshell: Remember Yori Kurita?

Yes, she of the AMAZING fame? Well, Theodore made a
gift of her to . . .
   . . Wait for it . . .
  *Me.*
Oh. *Joy.*
What else can go wrong?

# 8

## Imperial Palace, Luthien
## 15 June 3136

**E**arly morning, just a little past three AM: too soon for
birds and too late for crickets. The storm had washed the
air clean. Yori picked her way along the margin of a gravel
path flanked by light-wands, slipping in and out of fingers
of shadow. She'd been unable to sleep, her mind grappling
with the news that she would not be sent to Theodore's
command after all. Ah, but the coordinator was more calculating than she'd imagined. Waiting for her to fail?

"Well, I won't fail." Her voice sounded small against a
world she couldn't see beyond small nimbuses of light that
revealed the grass at her feet and a ghostly white ribbon
of gravel snaking alongside. "I will wait, and I will watch.
I haven't survived this long to grow careless."

A crunch of gravel coming from the unseen gardens
ahead and then a sudden ripple in the shadows made her
stiffen. She automatically reached round for a blade that
was not there, and she cursed herself for a fool. Letting
down her guard even for a second, walking the palace
gardens . . . Ears straining, she melted into the shadows,
flattening against a tree trunk slippery with lichen.

A thin pencil of light sketched the gloom, bobbing in
time with the intruder's footsteps. They were heavy steps,
a man's. Ahead and to Yori's left, a stone bench edged

the path, demarcated by a light-wand on either side. The intruder's light slid over the bench, and then he sat with a small sigh.

From her hiding place, Yori watched. She recognized him, and the jolt in the pit of her stomach wasn't alarm, but it wasn't relief either.

*What is* he *doing here?*

"Is someone there?" The man leaned forward, peering Yori's way. She felt as if his eyes were lasers, illuminating her where she stood. "Hello?"

Yori felt stupid, and she was angry she'd been caught out. "Hello." She carried herself with frosty gravity as she willed her feet across the gravel path. "You are out late, Shouriki-*san*."

Makoto Shouriki stood, and now his face was blurry. She heard the grin, though. "The pot calling the kettle black. What brings *you* out here? Can't sleep?"

*Affable enough, yet this no accident. So watch your step, Yori. Watch, wait, listen. Learn.* "I often walk at night."

"Ah." He was more than a head and a half taller, and sounded tolerantly amused, as if she were a small moppet he could pat on the head. This angered her. "Well," he said finally, "I know what insomnia's like. To tell you the truth, I'm always expecting a pager to go off, you know?"

"No," she said, "I do not know."

A pause. "Okay," he said, and now he sounded a little nonplussed. "Well, I just never need much sleep. Mind's always going."

"What is it you think about?" *Why am I asking? Why should I care?*

"Oh, all kinds of things. Experiments, mainly, genetics. One of the things I wish we'd get over in the Combine is this notion that because genetics is always associated with the Clans, it's something bad. Why, do you know that the number of inherited diseases we could treat with gene-targeted therapies . . ."

He rambled on. She listened, parsing his words, measuring his sincerity, the threat he might or might not represent. *Because this can't be an accident. Someone* had *to notice I was gone and send him to meet up with me. But why?*

She wasn't aware he'd asked a question until he said her name. "Sorry?" Angry at herself for being caught out.

"I asked whether you're happy about your new assignment."

*Hmmm. A spy for Theodore? To feel me out?* "I am not *un*happy."

"That's a funny way to put it."

Yori shrugged. "It's my way."

"Okay." Silence. "You don't talk much, do you?"

*I never talk much.* "I don't know you."

"Ah." Makoto hesitated. "Well, you don't have to worry about me."

*The person who reassures you that there is nothing to worry about is precisely the person you* should *worry about.* How many times had she been gulled with that argument? Several, and once not long ago that had nearly been the death of her. She said, "I am not worried."

"I don't believe you, but it doesn't matter. You must get lonely."

*Stop being so damned nice. I don't* want *to like you.* "Loneliness and the ability to *be* alone are two different things."

"That's true. But I understand your position better than you think."

"Why? Because you're a Kurita, too? Isn't it amazing that we never seem to lack for people willing to be our friends? Well, I'm not looking for a friend. Friendship is overrated, anyway."

"Why is that?"

"Because the man you call your friend may be the enemy you are forced to confront and destroy in the next battle."

"I'm not a warrior."

"Not all battles are fought with 'Mechs."

"True. But your attitude is pretty damned cynical."

"No, not at all," Yori said. "That is my life."

Later, on the way back to his room, Makoto Shouriki thought: *Porcupines.*

# PART TWO

## *Tenuki:* Elsewhere

# 9

Canned martial band music blared from loudspeakers. The pachinko regulars were already lined up two deep in a queue that snaked down the street and around the block. There were a few *pachi-puro*, pachinko professionals dressed in flashy designer suits. But most were elderly, slouch-shouldered men in baggy trousers, each convinced that he'd earn a special prize. The regular prizes—cigarettes, candy, food—they were nice. Legal. The special prizes were nice, too. They just weren't legal.

At ten, the doors opened and the regulars streamed in, conversations cut off in mid-sentence, expressions suddenly grim. In thirty minutes, the air was thick with blue smoke and noisy with rave music, sirens, the clatter of pins and the rattle of ball bearings cascading along plastic chutes.

Today was Katsuo Kirino's lucky day. He'd known from the moment he purchased his starter bin of one hundred and twenty-five pachinko balls and found that his favorite machine, fire-engine red edged with black, was free. Free! An omen because red was very, very lucky.

When he began five years ago, Kirino was an amateur, as likely to lose five thousand balls as win a hundred. His father would cuff Kirino's head and shout that he was the son of a *Shatei-gashira!* He was supposed to make money off of these idiots, not *become* one! That was why he had ventured out of his *oyabun's* territory to play here amongst the more loosely allied factions, safe from his father's prying eyes.

With a flick of his wrist, Kirino cranked the handle at the machine's bottom right. His first ball shot into the guts of the machine, a *Deji-Pachi* while Kirino controlled the ball's speed with careful adjustments of his thumb. Not too fast, not too slow, look out, look out! Then he grinned fiercely, as that first ball fell into a center hole and set the LCD's digital slot windows spinning. His gaze fixed on the blur of numbers. . . .

First number: 7. Then another 7. Then . . . a third. 7-7-7. A fever! The first pull of the day, and he was already churning out the balls! The machine's siren wailed, and a silver stream of balls spat out one after the other, a glorious stream that sounded like money.

His luck held. Every machine he touched went berserk. By noon, he'd filled five bins, easily forty to fifty thousand balls there. When he hauled them to the redemption counter and watched as the balls were emptied into an automatic counter, he knew he'd won a special prize.

Ears still ringing from the noise, eyes itchy with cigarette smoke, he clutched his precious chit and pushed out of the parlor. He stood a moment, blinking, a little sun-dazzled. Then he veered right and down a blind alley. Near the end and on the right was a rectangle of peach-colored brick. Kirino tapped on the center brick. The brick scraped to one side, and a pair of dark eyes peered through a slit. *"Sate, hajimeyou."*

Not wasting any time, Kirino pushed his chit through the slit. "A minute," the voice said, and the slit closed.

While he waited, Kirino thought of the women he would buy that evening. Indeed, he was so busy thinking about what he would do with all that lucky money that he didn't register the barrel of a laser pistol in his right ear until much too late. And then his luck?

It kinda ran out.

## Siang, Biham
## 18 June 3136

Another balmy day on Biham: hazy, humid. The air smelled like chemicals, courtesy of Yoshimatsu Chemical's corporate headquarters that lay west of the city. There was rain in the forecast, something people put about as much faith in as they did the second coming of Devlin Stone.

By midday, the open air market in a dusty town square was packed with shoppers browsing tables heaped with produce, sandals, pots and pans. Business was picking up, life was finally getting better. The terrorists had called a truce, and that had held for the last two months. Sir Reginald Eriksson could still draw crowds of disgruntled natives, and he spoke often. People kept waiting for the DCMS to shut him down, but they didn't.

Still, the DCMS occupying forces kept a relatively low profile, and lately people had started to relax. No conversations suddenly choked off in mid-syllable whenever the troops happened by. Occupation was becoming a way of life. Just about.

There was a popular open-air café about thirty meters from the edge of the market where a lanky musician coaxed something bluesy and lonesome from an alto sax. About twenty people stopped to listen, some tapping their feet, keeping time, others watching the musician's slow sway as intently as cobras mesmerized by a snake charmer.

The café specialized in Indian food and was the ideal spot to enjoy lunch and listen to the music. A trio of off-duty soldiers—two men, one woman—had just snagged one of the best seats in the house: ringside, in the shade, at a round table with wrought-iron chairs painted forest green. The rest of the café was busy, too, and so Nori Goto, a gawky young man of perhaps twenty, was run off his feet, carting large salvers piled with fragrant curries that smelled of coriander and cumin.

Goto was an orphan. His mother had been killed during the first DCMS attack wave. His father was MIA and presumed dead. Goto had dropped out of college about seven months ago when Sakamoto's people stormed the campus during a student protest and strafed the crowd. No real reason. Just because they could. Seventy students died, as did fourteen professors, the dean, and a golden retriever with a starred, Republic-blue bandana knotted round his neck. After that, Goto decided there just wasn't a lot of call for philosophy majors in a DCMS world.

The off-duty soldiers ordered *baigan bharta*, puffy rounds of wheat *pouri*, creamy *dal makhani*, and a spicy *aloo mut-*

*ter gobi*, the buttery tomato glaze glistening on the potatoes and cauliflower. The tray was very heavy, and Goto was careful. He wore a roomy, long-sleeved cotton *kurta* with bold purple and red stripes that draped to his knees over a pair of loose ivory cotton pants that tapered at his ankles. The clothes gave him the freedom of movement he needed for his work, especially today.

The soldiers were listening to the wail of the sax, the woman keeping time, the guys sipping icy cold Indian beer imported from Terra. When Goto arrived, the soldiers barely spared a glance as he served, kissing the plates to the table without so much as a click.

Only when Goto lingered did the woman look up. She jetted smoke out of the corner of her mouth. "You forget something?" she said.

"Yes," Goto said. He bowed, like a virtuoso after a fine performance. "Burn in hell," he said . . .

. . . As he thumbed the detonator strapped over his heart.

"How many of *our* people?" Plugging his left ear with his pinky, *Sho-sa* Daniel Spear strained to hear the medic's report through engine roar. His ride, a clunker of a Ranger scavenged from Biham's Republic stores, ground along with a sound somewhere between a ferrocrete mixer and a dishwasher. "And civilians? . . . Uh-huh. Hell. Okay, I'm heading back to base now. Keep me posted. Out."

To his right, Spear's aide shouted over the din, "How bad, sir?"

"Twenty of our people dead. About fifteen more shredded by flechettes. Medic estimated at least that many civilian casualties." He tucked his microcomm into his breast pocket. "Well, I'd say that Eriksson's boys have broken the truce. Just when we start letting off-duty personnel back into town, something like this happens. I don't get it. Don't these people understand we're here to help?"

"Maybe Eriksson had nothing to do with it, sir. *Tai-shu* Tormark wouldn't've let him come back if she thought he'd pull crap like this."

Spear bit back an observation about their illustrious *tai-shu* he'd likely regret. (He was a Sakamoto holdover, and no Tormark groupie.) Instead, he concentrated on the view. The Ranger was climbing, straining through a series of switchbacks. Spear held his breath, waited for the clunker to finally up and die. It didn't, thank Christ, and they crested a plateau stippled with scrub pine. Directly ahead, the calm sea looked like light blue glass. To the north and atop a series of berms were three massive, wide-mouthed stacks shaped like pedestal eggcups about sixty klicks distant from the city, fifteen klicks from the base. White clouds of steam billowed from two stacks. To the right, a freight landtrain coiled for the complex.

A nuclear fission plant: Who'da thunk? Long ago, Biham was a miner's wet dream: coal, oil, natural gas. The rolling steppes west of the city were once blanketed with oil refineries, and the mountains west were a honeycomb of ancient mine shafts. All the fossil fuels had been exhausted a long time ago, though. Not much choice except fire up the old fission plant.

His Ranger swung left toward Biham Command, a complex of Quonsets and tents sprawled in a small valley south of the plant, and Spear returned to the problem at hand. Countering resistance was part of his job description. Yet Spear had a sneaking suspicion there was more to this than met the eye: *Same problems on Galatea III, Ancha, and Sadachbia, all border planets. I wonder . . .*

As if he'd read Spear's mind, his aide said, "Sir, all the resistance cells occur along the border with this so-called Republic March. What if Sandoval-Groell's sending fighters, money and materiel across the border?"

"Damn good thought. What we need is some decent intel." A tiny, white puff blossomed very far away to his left, something he saw but didn't process. "Then we could . . ." His voice trailed away as his brain caught up.

*Wrong place for a steam cloud.* Spear's eyes widened, and his gut clenched. *Oh,* shit . . .

*"INCOMING!"* he screamed at the same moment that the Ranger's onboard diagnostic system also chewed through the information and shrilled a warning. "We've got . . . !"

## 10

## Siang, Biham
## 18 June 3136

**E**lla's Della was one of Tony Yamada's places, about a block away from police headquarters and the courthouse. The evening-shift rush was just ending, and the clink of cutlery and murmur of voices drifting to the storage room came on air fragrant with the scents of dill pickles, slaw, melted Swiss cheese, greasy fries and coffee. The table at which Yamada and Eriksson sat was slotted between molded aluminum racks, five meters long and two deep. The shelves were lined with restaurant-sized plastic containers of Russian dressing, mustard and ketchup, tins of hash and tuna.

Lighting his new smoke with the dying end of his last, Tony Yamada inhaled deeply, held it, and then let go, squinting against smoke curls. He'd picked up smoking right around when he dropped out of high school and joined the Red Dragons. He'd picked up other things from the Dragons: tats, how to use a gun, how to gut some asshole with a knife. Useful stuff. Twenty years later, he wasn't with the Dragons, but he still smoked and put his skill set to good use.

"Look, Eriksson, I know gambling," Yamada said. He'd had fries and now killed the butt in a glop of ketchup. "The house always wins in the end because the house makes the rules. I know how to win, and I know how to hurt people so they don't like it so much."

Eriksson's bald pate was ruddy with indignation. "I don't see how killing innocent civilians helps. Under other circumstances, Spear's death wouldn't have mattered, but I'd brokered a truce with the man. I can't work with the Dracs if you diminish my credibility."

Yamada's words floated on puffs of smoke. "They tolerate you. If Tormark wasn't watching your ass, they'd've squashed you, old man."

Eriksson drew himself up. "This is not open for debate. I organized this resistance. If we are to expel the Combine, then we must act together. We must think as one. We must remain united."

"United." Yamada made a rude noise, then leaned forward, his eyes slitting. "That's just a fancy way of saying *you* wanna call the shots."

"Even a resistance has rules of engagement. As long as I'm in charge, you will do as I say. If you won't, then I can't use a man like you."

Yamada's face felt stretched tight, like someone had hooked needles into his skin and pulled. "You think because you're a knight, you're better'n me? You take a crap, it stinks, right? You rattle around in your big fancy 'Mech, and anything you hit, it's got a metal skin. I bet you never looked someone you were gonna kill right in the eye and see how he *knows*," Yamada tapped a finger to his temple, "up here, he's about five seconds away from dying. But I do know. I'm *exactly* the kind of man you need."

Eriksson said nothing. Yamada smoked. Finally, Eriksson's knotty fingers flexed, unclenched, then flexed again around his cane's worn gold handle. "Perhaps," the old knight said, "but our relationship ends now. If you persist, I will be forced to stop you."

"How? Whatcha gonna do, old man, go to the police? The Dracs? Naw, you listen to *me*." Yamada leaned in until they were a hand's breadth apart. Close enough for Yamada to make out the milky-white stain of age clouding Eriksson's light blue eyes. "You try to stop me, and I'll stop you."

"Threats, Yamada?" Leaning into his cane, Eriksson hauled himself erect. Yamada saw how much effort the old man put into not betraying a hint of weakness—and he almost admired the man for it. Almost.

Eriksson said, "I may be old, but I am no one's fool, least of all yours. I survived Sakamoto, and I shall survive *you*. You do not want to see what will happen if I meet with some accident or other."

"Naw, Eriksson, naw. You don't get it." And now Yamada smiled, and his lips peeled back to reveal a pair of polished pointed incisors, filed to look exactly like a wolf's. "When it happens, it ain't gonna be no accident."

Yamada left Ella's around eleven. The night was humid, the air drifting in on a westerly breeze that reeked of acetone and cat piss: the chemical plant. He passed into a section where the buildings were a bit shabbier. Garbage in the streets. People in knots on a corner or sprawled on steps, guarding territory. The majority of windows on the tenement buildings didn't have glass, and even more were boarded up. Girls on the game strutted in thigh-high boots and glittery lace-up corsets. A slow parade of curb crawlers in sleek Avanti hovers slid by as unseen johnnies, hidden behind their polarized canopies, eyed the merchandise.

Yamada jogged up the steps of an aging brownstone with a neon light-globe hovering above the entrance: The Up and Under. Inside, he wandered over to the bar where a beefy guy with biceps like cantaloupes was polishing glasses with a white rag.

"Boss." The barkeep's name was Big Mark. Big Mark found an empty glass, loaded it with ice, spritzed in soda water, and finished with a slice of lime. "They're all here," Big Mark said as he nailed a napkin to the counter with the glass. " 'Bout ten minutes ago."

Nodding, Yamada turned, leaned his back against the counter, and sipped his soda water. The bar wasn't fancy, or very big. Smoky, wood-paneled. A smattering of round tables with chairs and eight booths evenly distributed parallel to the bar. The wall was halved by a narrow walkway that led to the bathrooms off to the right. There was a door off to Yamada's left, faced with black leather and black lacquered studs. Four patrons sat at the far end of the bar, and there were two women—and one clearly on the game, with a black lace bustier under a leather jacket—tucked in a booth to the far right. Yamada turned away as the women began to kiss. "How's business?"

"Good," Big Mark said. "Cops already been in. They got the usual."

"Okay." Yamada turned as a cocktail waitress pushed

through the black leather door trailing voices and the rattle of dice. The door flapped shut.

The waitress gave Big Mark a drinks order then said to Yamada, "He's back again, down sixty kay. No problem yet, but Kip wants to know how deep before we sand him."

"Let him dig to eighty and then call it. He drinking?"

"This'll be his fifth."

"Good. Come get me if there's trouble." Glass in hand, Yamada headed for the narrow walkway that led to the restrooms. Instead of turning left, however, he went right and then right again. The hall ended in a door faced with red leather tacked with brass studs. Usually, there was high-stakes poker behind this door. Tonight four people, two men and two women, sat in caster chairs around an oblong, oak Texas hold'em table faced with green cloth and rimmed with a wide bumper of black leather.

One of the women, small with a frizz of espresso-colored hair, looked up as he pushed in. "You're late."

"I got held up," Yamada said, dropping into a vacant seat. He told them about Eriksson. When he was done, there was a short silence, and then one of the men said, "He's got a point."

"About what?" Espresso Hair demanded.

"Down, Abby, down." Noah Bridgewater had a mild, good-natured face with clear brown eyes. "I'm just saying terrorism doesn't win wars. Never has."

The second man—older and with watery hound-dog eyes, named Conley—asked, "You're agreeing with Eriksson?"

"I'm just saying history's not on our side. No matter how much resistance has been mounted to past occupations, once the Dracs are solidly in, they stay. On the other hand, Tormark has a reputation of being pretty evenhanded. Why not give her a chance?"

"That's a non-starter," Yamada rapped. "We got to target the Dracs, put them in a world of hurt."

"Do you have anything like a plan?" Bridgewater asked.

Yamada looked at the second woman, who'd barely stirred. Her eyes were deep amber with green flecks, and very solemn. "Maybe," she said.

Bridgewater said, "Yeah? Maybe like *what*, Dasha?"

Dasha was stunningly beautiful: tall and capable, with a

mane of rust-red hair. Combined with her strange, sad eyes, she seemed ethereal, not altogether *there*. She fingered a tiny gold locket dangling around her throat. "Maybe, like, we've got a plan. Not ready for prime time yet."

"Uh-huh," Conley said, without enthusiasm. "So, what do we do in the meantime?"

Yamada's filed incisors showed in a grin. "I got a couple ideas. We set up food kitchens, maybe a free clinic or something, and then run our ops in the background. Makes it harder for the Dracs to shut us down. They'll be taking food out of the mouths of kids. That's real bad publicity."

Bridgewater, who was an EMT and the group's medic, said, "I can ask the Dracs to lend a hand. One of those goodwill things."

"What if Eriksson gets in our way?" Abby put in. "We'll still be running ops. I don't think he'd turn us in voluntarily, but he knows us. You and Dasha have real jobs. I got the gig on base, working the chow hall. Great for scuttlebutt, but I got to eat."

"We all do," Dasha said. "But I actually agree with Noah this time around. They'll send a new base commander, someone seasoned. We need to pull one or two more ops, and then we should let up awhile. Let the activity dribble away, and the Dracs will relax. Otherwise, they'll always be edgy and suspicious. That way, they won't think bigger. We don't want them thinking bigger."

Conley and Bridgewater looked at each other. "Bigger?" Conley asked. "How *much* bigger?" When Dasha shook her head, Conley threw up his hands. "Well, Jesus, give us a hint."

But it was Yamada who answered. "Big," he said. "*Real* big. Like . . . *boom*."

sworn to secrecy, but Shimazu was *yakuza*. So . . . yeah. "I have more important things to worry about than some gambler getting whacked. Right now, we have fireworks on Biham and the border worlds in proximity to this ridiculous Republic March." He looked toward the far wall. "Any idea what's eating them?"

"Other than the obvious?" Wahab Fusilli said. The O5P agent's normally swarthy skin was a queasy shade of washed-out yellow under the fluorescent glare. "They want us out?"

"I get that," Crawford said, irritated. Fusilli seemed subdued, his blue eyes more opaque than usual. The information Fusilli brought back this time was similarly dull. Maybe the job was eating at Fusilli, maybe too much solo recon. Yet even back in the fold, Fusilli wasn't close to anyone.

*Understandable given his past: Treason isn't something genetic, but you inherit the shame.*

Aloud he said, "Any idea how much Eriksson's calling the shots?"

"Not from the available intel," Fusilli said.

"Hunh," Parks grunted. He was a big man and very tall, with large hands, blunt fingers and rugged, suntanned skin. He stroked a wiry tangle of salt-and-pepper moustache and square-cut beard, like a professor mulling over a knotty problem. "I told you it was a mistake to let Eriksson go back. Don't look now, but that's come back to bite us in the ass. We should arrest the guy."

"Oh, *that* will win hearts and minds," Fusilli said. As an agent, he only wore his uniform when he flew his Balac Strike VTOL into battle. Today, he sported blue jeans, a black short-sleeve tee, and lace-up black boots. With the tiny diamond stud in his left earlobe, a fall of shoulder-length raven-dark hair, and those blue eyes, Fusilli turned heads—not always an asset for an agent. "We're Dracs, remember? Mention Al Na'ir, and everyone knows exactly what you're talking about. I was on Al Na'ir. I survived it, and *I* understand completely."

Fusilli had a point, a good one. Before Spear, they'd been at yellow: locked but not loaded. They'd upgraded to red: locked and loaded. Crawford said, "What about resupply? Julian Davion's close. Or maybe Sandoval-Groell."

# 11

**A**ndre Crawford was tired of canned air, fed up with recycled waste water that tasted like musty aluminum, sick to death of light-globes that were always too bright. Up to *here* with day after day spent in a labyrinth of tunnels beneath the skin of an ashcan planet where the air was argoncyanide, the star a red giant, and the light a brassy crimson. There were days when Andre Crawford wanted someone, *anyone*, to explain why they'd traded Proserpina for a sewer like Halstead Station.

Like today: He read the news bullet again and then squinted across his desk. "A guy gets blown away outside a pachinko parlor. So? Maybe it's just another *yakuza* killing."

"Just another *yakuza* killing." Draped in an office chair opposite, Lance Shimazu screwed his lips to a disdainful pucker. "I like the way you say that. Ho-hum, just those wild and crazy *yakuza* kids doing their thing."

"Hey." From the seat alongside him, Wesley Parks glared at the squat, burly *yakuza*. "Watch the mouth, kid."

"Stow it, Parks," Crawford said. A headache thumped his temples. Shimazu was the price they paid for trying to keep the *yakuza* factions on board. To Shimazu: "It isn't?"

"No. This guy Kirino, it's a message."

"I don't see how. Whoever killed him couldn't have had any idea we'd get wind of this in a timely manner. To outward appearances, we're just as blind and deaf as everyone else." A well-placed fiction: They had the black boxes. Katana had trusted very few with the information. Not even the coordinator knew. Of course, *Shimazu* knew and was

"I say we take the fight directly into that stupid March of theirs," Parks put in. "Plant our butts on Tikonov, if we have to."

"No can do," Crawford said, twiddling a pen like an anxious baton twirler. "We've got enough stealing Peter to pay Paul for the Dieron push. Take Biham: We've got roughly eight hundred troops responsible for seven-fifty square klicks."

"That's thin," Parks said.

"Yup. And that's why I want *you* to step into Spear's shoes."

"There are shoes left to step into?" Parks said, and then winced. "Sorry, that was a really bad joke."

"Crass," Shimazu agreed. "You'd make a pretty good *yakuza*."

"Can we stay on track here?" Crawford said. "Parks, I want you to take McCain along. He's a doc. We'd win brownie points if we set up mobile clinics, maybe help the civilian hospitals." He looked at Fusilli. "Eriksson ever see you when Sakamoto had you and Liz on Al Na'ir?" When Fusilli shook his head, Crawford said, "Then here's how we play it. I want you on Biham, where you're gonna have plenty of support, and I want you to check in regularly with Parks. No running black, got it?"

Fusilli held his gaze for a second too long, as if trying to read Crawford's intent. Finally, he said, "I will if conditions permit. They might not always be optimal. But I will."

There was a note of reproach in his voice. Crawford pushed past that. "Good. You find the contact person or people, but leave Eriksson out of it if you can. Last thing we need is for them to think we're worried. Our best bet is to shut down the receiving end. If Sandoval-Groell's the one, and things go black?" Crawford shrugged. "Tough shit."

*And if Katana's been successful with the Cats, he might have a lot more fireworks in his backyard than he's counted on.*

"What if Eriksson's the contact?" Fusilli asked. "He's a knight."

"Knight or not, if he's the guy?" Crawford said. "He'll wish he never got in our way."

Parks said, "What about the *yakuza*? How do we know that they aren't the ones doing resupply? I mean, we're talking money."

Shimazu shook his head. "The thing bugging the *yakuza* is you guys take them for granted. All this stuff, it's a signal. Kirino was the son of a man involved in *bakuta*, a gambling faction on Junction, but his *mother* is Eddie Alzubadai's step-niece."

"And Alzubadai is . . . ?" Crawford asked.

"Low-level. Runs operations out of Donenac, Valmiera, Ljugam . . ."

"Planets near the New Samarkand border. That's far enough away from Junction. What's the problem?"

"Just because we got different territories doesn't mean squat. Anything or anyone that cracks down on one group affects everybody. Now Kirino was only one guy, but there was another killing the same day Kirino went down. *That* was aimed right at Kamikuro."

*Oh, no.* Crawford went still. "Not Kamikuro, please."

"Naw, naw, these people are *kabuki-mono*; they're not nuts. The guy got whacked was Kamikuro-*san*'s banker. Head shot, right back here." Shimazu tapped the base of his skull where it joined the spine. "When he was in bed with a lady friend, you know, in her apartment. Brains sloshed all over the place. Popped the lady friend, too. But this is all a kick in the ass to get you to notice."

"Notice what?" Parks said. "What do they want, flowers and a thank-you card?"

"Parks," Crawford warned. He looked at the liaison. "*Tai-shu* Tormark rewarded the *yakuza* by promoting them within the DCMS."

Shimazu screwed up his nose. "Ahhh, look. I don't want to appear disrespectful, but . . . so *what*? I mean, really?"

Crawford was stunned. "Promotion into the DCMS is an *honor*."

"If you say so. That and a half-stone can buy you a beer."

"Hey!" Parks flared. "What kind of crap is *that*?"

"You asked. I'm telling you. That kind of stuff doesn't exactly make the rest of the *yakuza* go green with envy. Times have changed."

"Okay," Crawford said. He still couldn't believe his ears. When had things changed so much? "What's the issue?"

"What a lot of guys want now is to be on the winning side. Tormark doesn't look like she's winning so much as she's trying to plug eleven holes with ten fingers. All the *yakuza* got to do is look at worlds like Styx, Saffel, Ancha, *Biham* . . . like taking out an ad."

He was right, and Crawford knew it. "How many factions are we talking?"

"Three around Junction, and maybe Eddie Alzubadai's guys. Word's out they're *ronin*, freelancers."

"Somebody help me." Parks put his hands to his forehead and squeezed as if to wring Shimazu's words from his brain. "Why is this happening now? And why the Benjamin District?"

Shimazu rolled his eyes. "Let me ask you. How many of those conscripted *yakuza* are still in the DCMS?"

"A few," Crawford said, not liking how defensive he sounded.

"Translation: Not. *Many*. That's counting Kamikuro-*san* and the *Ryuu-gami*, right? See, you have to understand the basic conflict here. First, you got your business. Your business is what keeps you in power. You get a drain on your revenues because there's war, or you got your ships seized, and you piss off a lot of people. Plus, there's uncertainty. It's like the market and speculations. If people get worried, they get the yips. They get the yips, they cut down on orders. They do that, people lose money. As for Tormark, look, no disrespect, but she just isn't that popular with the suits. Most *yakuza* feel they gave you plenty and maybe you owe *them* a favor or two."

"Meaning they don't think she's got the backbone," Parks grated.

"Meaning they don't *know* her. Tormark or some of you guys—even you, Parks, you're their type—you guys go to a meet."

"They're welcome here." Crawford said.

"We'll even provide doughnuts," Parks said.

"They'd like doughnuts," Shimazu said. "But you got to go to *them*. Makes the *oyabun*s look weak if they come to you. But if you go, or Tormark . . ."

"That's where I draw the line." Crawford shook his head. "No can do. It's Viki Drexel and you, or nobody. Besides, Viki's dealt with the *yakuza* before. I'll send her with full authority to negotiate. That would be a way of showing respect. That we trust them not to get our heads handed to us on a platter."

"Yeah," Parks said sourly. "Just the inside of a refrigerated box."

## 12

*Katana's Journal*
*23 June 3136*

**S**omething I never thought I'd hear myself say, but Luthien in my rearview? Gotta love it.

I left Luthien much later than I wanted, but there are things a *tai-shu* just has to do. And one hard thing: sending the Old Master away to take care of my father on Mizunami. A *tai-shu* has an advisor, not a security blanket, and I've pretty much kept him under wraps, didn't include him in any of the official functions. Though I did catch Bhatia giving him the oddest look . . .

Anyway, the Old Master understood. Said he wondered why it had taken me so long. And then he said the oddest thing: "You, your friends, your enemies, are not in control of your destiny. You are stones in an ever-changing game of *Igo*. Depending upon where you are placed, either you are weak and vulgar or you add to a beautiful shape. You can't know until you are played and make your play in return. There will be times where you are squeezed, when your moves are *damezumari*, played with a shortage of liberties. There will be others when you are *sabaki*, light on your feet, ready to press an advantage with little warning. So, choose wisely."

O-*kaay*, that was cryptic. Choose what? I mean, if I'm just a stone? He didn't explain. Great. And it's probably important.

There was another official reception in honor of Theodore's appointment. That's when the weirdest darned thing happened. I'm stuck with the same guy who got to me the night I wore that *furisode*. Some noble so unctuous I wanted to wipe my hands. I couldn't figure a graceful way out when, all of a sudden, Makoto Shouriki shows up. Again. Very pleasant guy and easy to talk to, and you can tell that he's listening. Makoto reminds me of McCain: a genuinely nice human being who wants to help.

Anyway, he gave me an out: came up to my elbow, said something like, I've been looking all over for you. Like that. Then he steered me through the crowd and out to a balcony. We made small talk. But there was something on his mind, and so I decided to let a silence go. See if he wanted to talk. I don't believe in coincidence.

He bit. Makoto said, hesitantly, as if feeling his way, "I noticed something about *Tai-sho* . . . sorry, *Tai*-shu Kurita. Theodore. Did you?"

"Notice what?"

"He seems a little . . . *off*. Something in his manner, his walk . . ."

I played dumb. But I *did* know, exactly: had seen it when we were in the sim. Anyway, I generalized. Said I wasn't sure. Hadn't noticed. Things like that. Makoto just gave me this quizzical look, as if trying to read between the lines or peer into the space behind my eyes. Finally, he said, "Well, all right then. It's probably nothing."

I agreed, and that was that. We moved onto other things, and then I got busy and didn't see him again, and then I left.

Got a bad feeling about that. About Theodore. Just about as bad a feeling as I've got about the Kitten. How to deal with her? The Kitten's tough to read. She strikes me as a person used to hiding deep in the shell of her own skin, peering out at the world with these bright, sharp eyes that watch and judge.

We met the day before I left. Deciding exactly where and who should actually issue the invitation was a bit of a protocol nightmare. Lemme see, does *tai-shu* trump royal blood, five thousand times removed?

Anyway, I invited her to tea. Longest hour of my life. She actually critiqued my sim, the twit! Listening to that

little kewpie doll dissect each and every misstep . . . and
then I had to bite my tongue when she explained that she
was just being helpful. (Oh, yeah, right.)

Long and the short of it: She's got to gather up my Ronel
troops now posted to Sakuranoki in the New Samarkand
District and bring them bag and baggage to Halstead Station. I could use the men. Problem is Sakuranoki's hell and
gone. It'll take two months just to pack up and then six,
maybe eight weeks to make Halstead Station, maybe
longer. But they're more warm bodies.

Well, maybe the take-home is that things will happen
when they happen. I need to learn to relax. Like now. Most
people'd give their eyeteeth for a chance to travel in a
*Monarch*. This sleek little baby's built for comfort, not combat. When I went to Irece to beg the Cats for troops, I
took a *Fury*. But when you're in Luthien space, you don't
come armed to the teeth. The same way no one's allowed
weapons within the palace precincts. (Though Toranaga got
away with it, and isn't *that* interesting?) Oh, you can brag.
You just can't back it with muscle or . . .

Hang on. Captain's on the horn.

# 13

**Monarch-*class DropShip* Fury's Lease, *en route***
   **to Luthien jump point**
**Pesht Military District, Draconis Combine**
**23 June 3136**

**H**er comm shrilled again, a high-pitched whistle, and Katana toggled off her microrecorder and punched up the
comm. "Tormark."

"I think you better get up here, Katana-*san*." The captain, a grizzled Fury veteran and about as unflappable in a
pinch as they came, sounded tense. "We've picked up a

distress call from a DropShip but couldn't get the registry. Sounds like they've suffered some sort of catastrophic hull breach. Comm says no other vessels are responding to the emergency. Request permission to change course to intercept."

"Go," she said. She pulled the sleeve of her olive drab jumpsuit down over her microrecorder. Time for journaling later, but it looked like she'd certainly have something pretty interesting to log. "Best speed."

It took them forty minutes at full burn to pick up on visual. No one said much, and the bridge was silent save for the beeping of computers and the steady, basso hum vibrating through the deckplates from their fusion engines at max thrust. They were pulling three gs, one above the *Monarch*'s tolerance, and Katana felt gravity's fingers tugging at her skin. She stood to the captain's right, her left hand gripping the command chair, her eyes searching a myriad of stars on the viewscreen.

The captain picked out the ship first. "There," he said, pointing. "About one o'clock. That corona, looks like the plasma burn from exhaust baffles. Comm," he continued, turning to his communications officer, "adjust screen, center and magnify."

"Oh, my God," Katana said as comm complied and the stricken ship swam into focus. "What the hell is *that* doing here?"

The other ship was a sleek aerodyne *Achilles*-class vessel: half the tonnage of their *Monarch* but much more powerful, with weapons—autocannons and LRMs—out the wazoo.

*Shouldn't be this close to Luthien, only three days out. How did they slip past the security ships stationed at the jump point?*

A mystery that would have to wait: She saw at once that the vessel was in big trouble, the telltale ghost-white plume of vented atmosphere still spewing from a jagged hole, a good twenty meters wide, in the ship's port hull, aft of a cargo bay that normally held infantry on a combat drop.

"That's one big hole," she said. "Blew out the entire aft cargo door."

"Mmmm-hmmm." The captain's eyes slitted. "But look at the edges. See all those curls, that stellate scoring? They weren't *hit* by anything. Looks to me like something blew out."

"Munitions?"

"No, munitions stores are forward and deeper in the ship. Comm, you got a registry ping?"

"Negative that, sir."

"Then what?" Katana's eyes picked through the details, trying to reconcile what she saw to what she knew. *Still venting after all this time . . . Why haven't they sealed off the section? The plume's almost directional, jetting through the rip.* "Something's wrong here," she said. "You see that plume? That's coming out under pressure. Why haven't they sealed off that section? For that matter, where's the atmosphere coming from?"

The captain's mouth set. "I was kind of wondering the same thing. Whatever they're doing over there, they've got to be suited up, ready for evac. That's what I would do."

"But why haven't they launched escape pods?"

"*That* is a very good question. Let's ask them. Comm, can you . . ."

"Sir, *their* cap's coming through now."

"On speaker." The bridge filled with the fizz of interference, and the captain said, "*Achilles* ship, this is *Monarch* Delta-Charlie-Tango-Five-Niner, what's your status?"

The answer—a man's voice, Katana was almost certain, and she heard his panic even through the distortion— filtered through in spurts and pops: "*Monarch*, this is *Achilles* Helo-Foxtrot . . . we . . . unable to evac . . . shorted . . . we have suited up . . . request . . . station . . . !"

The captain scowled. "Comm, can you clean that up?"

"Negative that, sir. That's the best I can do."

Katana was gritting her teeth hard enough for her jaw to hurt. "I think they're requesting we go to stationkeeping."

The captain nodded. "That's how I heard it, too. That way, we can do an emergency dock, belly to belly. We've got the most tonnage, that's how it should go. There are a couple problems."

"You mean, beyond the fact that we're all going to be panting on the deckplates when we do a rapid deceleration, not to mention burning up obscene amounts of fuel and screwing up our schedule besides?"

"To name a few." The captain hooked a thumb toward

the viewscreen. "I don't like all that shimmy out there. This baby won't exactly turn on a ten-stone. We slow to stationkeeping—yes, panting on the deckplates—and they can't control that pitch and yaw out there . . ." He didn't finish the rest of that thought.

"Can they make it under thrust to Luthien?" Even as she asked the question, she knew the answer. Under full burn, the *Achilles* would take two days to make Luthien. The crew's environmental suits had enough air for thirty hours.

"You know they can't. So, either we match their course and speed as an escort and hope someone hears us. Or we dock. There's no in-between. Now, I can't think of a reason in hell why we should slow down just to listen to them die. So it's a dock. That's my opinion." His dark eyes fixed Katana's. "But it's your call, *Tai-shu*. Either way, we suit up just in case and dispatch an emergency distress, see if the cavalry comes charging over the hill. I don't think it will, or else it would've shown up by now."

It took Katana less than a nanosecond. "Suit up, Captain. Then let's go save their asses."

The captain's voice was thin and attenuated through Katana's helmet speakers, like they were kids talking through tin cans on a string. "Status, Helm?"

"Board shows we're at stationkeeping, sir. Stationkeeping thrusters optimal, and we are holding position." The helmsman, a youngish woman with a wedge cut of silky black hair, turned to look back at the captain. Katana saw that she'd sweated enough for a swatch of her hair to glue itself to her cheek. The rest was standing on end under the sudden weightlessness that had come when they cut thrust and lost gravity. "*Achilles* vessel has cut transit drive and engaged braking thrusters. Distance, twelve hundred meters. Speed is five minus five and slowing. Board shows that she's got maneuvering thrusters, but she's still got some pretty bad yaw there, sir. If she can't get under better control, I'm going to have to try to match the rate of her spin. Except . . ."

"Go ahead."

"She's smaller, sir. Not as much mass to move, plus they got that leak that keeps nudging them out of position. With our greater mass . . . Sir, this ship is going to be pretty mushy, and *that* ship is going to be moving much more quickly relative to us. I'm sorry, but this baby, she's not designed for pinpoint maneuvers like this. She's," and now the helmsman sounded almost apologetic, "she's a luxury liner, not an assault vessel. Sir."

"Understood. You just do your job, it'll be all right." The captain spared the helmsman a reassuring nod that Katana didn't think translated to his eyes. (That was okay. Her stomach was doing somersaults, too.) "It'll be fine. But if it comes down to them or us, I want you ready to move us the hell out of the way. No use getting dinged up when we got time to try this half a dozen times if we need to. You got that?"

"Got it, sir."

The captain looked up at Katana. "Now comes the fun part."

His tone gave the lie. There wasn't really anything she could say, so Katana just nodded, then cut her gaze to the viewscreen. The *Achilles* had slowed, yes, but it was jittering along its vertical axis, though it had managed to roll so its undercarriage grew larger in their screen. No damage there that Katana could see, and their docking collar looked intact. Now if they could just ease together . . .

Her mouth was desert-dry, and it hurt to swallow, but she was sweating like mad. So much so that when she took a careful step back from the captain's chair to stand behind it, her grip-boots grabbing hold to anchor her to the deck, two tiny droplets shook free from her upper lip as wavering globules that splattered in slow motion against her faceplate. She thumbed down her suit's temp, shrugged tension from her shoulders and blew out a breath. If she kept sweating like a pig, she'd have a hard time seeing past the smear.

*We can do this, piece of cake, just kiss that belly . . . But we gotta watch that damn vent, and I don't get that vent. Why is it still pumping?*

"Here they come," Helm warned, a knife-edge of apprehension cutting through. "Z minus thirty and holding. Distance, one thousand meters . . . ninety . . . Distance, eight-five-zero . . . Sir, they're starting to roll."

"Compensate, Helmsman. Keep our belly to 'em,

keep . . ." The captain's voice notched up in alarm. "What the hell?"

Katana gasped as proximity alarms screamed. "They're pitching, bringing their nose down! Are they out of control?"

"Negative that, negative!" Helm whipped round in her seat. "Sir, they've engaged maneuvering thrusters!"

*Nose is the most heavily armored section of the ship, and they're bringing up their speed!* Katana saw it in a flash. "Captain, they're going to ram us! You've got to get us out of here!"

But the captain was already half out of his seat. "Helm, engage our transit drive, burn those sons of bitches before they can—!"

"They're hot, they're *hot*!" the helmsman cut in, her small gloved hands flying over her controls. "I read a weapons' lock! I read—!"

"They're going to hit us!" Katana shouted as the nose of the *Achilles* vessel speared space and blotted out the stars.

"Brace for impact!" the captain shouted. *"Brace—!"*

# PART THREE

*Tsumego:* Life and Death

# 14

The autopsy room was very quiet except for the soft hum of specimen refrigerators along the right wall. The temperature hovered at a cool eighteen C, enough to chill the tip of Detective Harry Loveland's nose. The hospital laundry was just around the corner from the morgue, and the air smelled like soap laced with the sharper bite of fixative and the stink of decomposition mingling with the jagged tang of copper.

A fluorescent light-globe floated over a waist-high stainless steel autopsy table. A body, covered by a white sheet, lay on the table. The body might have been male or female. Loveland couldn't tell.

They'd gathered at the medical examiner's autopsy room workstation. "So are we talking about the same guy?" Loveland asked.

"Maybe." The ME was a round man with eyes small as ball bearings. "I've never run into a killer with three distinctive killing styles."

The man standing to Loveland's right said, "Every killer's different. Some evolve. But most serial killers eventually unravel."

Special Agent Richard Thereon said this with no hint of superiority, and Loveland liked him for it. No matter what the planet, Bureau guys shared a sort of cookie-cutter quality: the gray suit, starched white shirt, nice tie. Agents had 'tude, couldn't wait to show you what a moron you were. Thereon worked out of Ancha's Bureau of Investigation and was . . . different. He could've been a turd. Loveland's jurisdiction was Kordova on Towne. Detectives usually didn't work cases out of their jurisdiction. Loveland did because the planetary legate said he could. (Other planetary jurisdictions hadn't objected. Now they could blame Loveland if the investigation went south.) Anyway, Thereon wasn't a turd.

"Well, if he is, it's only sporadic." The ME poked at his computer. The screen filled with the body of a nude woman on an autopsy gurney. Her skin was puffy but not hideously swollen, with a bluish hue. The long hair was dark and limp as seaweed. A deeply purple-black bruise encircled the woman's throat right below the thyroid cartilage, like a too-tight necklace. Her eyes were gone, tags of bleached flesh highlighted against naked bone.

"Okay," the ME said, "I've had a chance to review all the cases that the Kordova ME, Doctor Slade, did. The Little Luthien killer's first vic, Alicia Lang, found 23 February 3134. Time of death was within the twenty-four hours prior to discovery. Cause of death was fatal brain anoxia secondary to ligature strangulation. The eyes were removed antemortem."

"Before death," Loveland said.

"Yup. But here's what's interesting. Your guy is ambidextrous *and* a pro. No nicks, no hesitation marks. The lids were cleanly sliced with a single-edged blade, likely a scalpel. Same with the second victim, except that woman had no ears, and the third, no tongue."

"See no evil, hear no evil," Thereon said. His eyes were gray, large and stormy, as if filled with heavy clouds. "A real joker."

"Yeah, except Chuckles got a kill buddy, Shu Imashinigi," the ME said. "Vic two had lots of hesitation marks, ripped skin. But by victim three—" Another woman, her mouth a bloody gaping maw. "Imashinigi's improved. Only nine cuts to get the tongue. But even at the end, his technique was still pretty crude."

Another click, and this time, there was an image of an adolescent girl in pieces. "When they found his daughter's body in his deep freeze, she was in pieces. But she was surgically dismembered, very neatly. That's Chuckles, not Imashinigi. That pelvic block dissection . . ." The ME was balding as well as plump, and he palmed his scalp, stroking the skin as if smoothing back hair. "I couldn't've done it better."

Loveland had investigated fatal rape cases where MEs

cored the pelvis. He didn't like the procedure now any more than he did then. In this case, that detail was kept back from the press as well as any hint there was a killing team. "Why the dissection?"

"To rub your nose in it, Harry," Thereon said. "He wanted you to know that this girl had been brutally victimized by her father. Our unsub is extremely intelligent, highly organized—and having the time of his life."

At the autopsy table, the ME peeled back the sheet to reveal not a man's face, neck and shoulders but a woman's. "Just like Slade, I kept asking myself how Chuckles did it. How did he immobilize these women? Because they were alive. Then I read Slade's reports, and then I got Agent Thereon's report on that Ancha prostitute, the one got her throat ripped out, and the Bureau ME's findings. So I looked at this lady—and I found it."

Loveland stared down at this Jane Doe, unclaimed, not missed. Her face was pulpy. Her nose had been broken by a blow delivered by a right-handed individual. Her chocolate-brown skin was dusky, with extensive marbling by dark green vessels ballooning with stagnant blood. The morgue refrigerator maintained the body near freezing to prevent further decay, but Loveland still caught a whiff of rot.

And the woman didn't have a throat. Instead, there was a ragged, bloodless crater. The trachea had been crushed, the left carotid artery severed, and the right pulped. As she suffocated, Jane Doe had seen her blood sheeting her killer's face.

A year ago, there'd been a prostitute on Proserpina, who'd died in *exactly* the same way.

But their killer was starting to make mistakes. On Proserpina and here on Ancha, he'd left saliva. Saliva meant DNA.

But while the bite marks matched, the DNA samples didn't. Both prostitutes had been murdered by the *same man* in the same *way* because the bite marks matched. Yet the DNA recovered in *this* woman's throat and beneath her nails was *different*. They had *two* cold hits.

And there was one more crucial detail that tied all the killings together across the prefectures, from Towne to Proserpina to Ancha.

Using his gloved hands, the ME gently turned the woman's head. Her hair was a spiked black tangle, but the running stitches, like the seam on a baseball, were clearly visible: the skin sutured after the skull cap had been refitted, and the woman's face and scalp pulled back over the exposed bone. "Right there," he said, peering through a magnifying glass. "Between the fourth and fifth cervical vertebrae. Impossible to pick up unless you knew where to look. The fact that all the victims since Proserpina have dark skin makes it that much harder to find."

Loveland squinted through the magnifying glass as the ME gently pulled the skin taut between two gloved fingers. Then Loveland saw it: the tiny lips of a circular wound invisible to the naked eye.

The ME said. "He must've used a stiff, strong wire and pithed her like a frog, except he didn't obliterate the brainstem. So she'd be conscious but paralyzed." The ME peeled the sheet to the woman's abdomen. "This poor woman didn't feel a thing, but she saw every second."

The woman's breasts were gone. Flesh and fatty tissue had been deftly sliced away to expose muscle the color of meat left too long in a grocer's display case.

"This guy of yours, he's a monster," the ME said.

"No," Loveland said. "Satan."

# 15

*JumpShip* **Kaminari,** *somewhere near Midway*
  *nadir jump point*
*New Samarkand Military District, Draconis*
  *Combine*
*22 July 3136*

**W**hen he had come to himself, he had done so in blood.
Lots of it. Blood globules—shimmering, wavering and ee-
rily alive in weightlessness—had spattered windows and
workstations, walls and books, rupturing into spidery
smears. More blood, tacky as an imperfect second skin, had
coated his face, seeped into his hair, dried on his hands.
Blood in his mouth, tasting of death.

Even now, a week later, with the ship clean and the crew
watching him with frightened rabbits' eyes, he had a hard
time remembering what had happened. He recalled smashing glass and hurling furniture, all in terrible, ceaseless slow
motion—and he remembered pain. Clawing his way back
to some semblance of rationality was agony, and once he
was there, the frenzy of his grief, as real and genuine as
any lover's, shook him to the core.

*Dead, dead, she's gone, and now I'm truly* alone. . . .

Before this catastrophe, he'd been lonely. (It had been a
mistake to kill Marcus: He'd discovered that within a day.
They needed one another. So he'd made a little shrine of
Marcus, played games with him. That helped.) He'd done
a murder here, a killing there, hopscotching from planet to
planet, restless, restless. Ravaging bodies only to discover
that his hunger grew, like something alive.

Briefly, he was Crawford's golden boy. He'd finally left
because he wanted Katana all to himself. He'd lived for
the day when he revealed himself, had fantasies of how it
would all happen. How she would look at him at the very,

very end. The scales would fall from her eyes, and she would see him as he truly was: the only man she wanted or needed, the only one she could trust. Katana would come to him, to his bed, willingly. Eagerly. Aboard his JumpShip and in the perpetual night of space, he'd spun fantasies of Katana in his arms, Katana's mouth against his, the slide of her fingers, the sleekness of her skin and taut muscles: fantasies that left him shivering with longing and lust.

The rub had been how. Even if the Kuritas were gone, there would be the others: Crawford, Parks and all the rest—and that accursed Kan Otome, the Old Master. (And if Katana only knew the truth about that old, *old* man . . . Everyone had a past.)

Yet none of that mattered now. Katana was dead.

The only thought that now burned his raging, grieving brain like a brand was how to destroy the Kuritas, each and every one.

But there'd been this godsend, maybe an omen: a message, encrypted, delivered through trusted couriers, deposited in a secure account. When he'd read it, he saw his path. He saw his chance.

Because in Vincent Kurita's garden, there was a snake named Ramadeep Bhatia.

## JumpShip Shadow, *Midway nadir jump point*

Ramadeep Bhatia floated before a portal and waited for the call. He'd gotten word of the accident—the *Monarch* reduced to a debris field and only a handful of bodies recovered from a ship with no escape pods or lifeboats—while en route to the Luthien jump point, the first leg of his long trip to New Samarkand, hell and gone. Thank the dragon, someone upstairs liked him because the news crackled from JumpShip to JumpShip—and right to Bhatia's very own. (Although those fools in Katana's command headquarters on Halstead Station probably didn't know yet.)

Gods, Toranaga's little gift showed such foresight! The *genius* of it! Had the man *known* the coordinator would refuse and post Yori Kurita to Katana's command? Because it was clear: Yori would assume command by right of blood. Oh, this Toranaga was turning out to be a much more capable man than even Bhatia had been prepared to admit.

A sudden thought so stunning that the realization was physical, an electric jolt that sizzled through his skin, quite took his breath away. Was this *only* coincidence? Did *Toranaga* have a hand in Katana's death? Dear gods. Bhatia released his breath, very slowly, his heart thudding in his temples. If so, then the warlord was even more cunning, more gratifyingly proactive than he'd imagined.

Yes, things could not be more to his liking. *Now* was the time to set *his* plan in motion. The plan was . . . well, *audacious*. Dangerous, actually. Because, as soon as he was a day out of Luthien, he'd sent a message through very secure channels—safeguards upon safeguards—to a man Bhatia never dreamt he'd call upon as an ally.

*But now, now is the time to strike! To rid the Combine of the Peacock once and for all!*

One dangling thread sobered him. What of the Bounty Hunter? Without Tormark, would he return to his heinous ways? Bhatia suspected the Bounty Hunter and Kappa—a man he feared more than he liked to acknowledge—were one and the same. Yet a follow-up report from his agent on Asta indicated that the rumors regarding the Hunter's reemergence proved false. No one had seen the Hunter, not on Asta or Halstead Station.

Bhatia was not a superstitious man, but Fate had dealt him this chance. Tormark was gone. Vincent Kurita and his family would join her. And then? Bhatia permitted himself an indulgent smile that was slow in coming, delicious in its essence. Yes, he would install the child, this Yori Kurita, who would see them through to a new era of glory and might such as the Inner Sphere had never seen.

The silence was rent by the shrill of his comm. The sound was as palpable as a set of icy fingers tripping up his spine, freezing his blood, stopping his breath.

*What am I doing? This way leads to madness. I can still stop this. I do not have to travel this road unless I am very, very sure because once done, there is no turning back . . .*

And then the moment of indecision passed. Ramadeep

Bhatia punched in. He listened to the background hiss of deep space, the cracks and pops of a solar wind—and waited on Fate. On his destiny.

On the whims of a monster.

Jonathan clicked off, pushed away from his console and drifted.

*Like a gift from the ashes. There is a time, and there is a place. A time to live, a time to die, and they will die because I've never felt this way, so empty. Hollow as if all my guts had been scooped out . . .*

The ISF director had been brutally succinct: "I propose nothing more than an alliance of convenience. We are enemies, but even enemies can work toward a common goal. Once Kurita is dead, you will disappear. I will not pursue you. Yet venture into my sphere again, and I will hunt you down."

*Well played, Director, nicely done.* Jonathan swam to a cabinet and paused, debating. The glass doors were expensive quartz crystal, the better to enhance the many minute, brightly lit fiber-optic filaments illuminating his collection. His eyes—hooded, gray as mist—ticked over the items, and then he selected a vial and secured the cabinet once more.

Humming tunelessly, Jonathan released the vial. It had a slight bulge in the center that created the perfect contact angle to prevent liquid from pooling at the bottom. The clear preservative bunched like thick lava, and the blue eyes with their thin stalks of optic nerve bobbed.

So Bhatia wished to use his services? Well, *Jonathan* had *his* conditions, and Bhatia *would* abide, or Jonathan would destroy him. Might do so anyway. He had no illusions. Bhatia would kill him the very second he was no longer useful.

And meet with the ISF director at the College on New Samarkand? He thought *not.* Oh, he'd *go,* but on his terms. If he used pirate points, he'd arrive before the third of September when the new class entered the college.

But there was something about September that bothered him. What was it? Somersaulting to a workstation, he did a search—and then his chest seized with sudden hope.

September was the month of *O-Bon:* the Festival of the Dead when restless spirits, the *kami,* wandered the earth, revisiting their homes and loved ones. Dear God, it was an omen! His heart filled with a preternatural certainty that spilled into a kind of ecstasy. His eyes stung, and when tears came, he dashed them from his eyes. The tiny orbs shimmered like diamonds.

Yes, he would offer *himself* to his darling. She would use *his* body as a vessel. Her soul would mingle with his in an intimacy beyond the merely physical. They would be *one*: his body *her* temple.

"Yes, Katana," he said. He let the vial spin free, the ownerless blue eyes bob away. There was only one woman he wanted, just one. He raised his fingers, stroking the air, as if pulling at invisible filaments. "Come to me, my darling. Fill me. Then you will *know* the man I've been, the one that I am—because I am here for you, my heart, my beloved Katana. I am *here*."

# 16

*Yamabushi Retreat, Ogano*
*Benjamin Military District, Draconis Combine*
*29 July 3136*

This high in the Ogano Mountains, alpine scrub gave way to shattered rock and naked scree. The air was thinner, something Theodore felt in the slow burn in his chest and ache in his joints. Sweat greased his face and neck, and his temples throbbed to the drumbeat of a headache. He rested, leaning against an outcropping of gray rock baked hot by a fierce and unforgiving sun. Unhooking his insulated water bottle, Theodore drank. Icy and sweet, the water tracked a cold finger down the center of his chest and into his belly. Yet his left hand jittered as he tried to cap his canteen, and he finally had to use his right.

*Eihei-ji* Temple was built into the mountainside. A

mountain river of glacier melt was tapped for water, and the monastery sported well-tended gardens of white stone and evergreens. The haunting melodies of *honkyoku,* meditation pieces played on *shakuhachi,* floated above the musical chants of the monks immersed in their meditations.

Now clean and refreshed, Theodore watched as three monks approached. They each wore simple geta, a black tunic and dark blue, ankle-length robes. Two of the monks were more substantial because they were O5P agents who, with four others, served as round-the-clock bodyguards.

The third monk was as tall as Theodore but without his ice-blue eyes. His head was shaven, and he shuffled. His shoulders slumped.

"Brother." Theodore grasped Ryuhiko's forearms. His brother was older by fifteen years, and his arms were surprisingly thick with muscle. His skin was bronzed by sun. Yet Theodore saw madness in those too-bright, hazel eyes. "You're big around as a *BattleMaster.*"

Ryuhiko laughed. "After prayers, there isn't much to do. Sometimes I turn wood to make bowls and boxes the monastery sells, but most of the time, I'm out and about. I'm getting as good as the Nykr goats."

"I'm impressed. Huffing up the mountain, I almost passed out."

Ryuhiko gave a negligent shrug that was somewhat abbreviated because of his posture. He gestured for Theodore to walk, but Theodore hesitated. His brother made an exasperated sound. "Oh, come on, come on. I haven't had a bad day since . . . Jamon, when was my last bad day?"

The taller bodyguard said, "Last week, *Tono.* You were . . . unwell."

"Was I? I don't remember. Did I hurt anyone?"

"Only me, *Tono,* and not badly. If you'd bitten instead of scratched, it would've been worse."

Ryuhiko barked a raucous laugh. "That will teach you! When I get an idea in my head, it won't shake loose until I've got what I want."

"Indeed." Jamon's tone was bland, but his eyes semaphored a warning to Theodore.

They walked, their sandals crunching over scree. Ryuhiko was still smiling and muttering, sometimes chuckling.

Soon, they came to a narrow, rugged path cut from the mountain's face. The right edge gave way to air and rocks below. Instinctively, Theodore moved to bracket Ryuhiko against the mountain. He was tired, but he trusted his step far more.

Suddenly, Ryuhiko said, "How is my father?"

A dangerous subject: Vincent Kurita never came to visit his eldest son. The cover story—that Ryuhiko preferred the isolation that was a monk's life—helped.

*Just as the official story of her wish to lead a contemplative life covers the truth about my mother: that she's hidden away in a hospital at the base of these mountains, her mind gone.*

Theodore resisted the temptation to look back for the guards, who'd fallen back a respectful distance. But he slowed a tad. "He's well. Why, a month ago . . ." He chattered about receptions and the nobles' squabbles.

His brother interrupted in mid-sentence: "What about you?"

"Oh, I just attend boring functions."

"I didn't mean that." Ryuhiko's voice was flat. "I meant: What about *you?* You, your body, *you* . . . What about *you?*"

"I'm fine."

"You're a liar." Again, that curious flatness. "You think I don't see? Your left hand shakes, Brother, and your face tics every now and again, but so fast you don't realize. But *I* see it. You're dragging your right leg—"

"I'm tired."

"*Dragging* your *leg!* So don't tell *me* you're well, Brother! If you are also ill, why are *you* free? Why must *I* stay here while *you*—!"

"We should go back." Theodore was uncomfortably aware that the guards were easily fifty meters behind—and aware of the empty space to his right. "I need to rest. The altitude . . ."

"Bullshit," Ryuhiko said, and made the word much uglier than it was. "It's because *he* favors you. Mother favored me, but Father always loved *you!*" Ryuhiko's face was a contorted mask of crazed hatred and grief, and it had all happened so fast, like a volcano exploding without warning. "You're free, and I'm less than dog shit!"

Out of the corner of his eye, Theodore saw the guards

hurrying down the path. Just a few more seconds . . .
"Come, Brother," he said, and then he did absolutely the
wrong thing. He clasped Ryuhiko's arm. "Come, let's—"

"Take your hands off me! I'm not a dog. I'm no one's
*puppet!*" With a wild cry, Ryuhiko launched himself at
his brother.

Theodore reacted, a fraction of a second too late. "Ryuhiko! No!" he shouted as he simultaneously tried to both
turn and plant his feet. To his horror, his right knee locked,
and then Ryuhiko was on him. His brother's momentum
staggered Theodore, sent him reeling. Desperate, Theodore
grabbed Ryuhiko's tunic in both hands and then went
against instinct. He willed his body to go limp, using his
weight to drag Ryuhiko down. His right leg was still rigid
with spasm, and Theodore cried out as Ryuhiko's left knee
drove into the taut hamstring. Then his brother's hands
were around his neck, the big work-roughened hands
squeezing . . .

But then the guards were on them, and the moment of
danger passed.

His brother didn't stop cursing him all the way back.

Night slammed down. The air was frosty, and Theodore
was numb with cold. He sat staring at stars wheeling
through the heavens—his right hand clasping his left to still
the tremor that had settled into his very bones.

In that instant when Ryuhiko had him, Theodore had
fleetingly thought of death. Death would be a release. A
few moments' horror, and then their bodies would burst
upon unforgiving rock, and *he* would die.

For a fraction of a second, Theodore had craved death.
Tasted it.

*Have even I given up hope?*

That frightened him because he thought that Makoto
Shouriki had tried to tell him the same thing in a different way.

Back on Luthien, the day they'd learned of Katana's
death, Makoto had found him beneath that spreading
cherry tree, and he'd said the strangest thing: "Dynasties
are like gardens, Theodore. They must be tended, cared
for. Most of all, they depend upon the land."

What was Makoto getting at? Though he liked Makoto, considered him a friend, *he'd* not said anything about the curse in their blood. For the first time, Theodore wondered if perhaps his *father* . . . "And?"

"And *your* garden is built on shifting sands. Forgive me, Theodore, but I must be blunt. I worry for the future of your house. True, your sister is formidable and should be next in the line of succession. But that is no longer a given. Yori Kurita is rising, Theodore. She is rising fast, like a comet breaking free of gravity."

Theodore had forced a laugh. "I'm not planning on going anywhere, you know."

"No?" Then, swiftly, Makoto extended his left hand in a handshake. Without thinking, Theodore extended *his* left, realizing his mistake as their hands touched—and held. "For the love of God," Makoto said, clasping Theodore's hand in both of his, "take care, and *quickly,* Theodore."

*Held my* left *hand because he* knows.

And now Emi's words, an omen: *You're the only one who can save us, Brother. The only one.*

# 17

*Copenwald, Halstead Station*
*7 August 3136*

Expressionless, Crawford listened as a white-faced aide named Meriwether delivered the news. Afterward, Crawford took five minutes alone, red hair cascading around his face as he wept: huge, wracking sobs he stoppered with a fist.

And that was all the time he could spare. Immediately pressing were alerting the various commands; marshalling troops for Dieron; awaiting and then digesting Fusilli's intel on Biham, where Parks and McCain now were also stationed; and alerting Viki Drexel, who'd left for Junction a week ago, about Katana's death. If he could even *find* Viki: Agents in the field specialized in making themselves scarce.

How ironic that news of Katana's death had coincided with a triumph. She'd succeeded in securing a galaxy of Cats to mount campaigns on Styx and Saffel, then had gone to Luthien to lay out their plan of action. She'd taken her place as a full warlord even as they battled to rebuild the district, but gone into that Black Room, her head high. Now, without Katana at the helm, the Cats might find a loophole to exploit. Better the Cats stay in the dark.

*By God, I am beginning to think like a politician.*

The same message also contained the coordinator's posting of Yori Kurita to Dieron command, and her elevation in rank to *sho-sho*. Like it or not, Yori now had command privilege by right of blood *and* rank.

*Yes, little girl, we'll take your orders, but the jury's out on you. When we strike Dieron, we will not take it for* you— *because Dieron is what* Katana *wanted, and Dieron she'll get.*


## Hoarder's Run, Sakuranoki
## New Samarkand Military District, Draconis Combine
## 20 August 3136

The dojo smelled of sweaty feet and wet leather, but Yori Kurita paid no mind, her attention instead focused on her opponent. Jirobi Katanga, late of Ronel and the Fury, was tall, with very long arms and a better reach. Already, he'd scored with well-timed cuts, parrying her bamboo blade with ease, taking advantage not only of his height but of the energy of *her* attacks.

Frustrated, Yori blinked away sweat. This type of free-form fighting, *keiko*, was much more demanding than the simple exercises of *kendo kata*. There, she *always* knew who was bad, and who *shidachi*. In *kendo,* the *uchidachi always* lost because the bad guy always struck first.

*As they have all my life:* Then *you see the attack coming, you know exactly how to parry and defeat his energy, turn it against him . . .*

There was a loud double rap on wood. Instantly, she and Jirobi came out of their stances. Grateful for the chance to cool down, Yori stripped off her *do* as a lieutenant approached, a folded sheaf of paper in one hand. She knew at once by the look on his face that something was very wrong. "A priority message from *Tai-shu* Toranaga, Kurita-*san*."

At her gasp, Katanga said, "What is it? Are you all right?"

Angry at her slip, she said, simply, "*Tai-shu* Tormark is dead. An accident when her DropShip attempted to aid another ship in distress."

The color drained from Katanga's face. She was stunned when she saw the shine of tears. Would anyone mourn her? Quickly, she squelched the thought as irrelevant and focused on what to do next. Tormark was gone, and this was *her* moment. Clearly, her patron understood, else he'd never have the news couriered so quickly. (And did he have a hand in this? That crocodile, she wouldn't put it past him.)

*There is a time to act, and a time to mourn. For now, I act.*

She dismissed the messenger, then turned to Katanga, whose tears rolled unashamed down his cheeks. She couldn't help feeling a twinge of satisfaction as she bent to retrieve her *do* and took up her stance—because the game had suddenly changed, and she knew *exactly* what to do.

"Enough," she said. "Make ready your *shinai*. Dry your eyes and fight. There is time for grief when the fight for Dieron is past, but now you are a warrior, and you will rise to battle. So, fight because that is what *Tai-shu* Tormark would demand. Fight for your dead leader's honor."

*And then tomorrow, at first light, prepare to fight for* me, *now your leader and very much alive—because I so command.*

# 18

**K**arl Pierpont was on tilt. He'd played way too many hands, tried too many wild maniac bluffs . . . and now this. He sat facing Tony Yamada in Yamada's back office: a small, extremely well-soundproofed cubicle. Gray walls, concrete floor. A drain in the center of the floor, just under Pierpont's chair. (Why, was that *only* rust he spotted?) A desk, metal, institutional gray. Yamada was smoking, his heavy lids at half-mast. Pierpont could've used a smoke, maybe another Scotch and soda. Maybe just bring the bottle.

Yamada said, "Look, man, what can I say? You've got a tab longer than my arm."

"But I'm good for the money," Pierpont pleaded. "I'll pay you back."

"With what? You owe seven-fifty kay, with interest, not counting tonight. You want more credit, you got to come up with a down payment."

Pierpont swallowed, tasting sour alcohol. "I . . . I can't do that."

"Then we can't carry you anymore. Now, I know you're a good guy." Yamada sucked more smoke. "Maybe I should talk to your boss, work out an installment plan."

Aghast, Pierpont said, "Man, are you *crazy?* I got a clearance, I got a decent job! You mess up my job, how am I going to pay you back?"

"What about your house? Or your old lady—she got money?"

"Naw, man, nothing like that. You take our house, where're we supposed to live? What about my kid?"

"Kid, huh? You got a picture?"

"Yeah." Suddenly hopeful, Pierpont fished a snapshot from his wallet and passed it over. He waited, literally, on the edge of his seat.

"Cute kid," Yamada said. "You know, I got some cute ones."

"Kids?" (Actually, Pierpont couldn't care less but, hey, if talking about kids got Yamada to extend his credit, they could talk about head lice for all *he* cared.)

"Yeah." Yamada nodded at one of two bodyguards stationed at the door behind Pierpont. The guard left. They waited. The man returned. He carried a clear plastic cage with a vented pink plastic top. In the cage was a tiny gray mouse with glassy black eyes and nearly naked pink feet.

"See, this is real cute, too," Yamada said. Screwing his cigarette into the right corner of his mouth, Yamada pulled open his center desk drawer, rummaged around and withdrew a pair of very thin, very sharp scissors. Yamada stood, reached into the cage and pinched the mouse up by the scuff of its neck. The mouse went *screeek.*

"Ain't it cute?" Yamada said, cigarette keeping time. Holding the scissors in his right hand, he squinted at Pierpont through a wavering curtain of smoke. "Cute little bugger. We catch a lot of these because times are hard, even for mice. They come in, work their way into the storeroom, eat, hide out. But, you know, mouse gets caught, and I think, Yeah, you cute little fart. Crap all over my storeroom, eat my food, how you gonna pay me back? No, you don't know? Well, let me show you."

Then Yamada snipped the mouse's right rear foot. The mouse jerked and let loose a loud, high *SCREEEEE!* Blood bubbled from the raw stump.

"Aw, *JESUS!*" Rearing back, Pierpont half-rose, but Yamada's men clamped down on his shoulders. The mouse was still squealing and dripping blood, thrashing as Yamada pinched it tight. "Man, *God,*" Pierpont said. Sour bile mixed with Scotch pushed into the back of his throat, and his stomach churned. "Jesus Christ, whaddaya *doing?*"

"You know," Yamada said, still addressing the squalling mouse, "I don't think that's enough, you little shit. I don't think you learned a lesson. You eat like a pig and leave me to clean up the mess. Here's what I say about that."

"No!" Pierpont shouted, as the scissors flashed and the

mouse screamed. By the time Yamada finally decapitated the animal, Pierpont had vomited into his lap.

"Man, aw, man, what do you *want?*" Pierpont mewled. The vomit was warm against his thighs, and the smell made him retch. "I'll do anything, whatever you want . . ."

"Yeah?" There was blood on Yamada's hands, and he plucked a tissue from a box, wiped away the gore, finger by finger, then made a tiny tent of the thin paper over the still-quivering mess on his desk. Then Yamada pinched Pierpont's photo of his daughter between his left thumb and forefinger. His right hand played with the scissors, snapping the blades, slicing air. "You mean that? You're not just playing with me, now?"

"Anything, man." Pierpont coughed, wiped his mouth on his coat sleeve. "Anything you want."

"Good," Yamada said. He smiled. "That's real good."

# 19

*Siang, Biham*
*25 August 3136*

The bourbon was paler than piss; there was so much smoke he got a nicotine buzz just breathing; and the pretzels were stale. Wahab Fusilli hunched on a stool just beyond the elbow of the bar. He kept an eye on the front door, because this was Saturday night and the place was busy.

Nursing his drink, he brooded. Fat lot of good Bhatia and the ISF were. Frankly, with Katana's death and Yori Kurita assuming command, Fusilli wondered now if Bhatia needed him at all. And did *he* need Bhatia? Fusilli fingered the diamond stud in his left earlobe. *Any* of them? Tormark was dead, and he wasn't even upset. He wondered if he'd even *liked* her.

*What do* I *want? Whose side, what first?*

First, he had another drink. As the bartender, a beefy man with huge biceps, fished up ice for another round, Fusilli considered that he'd done very well for a double agent, thank you. He was alive, wasn't he? He'd a certain aptitude for the work: negotiating that razor-thin margin between factions with great care, shifting blame, diverting attention. He'd been skilled as a child, too: *It wasn't me. It was them. I threw that rock because I was scared, and I didn't mean to put out his . . .*

"This taken?" A woman with a mane of long red hair stood at his right elbow before an empty bar stool.

He hadn't seen her come in. Bad. He had to stay alert. "No."

"Great." She wore very tight black leather pants and a black blouse, its first three buttons undone. Gold glinted at the hollow of her throat. She slid onto the stool, leaning his way as she adjusted the tails of a black leather jacket, and he caught her scent above the stink of cigarettes: sultry and sweet, like musk and warm honey. The bartender took her order for vodka on ice with lime. She eyed Fusilli. "You want another?"

He was barely through his second. "Sure." He waited until the bartender set down their drinks and moved away. "So what do we drink to?"

"Saturday night," she said, and they clinked glasses. Fusilli merely wet his lips, but the woman took a healthy swallow, sighed. Her lips glistened. "I've been waiting all day for that."

"Rough day?"

"Every day's rough on Biham." She traced the mouth of her glass with a forefinger. "You're new here."

"Haven't been planetside very long." This was true. The best way not to get tripped up by lies was not to tell more than he could keep track of.

"How long?"

"About three, four weeks. Work dried up on Proserpina after Tormark moved to Halstead Station." Fusilli made a face of genuine disgust. "Working tunnels, like a rat. I like real air, sunshine. I like stars."

"I'm with you." She stuck out her hand. Her grip was firm and surprisingly strong, and her fingers were long. "Dasha Miyagi."

"Shakir Jerrar," Fusilli said, and was startled. This was not the name by which Parks would know him. *Why did I pick that name?*

"So, Shakir." Dasha tongued lime from her drink and sucked the fruit. "Got a job?" When Fusilli shook his head, she said, "You must not need money."

"I got a cushion. I can afford to be a little picky."

She tossed the naked peel into her glass. "What kind of work?"

"A little of this, a little of that . . ." He rattled ice. "I was in the Drac Brotherhood back on Proserpina."

"What made you bail?"

"They bailed on *us*. Soon as the DCMS took over, they let us go. Assholes. Wanted us only as long as we were useful." He gave a humorless laugh. "What else can you expect from a Drac?"

"You don't sound grateful."

"Why should I be?" *Easy, don't push it.* "They needed us when they needed us, and then they blew their noses and walked away."

She had very large eyes, and in the poor light of the bar, he couldn't quite catch their color. But they were expressive and, now, very solemn. "What about now that Tormark's dead?"

"What about it?" Fusilli tipped the last of his watery bourbon into his mouth. Catching the bartender's eye, he pointed at their glasses then held up two fingers. "She's dead," he said. "Not as if they didn't kill plenty of people along the way."

But he wondered at a sudden flare of anger burning his chest. *What the hell? It's not like I ever felt at home there, or that they tried.*

Dasha looked pensive, a little sad. Her fingers went to her throat, twining round a gold chain with two tiny charms he couldn't make out. She didn't say anything until the bartender brought the next round. In the interim, Fusilli noticed that the bar had started to empty out. He glanced at his watch and realized with a jolt that an hour had passed.

He looked up to see Dasha watching him. "What?"

"You look like a man waiting for something to happen."

Fusilli picked up his glass. He was a little woozy, feeling the bourbon. Decided to hell with it. "I guess I am."

"So what are you waiting for, Shakir?"

"What we're playing at."

"I never play. Did you think I was going to invite you home?"

"I don't know," Fusilli said, disturbed that he'd flashed to *exactly* that. Even more disturbed to find that he was aroused. How long since he'd been with a woman? "I'm not sure I'm looking for that."

This time, she stared at him for a second too long. "Word is you're looking for people who make things happen."

For just an instant, he felt disappointment. The job again. Not *him* at all. Still, he had his part to play. "Are you one of them?"

"I'm a facilitator. Maybe we can discuss our mutual interests?"

The invitation was clear. He paid for the drinks and stood. She was much taller than he'd thought. When she moved, she did so with sinewy grace.

The night was warm but not unpleasant. The sidewalk was empty, though cars lined the curb. "This way," Dasha said, turning right. After a few moments, she said, "You seem nice."

*No, I'm not.* "I try to be."

"So, I'm really sorry." She brushed his right arm with her fingers. "Really."

Fusilli opened his mouth to reply, but then he sensed movement, heard a car door pop, and he half-turned. Later, he thought maybe the alcohol slowed him down. Or the bartender spiked his drink. Whatever, he turned achingly slow, as if underwater. A high, soft whine at his right ear, and then something punched his brain. The blow was as substantial as being hit with a club, but Fusilli had time for one last thought: *Sonic stunner.*

Then the darkness took him.

# 20

*Deber City, Benjamin*
*Benjamin Military District, Draconis Combine*
*25 August 3136*

**T**heodore couldn't breathe. His chest was tight, clamped in a vice of sudden, very real, very mortal fear. "Why now? What did I do to trigger it?"

"You didn't do anything." The doctor was young but with the gravitas of a much older man well-acquainted with life's tragedies. "But it's not all of a sudden, is it, *Tono?*"

"No." Theodore swallowed. His throat hurt. "Almost a year now. When we were on campaign . . . I decided . . ." He'd been about to say that the tremor had frightened him so much he'd decided against pushing for Dieron last year. He remembered how puzzled Katana had been, the questions in her eyes. Instead, he said, "I thought it was just fatigue."

"Fatigue would make paralysis agitans more severe. But the tremor, the spasms in your right leg combined with your difficulty walking—these are classic symptoms of Parkinson's, and you know it. Your mother is a carrier of the early-onset, familial form of the disease, an autosomal dominant, and your brother showed symptoms when he was twenty-eight. You're at the age where we'd expect to start seeing symptoms."

"What are my options?"

"Let's talk about the reality of your situation first. Parkinson's is a neurodegenerative disease attacking the central nervous system. . . ."

"I know *that*," Theodore said, angry now. "Don't you think I know *that?*"

The doctor was unruffled. "Your *brain, Tono:* Your neurohelmet depends on a neural interface. But if that interface begins to *change* . . ."

"Oh, God." He felt sick. He'd never considered that. "You mean, my 'Mech . . . Oh, God."

*Maybe that's what happened in the sim, the helmet not* responding . . .

"How long will the interface hold?" he asked.

"Impossible to say. It will fail sooner rather than later, I'd guess."

"What about drugs?"

"They all have side effects, some quite unpleasant, and drugs don't cure. They merely delay. Familial parkinsonism is quite unrelenting."

"Can I still control my 'Mech if I take drugs?"

"There's no precedent. These drugs work by changing the relative balance of neurochemicals. I don't know what will happen to the interface. Maybe nothing, or things might get worse. I just don't know."

*I can't just wait around to* die . . . "Is there any other way?"

"*Yessss,*" the doctor said slowly, but then held out a hand, like a traffic cop. "Experimental surgery using stem cells. These are pluripotent cells, capable of turning into whatever cell the body requires. Stem cells have been used to repair damaged heart muscle, for example. But the results for neural regeneration haven't been encouraging."

"*How* not encouraging?"

"There's never been a success," the doctor said bluntly. "Patients always get much worse since there's no way to regulate how many neurons regenerate. Of course, there's always the first time."

Theodore's hope died like a guttering flame. "But I wouldn't be it."

"Not with the aggressive familial form you carry. I'm sorry."

"But there *are* drugs. I'd still function for awhile, isn't that right?" *Long enough to wage a campaign?*

"Possibly," the doctor said, and then told him what the drug regimen would be. "*Tono,* your disease is quite aggressive. It won't be long before you have breakthrough symptoms drugs will not control. Within six, maybe eight months. Then people will know."

*God, right around my birthday, what a lovely gift.* He saw that the doctor wanted to say more. "Yes?"

"*Tono,*" the doctor began gently, "your death is many years away, but much will happen before then. You know from your mother and brother that this will be a long, slow and painful deterioration. To keep this from your wife is beneath your honor, and you must plan for the future: to ensure your legacy and that of your family."

Theodore stared at the doctor. *My legacy. My lineage: my mother who can't think or move, and my brother lost in his delusions. My future.*

And again, Emi: *You hold our destiny in your hands. You are the only one, Brother, the only one.*

## 25 August 3136

Theodore held Chomie as she shuddered in his arms, her grief so very much like the tremors he could not control. They lay on a low divan, with firm bolsters against which Theodore leaned to support them both. He'd called for lights out some time ago and had candles lit. Shadows danced in long black fingers.

Finally, Chomie gave a long, tremulous sigh, like a child exhausted from weeping. "It feels wrong," she said.

Her hair smelled like roses and was smooth as spun black silk. He cupped the back of her head with his left hand, his trembling fingers massaging the delicate egg of her skull. "This is the only way, my heart. We must do this and offset what will be common knowledge within the year. Likely, I'll invent a brain tumor." He added wryly, "I don't think we need yet one more Kurita suddenly called to a life of devotion."

Her body stiffened, and she pulled away. She was a delicate woman with features as finely chiseled as an exquisite cameo. "This isn't funny."

"Chomie, I'm running out of time. I'm a warrior, but I cannot beat an enemy I cannot see, and this, my *mind* . . . You can't imagine what this is like, to be losing your *self,* everything dribbling away, and knowing there is absolutely nothing you can do."

"You can fight."

"To what end? There are drugs I will take, but I will not win." He reached for her, cupping a hand to her abdomen. "Yet this, the warmth and safety of your womb, this is our chance. My love, I beg you," and now he let his tears come as he took her face in his hands, as he kissed her streaming eyes, her cheeks, her lips that tasted of salt. "Please. We've played this fiction long enough. Five miscarriages, when the reality is that the fetus carried the disease. This is our last chance. I will not force you. I could not. But, please, this is the one battle I cannot lose, and you are the only one, my heart, the only one who can help me, who can save *us* now."

After that, he said nothing more. Instead, he told her with his hands, his mouth, his arms how he felt, what she meant, what they must do.

And, in the candlelight, they bound their love with their bodies and tears.

# 21

*Armitage, Ancha*
*26 August 3136*
*0145 hours*

The nine drunk tanks were standard: three-meter cubes, faced with ferroglass, and three to a side. A single chair and table, bolted to the floor. A bench where the drunk slept it off. A drain in the middle of a concrete floor for hosing down vomit. The air always smelled like day-old puke laced with urine or feces.

A lone uniform was dictating when Loveland and Thereon walked in. He said "Pause" to his computer and faced round. "You the guys?"

Loveland did the introductions, then said, "You got guys we should meet."

"Yeah. Bill Reilly, he's the shorter guy in the middle tank," the uniform said. "Big guy at the end is Mack Strobel. Dockworkers, couple of priors, pissant stuff. Dust, mainly. Thing is, when I ran 'em, they'd already been tagged. But then I ran the tag."

"Problem with the tag?"

"Naw, it's legit, except it belongs to a patrol officer who skipped out eight months ago, name of Josh Petrie. Nice wife, cute kid. Girlfriend's what everyone figures. Thing is, the tag clocks in on twenty-eight February at oh-two-hundred-forty-five hours, but the wife reported him missing sixteen February. And get this." The uniform called up a file. "Spaceport says he left for Murchison on twenty February, eight *days* before these guys swear up and down it was a *cop* tagged them."

"Hunh," Loveland said. Taggants were microscopic, chemically inert compounds whose residua could last on skin for several years. Suspects were subjected to a sniffer: an ultra-sensitive device that could pick up as little as two parts per million. The catch was that patrol taggers were fingerprint-activated. Only Petrie could've activated the device, but if he was *gone* . . . "That doesn't compute. Did they say where and why?"

"That's where things got a little interesting. The way they were talking, I think they ran into that homicide I heard you been working."

"What about the cold hit, the DNA?"

"Sorry. These guys don't match, and it's not Petrie's."

"Okay. Let's talk to these guys," Loveland said.

"Sure. Which one you want first?"

Loveland and Thereon eyed the two men in their rumpled coveralls. The men stared back, but when Loveland walked to the middle tank, the little guy's eyes slid away. Loveland aimed a finger. "That one."

They used a small interview room, the kind with a one-way mirror, two chairs, a table and nothing else. Wrists in plasticuffs, Reilly was definitely sober now and reeked of day-old dust—a cloying, burnt-caramel scent. His eyes were red-rimmed; his nose was a roadmap of ruptured capillaries; and he had a duster's tremor in both hands.

His memory was just about as good. "Look, we was pretty messed up. I don't remember. But we ain't done nothing to that slag. She was all banged up, said a johnny done bashed in her mug."

"Yeah?" Loveland leaned back against the door while Thereon held up the near wall. "If she was as messed up as you say, you should've offered to help her, right?" He looked at Thereon. "*I'd* have helped her."

"Me, too," Thereon said.

"But you didn't help her," Loveland said to Reilly. "Plus, you and your friend got tagged. Now the only reason I can think of why a cop does that is because you were doing something to that woman you shouldn't."

"We didn't do nothing bad. Last time I seen her, she was okay."

"Was this before or after you raped her?"

"We was just playing round. Oi, Pie done me before. Wasn't like we wasn't acquainted."

This man wasn't their killer, but Reilly had contact with Petrie and that interested Loveland a lot. Otherwise, Loveland didn't really give a rat's ass about Reilly. "Listen," he said, "I don't really give a rat's ass for either you or your friend in there. I want to know about the cop."

Reilly screwed up his face like he'd finally got a whiff of himself. "And you ain't gonna try to pin this on me?"

"Not if you didn't do anything."

Reilly got a canny look. "What about tonight?"

"Can't help you there. Not my jurisdiction. You cooperate, I'll put in a good word. Best I can do."

His best was apparently good enough because Reilly thought for another moment, then leaned forward, as if to impress Loveland with his earnestness. "It happened just like I said. Me and Mack, we was hanging out by them old warehouses down by The Loading Dock."

"Loading dock?" Loveland said. "You were at the spaceport?"

Reilly shook his head. "No, no, *The* Loading Dock. It's a bar west end of town. Pie used to work it. Anyway, we was hanging round, not doing much."

"Really?" Thereon's smoky eyes looked sleepy, as if Reilly's story were of no more interest than a weather report. "February's pretty cold here, right? Can't see why two guys would just hang around."

Reilly reddened. "Mack and me, we'd scored a coupla lines, and we was hanging round, you know. And we was using, not selling."

"Oh, well," Loveland said, "that's a relief."

Reilly pushed on. "Anyway, Pie happens by. She was messed up just like I said. She told us what happened and then . . ." He trailed off.

"Yes?" Loveland prompted. "And?"

"Well." Reilly swallowed again. "Things got a little rough."

"How rough?"

"Rough enough." Reilly clamped down on the end of the sentence. Unsure if it was useful to go after the grisly details, Loveland eyed Thereon who made a minute *keep rolling* gesture.

"Okay, so things got a little rough," Loveland said. "Then what?"

"Then . . . well, Mack, he was holding Pie still-like, and I was . . . anyways, all a sudden, this Bob appeared outta nowhere. Only he didn't feel like no cop."

"How do you mean?"

Reilly's features arranged themselves into an approximation of what he must imagine passed for deep thought but only succeeded in making him look constipated. "Gets so you know who's a cop. It's like this sixth sense, see? This wanker, whatever he was, he wasn't no Bob."

"What was wrong with him?"

"He was just . . . *there*. He shouted, and then Mack, he done run off, and I tried getting away, only then he got me round me neck. That's when I knowed there was something wrong. After he touched me, after he had his hands on me, I was happy to clear out. Only it wasn't about not getting caught. It was about *him*. His *hands*."

"What about them?"

"When he broke us up, when he hauled back on me neck, his hands," Reilly said, "they was ice cold."

"So? It was a cold night."

"No, they's cold," Reilly said, "and then, they's *dead*. This Bob, he were a dead man walking."

# 22

When they were done with Reilly and Strobel, Loveland and Thereon went to a break room in the basement. The break room was empty except for two round plastic tables and mismatched chairs, vending machines, a microwave. The place smelled like burned popcorn. Loveland studied his vending machine choices, didn't like any of them, settled for a chocolate bar and black coffee. There were worse things than getting jazzed on caffeine and sugar.

"What do you think?" Thereon swigged from a cola can, then belched soundlessly. "You think Petrie's the one we're after?"

"Naw." Loveland unpeeled the chocolate bar and stared at a mottled, whitish discoloration speckling the candy. "DNA doesn't match."

"That's butter separating from the cocoa," Thereon said, catching his look. "It should taste okay."

Loveland decided to pass. He tossed the uneaten chocolate onto the table. The plastic was scored with orange cigarette burns. "You like him?"

"Petrie? No," Thereon said. "Like you said, not his DNA. Only I can't figure that tag. No way to fake that."

"Unless our guy picked out Petrie first, got a sample print and then found a guy to do the microsurgery."

Thereon made a face. "Here's what bothers me. Our unknown subject didn't *have* to call attention to himself. The unsub didn't *need* the tagger. He didn't *need* to mess with those two guys. He could've waited until they were gone."

Loveland stared at Thereon. "You're saying he *wanted* us to look at Petrie."

Thereon nodded. "I think so."

## 0845 hours

Cheryl Petrie lived in a modest neighborhood on the south side of town. The house was a low, well-proportioned clapboard with a neatly fenced yard, flower boxes in the windows, a fire-engine red tricycle on the porch. A FOR SALE ticker was tacked to the lawn, its red digital display flashing like a strobe.

Cheryl Petrie was an attractive honey-blonde of about thirty-five, with light blue eyes. She worked as a bank teller but had agreed to meet them when they called from the hotel at seven.

"Do you believe what the department's saying?" Loveland asked. "That your husband ran off with a girlfriend?"

Pain arrowed through her eyes. She crossed her right leg over her left leg, tugging at the hem of a black pencil skirt stretched around shapely thighs. "Josh and I had a rule. We never went to bed angry, ever. We always talked it out. Sometimes it meant we were both very tired the next morning. But that's the way our marriage was, Detective. And Josh was working toward a law degree. Did they tell you that at the station?"

Loveland shook his head. Thereon said, "He went to night school?"

She nodded. "That's why this doesn't make sense. The night they say Josh left the planet . . ." Her mouth worked, and she pulled in a tremulous breath. "Josh was in school. At least, I know he started *out* for school. He had dinner with us, helped with the dishes, then read to Suzy, our daughter. When he left, he had his books."

Loveland wanted to believe her. "Did he show up for class?"

Her lips wobbled. "No. But that was the first time, Detective, the *only* time." She added faintly, "The last time."

"When did you involve the department?"

"Josh was like clockwork, home by quarter after twelve. When one-thirty came and went, I called the precinct. Then, the next morning, Josh's lieutenant and sergeant came to the house." Her blue eyes were suddenly liquid. "You have to understand. When a cop's wife sees a city car pull up, she thinks . . ." She broke off, knuckling away tears.

Loveland *did* know what wives thought. He'd been along on some of those rides. "Just a few more questions."

"Sorry. I try not to cry. It's not good for Suzy." She smeared away runny lines of mascara with her fingers. "Josh's lieutenant came to tell me that Josh had *resigned* and left a forwarding address on Halstead Station."

"Halstead *Station?*" He and Thereon exchanged glances. Loveland said, "Did you try to contact him?"

"Of course. I was frantic. If not for Suzy, I would've left for Halstead Station on the next shuttle. With the HPGs down, it was two months before I heard anything. The message was very matter-of-fact. He'd met someone, he wanted a divorce. He even left the number of an attorney here with whom he'd already filed. He said I could have everything. I was so stunned, I didn't know what to do at first. But then I contacted the attorney, and he showed me the papers. It was Josh's signature all right. I wouldn't sign them. That's the last I heard. I sent a follow-up message to Halstead Station, but Josh never answered. The department checked into it, but . . ." She spread her hands, a helpless gesture. "They let it go. I guess men leave their wives all the time."

Loveland thought of his two failed marriages, then weighed Cheryl Petrie against them. Maybe it was unfair, but he couldn't see anyone leaving this woman. On the other hand, the department eventually would've shrugged it off. Like she said, people left people all the time.

Thereon said, "There's a For Sale sign in your front yard."

"I just put it on the market. I can't afford the mortgage anymore, what with child care added in. The department's under no obligation to provide anything. So I have to sell." Her eyes filled again. "It feels like giving up."

They walked down the porch steps, across the tiny, neat yard, past the sale ticker. Thumbing the remote, Loveland went around to the driver's side as the locks popped.

Thereon said, "What do you think?"

Loveland paused. Behind Thereon, he could see Cheryl Petrie watching them from the porch. A little girl with blond ringlets stood on her right, a forefinger plugged in her mouth.

Loveland looked at Thereon. "I think she'll be getting that death benefit."

It was Thereon's idea to follow Petrie's beat. "Canvass the neighborhoods. Someone's got to remember him."

Petrie's beat was northeast, a neighborhood where the buildings got shabbier, the broken windows more numerous and the graffiti more frequent. No one—especially not the men squatting on stone steps and either smoking or drinking, or both—remembered seeing Petrie that far back. By three in the afternoon, Loveland's feet were screaming, and he was swimming in sweat. He dropped into the driver's seat and cranked up the air. "There's a reason I went for detective."

"What, you don't canvass?"

"Yeah, I canvass. I just don't do this *many*."

"Well, cheer up. I predict our witness will be in the last place we look."

"Christ, you're killing me," Loveland said as he pulled away from the curb.

On the seventh floor of an eight-story apartment building, they found their witness. She was an extraordinarily frail woman named Edwina Jeffries who looked about two hundred years old. She wore a tatty sweater even though the temperature in the apartment had to be near eighty. The apartment smelled as if the walls leaked cat pee and onions.

"Oh, yes, I remember Officer Petrie." She spoke with an old woman's quaver. "A very nice young man. He usually came around at about the same time as my meals."

"Meals?" Loveland asked.

She explained that she received hot meals once a day from a local charity. "Officer Petrie used to bring my meals up. Not all the time, maybe six, seven times a month. Just to say hello, see how I was getting on."

That sounded like the man Cheryl Petrie described. "And the last day you saw him?"

The old woman tugged her wattle as she thought. "Sometime in February, late, I think. I remember because I thought then that maybe he was sick."

Loveland's ears pricked at that. "Sick?"

"Well, just not *right*. He always whistled a little jig coming and going up those stairs, the same one all the time. I wait by the door when my meals are due. Usually, I crack the door a bit so I can hear and see who's coming. It was him, only he didn't whistle, and he didn't stop by. Didn't even look my way. That wasn't like the Officer Petrie *I* knew. So I said to myself, I said, Weena, you march right to that window and see what's what.''

"What happened next?"

"I got to the window over there." She pointed to a glass lozenge sheathed in a white aluminum blind. The blind was snugged at the head of the window, and two casement windows were cranked wide open. "And I looked down, and I saw him leaving. I recognized his uniform except . . .''

"Except what?"

"It was the wrong coat." The way she said it, she sounded almost put out. "There he was, with that long uniform coat buttoned all the way up."

Loveland shook his head. "I don't follow."

"Officer Petrie never wore anything but a little leather patrol jacket unless it was snowing. But it wasn't snowing that day."

"How can you be so sure?"

"Just because I'm old doesn't mean I don't remember things. I remember because of a warm snap we had right before the end of February. The smell of garbage coming up from the alley was so strong I called the super to complain. You could still smell it in the vents, like something up and died. Up there." She pointed toward the ceiling. "Well, it took days, and by the time the super got his fat bum up to check the vents, the smell wasn't so bad, and he couldn't find anything. But even the people who leave my meals smelled it. They asked if maybe my cat caught a rat and took it into the air ducts."

Until that instant, Loveland was convinced this was a waste of time. Now he sat forward. "Can you show us where the smell was the worst?"

That turned out to be the bathroom. The bathroom had one casement window of rainwater glass that overlooked the alley between this apartment house and the next. Jeffries pointed with a gnarly finger. "Right there."

Loveland inspected the ceiling of low-hung acoustical tile, the kind someone might use in a basement to obscure pipes. "I'm going to step on your toilet, Ma'am." Before Jeffries could object, he was straddling the bowl, closely peering at one tile.

"What?" asked Thereon.

"Here." Loveland stabbed a finger at an irregular, light brown stain. The stain looked like a watermark. "These are individual tiles. I ought to be able to . . ." Cautiously, he spread the fingers of his right hand, palmed the center of the tile and pushed up. The tile moved fractionally, enough so Loveland caught that faint but familiar whiff of decay. "Who lives in the apartment above yours?"

"Oh, an invalid," Jeffries said. "Well, used to. He moved in earlier this year, and not for very long. He was in a wheelchair, and very unfriendly. Said he didn't want to be bothered and had a nurse, though I never saw *him* until the night they moved out."

"Night?" Loveland said. "That's a weird time to move."

"Last I saw of him, his nurse was carrying him all bundled up, just like a baby. Our elevator wasn't working that day, I think. That's not such a surprise. Such a big man, too, the nurse. But I remember thinking that something wasn't quite right."

"In what way?" Loveland asked. "Something about the nurse? The guy in the wheelchair?"

"The one in the wheelchair. I'll show you." She led them back into her living room. "Through the window, you see that light on the corner?"

The window was old and the glass a little warped, so the street lamp on the far right corner was outlined in a faint, rainbow penumbra. "I see it," Loveland said. "He carried him down the street?"

"That's where the hover was. When they got to that light, and it shone on that poor sick man?" She leaned in. "He didn't have a *face*."

The invalid's apartment was still on a year's lease, though the manager said he'd never met the occupant in person. At first, Loveland thought they'd have to get a warrant. Then Thereon mentioned the stink in the ceiling, the health department. "I notice your elevator's not working," Thereon said. "Now, you don't want the building inspectors to come by."

The manager didn't. They got in.

The apartment was virtually identical to Edwina Jeffries'—except for the wheelchair parked at the door to the bathroom. Pointing the way, like an invitation to come on in. They did—and that's when they found the square that had been cut out of the bathroom floor.

They found a decomposing body wedged beneath. The body had been wrapped in pryolene, but as the body had bloated, the edges had pulled apart, allowing fluids to seep into that acoustical tile in Jeffries' bathroom.

The next day at the autopsy, the ME concluded that Officer Josh Petrie had been alive when his hands had been flayed, and the skin stripped like gloves. And he had still been alive when he was bagged and left to suffocate.

## 23

*Bore's Hell, New Samarkand*
*3 September 3136*

**W**hen the recruit dashed in, Jonathan peered down from a spider's-eye view. (Sun-baked, rough brick made for a splendid grip surface.) Then he dropped. The recruit gave a startled yelp as Jonathan flipped him over. The recruit was a boy, really, and he got *angry* about how *Jonathan* was going to screw things up. What the hell was *he* doing . . . !

Jonathan laughed so hard he nearly lost his grip; he laughed until there were tears; and he was still laughing as he slid his KA-BAR between the boy's left fourth and fifth ribs. The boy jerked like a huge game fish hooked on a heavy line as the knife skewered his heart. His eyes bugged, and red bubbles frothed from his lips. Still giggling, Jonathan ripped the recruit's uniform shirt apart and dipped his fingers in the blood. He inhaled that rich, full aroma and then slowly, deliberately, tasted each finger.

As the boy died, Jonathan stripped off the recruit's helmet and uniform. All the participants in the exercise wore multiple laser integrated system gear both for ID and to record laser tags. Jonathan wasn't planning on playing dead, but he needed to light up at just the right moment. He also snapped off the recruit's smoky gray goggles. The high-impact ferroglass lenses were low-profile and designed to withstand bursts of shrapnel. This was not a live-fire exercise, but the goggles would obscure his face until the proper moment.

To play this game, he'd cut his hair military-short and dyed it brown. That *really* hurt. He liked to look at himself, all that black hair cascading over hardened muscle and bronzed skin. His favorite pastime aboard ship, under acceleration: rubbing in oil, his fingers sliding over toned flesh, the sensation so erotic he shivered with lust as he followed the hills and valleys of his arms, his hard abdomen and taut thighs. (He was in the best shape of his life now, his body a temple for *her*.)

Jonathan washed his hands with sand and mounded debris over the body, then slung the recruit's Zeus laser rifle over his shoulder. By the time anyone missed him, vermin would've been done with the boy's face. By then, Jonathan would be long gone.

Now he crouched below the edge of a sandy berm, snuggled in his sniper's nest. The sand, dun-colored and very fine, like baker's sugar, was very hot against his exposed skin. (Thank heavens *this* sand was harmless, not like the caustic moat of diacetylsilicate surrounding the college proper.) He'd stripped down and then slapped on a jump pack. He buried the knapsack in the sand. From a munitions belt snugged round his waist, he withdrew magnetic quick-hitches that he fitted to his boots and wrists.

Seven hundred meters away, the air was alive with the staccato flash of ruby laser fire and the faint shouts of recruits. His company was in retreat, and enemy reinforcements were not far behind. He spied all those lovely targets milling around like ants, and his fingers tightened around the Zeus.

*A flick of a switch, that's all, and then I'd be at full burn.* That was, however pleasurable, an unnecessary risk. Yes, but what about the recruit? He really hadn't needed to kill the boy. He'd have accomplished the same thing waiting here.

*Acting as if I need to prove I've been here. This is like Towne all over again. I want Bhatia to know and fear me.*

But Bhatia did. He could bring Bhatia down. So, why this *hunger* for recognition? Because there was no Marcus to need and admire him?

In the next instant, he was furious. What a fool. He wasn't alone! He had Katana. He had to stop thinking like this. These kinds of thoughts fomented doubt, and doubt would get him killed. Or worse: caught.

*Bhatia would peel my mind, a layer at time. He'd keep me like a fly in amber, to learn how to make more of me . . .*

A throaty rumble shook him from his thoughts. Tracking left, he spied a DI Morgan clanking into the city. The enemy reinforcements had arrived. He'd had a chance to study the recruit's mission specs. The tank really didn't interest him and neither did the squat, jungle-green VV1 Ranger skirting the tank's right flank, its turret swiveling in a classic sweeping maneuver that would bring its eight machine guns to bear in a heartbeat.

No, his quarry was coming from the southwest. Vibrations jarred sand into tiny avalanches that spilled around his body, with a sound like rice. He flattened, looked right—and *there.*

The *Rokurokubi*'s massive form was so starkly outlined against a blinding blue sky it looked scissored out of paper. Wedded to the 'Mech's right fist, its *katana* blade gleamed a dazzling white. The gold accents of its oxblood red *kabuto* winked and twinkled as it strode forward. Behind it, its shadow was a long, inky stain on the sand.

Then, in the 'Mech's wake and high above, Jonathan spotted a Balac Strike following as if tethered by an invisible leash. An instant later, the sound caught up, that telltale *whopwhopwhopwhop* of blades slapping air.

He waited, clamping down on his desire, biding his time. He watched as the *Rokurokubi* ate up the distance between them. The pounding grew more violent as the 'Mech continued its relentless advance. The air filled with the ear-shattering roar of autocannon blanks spewing from its left arm. The air was close now with swirling sand scuffed by the 'Mech's feet, and the acrid smell of lubricant and ozone mingling with 'Mech coolant. When he breathed through his mouth, his throat rebelled, the muscles clutching against the burn. He spat, tasting grit.

*Ready.*

He laid the Zeus aside—no need for it in what he had planned—then dug into his munitions belt and reeled out a clawed grappler. Snapping the reinforced cable to a quick-release, he raised himself to his toes, crouching on his haunches, every muscle quivering as he watched the giant machine's left foot kick past. The 'Mech's pilot was likely oblivious to his presence. Probably didn't care even if he wasn't. After all, what was one man?

*Don't let it get too far ahead, or you'll never catch it. Do it now!*

In a flash, he was on his feet, up and over the berm, slithering to level sand hard-packed by the 'Mech's passage. He ran as fast as he could, lungs screaming against the superheated air, heart pounding against his ribs, legs churning sand. Then, as he crossed behind the 'Mech, he thumbed his jump pack to life. The lifters ignited with a growl, and he was airborne, wind as hot as dragon's breath scouring his face, his stomach bottoming out as he rocketed for the machine's undercarriage.

*Now, go, go!*

He swung the grappler, hurling it with all his might. The weighted hooks shot forward, clanked against armor, slid— and held, snagging the 'Mech where the left leg joined the machine's gyroscope housing. Instantly, he cut thrust and tripped the cable's uptake wheel. The metal spooled with a zipping sound, and as he came within two meters of the gyroscope housing, he swung back then forward, disengaging from the grappler and then flipping like an aerialist. For a heart-stopping moment, there was nothing but air— and then he made contact, his magnetic quick-hitches securing him like an insect in a spiderweb.

Jonathan let out his pent-up breath in an explosive *whoosh*. He'd done it, he'd *done* it—a lone man, no battlearmor, equipped only with lifters and quick-hitches! By all that was holy, he would put the fear of *God* into Bhatia! *This* was his destiny. How strong Katana and he were together!

He began clambering up the 'Mech's back, still using the

quick-hitches. But he wasn't prepared for how scorching hot the 'Mech's armor was, didn't suspect until his right forearm brushed metal. Pain boiled red and hot down his arm and blacked his vision for one perilous second. If not for the quick-hitches, he'd have fallen. He clung there, pulling in air so thick with heat it was like breathing in the exhalations of a blast furnace.

That brought him back to the reality of his peril, to mortality. He continued on, feeling it now, his breath slashing and hacking his throat with lava tongues of heat, his muscles bulging with effort. Every jolt and bang of the 'Mech's passage detonated in his joints. Sweat poured down his arms and neck, dripping like molten armor cooked by laser fire. The thunder of autocannons was deafening, and he was tiring, his limbs going watery.

*Can't fail.* Grimly, he stretched his right arm so far the tortured joint protested. He felt the solid thunk of the quick-hitch catching, and he scrambled up another meter. Above, he saw the flare of the *Rokurokubi's* helmet.

*Nearly there, mustn't fail, just concentrate . . .*

Roaring with the strain, he threw his last hitch, hoisted himself the last few meters . . . Just a *little more* . . . and then he clamped onto the pole of a banner fixed on the 'Mech's right shoulder.

Done it! But he had to rest, he had to, and as air whistled into his tortured lungs, he prayed: *Please, Katana, my love, please, do not abandon me now!* But, oh, God, he was so tired . . .

Then—somehow—he was atop the machine's head. He blinked, suddenly confused. How? He couldn't remember how he'd gotten here. No, he couldn't worry about this now. Time to finish this.

He swarmed up and crested the *suji kabuto.* At the helmet's lip, he inched forward. Instead of a *menpo,* the 'Mech possessed a face mask of ferroglass. Moving quickly now, he belayed over the lip of the steel armor visor, dropping down on myomer-reinforced flexible cable.

It gave him a vicious thrill when the MechWarrior caught sight of him. The pilot's surprise was instantly translated into movement as the *Rokurokubi* flinched, its arms automatically jerking back. Slapping molded plastique onto the ferroglass canopy, Jonathan disengaged his belay at the same moment that he banged on his lifters.

The *Rokurokubi*'s blade sliced air as the MechWarrior tried, unsuccessfully, to swat Jonathan from the sky. He twisted in midair, his vision swirling, and bared his teeth in triumph. *And now, and now . . .* He counted out the seconds, his heart beating a counterpoint, his thumb poised over the detonator. *And . . . now!*

A *WHUMP!* Brilliant yellow paint sprayed over the ferroglass and spattered the 'Mech. A clean kill.

*For you, dear Director.* Jonathan turned his gaze heavenward toward the Balac Strike even as he fell to earth. *So you may know—and fear.*

# 24

### Internal Security College, New Samarkand
### 3 September 3136

"Well, I'd never thought we'd find ourselves here," Toranaga said. He held a steaming bowl of plump soba and slurped noodles.

"And where is that, *Tai-shu?*" Bhatia said with a twinge of nausea. The noodle looked like a worm slithering down the gullet of a ravenous bird.

"Tormark gone," Toranaga said around a noodle. "A big bang, and she's a plasma smear."

"Indeed." Was Toranaga fishing to see whether Bhatia had anything to do with it, or whether Bhatia suspected *him?* Could he risk directness? After all, they were in his private quarters located in the very heart of the ISF complex and under heavy guard. They were well soundproofed. He'd modeled his system on the Black Room, a design he had also overseen and whose flaws, deliberately placed, he exploited when necessary. (He hated surprises he hadn't planned.)

Then Bhatia found his opening. They were attended by a single servant, a youth with dark cinnamon eyes hooded by luxuriant brown-black lashes. No boy, Cameron was a young man. Midway through the meal, Cameron offered a small platter of crisp mountain yam rolls. And that's when Bhatia saw it—the way Toranaga reached for a roll but trailed his fingers along Cameron's hand. Just the whisper of a touch, but it was there.

*Ah, is this what you dream of, Toranaga? The slender limbs and ripening body of a warrior, and the pleasures of Bushido?*

"May I ask you something?"

Startled, Bhatia covered by taking a sip of ice water. "Of course."

"As a warlord, I had reason to despise Tormark. But why you?"

"Suffice it to say Akira Tormark and his defection dealt a blow to my concerns." He paused. "More to the point, where do *we* go from here?"

Toranaga's eyes narrowed. He held out a mug to the youth, who filled it with strong, sweet potato liquor. "We?"

"Yes. Tormark is gone. Your protégée will command Tormark's forces and lead them to Dieron."

"Hunh." Toranaga's eyes were a little glassy, though he'd not had much to drink. "I've a suspicion that whelp Theodore will claim the prize."

"I think not. *Tai-shu* Kurita will leave Dieron to Yori. He'd look greedy and impolitic if he took over the reins. Yet, if she does well . . ." He let the rest hang, but a sudden gleam of avarice lit Toranaga's eyes.

*For that, I must thank that opiate I added to your liquor, my dear Toranaga. You may think yourself cunning—but I am more cunning still.*

Toranaga stared at Bhatia for a long moment. The ISF director could almost hear the wheels and gears turning, clicking, spinning. Calculating just how far he could go and still leave this place with his head screwed to his neck. Then Toranaga's jet-black eyes slid to Cameron still in attendance. "You really want to talk about this now?"

Bhatia was pleased when the young man didn't even blink. "Cameron's perfectly safe. Keen on being a recruit. His parents died suddenly, but he's become my good right arm, haven't you, Cameron?"

*"Hai."* Cameron gave Bhatia a reverent bow. "You are most kind, *Tono.*"

"That's a good boy. So." Bhatia gestured at his guest. "Tormark's demise—"

"Is the void which Yori will fill. Yes, yes, that's obvious." Toranaga pursed his lips, took a gulp of his liquor, said, "The question *now* is how far to take this, eh? Kurita's a peacock, and I don't see Theodore amounting to much. They've got uprisings on worlds he and Tormark declared secure."

"They *did* occur on Tormark's watch," Bhatia demurred. *Though I'd give my eyeteeth to know who's engineering those; I might send him chocolates.* "Are you implying, perhaps, a *renegotiation* with the coordinator?"

"No," Toranaga said bluntly. "I'm saying Vincent Kurita must go."

"I do not believe that Vincent Kurita has any intentions of stepping aside. And there is Theodore to consider."

"Then the same thrust must eliminate both. Doesn't much matter which goes first. But only one individual must remain to fill the void—and her name is not Emi."

*By the gods, this* is *the man.* Bhatia's pulse thrilled through his veins, and he was nearly breathless with exhilaration. "And then?"

"Then we will rule with a fist of steel and a will of titanium. When the Dragon roars, the Inner Sphere will *tremble.*"

Bhatia gave a delighted, breathy laugh. "I never thought you lyrical."

"No?" Toranaga tossed back the last of his drink. "Then let me tell you about the requiem I've composed."

When Toranaga was done, there was a small silence. Then Bhatia said slowly, "This is treason, Warlord. Be very clear about that. There is nothing subtle in this."

"No," Toranaga said. "But I think you agree: The time for subtlety is past."

The desert had relinquished the last of its heat. The college's lights turned the horizon amber. A cooling breeze raised gooseflesh along Bhatia's arms—or maybe that was still the excitement of it all.

*If Toranaga can make good on his plans, then I must cause enough havoc to cramp Tormark's troops so that Yori's arrival looks like a godsend.*

But how? Best intelligence indicated that Tormark managed to wheedle a galaxy of Cats to deal with Saffel, Styx and Athenry. Likely, the little slut had attached a codicil about what should happen if she died.

"Yes, *but* . . ." Bhatia trailed a forefinger along his chin. "The Cats are very respectful of these *mystics,* and if one or two were to *die,* these Cats would see this as a very *bad* omen. . . ."

All right, then. Eliminate the Cats but blame it on resistance movements on the border worlds with the Republic March . . .

He spoke to the night. "Then what about you, Theodore? You'll worry. How would it look for the granddaughter of a bastard to take Dieron? So how to interest you in *Altair?* Then *you* could legitimately claim you'd cracked The Republic's titanium curtain. You'd not be diminished in the slightest. At your funeral, they'll call you a hero."

Because when Theodore *died*—because die he would— everyone would mourn, and none more so than Yori, who would be the media's darling. He'd see to *that.* He'd rip out her nails one by one if he had to.

His thoughts were interrupted as the door whirred open. "Cameron," he said, turning, "did you make our esteemed warlord *comfortable?*"

Cameron looked confused. "*Hai,* I saw the *tai-shu* to his escort."

"Ah." Toranaga had resisted, when his *gift* of this young man could not have been clearer. But that sly touch of the hands . . . *Could that have been for* my *benefit? To tweak me?* He nearly chuckled. Oh, this Toranaga was a deep one. He'd enjoy working with him.

Ah, but to business. "Tell me, Cameron, what did you hear this evening?"

"I heard nothing, *Tono.*"

"What did you see?"

"Nothing, *Tono.*"

"And what have you learned? What is the single, most important lesson applicable to any clandestine operation?"

"I . . . I do not know, *Tono.*"

"Think hard, Cameron. Much depends on this."

"I . . . I am sorry, *Tono,* I have not studied . . ."

"Well, it's no matter. You have done well to be so honest." The look of relief on Cameron's face made Bhatia pity him a little. "Thank you, *Tono*. You know I would do *any-thing* to please you."

"Yes? Well, here," he said, stepping forward and extending his hand, "this would please me." Cameron eagerly clasped Bhatia's outstretched hand, and Bhatia grasped Cameron's right hand. "I will enlighten you," Bhatia said, then tugging the youth closer, whispered: "The single, most important lesson is this: No *witnesses*."

Quick as lightning, Bhatia clamped down on Cameron's wrist with his left hand and pivoted. Air rushed from Cameron's lungs with an explosive *HUNH,* and then Bhatia sent him spinning from the balcony.

Cameron screamed: a high keening wail that cut out after only a few seconds as he hit the diacetylsilicate sand surrounding the complex. Unfortunately for Cameron, the fall didn't kill him. His screams bubbled into razor-edged shrieks as the sand began its gruesome work of dissolving flesh from bone. Cameron's death would be agonizingly long, and Bhatia would have the youth's screams as his night's serenade. That was fine.

"Because there can be no witnesses," Bhatia said. He smiled. "Absolutely none."

As Bhatia made his way out of his private dining room to his bedchamber, his mood blackened. No word at *all* from Kappa. Bhatia could not believe he'd misjudged this mission's appeal. He suddenly remembered that lone recruit who had taken on that *Rokurokubi*. Could *that* . . . ?

As Bhatia approached, his personal guard saluted, palmed the door and executed a flawless bow as Bhatia breezed past. The outer door scrolled shut. Bhatia stood within a small featureless alcove, a single scanner winking to his right, the still-sealed inner door to his bedchamber directly ahead. Bhatia stood motionless as the retinal scanner read the pattern of vessels, sorted through those individuals allowed access—himself and his personal guards—and confirmed his identity. His inner door slid open with a faint sigh. Calling for lights, Bhatia continued to his private office—and stopped cold when he saw his desk.

Identi-tags. A bloodred data crystal. And a single human eye, tacked to the desk with a stiletto through an optic nerve now dusky as a dead worm.

Bhatia's fingers shook as he fit the crystal into his player. A tiny click as the crystal engaged, and then a voice issued forth, one he knew but to which he could not put a face.

"Good evening, Director. Thanks for the good *look* around, if you'll pardon the pun. I accept your offer, on the following conditions . . ."

Bhatia listened, his shock slowly shading to a sort of admiration. Why, this was one step better than *he'd* thought of. *But there still has to be a way to track him, there* has *to be.* Then another more alarming thought: *If he got in, he had to get the codes somewhere. And how much did he* hear?

"Anyway, you know how to send a reply. Only don't delay, Director, or I might get peevish. And, oh, I hope you enjoyed this morning. Sorry about the boy, but he wasn't going far.

"Another thing: You must talk to those guards of yours. I don't want to tell tales out of school, but I'll wager the guard I met has some interesting stories to tell about just how I managed to get in. And he got a good long look at me. He might provide a very nice description."

A pause. "Or then again—maybe not."

# 25

***Shadow Rock, New Samarkand***
***4 September 3136***
***Just after midnight***

Looking into his mirror, Toranaga adjusted the folds of his silk robe. He enjoyed the feel of the slick fabric against his bare chest. He'd ordered a multitude of fat candles lit, and fingers of shadow softened his features. The ever-changing play of light and shadow made the black silk shimmer.

Toranaga's eyes shifted to the image of his spymaster lingering near the door. "I want to make one change, Hamada."

"Changes frequently wreak havoc on an operation."

"Nevertheless. I want *you* to take charge of delivering the package personally. If you're worried about your neck, be so kind as to remember that my head enjoys keeping company with the rest of me."

"Something could still go amiss."

"If it does, then you should take care to gut yourself, and quickly."

"Even my death will bring you ruin, *Tono*. They all know that I am your man."

"We are through discussing this. You will take charge." Toranaga waved a hand without turning. "You are dismissed."

Hamada's lips parted as if he would speak, but instead he bowed and retreated. Toranaga watched his spymaster's reflection glide out of the room, and he knew that this—bringing Hamada into it, *personally*—would actually work to his advantage.

*Because you do not want to die anymore than I do, Hamada, so you will be certain there are no mistakes.*

Barefoot, he padded round the room, eyeing the scene the way a director muses over a shot. Yes, the window was open just enough for a teasing breeze to stir the gauzy draperies round his bed. He'd started a few sticks of incense, enough to titillate the senses. On a lacquered tray, wisps of steam still curled from an earthen decanter of hot sake, and one cup lay ready. Yes, this would do handsomely. Who said duty was not a pleasure?

That ploy, Bhatia bringing in that young man, was as transparent as the youth was appealing. All smooth skin and supple limbs. Bhatia likely didn't know the rivers of lust that Cameron had sent coursing through Toranaga's veins, licking his thighs with heat. But fall for a pretty plaything? Trust Bhatia with his neck? Toranaga thought not. Oh, Toranaga had been honest enough. Why, at least *half* of what he described as his plan was true. And if it *worked* . . . all eyes would turn to Yori.

A polite yet soft rap upon the wood frame of a shoji, and Toranaga turned as Hatsuwe, clad in a simple gray kimono, entered. "Ah, my young samurai, thank you for responding so quickly. You have been quite . . . patient."

Hatsuwe's brow crinkled in a nearly imperceptible frown. He bowed. "I wait upon my lord. You know I have no other wish than to serve."

Toranaga waved the young man's words away. "Come now, you are being too modest." He slid a few steps closer, lowered his voice to a seductive whisper. "Do not deny your desires, Hatsuwe."

His lips parted, and Hatsuwe swallowed. "Desires, *Tono?*"

"You know what I'm talking about. You wish to supplant Yori Kurita in my esteem."

In the candlelight, Toranaga saw that the samurai's neck and face were hectic with color. Suddenly, Hatsuwe knelt and prostrated himself full length, in total submission, as one would before the coordinator. "I am yours, *Tono.* Ever I will be yours."

Towering over the samurai, Toranaga savored the moment and knew the future was his to seize. "Understand this, Hatsuwe. I am unchangeable, the rock that endures throughout time. Yori Kurita is a tool, and she is one that you *will* suffer to live." Toranaga paused. "But for you, I have reserved a special place, a sacred duty and a path we will journey together, a way most beautiful—and we will pleasure one another."

Hatsuwe still did not look up. "Anything, *Tono.* I have waited patiently to honor you in the way of the samurai who revere their masters."

"Yes?" Toranaga gave a silent laugh. Then he turned aside, plucked up the decanter of sake and tipped the still-warm liquid into a waiting ceramic cup. He brought the cup to where Hatsuwe still lay, and then Toranaga knelt. His heart quickened, and his lust, tamped earlier, stirred. Yes, he would have this, take what was his. "Look at me," he said. "I command you to look."

Slowly, Hatsuwe rose until he faced his lord. They were so close Toranaga saw the pulse bounding in the man's neck.

"Now," Toranaga said. He sipped once from the cup and then proffered it. "Drink. Share with me as you will share my bed. I will show you the beautiful way, the *nanshoku* reserved for samurai alone and then . . ." Loosing his sash with his free hand, Toranaga let his robe slither from his nakedness in a whisper of silk. "Then I will show you how you may serve your lord. But for now, drink, my samurai. Drink."

Hatsuwe slept. The candles guttered, but Toranaga did not care. As sweat evaporated from his skin and the feel of Hatsuwe's passion slowly faded from his body, Toranaga smiled into the gathering darkness.

# PART FOUR

## *Yosu-miro:* The Choice

# 26

**W**ahab Fusilli jerked awake. He lay a moment, heart thumping, his nightmare thinning to shreds. As always when he woke, his eyes tracked the familiar contours of the room—enough to know that nothing had changed.

The room, no bigger than a jail cell, smelled of damp earth and new paint. The windowless walls were drywall painted a stark white. There was bare floor, also white. His aluminum cot was snugged against the right wall, its pillowcase, sheets and blanket snowy white. Through a door cut into a drywall partition, there was a full bathroom. Everything was white, even the comb and brush. Clothes, too, exactly his size and, blessedly, not white: olive drab trousers, a black t-shirt, a faded olive camouflage shirt, underwear, fresh socks. Boots but no laces. Just in case.

He figured they watched, or perhaps only listened. He'd searched, found nothing. He'd also looked for a weapon. Anything he could easily take apart—the towel rack, the toilet-paper dispenser—was plastic. The cot's aluminum frame was molded, as was the single chair. Nothing.

Now, a knock on the door. Fusilli pushed to a sit and stood. The door swung in. The guard was dressed in olive fatigues. He carried a tray: a sandwich, an apple, a double handful of small carrots. A bottle of water and a mug of steaming hot coffee with two containers of creamer, no sugar. The way he liked it. They'd done their homework.

The guard had no rifle. That meant more guards a few paces away. "Step to the far wall, please," the guard said. He said the same thing every single time, and Fusilli made him say it every single time. It was the only way to get a conversation going.

Fusilli said, "I demand to talk to someone in charge. I

don't have money, and I don't have a rich family that can pay a ransom. I want to talk to someone now." The same speech he gave every single time. So far, all he'd gotten was an emphatic monosyllable: *No.*

This time, though, the guard smiled. "You want to talk to someone?"

This was not in the script. "Yes."

"Well, maybe you're gonna get your wish."

"What do you mean?"

"We got us a couple of Dracs. So, maybe you're outta here. Now, enough with the chatter. Get against the wall," the guard said. There was no mistaking his tone, and Fusilli backed to the wall. The guard centered the tray under the light-globe, backed up without taking his eyes from Fusilli. "Go on. Eat up. And you might want to, you know, *enjoy.*" The guard's lips curled in a cruel grin. "Maybe, you know . . . last meal."

He didn't have to wait long. As he did, he fingered the diamond stud in his left ear, considering . . . then let his hand fall. Not yet.

This time, two guards came. Both had rifles. One held him at gunpoint while the other zipped plasticuffs around his wrists. Then they led him out of the room—which, he now discovered, was a converted cellar. They led him forward only a few steps before turning right and ascending a flight of stairs. The wet earth smell was strong, and then Fusilli winced against a slant of sunlight.

He pushed into open air. The cellar lay along the west wall of a squat, anonymous, gray rectangular structure of corrugated metal. There were trees all around, and he saw clouds through breaks to his left and a higher peak to his right. The day felt late, near dusk. In the mountains, he thought, far west of the city and easily eighty klicks from base.

His guards marched him to a clearing. There were more people there, men and women, all in green fatigues and all with rifles. They stood in a rough semicircle, and in the center Fusilli spotted Dasha, in fatigues and black tee, a slugthrower in a quick-draw holster at her right hip. To her left was a man he'd never seen, also in fatigues and a black tee that was tight as a second skin and showed the leading edge of a tattoo on his right bicep. He was lean and a little wolfish. His black hair was military-short and styled into black spikes. *Yakuza* material: He reminded Fusilli of Lance Shimazu.

Dasha didn't smile when their eyes met. She didn't look angry, either. She was still stunning, her rich copper hair drawn back from her face, accentuating a widow's peak, and remarkable amber-green eyes. She said nothing. After a moment, her eyes slid away.

The man stuck his hand out and flashed a smile. "Tony Yamada."

Fusilli saw the filed incisors. He didn't take Yamada's hand. He said nothing. He waited.

Yamada wasn't fazed. Instead, he glanced down at Fusilli's cuffs. "Hey, what's this?" Pointing at the cuffs now, looking at the guards. "Get these off, huh? Hey, and get him a chair. He looks kind of used."

A guard cut the cuffs. Fusilli said nothing. He kept his eyes on Yamada. When the second guard produced a folding camp stool, Fusilli didn't even look at it. He kept his gaze on Yamada. He waited.

Yamada nodded. "Right, shoulda thought of that. Psychologically, wouldn't make sense for you to sit down, right? Makes you submissive."

Fusilli said nothing.

Yamada pulled a noteputer from his hip pocket. "Ho-kaaay, so we checked you out. You're"—fiddling with the noteputer—"Shakir, right? Shakir Jerrar? Born on Ashio, parents dead, blah, blah. Moved to Proserpina, blah, blah, blah . . . served in the Brotherhood. But here's what I don't get. You told Dasha you left Proserpina because the jobs dried up. Only *here*, it says here that you killed your squad leader. Something about a bunch of you Dracs getting into trouble."

Fusilli spoke for the first time. "I'm not a Drac. I was in the Brotherhood."

"So what happened?"

"Like I told Dasha: The Fury left. Most of them, anyway, or maybe just the good ones. The ones leftover were vintage Dracs."

"And?"

"And I didn't like the way a sergeant was treating someone."

"Record says you were insubordinate, and when

*things*"—he made quotation marks with his fingers—"escalated, you popped your sergeant."

"That's about right."

"Ah-hunh." Yamada cocked his head the way dogs do when trying to make sense of something. "You interested in what I found out?"

"Not really. I already know what happened."

"Ah-hunh," Yamada said again. "Well, here's what I found out. Apparently, this sergeant and another guy were coming on to a couple of the local women. But you didn't think it was so funny. You broke things up, got those women out, and then things got hot. Next thing you know, BAM! You shoot your sergeant. What, he was having fun with your sister?"

"I don't have a sister," Fusilli said. "Rapists and bullies just happen to be low down on my list."

"So how come you're still alive? How come they let you go?"

"They couldn't catch me."

"You that slick, Shak?"

"I'm that lucky."

"I'd think you'd hightail it as far away from the Dracs as possible."

"Maybe I'm also stupid. Or stubborn. I've been accused of both."

"Uh-huh." Yamada tossed a quick look at Dasha, who responded with a slight shrug. Yamada turned to Fusilli. "So what do you want, Shak? Hunh? You want to fight the good fight? You want to play soldier boy?"

Fusilli stared at Yamada for a few moments before replying. "If I'd wanted to play soldier, I'd have asked around for Eriksson."

"So you want to *kill* you some Dracs, Shak?"

"As many as I can get my hands on. After I left Proserpina, I stopped off at Al Na'ir to check up on my brother and his kids, his wife."

"I thought you said you were an only child."

"No, I said I didn't have a sister."

"True," Yamada said, and the way he said it, Fusilli knew Yamada was listening for inconsistencies, little details that might trip Fusilli up. "And?"

"My brother's family was in Phoenix Dome." He paused

to let that sink in. "Next time I get my hands on a Drac, I want him cuffed, and I want him to see it coming. I want to see his eyes. And I want to do that a couple hundred times."

Yamada's lips split in a lazy grin. "Well then, Shak, today's your lucky day."

That seemed to be a cue. There was a general shuffling, and then the audience parted like a human sea—and Fusilli's stomach bottomed out.

The lieutenant's uniform was torn and bloodied. Her brown hair was matted with filth. She had brown eyes, an angry gash on her right cheek. She was a tiny woman, barely a meter and a half. Her plasticuffed hands were thin, the wrists like twigs. Her ankles were cuffed. She couldn't run. She smelled of fear.

And Fusilli knew her.

*Oh, dear God . . .*

Nancy Compton: a nurse attached to command headquarters back on Proserpina. He didn't know if Compton would recognize him. She'd been relatively new, and he'd been away from Proserpina for the better part of the last year. If she recognized him, she would not know about his mission. She probably didn't know he was on Biham. Compton's liquid brown eyes skipped from Yamada and Dasha to Fusilli. He couldn't breathe. He kept his face absolutely still. She stared at him for a second longer. He couldn't tell whether this was because she *did* realize who he was or because she was trying to place him. Then her eyes returned to Yamada.

Wordlessly, Dasha pulled a semiauto pistol done in a black matte finish from its holster. She checked the safety, then held it by the muzzle, offering the weapon to Fusilli.

Yamada was smiling again. "Okay, Shak. It's showtime."

Fusilli didn't move. Couldn't.

Yamada said, "Know how to use one of those, Shak?"

Fusilli said nothing.

Yamada said, "First, I thought laser, except all you do is cook the bastard. A Drac, there oughtta be blood. Brains splattered all over the place."

Fusilli was silent.

"Your big chance, Shak. You want the whites of her eyes, go for it."

Fusilli willed his face to stone, but his mind was frantic, desperately riffling through various options, searching for something to get him off the hook—and, just as importantly, get him away from Compton. But he couldn't think of anything. He'd been condemned by his own words, his cover story. No way out, not after that little speech.

A small voice he recognized, belatedly, as conscience: *Every second she's alive is another second she might betray you.*

They were leaving him no choice. He couldn't refuse.

*Better her than you, better her.*

Expressionless, he took the gun from Yamada. The gun was heavier than he expected, and the grip was stippled and blocky. Turning aside, he pointed the muzzle toward the ground and ejected the magazine, checked the nine-round clip. Then he pressed the magazine back into the grip with the butt of his hand—not tough-guy fast but smoothly until the magazine clicked. Jacked the slide and chambered the first round.

Fusilli faced Compton. They were perhaps two meters apart. She was shivering. Her knees buckled, and she would've collapsed if the two guards hadn't gripped her forearms. Her eyes rolled like an animal's. A tiny moan dribbled from her mouth when Fusilli thumbed off the safety.

"Pointblank, Shak," Yamada said. "Right between the eyes."

Fusilli closed to within arm's reach, and as he did so, the two guards drew their weapons—aimed at his head. The warning was clear.

He pressed the muzzle against the nude space between Compton's eyebrows. He eased back on the trigger, balancing the trigger pull on the pad of his right index finger, knowing the first pull would be the longest and require the most pressure. So he had time . . . for what? He didn't know.

*Either her or me. They're making me. I don't have a choice, I . . .*

"Wait!" Yamada shouted. "Hold up there, Shak!"

Fusilli flinched. Not enough to take up the rest of the pressure, just a jerk of the head and arm. Compton sagged a little and let out a small sound that was not quite a sob.

The guards each broke at the elbow, aiming their weapons at the sky. The watchful crowd said nothing.

Fusilli turned as Yamada strode up. "Give me the gun," Yamada said.

Something unknotted in Fusilli's chest. *A test. He'll keep her alive, a hostage, but that still doesn't help if she knows me, if she talks . . .*

Yamada's voice knifed into his thoughts. "You're pretty pissed off about Al Na'ir, right? Well, a guy's that mad, he wants to kill with his bare hands."

*No.* Fusilli's blood iced. *Oh, no, no, don't make me do this. . . .*

Yamada's eyes were bright, like black coins. "A bullet's not hands-on, and you look like a real hands-on guy, Shak. So here's what I think. I think you should strangle the bitch."

Dasha spoke for the first time. "Tony, I—"

"Shut up, Dasha." Yamada didn't even turn around. His gaze pierced Fusilli like a dagger. "Whaddaya say, Shak?"

He didn't answer because he knew it wouldn't matter. Somehow—he didn't know when it happened—Compton was secured to a tree, and now he stood before her, the eyes of the others on his back. Compton was crying and moaning: "Nopleasepleasenonononono . . ."

*One of us has to die, or we'll both die. No choice, it's her or me.*

"Go on, Shak." Yamada again, close by, right alongside, whispering as intimately as if they were best friends, or perhaps lovers. "Do her, man."

Then Compton said one word: "No." But there was no terror. It was the voice . . . of astonishment. Of wonder. It was the voice of Death—because Fusilli saw in her eyes that she had recognized him at last.

"No," she said, "no, you can't do this, Fu—"

He caught her throat with both hands, choking off those last treacherous syllables—and then he squeezed with all his might, sweating, grunting like an animal. Because strangling the life out of someone is hard work and takes a very long time and is much more horrible than anyone can possibly imagine.

No one else spoke. No one moved. Compton struggled, soundless, in a losing battle for her life. Near the end, when her face was black with blood, he felt a sudden give when he broke something in her throat, and she quivered in her death throes.

By then, he was weeping.

# 27

**Dieron**
**Former Prefecture X, Republic of the Sphere**
**5 September 3136**

Commanding General Tina Magnusson-Talbot stood with her arms akimbo, an unlit cigarette clamped between her teeth. She was trying to quit, and the DropShip pilot fussed about her smoking on board. She was a big-boned woman with nicotine stains on her fingers and a whiskey burr in her voice, and she usually didn't take any crap from anyone, let alone a pilot. But she settled for chewing nicotine-spiked gum. Stuff tasted like a dog's butt.

They were coming in from the east and were low enough for the northern mountains to have resolved into snow-capped peaks. Any other time, she might've enjoyed the view. But she was too keyed up.

Talbot wasn't a superstitious woman and didn't believe in anything she couldn't see or touch. So no matter what the scuttlebutt was about that Tormark biting the proverbial dust, Talbot wasn't buying that the Dracs weren't gunning for Dieron. A heck of a lot of people, with just about as much brass but not the balls, figured the Dracs were gonna lie low for a long time, regroup and all that crap. She didn't believe it. So Dieron was going to be ready, come hell or high water.

She flipped gum with her tongue, cracked the wad against

a row of rear fillings. *Crack-crack-crack-crack!* Like pistol shots.

The DropShip skimmed a ridge, and then her stomach bottomed out as the ridge fell away to a gorge edged with rock and scrub pine. A silver ribbon of river cut through the center, but she could see at once that the flow was reduced, and the once-submerged land was now inhabited by meandering trails of people movers and artillery vehicles radiating like spokes from the central hub of a bulbous DropShip.

"Look at that," she said. "Six months in the making, that base. Hell of a turnaround time, but look at it."

Her aide, Coleman, said, "It's a nice base."

"You don't sound very enthusiastic, Coleman. Something stuck in your craw?"

"Well . . . You really think they'll come, General?"

"Count on it. No stopping the Dracs this time, no matter how much The Republic throws their way. Hell, if I was a Drac? I'd come on like gangbusters. Why? You'd rather they didn't?"

"I like it when people aren't shooting at me."

"Can't disagree with you." She squinted up at Coleman as if through a veil of cigarette smoke. "What's on your mind, son?"

"Well, all this build-up for a base that's as indefensible as a dome . . . I don't get it."

"How do you mean?"

"How do I mean, Ma'am?" Coleman looked a little stunned. "The base is in a valley. We're sitting ducks, General."

"No, son, not ducks," she said, and then decided, hell with it. Pilot could open a window or something. She fished out her lighter, flicked it to life. Didn't spit out the gum, figuring a double whammy might be kind of interesting. She touched the flame to her smoke, sucked greedily, and inhaled a lungful that instantly went to her head in a blissfully pure nicotine buzz.

"Not ducks," she repeated, snapping off the lighter. She cracked gum. "Bait."

# 28

There was a cop's butt parked on every available stool in the diner, but they snagged the last vacant table, tucked in a far corner. An overweight blonde with hair from a bottle arrived with two heavy white porcelain mugs and a pot of fresh-brewed coffee. Thereon ordered cherry pie; Loveland chose lemon chess. He watched as the waitress chunked out a wedge and then laid his plate on the table without it making a sound. Prolonging the moment, Loveland inhaled, smelled lemon and buttermilk and sugar, then forked off a bite into his mouth. The tartness made him moan.

Thereon just ate. He was a man who understood that food was fuel, and that was it.

Loveland was on his second piece of chess pie when he said, "So what do you think?"

Thereon's smoke-gray eyes fixed him over the rim of his coffee mug. "I think Petrie bagged us a cold hit that matches the hit on our Jane Doe. I think we got some kind of armor lubricant is what I think."

"Yeah, but those are facts," Loveland said, his mouth full of pie. "And what the hell sense does body armor make?"

Thereon shrugged as he pulled out his noteputer. "It doesn't have to make sense. It's a finding awaiting an explanation. We know our unsub is methodical. He plans. We now know for sure that he's got surgical experience because he had to strip Petrie's hands without making a mistake, and the arterial supply to Petrie's skin was both cauterized and knotted. Throwing a surgeon's knot with suture isn't easy."

"Meaning our guy could be a surgeon. Or a lab tech. A

surgical nurse. Even a forensic pathologist." Loveland stared moodily at his unfinished pie then slid the plate away with his thumb. He'd lost his appetite. "Man, I don't want to think about that."

"We're going to have to because not only is this guy smart, he's changed, a *lot*. The common denominator for the women on Towne was location. Now, since that Proserpina killing last February, they've all been prostitutes, all dark-skinned, most of them tall." He waggled his noteputer. "Do me a favor. Beginning with the Proserpina killing, when he went strictly to darker women, chart out the murders in sequence. Eliminate Towne; eliminate the outliers on Devil's Rock and Irian."

"Okay." Loveland fished out his noteputer, thumbed it to life and tapped in data. "What am I looking for?"

"With this many dots, there's got to be a connection. Up to now, we've looked at the victims. But maybe it's something about the *sequence* we're not seeing."

Loveland watched as his computer icon told him how hard the computer was working and he'd just have to hold his horses. "Like what?"

"If I knew, I'd tell you. But I was thinking about what that old lady said. That guy in the wheelchair not having a face. Remember that?"

"What? You think our guy stripped off the face like he did Petrie's hands?"

"No, I don't think that's it. What I want to know is why he took that person but *left* the wheelchair. This is a guy who only takes what he *needs*."

"So you're saying maybe he needed this guy."

"But not his wheelchair. He left that for us. He knew we'd eventually find Petrie. What if Wheelchair Guy was dead? Dead weight's heavy, but we already know our unsub is big because Petrie was big. He lifted weights; he was in shape. And that lubricant, it's for armor, right? So what if Edwina Jeffries couldn't see a face because it was behind a visor or helmet?"

Loveland opened his mouth to reply, but his noteputer dinged. "Okay, all I got here is a bunch of dots. What am I supposed to be seeing?"

"Have your noteputer connect the dots sequentially."

Loveland's brows knit. "Why?"

"Just a hunch. Try it."

"Okay." Loveland shrugged, poked buttons, watched as his noteputer drew a straight line from Towne to Murchison to Halstead Station, and then another line that began at Proserpina and swooped like a scythe, cutting through David, Galatea and back to Murchison, then arcing through Galatea III . . . "What am I supposed to be seeing?"

"What does the figure look like?"

"Well, it's a line, then an arc, then . . ." His voice died. "Holy shit."

"Yeah." Thereon's voice was flat. "You see it?"

"It's a *K*. A cursive, goddamned, capital *K*." Loveland uncapped a pen, snatched up a napkin and quickly scratched out an elongated capital *K* in black ink. "The murders follow the sequence of strokes required to make a *K*."

"*K*—for Kappa."

"No," Loveland said, "not just Kappa. Who's been to all these planets? Who uses armor, *battle*armor?" He didn't wait for Thereon to answer. "That's a *K* for *Katana*: Katana Tormark and the Fury. Because what about her is the *same* as our murder victims?"

"My God." Thereon stared. "*Skin* color. Tormark's skin color is . . . was roughly the same as every single victim's since Proserpina. And *Petrie* . . ."

"Told his wife he was going to *Halstead Station* where Tormark's people are headquartered," Loveland said. "Jesus Christ, Thereon. Kappa, our unsub . . . he's one of *them*."

# 29

## Kendall Mountains, Biham
## 17 September 3136

"**Y**ou think this is such a good idea?" Yamada asked. He pinched a cigarette in his right hand. A gray tube of ash drooped like the wilted stem of a flower. "Kind of fast, you ask me."

"He's been here for three weeks, Tony," Dasha said. She sat on a camp stool, perched on the other side of a metal desk painted a dingy institutional gray. "His story's checked out. He's drilled with my squad. He's excellent on the firing range. You can tell he's had training. I think tonight's a very good time for him to get his feet wet." When Yamada didn't respond, she added, "For Christ's sake, he strangled a Drac with his bare hands. What more do you want?"

"I saw it." Yamada took a quick puff, shattering the tube of ash to gray dust. Smoke spurted from his nostrils as he swiped away ash with the side of his hand. "That's what bothers me."

"Why?" She'd forced herself to watch every terrible second even as the full horror of what Yamada was doing to Shakir, to all of them, blasted through her body like a cold, merciless wind. "I couldn't have done it, not even if you pointed a gun at my head. I don't think any of our people would've. It's more like murder." *It* was *murder*.

"*That's* what bothers me. He just did it, like a good soldier."

"What would you have done if he refused?"

"Kill him, and do it myself. Would've been fine."

She said nothing. He wasn't kidding. Yamada was cold, calculating and ruthless. For him, murder was just the price of doing business.

Another puff and then Yamada scratched at his chin with

his thumb. "Here's the thing. Shak was in the Brotherhood, right? Took orders from the Dracs? So here's this lieutenant, and he kills her. Just like that."

"He shot a sergeant."

"Who was raping a civilian. Totally different. I don't care how bad you want revenge. Most people, there should be hesitation, or they should refuse. Shak got cold. Just . . . cold. Weighed the odds, made the choice."

"He was a soldier."

"He was a *grunt*." Yamada paused. "If he's really a Drac, they could've set it up, planted records."

Dasha thought about that. The thing was she liked Shakir, and it didn't hurt that he was really quite . . . handsome. That long black hair and ice-blue eyes, coupled with a sensitive mouth and high cheekbones, and a physical presence that sent a charge of sexual attraction sizzling through her veins. Back at the bar, it hadn't been all bluff. Now that she knew him better, she thought about him when she had to go to work. She enjoyed spending time with him when she was here. He didn't say much, but when he did, she sensed sadness deep down, the same kind she felt: that emptiness where joy used to be. Whether he knew it or not, Shakir was a lost soul, at home nowhere, untethered just like her.

As if he'd read her mind, Yamada said, "You sure the only reason you want him along tonight is because he's ready to see some *action*?"

Caught off guard, she flushed under Yamada's intense scrutiny. "What's the matter, Tony? Jealous?"

She didn't like the way Yamada's eyes flared, and she was stunned at the thought that maybe she'd hit Yamada in a soft spot. But the moment passed quickly, and Yamada covered his anger with a harsh bark of laughter. "Dream on, babe. I got women coming out my ears."

"Lucky you. Listen, don't worry about me. Between this and my job, I'm so tired I can barely stand."

"Yeah?" Yamada said, and his tone turned a little nasty. "Well, you get to know Shak better . . . maybe you won't be doing a lot of *standing*. Maybe doing that old horizontal mambo, you know what I mean?"

"God, you are so unbelievably crude. Look, I'll sleep

with whomever I choose. If it turns out to be Shakir, it's my business."

His face was stiff with anger. "It's my business if it compromises my operation."

"*Our* operation, Tony." She paused. "Look, if Shakir's a spy, why haven't the Dracs come swooping down?"

"Maybe the mission is to figure out our capabilities. Maybe his mission is to find out where we're getting our matériel. Then the Dracs take us out and go hit the March. The thing is, we can't let them stop us, not now. We know how this has to end."

She let the silence hang a few beats. "Nothing's going to change that. You know that, when the time comes, I'll go through with it."

Yamada ground out his smoke. "If they let us, babe. If they let us."

Fusilli waited outside Yamada's camouflage-green Quonset. He sat on a flat rock beneath an evergreen, leaning back against the coarse bark. The day was cloudless, and the sun was directly overhead but not hot. Dappled light transformed the woods into a shadowy haven. There had been a lot of rain in the last few days, and the air smelled wet and a little like resin, and was cool this far into the mountains. A peaceful place, really. Not a place where a man strangled a woman with his bare hands.

He rested his head against the tree and closed his eyes. God, how he wished he could purge that from his memory, his nightmares. But maybe he wasn't supposed to forget something like that.

*Not my fault about Compton, they made me do it. I had no choice. . . .*

Which way he now tipped should depend on his loyalties to Ramadeep Bhatia, his duties as an agent of the ISF. This assignment couldn't dovetail better with his original mission to cripple Katana Tormark's troops and defeat her people from the inside out.

Except now . . . there was Dasha. His lips twitched into an unconscious half-smile. Like Yamada, she seemed to have another life out there about which she was reluctant to talk. But he liked her, a lot, and he thought the attraction was mutual. When was the last time he cared about anyone or anything other than himself?

A voice he associated with self-preservation niggled: *She's just a tool. Watch out for yourself because you're the only one who can and will.*

Yes, but what would it be like to *care* for someone that much? Oh, but he had a mission, right? He gave the lobe of his left ear an absent stroke as he thought. The stud was gone. He'd removed and carefully slid the gem into a tiny waterproof packet he carried in an inside pocket, over his heart.

Whose side was he on, anyway? Say he facilitated these people in their goal of taking down Katana Tormark's command. But to what end? Katana was dead. Whatever reason Bhatia had for wanting to oust her was irrelevant. In a very real sense, that part of his mission was done.

Facing that harsh reality also made clear another. He was stuck here, in the Dieron District, for the foreseeable future. Bhatia couldn't very well recall him, and he could not just disappear. He could never hide for long from Bhatia, or Crawford and the O5P. Crawford would hunt him down if he discovered Fusilli's treachery: how he'd allowed Liz Magruder and all his comrades to die on Al Na'ir.

So then the choices were between DCMS and Dieron Command, and between Dieron Command—and this woman. Yet would he ever allow her to really know him? How stupid. Of course, he couldn't reveal who and what he was: the man he was now or the traitor's name he'd taken.

And of all his damnable *perversities*, that name . . . why choose *that*?

"Shakir?"

He opened his eyes. Dasha looked down at him. A little embarrassed, he pushed himself to his feet, brushed pine needles from his pants. "Sorry. Just woolgathering. Was Yamada all right with it?"

"Not really. Yamada was a *kuso atama*."

"What did he say?" When she didn't answer, Fusilli touched her arm. "Hey," he said gently. "*I'm* not the prick. Yamada is. What's the matter?"

She pulled in a deep breath. "He thinks you're a spy."

It was the suspicion he'd been expecting. Sooner or later, someone always questioned. So he knew how to reply. His tone was belligerent, challenging, and he didn't have to feign anger. "Yeah? Well, let him come and talk to *me*. How many people does that asshole want me to strangle before he figures out that I'm not a spy?"

She put a restraining hand on his chest. "Relax. You'll get your chance." She debated, then added, "He also thinks I like you, and that that's affecting my judgment."

This he had not expected, and his anger evaporated. He didn't know why he should care what this woman thought about him, but he was acutely aware of her: of those mysterious eyes, that lush copper hair, the length of her throat. That thin golden chain with its gold locket and key. "And?"

Dasha didn't reply. Instead, they stared at one another. He saw the turmoil in her face, and he wondered what he looked like to her. They were so close, all Fusilli had to do was lean forward and kiss her if he wanted. His brain screamed that he was losing his objectivity; there was his mission, and only a fool would fall in love with the enemy. But he didn't care because he felt something else he hadn't in a very, very long time: desire. And maybe the promise of something more.

And what mission, what damnable *mission*? This was his *life* they were playing with now. *His* future.

It was Dasha who made the first move. She took a step back, and the moment was gone.

"Just do me a favor," she said, turning on her heel. "Don't screw up."

# 30

*17 September 3136*

**T**he night was a forest of shadows. Heavy clouds pressed overhead, and the air smelled like aluminum. Fusilli squatted behind boulders ridging a valley about three hundred meters deep and studded with scrub. A meandering two-lane road was barely visible through night-vision digital binoculars. Squinting at the green-and-gray electronically enhanced image projected upon a phosphor screen, Fusilli frowned. "You're sure?"

"Uh-huh," Dasha said. She was no more than a half meter away on his left, crouching so close her arm brushed his. "Bridge washed out by rain along the main road from the spaceport. That checks out. A resupply DropShip's got perishables. Medical supplies mainly. A Drac's coordinating with the main hospital to open up clinics."

That tallied with McCain's plan. "And the convoy?"

"Three VV1 Rangers, refit for hauling supplies, no air escort."

And that did *not* tally. Rangers were light infantry wheeled vehicles with turret-mounted machine guns and four front-mounted lasers. They were designed mainly as antipersonnel weapons. Fusilli couldn't see the Rangers doing much against a long-range assault, and Dasha's platoon had the advantage of elevation. Counting him, her platoon was seventeen strong, armed with five Carl G M88 recoilless rifles firing HEDP rounds. The high-explosive dual-purpose shells could punch through armor and gouge craters into the road, cutting off the tanks' escape route. Each M88 gunner was grouped with a spotter and another fighter for cracking the Venturi aside for reloading. Everyone but he had M12 carbine assault rifles, and they could potentially overwhelm the Rangers within minutes.

"Convoy doesn't strike you as a bit thin?" he said.

"You mean, do I think this is a trap? Sure."

"Then why are we doing this?"

"Because," she said, retrieving her binoculars, "we can."

Hunkered behind cover, *Sho-sa* William "Buck" Bruckner tongued his chaw to the other cheek and worked the tobacco something fierce. Palming his coal-black Stetson, he dug at his scalp in a good, long scratch. Then he screwed on that Stetson and worked his chaw. Would've felt better with his lucky whitey, but a bone-white Stetson at night? Like an ad: *Shoot me.*

He aimed right and squirted tobacco juice into the darkness. "You got 'em?" he growled into a microcomm secured around his wrist.

A whispered voice in his ear from Tactical: "Got 'em on

thermal imaging. On the right ridge. I count eight . . . no, make that nine targets."

Nine pairs of eyes staring into the valley. Buck's long experience as a tank commander told him that for every bad guy you see, expect an evil twin. If *he* were doing the ambushing, he'd opt for LAWs or M88s. Well, no way his people were gonna be *that* easy to squash.

"Okay, people," Buck said. "Here's the drill."

"Here they come," Dasha muttered into her microcomm. Her goggles made her look like an extraterrestrial from a bad horror holovid.

Fusilli heard engines rumble as the ghostly green tanks surged, picking up speed. Each hauled a flatbed unit capped with a hard shell.

*If it's Bruckner, he'll vary their speed. That's what I would do, only I wouldn't be here* at all, *or I'd have air support,* something.

"Wait for it." Dasha on her haunches, peering over a hump of rock. "Don't target those flatbeds. Remember, we're here to get supplies, too."

Later on, Fusilli would remember that little *too*. At the moment, though, his nerves sang with anxiety. He probably knew some of those people. What if McCain had gone to oversee the off-loading of supplies?

*Bruckner, be smart. It's an ambush; you've got to* know *that.*

The lead Ranger was now nearly midway through the valley. The other two followed, spaced like green beads on lengthening string. The lead Ranger gunned its engine with an audible grind of whining gears.

Dasha inhaled, short and sharp. "Now."

Tactical: "I read tracer fire!"

"Throttle down!" Buck barked. "Two seconds, then punch it up! Keep it unpredictable, people, watch your distance, watch . . . !"

"Incoming!" Tactical said. "Sir, we've got two . . . !"

"Gunners, return fire!" Buck shouted. "Return . . . !"

Tiny red-orange sparks flared in arcs of subdued tracer fire. The tracers rained down, followed by the dull *pomph-*

*pomph-pomph* of HEDP rounds rocketing from the maws of M88s, pulling tails of orange-yellow flame. The M88 to his left let go, and Fusilli felt heat from a back-blast of superheated gases, smelled the stink of explosives. Below, muzzle flashes spurted from the Rangers' machine guns followed a split second later by the unmistakable *tatatatatatat* of weapons fire.

Something weird about the flashes . . . Fusilli couldn't put his finger on it. He couldn't see well even with subdued tracers. He heard the zip and crack of bullets punching rock, and he ducked as something hummed a groove over his head.

He'd seen enough to know that the lead tank had taken the first hit just forward of its machine-gun turret. The armor was still intact, as was the front right wheel, but whoever was inside would be banging around like a pea in a tin can, and the temp ought to be spiking pretty fast.

*What can I do, what can I do?* Fusilli's brain raced through his available options. No, there was *nothing* he could do. He didn't know if he wanted to. But then he thought: *That machine-gun fire, something* wrong . . .

He inched up. The air was alive with the fizzle of tracers, the thump of M88s and the *pockpockpockpock* of bullets scoring rock, chunking out shrapnel. Then he saw the problem. First, no laser fire. Each Ranger had four. Why not lay down a suppressing fire to keep the fighters from swooping down to take control? Or maybe Buck was holding lasers in reserve.

Second, he counted only *six* machine guns per tank. That was wrong. There were *eight* on every Ranger. So where were the missing guns?

All three tanks, scored from multiple hits, had nonetheless managed to make it to a spot directly beneath their position—and now did the incredible. They *halted*. Dead. Stop.

*Maybe something wrong with the lead's drive train. Road's so narrow, no way the others can get around* . . . The road behind was pocked with craters, though the road ahead was still maneuverable. Then he saw the strategy. The elevation worked both ways now. The Rangers couldn't return fire as efficiently because of the angle, but the M88 gunners were having just as much trouble. The gunners were on their feet, their spotters grabbing each at the waist as the gunners braced against the rock to lob their rounds straight down. They could get off shots but with the higher risk of exposure. Good tactical sense would've been to shift right, move some gunners ahead of the tanks. But the gunners were staying put.

He was puzzling over all this when he felt someone touch his right elbow. "Time to go," Dasha said. She'd parked her NVGs on her forehead.

"Go?" That made no sense. If they were intent on getting the supplies or, at the very least, those tanks . . . On the other hand, wasn't this precisely what he had hoped for? So the tanks could get away? *Who am I? What have I become?* "You mean you're aborting the attack?"

Shaking her head, Dasha shouldered her rifle. "Not on your life. But you're coming with me."

"What about your people?"

"No time to explain." Dasha was already moving off. "Come on, Shakir. My people know the score. Just do what I say."

Fusilli stared after her retreating form for a long moment. Then he pushed himself to his feet and did what he was told.

There was a few seconds' silence broken by splutters of static. Then Tactical: "No tracer fire ahead. Fire's concentrated directly above us."

"Okay, so they're not moving." Chewing, Buck spat, then drawled through his comm, "Shadow? You in the loop?"

"Roger that." Shadow's reply was fringed with only the faintest whisper of the usual throb and thump Buck was accustomed to. "Practically on top of you guys."

Buck glanced up, saw nothing. Shook his head. *Sweet.* "Anything?"

"Two targets on thermal, moving on a northeast vector. I'm off."

"Good hunting. We'll warm a couple of asses down here, give 'em something interesting to look at. Out." Buck reeled in a breath. "All right, people . . . Pop those tops and let 'em rip."

# 31

They wove uphill through trees, their footfalls dulled by a thick carpet of pine needles. The staccato chatter of machine guns and dull *whump*s of M88s faded. His flak vest added weight, and Fusilli was sweating. They'd light up on aerial surveillance—if anyone was looking.

A far-off *boom* balled like thunder. He pulled up a second, waited, heard the boom again and turned back the way they'd come. Through gaps in the trees, the diffuse glare of an explosion smudged the horizon amber. A breeze gusted past, tugging the stink of scorched metal.

"I don't know that sound," Dasha said.

"I think one of the tanks went." He was suddenly sickened, angry that he'd not helped Parks' men somehow. But what could he do? The fault lay with Parks, and whatever cockeyed plan he'd dreamt up. "Hell should I know? You've got a microcomm, call them."

"We maintain silence until this is over."

"Until it's *over*?" His face was so tight he thought his skin would split. "That explosion sounded like it *is* over for somebody."

"And if it's the Dracs, that's fine."

*Get control.* "Where are we going?"

She started off again. "You'll know when we get there."

As they neared what Fusilli thought must be a summit, he had a sense of a clearing just ahead, and it was cooler. Seconds later, his ears pricked to the gurgle of water. They followed a stream, then veered right. A short time later, Dasha gestured to a natural blind: a huge root-ball from a toppled pine. Fusilli hunkered down next to her. "What is it?" he whispered.

Dasha held up a hand for silence. Cautiously, she peered round the root-ball. Ducked back. "Ahead, about fifty meters."

His NVGs picked up the unambiguous signature of a cooling engine that resolved into the outlines of a lone soft-topped, wheeled vehicle. A military ambulance: There was a dark cross drawn against a much lighter background. Then his gaze sharpened on an icon on the driver's door. "Dasha, they're DCMS!"

"No, they're friends." Still, she leveled her rifle at her right hip and thumbed off the safety. Almost as an afterthought, she pulled a handgun from a hip holster and handed it, grip first, to Fusilli. "Just in case."

"You're not worried I'll shoot you in the back?"

"Shakir, you do that, you'd better not miss," she said. "Because I sure as hell won't."

Two men appeared, also wearing NVGs. They stood perfectly still, weapons at the ready, as he and Dasha approached. He did not believe these were DCMS soldiers or resistance fighters. Mercs? No, Dasha had called them friends. Mercs had no friends. So these were *allies*. From where?

When they were about six meters away, Dasha flipped up her NVGs and tapped Fusilli on the arm. "Let them get a look at you."

He did what she said. Instantly, he was plunged into darkness, a disconcerting result of having used the NVGs. He waited for his vision to clear, aware as each second passed of his disadvantage. Then he was dazzled by the sudden flash of a torch. He heard one of the men: "Who's the guy?"

*Accent.* Fusilli concentrated, trying to place it. *Heard this before . . .*

"New recruit." Dasha's face was bone-white in the glare. "Shakir."

"You've never brought anyone before."

"You got two packages." Dasha shrugged. "So I got me a mule."

"Yeah, I'll bet he's a real *nice* ride. A real *bull*." His laughter was nasty. "All right, c'mon over."

*Got it.* The light moved off Fusilli's face. He blinked away purple afterimages burned onto his retinas. *Tikonov.* Flipping on his gun's safety, he tucked the weapon into his waistband at the small of his back. His vision was clearer, and when he got close, he heard the *tick-tick-tick* of the truck's muffler. So, *these* two had arrived not too long ago.

The taller played his light over the ground. "There you go."

There were two large, bulky green rucksacks on metal frames. Shouldering her rifle, Dasha knelt by one sack. Her deft fingers worked the straps from metal cams, flipped back the flap and reached inside. She tugged out a rectangular case that was perhaps one hundred centimeters by forty by ten. The case was plastic polymer, like a small suitcase, and had twin metal clasps that Dasha flicked open. She lifted the lid with both hands and, in the glint of the flashlight, Fusilli caught a glimpse of a metallic cylinder perhaps eighty centimeters long in an eggshell foam cutout.

"Give me your light," Dasha said. The tall man handed his over, and Dasha hefted the cylinder, fanning light along its length.

Fusilli spotted a seam around the cylinder's middle. *Canister.* "What is that?"

Dasha didn't reply. Instead, she replaced the canister, snapped the lid, slid the case back in and cinched the sack. The second backpack held an identical case and canister. "Okay," she said to the tall man, and handed him his light. Hoisting one sack, she hefted the pack to her back and motioned for Fusilli to take the other sack. "We'll take it from here."

"Suits me." The tall man and his partner placed their goggles over their eyes. "We got to get this back to the hospital before anyone misses it."

*Hospital.* Fusilli shrugged on the second sack. The rucksack was very heavy, and that, plus the added bulk of his armor, made him feel as if he'd sunk into the ground up to his ankles. *Spies who've infiltrated the base?* Then he thought of the accent. *No, probably civilian. McCain must've loaned the ambulance.* But that meant Tikonov operatives were in the city.

He was so busy working the problem that he didn't notice the change in the air. The change was subtle, like a . . . gathering. He went still, every nerve tingling, aware that this wasn't quite a sound but more like air being pushed and bunched. That sound, this *feeling*, he *knew* this . . .

"We have to get out of here." He turned to Dasha. "Right *now*."

Dasha froze, her hand halfway to her NVGs. "Why? What's wro—"

"Something's coming." Frantic, he tugged his NVGs into place and craned his neck back, scanning the sky. "From the air. I hear it. I *feel* it."

"What the hell . . . ?" said one of the men.

"Quiet! It's *there*, it's . . ." Frustrated, Fusilli concentrated on the feeling, reeling in data from his senses. No rotor or engine noise, just the *impression* of something moving. Whatever it was, it was moving fast. Something light, highly maneuverable and lost in all that dark . . .

"Black," he blurted. "It's a black copter, stealth mode. They've rigged a copter to run virtually silent. Not totally, but it's been too high for us to hear. Only I *feel* it getting closer. They must be tracking us with thermal imaging. That ambulance, the engine's still hot. We're lighting up down here. We've got to get away," he said, already tugging at Dasha, trying to get her to move, *move!* "There, *there*! You *hear* it? Do you hear it now?"

"I don't . . ." Then she gasped, and now Fusilli could tell from her expression that she *did* hear what he'd detected before any of them—because he was accustomed to the sound and knew it well: the faint *whupwhupwhup* of a copter thumping air. "I *hear* it," she said. "Could it be reinforcements? Dracs going for the convoy?"

"No. Those Doppler crescendos mean it's getting close!"

"*I* hear it," the taller man said grimly. His hands fisted around his rifle. "By God, I hear it."

Now they all could: the long blades of a main rotor slapping air in an irregular rhythm. "Oh, God," Fusilli said. His NVGs revealed the unmistakable outlines of a Warrior H-7: a premier attack helicopter used by the Lyran Commonwealth. *Autocannon and LRM 4-pack . . . If it uses anything, it'll be the autocannon.* Even as he watched, the Warrior bumped, porpoising up and then down in an attack dive. Bright orange spurted from the nose.

"Come on, come *on*!" he cried, catching her by the arm. "Dasha, we need to . . . !"

A thin, high-pitched scream, like the dying agonies of some magnificent bird, sliced the air, and then the forest erupted with a roar.

# ═══ 32 ═══

The blast punched his chest, sent him flying. Hot wind sheeted his body. He smelled the acrid stink of scorched hair and burnt metal as superheated gases licked his face. He landed on his back, the metal rucksack and heavy case smashing his spine. A bolt of pain whip-cracked up his back, and he wheezed a half-scream, half-grunt of pain.

Somehow he made it to all fours, pulled air into his lungs, gagged against pain. His goggles were gone. The autocannon incendiary slug had exploded perhaps fifty meters shy of the ambulance, igniting the trees. The air was alive with the crackle and *hoosh* of flames. Streamers of sparks erupted like fireworks. Fire backlit the ambulance. One man was down. He didn't see the other. Above the sputter of the fire, he made out the dull *whupwhupwhup* of the Warrior as it circled, maybe in a search pattern.

They had a small advantage. The ground and trees were too wet to sustain a fire for long. Already, gouts of dense black smoke billowed from the forest floor where the fallen pine needles stubbornly smoldered.

"Dasha?" He tried to remember where she'd been standing when the blast came. To his right, just behind . . . Where was she? He willed himself to his feet, and his head swam. Swaying, he grabbed a spindly ash and clung to it until the dizziness passed. The left side of his neck and jaw were wet, something trickling. He wiped his neck with his arm and then gaped at the black stain on his sleeve. His fingers crawled to the base of his scalp. His black hair was matted and sticky, and he winced as his fingers found the edges of a jagged wound perhaps five or six centimeters long. *Shrapnel, all this wood exploding, it's like needlers going off all around.*

He had to find Dasha and get them out of here. He stumbled, wrestling with the pack to keep his balance. For just an instant, he was tempted to leave the pack, but he remembered those weird cylinders and knew they were important. Certainly of enough value that Dasha had mounted a diversionary raid to cover this exchange. "Dasha, for God's sake, can you hear me? Where are you?"

Then, over the pop and hiss of the fire, weakly: "Shakir! *Here!*"

He pivoted right, squinting against dancing shadows. Then he spotted movement near the shadowy hump of that root-ball. As he staggered over, she lifted her face. His breath hissed through his teeth. "Oh, God," he said. She lay sprawled on her stomach, pinned by the weight of the backpack. Blood slicked her face. "Can you move, Dasha? Can you get up?"

"N-no." Her voice hitched with pain. "I can't . . . right . . . *leg* . . ."

*God, no, not broken, please* . . . No bone that he could see, but there was a ragged hole in her camis along her right thigh and a lot of blood. "I've got to turn you over," he said.

As he rolled her to her back, she moaned and then struggled to her elbows. "What . . . ?"

Fusilli was amazed at how calm he sounded. "There's a large piece of wood in your thigh, like a spear. I think it missed the bone, but . . ."

"Is it pumping?" Her face, shiny with blood, twisted in pain and, now, fear. "If it's an arterial hit . . ."

He was already stripping his belt. "I don't know, but I'm not taking chances." Wrapping the belt around her thigh, he cinched it down as tightly as he could. Dasha's teeth showed in a grimace, and the cords of her neck stood out like ropes, but she didn't utter a sound. When he was done, he said, "Make a deal with me."

"What?"

"When we get back, I want you to show me what's in that locket." He smiled down at her as his fingers closed on the jagged wooden dagger. "Okay?"

"The locket? Well, I don't . . ." She broke off with a sudden scream.

"I'm sorry, I'm sorry," Fusilli said, and then he showed her the wood he'd jerked from her thigh. The shard was almost as long as his hand and half as thick. It glistened in the firelight.

"Damn you," she said shakily, trying to smile.

"Is that any way to talk? I still want to collect."

"Maybe." She was panting now, the effect of blood loss and shock overtaking her. "You've got . . . got to get out. There's no time, you . . ."

Her words were cut off by another burst of autocannon fire. The incendiary slugs shredded wood, and two trees erupted in flames. Fusilli threw himself over Dasha as splintering wood nipped his arms and back.

As the Warrior swooped away, he heard a gargling screech of agony. Fusilli's gaze jerked left, snagged on the tall man who was lurching for the ambulance. Then he fell, his rifle discharging as he hit, a wild spray of muzzle flash spitting harmlessly into the sky: *bapbapbapbapbap!*

Fusilli looked down at Dasha. "I'm not leaving you. It's not an option."

"It *has* to be!" Dasha's words rode on hisses of pain. Her hands scrabbled over, then fisted in his shirt, and she pulled him down until their faces were only centimeters apart. "We arranged all this ahead of time. My people pulled back . . . once we were clear. I . . . I don't know what went down back there . . . but they're waiting for me to call through on my microcomm, then they pick us up. I can't make it, but you can. Take the microcomm, get these packs to Yamada. They're important, they're everything, they're . . ."

"No," Fusilli said roughly. "*You* are." And then he gathered her to him in a fierce, desperate kiss. He felt her stiffen, tasted her blood, but then she returned his urgency, answering his hunger and need with her own. When he pulled back, he was breathing hard. "I'm not leaving without you." His voice was hoarse with fury and emotion. "You *got* that? You *understand*? It's not negotiable."

"Yes." She sounded out of breath. "Okay. But the packs . . . there's no choice about those either. Trust me, Shakir, there just isn't."

"What's so . . ." He began, but then his voice was cut off by the roar and rumble of an engine. Not the Warrior, but what . . . ?

Dasha gripped his shoulders. "The ambulance! It's moving!"

The other man, Fusilli realized. He must've made it back to the vehicle and kicked it to life, hoping to escape. Of course, *he* should have thought of that. Fusilli let go of Dasha and twisted round. "Hey!" he shouted. He waved an arm. "Wait!"

But the ambulance was already lurching away, wheels spitting dirt and rock, engine straining to pick up speed. There was a squall of metal as the vehicle jounced against wood, and the ambulance shimmied, as if on glare ice, slewing sideways. But somehow the driver wrenched the vehicle out of its skid, and then he was moving off.

"There's no cover that way," Dasha said. "He'll run out of trees in about three hundred meters. They'll get him as soon as he's in the clear."

"That must be what the Dracs want, why they're driving us south. We've got to double back. Come on," Fusilli said.

She tried to take as much of her own weight as she could on her left leg, but she was weak, and the weight was crippling. Still, Fusilli pushed on, half-dragging, half-carrying Dasha. Without his goggles, he had trouble finding his way. Then he heard a gurgle and knew where they were.

How long had they been walking before they hit the stream? He couldn't remember, but they were headed downhill. There was the stream, so this must be the right way. But was this the right thing to *do*? Even if it was, might not Dasha's people be dead?

No choice, he had to hope someone had survived. He labored on. Sweat poured down his face. When he slicked his lips, he tasted watery salt and clotting blood. They were moving into the wind. Though the breeze was very light, he was reasonably sure that the fire, at least, would not be chasing them. In fact, the fire was guttering, its orange-yellow flames no longer arcing heavenward, and there was more smoke. The Warrior hadn't touched off more trees, so it was clearly pursuing the ambulance, which it should overtake, and very soon. That might have been its mission all along: run black, follow them to the meet, then take the am—

He stopped dead. "Wait a minute," he said. "If they followed us, they've got thermal imaging, and if they've got *that* then . . ."

*Then* the farther they were from the fire, the more visible they'd become. They'd likely be visible well before the fire was out.

But . . . *why* was he running? These were *his* people. He could give them Dasha. She was Yamada's second. She knew a tremendous amount . . . like what was in these packs, why they were so vital.

He stood, uncertain, his heart hammering in his chest, his mind running in circles until his thoughts were a tangle he couldn't unravel. Or maybe he was—finally and perhaps irrevocably—making a conscious choice that did not depend upon the whims of an unseen master.

"Dasha." Urgency pulsed in his voice like the throb of blood. "Dasha, where's your microcomm? Do you have it?"

It took her a moment. Her head hung so her loosened hair fell across her face. "Yes," she said, but her voice was a whispery slur. "But they'll hear . . . they'll . . ."

"I know." They couldn't risk the microcomm just yet. They had to wait until he was certain that the Warrior had moved off. All he had to do was wait. And figure a way where no one could see them from the air.

Shadow never had to fire another shot at that ambulance. The vehicle emerged, and he urged his Warrior down. Orders were to take the merchandise, maybe prisoners, if he could. Torching just enough trees was tricky, but he thought he'd managed it. The fire seared an irregular C-shape against the surrounding darkness, belching streamers of dense smoke that twisted into black columns. As Shadow watched, the ambulance lurched, jerked. Halted. It didn't start up again. Whoever was behind the wheel had either passed out or died. He didn't really care which.

Instead, he vectored back and slewed east. His forward-looking infrared *had* detected what looked like two separate targets, blossoms of bloodred haloed with yellow. But he couldn't see them now.

*Damn.* He cut north to south again. *Could've sworn . . .*

But the only thing he saw moving was the fire, and that didn't count.

Shuddering with cold, Fusilli listened to the Warrior crisscross the sky. Now that he knew what to listen for, he wasn't having as much trouble tracking it, though the rush of the stream was very loud. But he thought that the copter's search radius was increasing, passing in wider and wider arcs.

*Meaning he can't see us.* Relief surged through his body and almost beat back the cold. *It worked, it actually worked.*

Then Fusilli was seized with another shiver so violent his teeth chattered. The shivering would continue because his body was trying to generate enough warmth to keep him alive. He was a strong man, in good condition, but he knew that physical strength was no match for hypothermia. So he hoped he wouldn't have to wait too much longer. His feet felt like blocks of ice, his legs were numb. Worse—he didn't know what the cold was doing to Dasha. "Dasha," he said, then again, "Dasha?"

"C . . . co . . . coal . . . cold," she said very faintly. Her head rested on his left shoulder. She shuddered weakly in his arms. "*Cold.*"

"I know, my darling, I know," he said, though he didn't think she could hear him. Maybe that was why he said it. He boosted himself a few more centimeters from the icy stream. He'd cradled her against his chest as he lowered them into the water and then stretched himself out until the water washed over her legs and buttocks. He stopped there because he didn't want the water to suck the remaining warmth from her heart, her brain. He'd warm her with his body heat, and he had to pray that her body would shunt blood from her arms and legs, and keep her vital organs going.

But *what* was he doing? This overwhelming tenderness he felt for this woman had ambushed him, sideswiped him from . . . What? The road he was meant to travel? He was rootless, without purpose, going through the motions for a cause he no longer believed in, if he ever had. Compassion was an alien emotion. And love? He'd never known love. But he knew what he felt for Dasha. Nothing and no one was more important, nothing. He would save her even at the cost of his life. This he was strong enough to do.

*Please.* His eyes burned with sudden tears. *I can't lose this. I can't lose* her *because now I finally understand what it is to care about something more than myself.*

"Almost." His lips pressed her chilled flesh. "Hang on, my love, please. I'll get you out of here, I promise."

*Because I choose . . . for us.*

## 33

**18 September 3136**
**0130 hours**

Okay, he hadn't cleared it. Why? 'Cause Crawford would've nixed it. But Parks was pissed. Compton made him see red. So, better to do something than sit with his thumb up his ass.

Still, with what they'd gotten? A clusterfuck.

Wesley Parks splashed coffee into a black mug with the DCMS logo stenciled on it in Kurita-red. He inhaled a mouthful. The coffee had been stewing all day and was rancid and sour. "Anything?"

"A whole lot of nothing," Buck said, his black Stetson parked back from his forehead. He smelled of dust and engine oil. He nodded when Parks offered the pot, held up his hand to say when. "I got guys in there now, but I think they caught on right quick when we blew that ridge. Rangers took some damage. Not bad. But I'd've *loved* to see their faces when we popped those tops via remote and let those Gauss rifles rip. Probably they never figured we could slave 'em to a Ranger as long as we disabled the lasers and one of our turrets to draw power—*and* run the whole she-bang on remote."

"You realize you could've used PPCs and saved yourself the trouble of punching big rocks into little ones."

"I'm a tank jock. I like things that go boom. And, hell, ended up the same. Those grenades weren't spit balls."

They drank coffee for a few more minutes, Buck giving Parks the rest of his report. Then Parks sent the tank commander on his way to clean up and get some shut-eye. Once Buck was gone, Parks drank more bad coffee.

The entire exercise had been devised based on semireliable intel from a source at the spaceport that a meet was going down. Exactly where in those hills, they weren't sure, but they figured if they ran their diversion at the same time, a recon Warrior running black might flush out just who was giving what to whom. Shadow got two solid contacts on thermal imaging: resistance fighters who broke away from the main group. Shadow had followed long enough to establish the location of the meet and even that there were four individuals, but he'd lost two. Right now, all they had to show for their trouble was one crispy critter, the ambulance driver who'd eaten his weapon before he could be captured, and one scorched ambulance. (A loaner to a civilian hospital—and how much of a pisser was *that?*)

Not good news for a ploy that Parks had hoped would garner more. He wasn't that concerned about those Rangers. They were on their last legs. Biham wasn't even that important in the grander scheme. But couple Biham with resistance along other border worlds, and they might have serious problems, have to divert troops, and that could deter a push for Dieron.

Biggest problem? No Fusilli, after two months of being gone. No check-ins, no nothing. Could Fusilli be dead? Sure. But maybe he got killed with his cover still intact. Might explain why his body hadn't shown up the way that Compton's had: her hands still cuffed, her body unceremoniously dumped along the main road leading to base. McCain said she'd been dead for about three days. No mystery about how she died: The bruises around her throat were visible despite the bloat, and her hyoid bone was broken. From the condition of her—the way the plasticuffs had sawed into her flesh—McCain thought she'd been cuffed while being strangled.

"And what kind of animal," Parks muttered, "does something like that?"

## 34

**18 September 3136
0400 hours**

After Bridgewater finished stitching her up, Dasha hadn't wanted pain meds. Her thigh was letting her hear about *that*, throbbing in time to her pulse with a liquid, searing heat. But she and Yamada had to finish this now, because everything had changed.

She said, "If he was going to turn, that would've been the time. All he had to do was kill me then take the sacks. But he didn't."

Yamada grunted. His eyes were puffy, but lack of sleep had energized him. He paced, jingling loose change. "Yeah, but the Dracs were right on top of you. And that was a nifty little trick, hiding those Gauss rifles on flatbeds. Maybe Shak got a message through to his Drac buddies."

"Tony, the Dracs aren't stupid. They had a surveillance copter. Shakir didn't have a clue what was what and still doesn't." She sighed in exhaustion and pain. "Look, we have a bigger problem. I can't go in like this, not for a couple days. And it's too late to tell me you told me so. I'm the only one who could verify that what we needed is what we got."

"And did we get it?" When she nodded, Yamada cupped the back of his neck with one palm and massaged out the kinks. "So we're committed. You got some vacation time, sick leave you can take?"

"Yeah. Maybe a week. I can do that. But with me out of action . . ."

"Pierpont."

She nodded. "I won't be hanging over his shoulder. You'll have to keep up a presence, or he's going to relax. Worse, he might tell someone. And . . . we need to bring our people into the loop. With everything that's happened, we have to. Shakir, too."

"Yeah, but there's something about that guy I just don't like."

"You've never liked him, but if we pull this off, you've got *him* to thank. I'd be dead by now or captured—and either would kill the mission."

Yamada debated. "Okay, we bring people in but not all the way. No names and sure as hell no details."

"If you don't want them to turn us in." Dasha nodded. "Of course, that goes without saying."

Abby finally broke the silence. "You're sure about this guy?"

Dasha nodded. Her eyes were smudged with fatigue. "If I were as good with computers as this guy is, I'd do it. But I'm not."

"This guy, this guy," Bridgewater said, irritated. "Who's this guy?"

"You don't need to know that."

"Why not?"

"For the same reason that he doesn't need to know about you."

"But you're asking us to get involved in this crazy scheme—"

"It's not crazy," Dasha said softly. "It's just dangerous."

Bridgewater flushed. "Gee. Okay. So, since this might get us all killed, we have a right to know who he is."

"No, you don't," Dasha said. "Whether his name is Smith or Jones or Devlin Stone, it doesn't matter. I'm not compromising an inside source."

"You don't trust us?" Bridgewater asked.

"Trust is irrelevant. If this leaks, then our entire operation grinds to a halt. I'm telling you because we *do* trust you—"

"Enough to tell us when it's too late."

"We trust all of you. That's why we decided to bring you into the loop. What's done is done. We need to move past this."

"Well, okay," Conley said. "I have a couple questions. I

sure as hell never studied anything as ancient as a fission reactor. But I'm not a total idiot. You want to cut power, take out the emergency backups, then threaten to blow the reactor if the Dracs don't back down. Well, if you cut power that could be bad, right? Like don't these reactor rods or whatever, I mean, don't they need water or something to keep cool?"

"That's true," Dasha said. "But our primary goal would not be to totally cut power to the reactor. That would be suicide, and I have no intention of killing myself. The idea is to interrupt the power grid."

"How will that work, exactly?" Bridgewater asked. "I mean, this whole reactor thing?"

"It's complicated, and a little dangerous. A reactor works because control rods absorb energy without decaying. They control the rate and amount of decay of uranium and plutonium. In this case, the rods are graphite in vertical honeycombed columns. When they're lifted a certain distance, a partial chain reaction occurs, the intensity of which is determined by the number of control rods lifted via magnetic field and how high."

"So what's dangerous about it?" Abby asked.

"Steam. The reactor heats water to steam and this provides power. Even if you scram the reactor, there's still heat, and so there's more and more steam. There are backups to either vent steam or send more coolant to bring down the heat. But if these backups fail, the steam bubble gets bigger and bigger. Or if the water all boils away and there's no more coolant, the rods melt. *That's* what's dangerous."

"Dangerous as in the thing blows?" Abby said.

"From the steam bubble, yes, because it will release radioactivity into the open air. But it won't come to that," Dasha said. "Now, Reactor Two's next scheduled maintenance is November, and that's good because there are fewer personnel on. We've got until then to get ready. We need to be on the same page when we go in. No mistakes."

"Speaking of same page," Bridgewater said. "Something as big as this, we should bring in Eriksson. I'm not saying he has to be part of the actual takeover. But if he knows it's happening, we can use *him* to negotiate with the Dracs. We should at least talk to the guy."

Yamada looked thoughtful. "Yeah, maybe you're right. You volunteering?"

"Sure," Bridgewater said.

"Attaboy." For the first time that evening, Yamada smiled. "Then this is what I want you to tell him."

Fusilli lingered after the others left, ignoring a pointed look from Yamada. Fusilli helped Dasha move to a cot and then, turning the lights very low, perched on a camp stool. Her face was very white, and her hair, fanning her pillow, was the color of dark blood. She wore a loose, black scoop-neck tee and the gold chain pooled in the hollow of her throat. He thought he'd never seen a more beautiful woman and his heart squeezed with longing. He said, "Dasha, there are things I need to know."

"Like?" Her voice was edged with fatigue.

"Who you were before all this, and what you are now." Her green eyes sharpened. "Why?"

*Because I'm afraid that this will get out of control. I'm afraid I'll lose you, and I've already lost more than you can possibly know.* "You did a background check on *me*, right? Turnabout's fair play."

"What do you want to know?"

"This talk about reactors . . . You work at the facility?"

"Let's just say that I'm a nuclear engineer."

"And we're to take over the facility as a sort of hostage," Fusilli said. "A way of bargaining with the Dracs for more autonomy?"

"Not *more*. Total."

"They'll never give in. You don't understand the Dracs. Biham, all this, we're insignificant. We'll never stop the machine that is the Combine."

"Well, I have to try. Our lives aren't garbage. We're not disposable. We have lives, desires." She searched his face. "Are you having second thoughts?"

*Not about you.* "I'm trying to help you see the reality of your situation." He debated, then said, "Those men we met weren't from Biham. They're from Tikonov. I know because of the accent." When she neither confirmed nor denied, he said, "Don't you understand you're being used?"

"Everyone uses people, Shakir, just like everyone has a past. The hard part is to know what to keep of the past and what to discard. The things that seem precious now aren't always. I don't mind being used this way if it gets me what I want."

And what did he want? What kind of past was he shedding, and what was this that he rushed headlong to embrace? He'd been on the outside looking in—at the Combine, at the Fury—for years. His whole life. The Combine should have felt like home, but it didn't. The Combine had ceased to be a home the moment he'd chosen a traitor's name for his own, a man executed for his crimes: Fusilli's great-grandfather.

He wasn't aware she'd spoken until she gently shook his arm. "Shakir?"

He snapped back to attention. "Sorry. Just . . . thinking."

"You're always thinking, Shakir." Her eyes searched his face. "What is it? What's troubling you?"

"Things. What we're about to do. Funny, but it's almost as if *this* is the only reality I know. I don't even remember what my apartment looks like." He tried a smile. "I don't want to talk about me. I'm boring. You're not, and you promised me something. Do you remember?"

Wordlessly, she nodded. "Then show me," he said gently. "Tell me."

Slowly, her fingers found the pendant locket, the gold reflecting in a nimbus at her throat. She slid the edge of a thumbnail into a thin gap and popped open the gold case. The light was behind Fusilli, and he sank to his knees at the head of the bed. He squinted, bringing the two pictures, one snugged into either half, into focus. What he saw made his throat constrict in sudden, anguished understanding.

One child, perhaps five years old, had a head of flaxen curls lit by a setting sun; the other, older girl had her mother's hair and the fine cast of her jaw, and a haunted expression that hinted at tragedy.

He didn't have to ask who the girls were. Instead, he asked, "When? How?"

Her eyes were very bright. "I can't. Not . . . yet. Maybe not ever. I just can't."

He had no right to expect any more. Instead, he smoothed hair from her forehead. "I'm so sorry for your pain, Dasha."

She tried a smile that failed. "It scares me sometimes,

but I have trouble remembering what my girls looked like. I don't know why. You always think there's a tomorrow, and then there isn't."

"And now?" he asked hoarsely. "What about now?"

"I don't know. I don't plan anymore. I learned not to, except . . ." Her fingers traced Fusilli's left cheek. "Now I'm not so sure I wouldn't like to."

Just that slight touch made his mouth go dry, and a hunger in his soul roar to life. It was as if all the barriers melted away, or perhaps he simply ceased caring. Without thinking—because he'd moved past that the instant he'd lowered them both into a freezing stream and held her close—he held himself above her, their faces only centimeters apart. The moment lengthened like the elastic strand of a spider's web, and still he couldn't move, didn't dare.

*I'm on the brink, but it's not too late. Only a fool leaps into the abyss.*

"Yes," Dasha whispered. Reaching for him, her fingers in his hair. Gingerly tracing the line of stitches Bridgewater had sewn to close his wound . . . And he burned with longing just short of true pain. "Please," she said.

And so he fell, willingly. He gathered her in his arms and felt her body arch, and then the hunger took over, because there was this, there was only this: this moment, this woman. The feel of her mouth, the tear-stained hollow of her throat and the tender domes of her breasts . . .

He fell, drowning in sensation. And he didn't care. He didn't.

# 35

"**A**hhhh . . ." The MP, a *sho-sa*, looked unhappy. "I can't authorize this."

"Why not?" Loveland asked testily. "Everything points to someone in uniform or attached to the DCMS."

"Well," the *sho-sa* drawled, "coulda been a civilian hire. We've got all kinds of positions here on base filled with civilian hires. Chow, hospital, garbage dump. This couldn't be one of ours. You're wasting your time."

"That's okay," Thereon said. Unlike Loveland, he seemed genuinely relaxed. "Ours to waste, right?"

Now the MP looked annoyed. "Listen, this is DCMS territory. You're subject to our rules. Any criminal investigation has to coordinate with ISF."

"We're not interested in that," Thereon said easily. "I don't think you're really interested in that, especially if we're right. Besides, commit a crime off base, it's ours *even* if the unsub's one of your boys. Now, you can stall us. You can talk circles. You can pick your nose. I can wait." Thereon glanced at Loveland. "Can you wait?"

*No.* "I can wait," Loveland said.

"We can wait," Thereon said. "While we wait, we'll make calls, see a coupla newsies. Maybe you'll get free advertising."

"Look, look." The MP held up both hands. "I got to go through channels, get authorization. That'll take time."

"But you can expedite, right?" Loveland grated.

"Depends."

*On what?* Loveland hooked a thumb at Thereon. "Then

it's like he said. We'll pay local law a visit, and the news guys, show 'em what we got."

"They don't have jurisdiction."

"*I* don't give a flip. Word is gonna get out that one of your boys likes chopping up women, and you guys are *protecting* . . ."

"We'll deny it."

"Yeah, well, judging from the news bullets coming out of here, you guys are just beloved." Loveland put up a hand. "I know, I know. I feel for you. *You* want to see justice done, Major, I know. *You* want to see justice done, right, Thereon?"

Thereon, deadpan: "I want to see justice done."

"Makes three of us," Loveland said. "But word gets out, you're gonna have more to worry about than an image problem."

The *sho-sa* said, "Ahhhhh . . ."

Crawford lasted fifteen seconds. "I can't be bothered with this crap! Shut them down."

"*Well* . . ." The *sho-sa* glanced at Crawford's aide, Meriwether, who only shook his head. The MP said, "Thereon's Ancha Bureau. They got authorization, this reciprocity between planets, that's the way it works here."

"They're serious about going public?"

"As a heart attack, sir."

Meriwether stirred. "Actually, this might work to our advantage. It's probably not one of *our* people, sir. Not one of the Fury, I mean. We all know that Sakamoto was a tyrant. So, worst case scenario, we hand him over and let them kill the son of a bitch. We come out looking good, and that counts. But if you stonewall . . ." Meriwether trailed off.

"Christ." Sighing, Crawford wiped his face with his hands then looked at the MP. "How solid is their evidence?"

"I need to review it. They've got a lot of paper."

"And you're understaffed, don't forget that," Crawford said. "And overworked. And then there are records of our own to collate—"

"Troops have already been redeployed," Meriwether added.

"That's right," Crawford said. "So, Major . . . two months to go through their records? Conservatively?"

The *sho-sa* opened his mouth, thought better of whatever he was going to say, and said instead, "*Hai*, however long it takes, sir. *Buuuut . . .*"

"What?"

"Sir, it's the DNA. A quick cross-match takes a week, maybe two at the outside. Even if I got our people to double-check. No way I can slow that down, not unless we have an equipment malfunction or something."

"That could be arranged."

"Sir, even then, I can maybe only stall about two, three weeks more. Besides, if it's not one of us, we've got nothing to worry about. Only—"

Crawford looked black. "Only what?"

Looking for help, the *sho-sa* glanced at Meriwether, who evidently did not harbor a death wish and merely stared back. Sighing, the MP said, "Regulations stipulate that the ISF contingent attached to command be informed of the query. I can't get around that, sir."

Crawford saw the problem. If this killer was a DCMS née Fury, ISF (read: Bhatia) would gladly topple the current command structure. So the trick was how to cross the ISF and not get caught. "Of course, we inform them. Just not right away. Not if you haven't got anything, right?"

The MP said, "Would you put that in writing, sir?"

"No," Crawford said. "And we never had this conversation."

After the *sho-sa* was gone, Meriwether retrieved a stack of signed directives, butted them together, and made a general fuss until Crawford said in an annoyed tone, "Are you loitering for a reason?"

"I just wanted to know if your uniform trousers got extra padding," Meriwether said. "Because if ISF finds out, they're going to take a big bite out of your ass. You won't be able to sit down for a month."

"I'm just being efficient," Crawford lied. He changed the subject. "What about Fusilli? Any word from Biham?" When Meriwether shook his head, Crawford asked, "Do you have *anything* cheery?"

"Scuttlebutt from Benjamin says that Yori Kurita and

her troops detoured there first to meet with *Tai-sho* Kurita."

"Ten to one, they're figuring out how to carve up the campaign between the two of them. Where is *Sho-sho* Kurita now?"

"Shimonita command reports that they're at Kurhah for recharge. They'll be at our system jump point within a week."

"Swell." Then he thought of something. "What about Drexel? Any word?" He read his aide's expression and said, "Wait a minute, don't tell me. She tripped into the same black hole as Fusilli."

"And pulled in the event horizon right after, yessir. She didn't show for her last contact."

"Why wasn't I told?"

"I *did* tell you, sir."

"What did I say?"

"That we couldn't send people after her because negotiations take a long time."

"*I* said that?"

"Yes, sir." A pause. "You still mean that?"

"Trust me. If we go charging in and screw things up for Viki?" Crawford picked up the next memo with a crisp snap. "I won't be able to sit down for a year."

# 36

*Pirate's Prairie, Ludwig*
*28 September 3136*

Lance Shimazu was ahead, pounding down a dimly lit hall that smelled of urine and mold. As he dodged right, Viki Drexel heard the *thwap-bang* of a door crashing against drywall and shouts. More *yakuza*—maybe *Yurei Tou*, Ghost Clan, maybe *Hachiman Buke*—swarming after them, just behind, coming fast! She put on a burst of speed, running flat-out, air screaming in and out of her lungs. Just as she cut right at the stairs, a spray of automatic weapons fire exploded. The sound was deafening in the confined space. Bullets chunked drywall. Stumbling, she fell up the stairs. Pain detonated in her leg as her right knee slammed into a stair so hard it felt as if someone had smashed a sledgehammer into her kneecap.

*Get up, get up!* Struggling to her feet, she half-hobbled, half-crawled up the stairs. Her right leg wasn't working right; her knee was on fire. She crabbed her way up, hit the last step with her left foot and then flinched left as another staccato round of weapons fire ripped the air wide open. Bullets skimmed seams above her hair, punched craters into plaster: *pockpockpockpockpock!*

She fell, absorbing the force of the fall with her left shoulder, and rolled, her gun hand free, coming around. On her haunches now, right knee still roaring, she tapped out three quick shots: *pop-pop-pop!* She heard curses, a general jostling as the guys jamming the stairs jockeyed for position and then answered with a round of gunfire. She scrabbled away on hands and knees, working to get to her feet. She risked a single glance over her left shoulder, saw the head of one of her pursuers, caught the bore of a weapon swinging round for a shot.

"Viki, *down!*"

Instantly, she flattened just as a lancet of ruby laser jabbed the air. She heard a scream, smelled the stink of burnt hair and flash-crisped skin. She jerked right, saw Lance Shimazu, his laser pistol spitting blood red darts of death: "Viki, move, *move!*"

Picking herself up, Viki bolted. Her right leg was better, functional but throbbing. Together, they wheeled right and clattered down the hall toward a T corridor. Viki huffed, "I got what's left in this clip, and then I'm out. Got to be a way out of here!"

"I'm hearing ya," Lance said. At the end of that hall, Lance skidded to a halt, took aim with his laser and scored the lock before giving the door a sharp, violent kick. The door slammed open, releasing a balloon of screams. Lance pushed Viki through. Viki caught a blur of fading cream-colored wallpaper and a heavy mahogany dining-room table, and people cowering beneath. They jogged from the dining-room to a short hall and then into a bedroom. Lance reeled her in, then slammed the door, jamming a chair beneath the knob. "Fire escape!" He whirled, pointing at a far window. "Let's go, *go*!"

The window was double hung, the wood sash old and swollen with rot. Straining, putting muscle behind it, Lance forced the wood. It gave grudgingly, squalling with indignation, before stalling three-quarters of the way up. Just enough space: Lance pushed Viki out first and then followed. Their boots clanged on wrought iron. The landing was narrow, barely wide enough to accommodate them. The fire escape serviced the east side of the building that faced another tenement. The alley opened at both ends. They'd come out on the third floor, an easy fifteen meters above the ground. Lance urged her down, and Viki took the steep stairs as quickly as she could, her bad leg feeling every jounce and jostle.

Laser fire rained from the bathroom window above. "No choice! Jump, jump!" Lance shouted, and before she had a chance to object, Lance yanked her from the fire escape.

They fell like stones. Air whistled past her ears, and the cobblestone alley rushed toward her face. *Think skydiving: go limp!* Viki slammed feet-first on the ground, the impact jolting through her legs and into her spine. Dizzy with pain, she instantly buckled, trying to absorb the fall in a roll. Then something tore in her right hip. She screamed.

"Come on, come on!" Lance boosted her to her feet. "Move, Viki!"

Dazed, every fiber in her body shrieking with pain and exhaustion, she lurched down the alley, Lance bearing the brunt of her weight. "Leave me behind!" she gasped. Each time she came down on that right leg, pain knifed her bones. She felt sick. "I'm slowing you down!"

"Shut up," Lance grunted. Sweat gleamed on his face and neck. "If we can get out of this alley . . ." He stiffened. "Oh, shit."

Viki followed his gaze. A car—black, tinted windows—skidded to a screeching stop in the mouth of the alley. All four doors popped open. She looked frantically, right, left—and there! "Service door, left, *left*!"

Lance kicked once, twice. The door popped. The service

corridor was dark and narrow. To their right was a door that led down to a basement. Lance fried the lock and kicked the door as a diversion before taking off down the hall, hauling a limping Viki.

*Not going to make it.* Any second, she expected a bullet to slam into her back or a laser to burn a hole into her spine. Then, just as they reached the connecting door to the lobby, Viki caught movement out of the corner of her left eye. Before she could shout a warning, their attacker launched a fierce turn-kick that hammered Lance's chest. Off balance, Lance reeled as their attacker followed with a crescent kick to Lance's face. The blow connected with a crackling sound like smashing eggshells. Blood spurted from Lance's nose, and he caromed off of Viki. They tumbled to the floor.

Viki came down on her right hip. She screamed, and her pistol spun away. Frantic, fighting against a sudden swell of vertigo, she fumbled for the gun—too late.

Their attacker scooped up the pistol and jammed the weapon so close to her face that Viki smelled burnt metal and spent powder. Her eyes clicked from barrel to hand to face—and then she froze as both she and her assailant gasped.

*"Tai-shu?"* Viki whispered. Then: *"Katana?"*

# PART FIVE

## *Shibori:* Squeeze Plays

# 37

The coordinator's room was completely dark. Aided by NVGs, the guard swept the room for the intruder. Weapon at the ready, he eased toward a set of inky silk draperies, nudged them aside. Nothing there. Turning, the guard took a step, then two more, but suddenly halted at a minute rasp coming from his right. Slowly, he pivoted. . . .

A green blur that resolved into a hand clamped his chin, tipped his head back. And then the knife sliced through flesh, and the guard couldn't breathe. He was drowning in black blood that sprayed—

"Stop playback." The holovid paused, the guard suspended in midair like a collapsing marionette. Pushing back from his console, Jonathan stretched, like a languid, weightless cat. Lovely holo, like a finely directed play he never tired of watching. What a waste that, in a little over two hours, that wonderful mock-up assembled in a barren stretch of desert and all the bodies would disappear. (Actually, vaporize. He'd packed the mock-up of the Imperial Palace with *that* much explosive.)

The fact that Bhatia had been *so* helpful in planning the assassination—supplying him with guards in need of "remedial training" as well as detailed blueprints and security protocols—also meant that the ISF director was playing for keeps. Probably Bhatia had already arranged some secretive little alarm that would bring guards running at precisely the right moment: too late to do anything more than lop off Jonathan's head and mop up the blood.

But Bhatia underestimated him—because Jonathan was changing. Metamorphosing. Drifting to a full-length mirror, he studied his naked body in minute detail, running his fingers over his skin, tracing the curve of every muscle, every hollow, every line and seam. Thinking about *her* living just behind his eyes excited him. His skin grew electric with desire, his hands provoking frissons of grief and fiery lust. Yes, the transformation had begun: of Katana's restless *kami* in every fiber, along every nerve. She was growing, swelling like a hand animating an empty glove. Her heat throbbed against the sensitive drum of his skin stretched tight over muscle and bone.

"But not yet," he gasped, crushing his desire with an iron will. "Not quite yet." Because first things first: He would give an impromptu performance, courtesy of Bhatia and what Jonathan had gleaned from a very helpful recording made during Toranaga's visit. Bhatia had chosen Jonathan's next targets. Jonathan could not fail. Not when he had such power. Not when he and Katana were one.

Time to hunt down some cats.

The shower was an ingenious contraption: foot and hand stirrups, an airlock seal to contain the water delivered under high power and pressure before being suctioned away so he wouldn't drown. Surrendering to a punishing spray just the near side of scalding, Jonathan considered two tidbits of information that had wormed their way to him.

The first came from a source on Devil's Rock: an obliging detective well reimbursed. Then the second on Ancha: When they'd run Petrie's ID-link and activated a trip wire, he'd known. Loveland was a blast from the past. But the Bureau agent, *Thereon* . . . Drop the *e*, and that clinched it. To quote his dear, departed Marcus, a blind man could see it with a cane.

"Oh, I'll just bet you can't guess what I've got in store for you, Thereon," Jonathan said, tingling with heat. "I'll just bet you can't."

# 38

For a good hour, it sounded like a herd of OmniMechs on a rampage. Heavy feet clomping back and forth that sent showers of dust and grit raining into Viki's face. They'd ducked into a crawl space secreted beneath the stairs where Katana had ambushed them. The crawl space was dark and very tight but ventilated, so the smell was only musty, not dead.

Lance breathed in wheezy, blubbering snorts. His nose was broken. On the other hand, Viki thought Lance was lucky he wasn't blowing his nose out the back of his head. Any other guy, Katana would've killed him.

"You don't remember anything about the accident?" Viki whispered.

"Not much," Katana said. "I remember the captain shouting something about a hull breach, but I blacked out. Next thing I know, I wake up in a holding cell."

"So, these *ronin*, they aren't *Yurei Tou*, are they?"

She felt Katana's surprise. "Yeah, Ghost Clan," Katana said. "Run by some guy named Eddie Alzubadai. How . . . ?"

"You first," Viki said grimly. "Do you know where they come from?"

"Shaul Khala, in the New Samarkand District. I got a good long look from the air. Ghost Clan's got this compound spread over a desert valley surrounded by mountains. Kind of weird. The place is like a bull's-eye, like it's daring you to take a shot. I was there about a month."

Lance said, "Dat's Sorrymut."

Viki bit down on her lower lip to stifle a laugh. (Well, it *was* funny.)

"Saurimat?" Katana asked. "Who are the Saurimat?"

"Mercs and hashashins," Lance snorted, then cleared his throat. "Assassins," he said more clearly.

"I never heard of them."

"Dere secred."

A secret society of mercs and assassins? Viki said, "We've been trying to figure out who these guys are. So they're *all* Saurimat?"

"No," Lance said, still stuffy-sounding but clearer than before, so that when he spoke, Viki automatically understood. "The Ghost Clan's a splinter group. More like go-to boys."

Katana said, "I figured they were holding me for ransom. Then they started moving me around to different planets. I have no idea why. Things started to deteriorate once we got to Ludwig. Some seemed to be in favor of whatever they were figuring to use me for, but a couple of them talked about how keeping *two* of us wasn't the original deal."

Viki was instantly alert. "*Two*? Do you know who the other person is?" *He's got to be alive, or we're toast.*

"No. Anyway, they dropped down to one guard at night. He . . . made a mistake. So, I killed him and took his weapon," Katana said, without a flicker of emotion, as if this were just another tick off the old to-do list: *Eat breakfast. Wash dishes. Kill the guard.* "Since then, it's been cat and mouse. But now I know why they were so torqued. It was because of you. How did you know I was here?"

Viki said, "Ah, well, we didn't."

A pause. Then: "You didn't?"

Quickly, Viki sketched their mission. "Lance said these *ronin*, these Ghost Clan guys, were hitting those clans that have supported you in the past. That's how Lance and I got involved. We made it to Junction—and walked right into a *yakuza* free-for-all."

Kamikuro's mansion was palatial—three tiers of bone-white mortar walls and gray-tiled roofs edged with elaborate iron scrollwork. His estate was east of the city and hugged the lakeshore. They'd been shown into Matsuro Kamikuro's study, virtually unchanged from the last time Viki had visited. But Kamikuro's sharp gray eyes looked a tad cloudier, his gait just a little slower, and worry lines creased his forehead. Kamikuro's *waka-gashira*, Tony Ito, was the same: burly, muscled, his small almond-shaped eyes beetle-bright with suspicion and not a little hostility.

There was one other: a heavy-set man built like a *Ryoken*, squat, wide. Gray, bushy eyebrows that curled like caterpillars.

Ito got down to brass tacks. "The other clans, they're starting to muscle in on our territory. No Sakamoto, it's a land grab. We started late out of the blocks because our people were fighting for you. Hard to defend territory you don't got no guys or ships, thanks to you."

"Respect," Kamikuro said sternly, and Ito subsided. Kamikuro said to Viki, "It is not that we are ignorant of the great honor *Tai-shu* Tormark has bestowed upon us. But we cannot eat honor, nor will that pay the many expenses of our operations. I am being . . . pressured."

"By whom?" Viki asked.

The *Ryoken* spoke up. "By me."

"Ah," Viki said, not liking this one bit. "And you are?"

"He is Mori Nobaru, my *saiko-komon*." Kamikuro's smile was almost apologetic. "Even I must bow to reality."

"And high time, too," Nobaru said. In contrast to his great bulk, he had a light, almost effeminate voice. "We have had more than simple revenue losses. We have endured raids upon our freighters and hits on key personnel clearly organized by other clans."

"Yeah, I'll bet you took that lying down," Lance said.

Nobaru's gaze had sharpened on the smaller man. "We've taken action," he said. "Some we *disciplined*."

"Discipline." Lance looked at Viki. *"Yubitsume."*

Nobaru grunted. "Let us say that Kamikuro-*san*'s got enough fingers for a necklace."

Katana said, "So what did you do?"

"I offered to negotiate on their behalf. Crawford gave me the okay before I left HQ."

"Uh-huh," Katana said, and when Viki didn't continue: "And?"

"Well . . . I said that since you clearly had enough cash and materiel to secure a galaxy of Nova Cats, you might be willing to part with more . . ."

Katana said, loudly, "What?" Then, whispering again,

"*Viki!* How *much*?" When Viki told her, Katana spluttered, "Where am I supposed to get that?"

"I was being creative. I figured maybe we could petition the coordinator, or Theodore. I was thinking on my feet."

"Tell me you didn't *sign* anything."

"No," Viki said, relieved, although the idea *had* crossed her mind. "We agreed to a truce and a meeting on Ludwig because it's neutral territory. Two other clans besides the *Ryuu-gami*: one from Reisling's Planet, and the other from Donenac. But no one else showed except Ghost Clan, and that's when we figured out their real agenda. First, they hit us with you being dead." Viki paused. "We weren't exactly prepared."

"Yeah." Katana let the silence go for a bit. "So, what was the real agenda? It wasn't about the money?"

"No." Viki shook her head. "It wasn't about the money at all."

# 39

## Katana's Journal
## 28 September 3136

The black boxes. Someone leaked. Thank God, Viki kept her cool and didn't confirm their existence.

Viki filled in the rest. She said Ghost Clan upped the ante by kidnapping Kamikuro-*san* right after Lance, Viki, Ito and some of Ito's men left Junction for Ludwig. Then Ghost Clan tried to grab Viki, but Ito's men busted her loose. As far as they know, Ito's still on-planet. Lance, Viki and Ito set up an emergency rendezvous point, just in case.

Then something clicked. "Wait a minute," I said. "All this escalation started before I was snatched, right? By about two weeks, give or take?"

"Yes," Viki said, "but why is that important?"

"Because that means that whoever *started* the trouble knew *ahead of time* that I'd disappear. You don't escalate unless you have a hold card."

"These guys—" Viki broke off as footsteps crossed outside then faded. A door slammed. Then nothing. We waited a few minutes to be sure.

"Time to get out of here," I said.

"I'm up for that," Lance bubbled.

"Wait," Viki said, "we have to have a plan. Alzubadai's guys are *ronin*. They're work-for-hire. So who are they working for?"

If it'd been a snake, it would've bitten me in the ass. I'll bet he'd ordered me killed. Except this snake forgot that when you're dealing with *ronin*, it's what the market will bear. Probably Ghost Clan figured to use me as persuasion in case Viki balked at coughing up the black boxes.

I said, "Ghost Clan is from Shaul Khala, and Shaul Khala's . . ."

"In the New Samarkand District," Viki said grimly. "Toranaga." She fell silent a moment. "So what do we do now?"

"We find Tony Ito. Then we get the hell off this rock— and take the fight right down Alzubadai's throat."

"But how do we find him?"

I tapped my microrecorder bracelet. "I kept notes. Just in case."

# 40

**Deber City, Benjamin**
**7 October 3136**

The surgical suite was cold and smelled of antiseptic soap. Chomie gathered a green surgical drape around her neck and shivered, mindful of the IV line taped to her wrist.

Standing alongside her, Emi frowned. "Cold?"

"No," Chomie lied. "Just . . . worried."

Emi's eyes crinkled above her mask. She was also gowned, and a blue cap covered her hair. "Don't worry. He's a good doctor, and I'm here. I'll stay with you through the first trimester. Longer, if you want."

Chomie was grateful for her sister-in-law's presence. Yet there really was only one person she longed for. But Theodore had departed for the Dieron District to aid Yori Kurita in her campaign for Dieron.

All the procedures of the past several months: the endless array of pills, then harvesting eggs as her ovaries yielded their bounty. When the doctor performed the intracytoplasmic sperm transfer, she'd watched, awestruck, as chromosomes from one of Theodore's unaffected sperm was injected directly into a harvested oocyte. That had been five days ago. She'd seen the tiny . . . what was it called? Blastocyst? Yes, that tiny ball of cells the doctor said was perfectly healthy and minus the dreaded Parkinson's gene. She'd stared, absolutely stunned, at the tiny cluster of cells that would be her son—their heir.

Movement at the foot of the gurney caught her attention, and she saw that the doctor, in blue scrubs and cap, had appeared. "Here, I stole this from the autoclave," Makoto Shouriki said, and then he tucked a warmed blanket around her body. "I keep forgetting that while I'm doing all the sweating, you're probably freezing to death."

"Thank you," she said gratefully. She watched as he selected a syringe from a nearby tray, checked the level of fluid and then cleaned off a rubber-capped port on her IV line with an alcohol swab. "What are you doing?"

"Giving you a sedative."

Anxiety spiked her chest. "But I don't want to sleep."

"You won't," he said, pushing in fluid, then withdrawing the needle. Then he clasped her chilled hands. His fingers were very warm. "This will help you relax. Be at peace, my lady. Emi is here, and I won't let anything happen to you or your son."

Later, a little dreamy, Chomie stared past the lights at the ceiling as Shouriki worked. She felt no pain, just an expansive sense of well-being, as if her mind were free of her body. She imagined her heart rose, too, and called to her husband across a void that only love could bridge.

*I do this for you, my love. I do this for us all.*

## Imperial Palace, Luthien
## Pesht Military District, Draconis Combine
## 15 October 3136

The data crystal contained an encrypted, holographic message from Shouriki: "While the next few months will be critical in terms of potential for miscarriage, I am optimistic. Preimplantation genetic testing confirmed that the embryo was free of disease, and the fetus is developing normally. Our prince will have his heir, and he will be pure, *Tono*. He will be free."

The message terminated. The crystal disengaged with an audible click. The pillar of light collapsed like a pirate's spyglass and winked out. Yet Vincent didn't move. Couldn't because he was afraid this was a dream.

*But no, this is a miracle wrought by men, not a sometime god. If such a thing is possible for mere mortals, then we shall yet endure.*

He rose from his desk and padded to the alcove where his gold-inlay black and Kurita-red samurai armor stood next to a double katana stand of carved ivory. Alongside it squatted a low rosewood table. Kneeling, he tugged open its single long drawer. The drawer held a series of rice-paper scrolls, each bound with red ribbon and outwardly indistinguishable one from the other. But he knew the scroll he wanted. Gently pulling away the red ribbon, he carefully unrolled the paper.

The demon painting pulsed with raw malevolence. Why he'd kept it, he hadn't known until this moment—until he felt the sting of tears in his eyes and the wet on his cheeks. Still kneeling, he used both hands to pull open his black kimono and bare his breast. Then he plucked his katana from its ivory stand. He held the sword with outstretched arms, the weapon's sterling silver dragon-head *tsuke* in his left hand, the leather-wrapped *saya* in his right. Pressing the sword's handguard with his left thumb, he pushed the blade from the scabbard's throat and, in one fluid motion, drew his sword.

The weapon felt good and solid in his hand. Its scent was of fine, acid-free camellia oil. Vincent raised himself on his knees, took up his katana in his right hand and fixed his streaming eyes upon those mocking demons.

"Not yet," he said. "You may snatch the best and the brightest; you may think you've won or that you will, that you will bring me and my house low. But I tell you now, and before all your dark lords, I make this *vow*."

Vincent drew his blade across his breast. He did this slowly, deliberately. The weapon bit his flesh, and he savored that hot spike of pain, derived a savage delight from the line of bright crimson that welled up to stain his blade. Vincent cut deep, and he cut true, welcoming pain as a long-lost lover. He cut silently, in a kind of ecstasy.

Then, leaning over the painting, he drizzled his hot life-blood so it seeped into the paper, branching along filaments and fibers. And with his blood came his curse as his defiance bloomed to its full fury.

"Bring your demons and your spells! Bring on the fire! *No* man draws my blood or blood of my kin and lives, nor will I suffer any demon to believe that he may defeat me or mine. So I swear now with what I have drawn by mine *own* hand. By *my* blood," Vincent said, "we are not finished *yet*."

# 41

*Copenwald, Halstead Station*
*Dieron Military District, Draconis Combine*
*15 October 3136*

**"M**eriwether, whenever you knock, it's bad news."

"This time, it's a bit of both." Meriwether handed over the noteputer. "Things on Biham actually seem to be dying down. *Chu-sa* Parks set up a tank convoy as bait based on some intel he'd gotten regarding weapons deliveries to the resistance fighters."

"Uh-huh." Crawford could see how it went: seven fighters dead, none captured, a torched ambulance, a crisped . . . "No authorization, of course."

"I think the theory was to ask for forgiveness later," Meriwether said. "The ISF team attached to Biham crawled all over that ambulance. The forensic report's in that attachment. Here." Meriwether blithely plucked the noteputer out of Crawford's hands and thumbed his way to the appropriate document.

Bemused, Crawford regarded his aide. "Tell me again why I bother to read anything? Considering you've memorized everything I need to know?"

"Why, sir." Meriwether was the picture of injured innocence. "It's in my job description. If you read everything, you'd never get anything done."

"I thought I *did* read everything."

"Most everything."

"Uh-huh." Crawford scanned the highlighted document. "Ceres Metals?"

"That's what the taggants said. The ISF people found them in the truck, meaning that the thing had been carrying explosives. Most commercial explosives manufacturers embed taggants in their products. But dysprosium is only used by one manufacturer: Ceres Metals."

"On Tikonov," Crawford said. "I'll be damned. It's Sandoval-Groell."

"*Chu-sa* Parks wants to know what you want to do about it."

Crawford opened his mouth. Closed it. Said, "Well, that's not up to me, is it? Especially since *Sho-sho* Kurita shows up in," Crawford checked his watch, "three hours."

"Ah," Meriwether said.

"Right," Crawford said dryly. "Ah."

One other thing about that report caught Crawford's eye: Wahab Fusilli. Well, more like his absence. Meriwether stood silently as Crawford read Parks' official version: the length of Fusilli's silence, no contacts, no request for extraction. If this were any other situation, Crawford wouldn't necessarily have been concerned. Fusilli had been absent for months at a time gathering intel. But there was a difference between intel work in the field and deep cover on the same planet where an agent was expected to check in. Crawford's gaze lingered on a personal note Parks had appended in his characteristic scrawl: *Something's up. I want to bring him home.*

Crawford homed in on that. Yes, something *was* up with Fusilli. He'd felt it for months. *Been eating at me ever since Al Na'ir, since I got a good long look at him here.* He'd never allowed himself to think about this too much. Sure, Fusilli proved his loyalty by telling them where Sakamoto was going. But his information on other serious issues had been faulty, and his survival on Al Na'ir just a little too convenient.

Meriwether cleared his throat, and Crawford blinked back to attention. "What?" Crawford asked. "It gets worse?"

"Yes, sir. Page eight. About . . ." Meriwether hesitated, "about Sir Eriksson."

"Oh, no," Crawford said. Eriksson was dead: found assassinated in his study. Eriksson's valet had miraculously survived and identified the assassin as a member of the very resistance movement Eriksson had founded. He gave a name: Noah Bridgewater. Local police authorities hadn't found Bridgewater, and they'd refused Parks' offer of assistance.

He remembered what Katana once told him, something the proud old knight had vowed: that *he* would be the engine of her destruction. Old grief tugged Crawford's heart. Looked like someone had beaten the old man to it.

Crawford handed back the noteputer. "Anything I have to sign, Meriwether?"

"Yes, sir. I'll put it on your desk." Meriwether shuffled his feet. "There is one more thing. Actually, someone to see you."

Weary, Crawford gestured at his door. "Show him in." As the MP entered, Crawford checked his watch. "I seem to recall I said two months."

"No way to sit on it that long, sir. Anyway, I have some good news. The DNA doesn't match our database, Fury, DCMS, anything."

"But . . . ?"

"It's the lubricant, sir. It's not pure. The first substance we isolated is for battlearmor, and it's quite unique. Only one kind of battlearmor requires this particular lubricant: the *Kanazuchi*."

"That *clears* us!" He felt like giving the MP a high five. "We don't *have* any *Kanazuchi*. Sakamoto's shock troopers used that on Normandy and Ancha, right? That was before the Fury merged with DCMS."

"Except we've got the oil in stock."

Crawford's elation evaporated. "We do? Why?"

The MP cleared his throat. "Because the Bounty Hunter requested it."

"But the Hunter's been gone since February," Crawford said stupidly.

"Yeah, and these guys have a whole bunch of fresh kills since then," the MP said. "And there's something else in the lubricant that clinches it. You're not going to like it."

"I already don't like it."

"Yeah, but you're *really* not going to like this. The contaminant is camellia oil."

"Oh, no," Crawford said.

"Oh, yes. Camellia oil is exclusively used for katanas. I checked distribution to see who actually put in a request. *Tai-shu* Tormark, of course, and several of the officers. But, sir, so did the Bounty Hunter."

Crawford closed his eyes. "That's the reason the DNA doesn't show up. Because the Hunter's not in the DCMS system and never has been."

"Maybe, but there's nothing to confirm or refute. No Bounty Hunter, no way to take a sample," the MP said. "So what do I tell them?"

Crawford was silent. He was surprised to find that he wasn't that shocked. There'd always been this barely suppressed air of violence about the Hunter, ever since he'd reappeared after dropping out of sight last March. Like something bad had happened . . .

*But we owe him more than we can possibly repay. Something I never told Katana, but I know he engineered Sakamoto's death, and he did it with my blessing. The hell of it is I'd use him again because he's that good.*

He supposed he ought to feel guilty, but he didn't. Whatever it took to get the job done. He said, "Tell them what they need to know: that the DNA doesn't match, and the lubricant matches the type used on a model of battlearmor we don't use."

"What about the camellia oil?" the MP asked, then must've read the answer in Crawford's face. "No, sir, I guess they don't need to know that."

"Nope," Crawford said. "They sure as hell don't."

Loveland chewed over it in the underground tram they took to the spaceport. "Did you see that MP? They're holding something back."

Thereon's smoky eyes held a faraway look. "It might not be important."

"Yeah? Well, if you've got something, don't keep it a secret."

"I keep going back to that old lady on Ancha, the one who saw that guy in the wheelchair. She said the nurse was big, right? And that the guy wrapped in those blankets didn't have a face."

"And maybe he wore a visor, and maybe it was armor." Loveland gave an irritable shrug. "We know all that. So what?"

"And Ancha's where we found the oil, and where we got that cold hit, the one that says there's a third man whose DNA isn't Imashinigi's and *isn't* the cold hit that popped up on Proserpina."

"Yes," Loveland said. "And? Where are you going with this?"

"We're going back to Ancha. We got to talk to the ME again."

"What for? We already have the cold hit. We already got a zillion cold hits."

"Yeah, that's just *it*." A sudden gleam of comprehension fired Thereon's smoky eyes. "They're not just anonymous. They're *cold*."

# 42

**T**hree days of electrolyte replacement solutions and nutrient bars had left Crawford's mouth tasting sour and gluey, and his bowels in knots. What he needed was exercise and movement. A stinging hot shower to sluice away sweat and grime, and a chance to brush his teeth. A decent meal and several glasses of ice-cold water would've helped, and he was damned tired of his own stink. Instead, what he'd had up to about four hours ago were sore neck muscles from the weight of his neurohelmet, and shoulders stiff as steel from gripping control sticks.

Now he was invisible, all but the most essential of systems shut down. His cockpit was dark, the only illumination an eerie green computer glow from his secondary viewing screen. He waited, a scant ten meters below the surface, one giant foot of his *Black Knight* braced against a rocky ledge, poised to spring as quickly as a sprinter in the blocks. Hiding underwater in a near-total systems blackout was a calculated risk Crawford was glad to take. He wasn't so far down that his comm systems were hampered, and the splutter-crackle of comm chatter bleeding through was soothing. Plus, his temps had come down. He was even a little chilly.

*Well, that's gonna change. Only I'm not gonna be on the hot seat.*

He'd never been in a submersible in his life, but co-cooned in his 'Mech with the battle raging above was surreal, like a dream. The muffled *boom-boom-boom* of SRMs punctuated a more constant, background susurrant rush of water. The water transmitted every shudder of artillery fire. Overhead, blaze-orange tracer fire sketched arcs like shooting stars.

Then a crackle in his neurohelmet: "*Tai-sa*, at present speed, estimate seventy seconds to target intercept."

"Roger that, Benco." Crawford spoke in a whisper though they were on a secured channel. "Keep up that artillery barrage but stay out of range, you copy? The idea is to drive them before they figure it out. How's that *Panther*?"

Benco, his artillery chief, made a dismissive sound. "Pretty banged up. We scored hits along its right torso, right at the fusion reactor. He's cooking."

"Excellent. Deep One, what's your status?"

A short pause, and then his lieutenant commanding a squad of SRM storm troopers replied. "Locked and loaded. Two flanking, right and left. Ready to go on your mark, sir."

"Good. Once I've engaged, I want you to spread out, then cut back and cover the rear. Make sure that sucker's got nowhere to go." *Just about showtime.* "Wait for it . . . Benco?"

"Fifty seconds, sir. Target holding steady."

"All right," Crawford muttered. He felt his calves tense in anticipation. A flick of his eyes to the left showed that his weapons status was as good as it was going to get, all eight lasers primed. He shifted, shrugged his shoulders to adjust his neurohelmet and cooling vest.

Now the water told him their prey was close. He still heard the muted sounds of battle, but now with a difference: a rhythmic *boomboomboom*. Thuds translating into shivers from vibrations transmitted first from land and then into the water.

Benco: "Thirty seconds, no change in course or speed . . . twenty."

Crawford reeled in a long, cleansing breath, then let it go. Out with the bad . . . Resting on his joystick, the fingers of his right hand grazed the nubs of his firing buttons. *Wait for it . . . wait . . .*

Benco's voice ratcheted up a notch with excitement. "Ten seconds, sir . . . nine, eight, seven . . ."

"Deep One," Crawford said, "on my mark. Remember, suppressing fire until I'm clear."

"Four, three, two . . ."

"Go!" Crawford banged his systems to life. He hammered his foot pedals, felt the surge of power through his cockpit. The water outside his canopy boiled as he heaved up his 'Mech's bulk in one massive push, the lake breaking apart as he shattered the surface.

In the open air now: His four storm troopers, hidden beneath thin shells of ice, had blasted free on jump jets. They were already firing as they spaced apart, flanking right and then left, circling around like shiny satellites. Sleet battered Crawford's cockpit, but he was so close he saw, through a sheen of ice over his adversary's cockpit, the MechWarrior's flinch of surprise. His prey: a huge, boxy *Grand Dragon.*

"Jesus," Crawford said as his targeting reticule burned hot and golden and very bright. "You are one butt-*ugly* 'Mech."

Then he and his storm troopers killed Yori Kurita, and he enjoyed every second.

## ═══ 43 ═══

**Y**ori stabbed a control. The recording froze just as eight concentrated streamers of red death skewered her *Grand Dragon* an instant ahead of four short-range missiles. Though she'd seen the recording twice and lived through it once in the sim, her humiliation burned just as bright and hot.

"That was ingenious," she said coolly. "How did you think of it?"

Crawford shrugged. "It seemed about the only place I could spring an ambush. I didn't have many options after you cut my lancemate to pieces."

She permitted herself a small smile. "That was the idea. We can't always attack or defend with superior numbers."

"Ah, spoken like a textbook." Crawford's smile was strained. He hesitated. "Permission to speak freely?"

She tried a light laugh that sounded false even to her.

"Of course, you're my second. I'm a Kurita, but I don't bite."

"Look," he said, leaning forward, "you're trying too hard. I don't blame you. This has got to be uncomfortable for you. It certainly is for me. It's tough taking over a command after a woman like Katana."

*Don't be so damned nice. I don't want to like you. A Kurita has no friends or allies.* Her tone was frosty. "I didn't know her well."

"Well, we did." There was no mistaking the sincerity or the pain in those startlingly clear jade-green eyes. "*I* did. I won't forget her, ever. And, much as I regret this . . . you will never *be* her."

Despite what she'd told herself over and over again, that she didn't care, she didn't—his words cut. "Colonel, I am well aware . . ."

He didn't let her finish. "And you don't *have* to be her. We need you . . . *I* need you to be yourself. What's more, you need it, too. *Sho-sho*, we have a long time together ahead of us. Let me work with you. I'm not your enemy."

*Yet you are not my friend.* How odd, she thought of Makoto Shouriki, and—stranger still—she wished he were there, so they could talk, maybe . . . She cut off that train of thought. Killed it *dead*. No weakness. She could afford absolutely none.

"I know you're not," she said, almost believing her own lie. *But you are not my friend and never will be.* "And I have an idea."

An hour later, Yori stood, naked, in a curtain of lavender-scented steam rising from her bath. She dipped in her toe, testing the water. Hot, just the way she liked it. She eased herself into the bath a little at a time, the water so hot that pain and pleasure mingled. At last, she was in all the way. *Up to my neck in hot water.* She laughed aloud. *And lavender bubbles.* Sighing, she stretched out, resting her neck and head against cool porcelain.

"I wasn't expecting this," she said, to no one. "No one expects this."

Just as Crawford had not expected what she wanted, how they would work together. *Crawford, in my lance . . . If that isn't a tacit signal that he is* mine, *I don't know what is.*

Sweat started on her upper lip, and she felt heat from the bath seep through her skin and into her veins in a heady flush.

*But they hate you;* he *hates you because you're not* her. *Well, I will break him, and they* will *respect me. I'll show them I am no one's puppet.*

A lie: She was. She felt her unseen master's strings plucking even here. She'd arrived more than a week ago, not just with the Fury soldiers and their armaments but with a battalion each of vehicles and battlearmor, a wing of aerospace fighters, and two battalions of infantry in tow, not to mention a WarShip and two DropShips. A bounty to the starved Dieron command, and a loan from her patron, who must be certain she'd make *tai-shu* when all was said and done.

Yes, Toranaga was pulling her strings. They all were, even Theodore Kurita. Toranaga's idea again, her visiting him on Benjamin. Though for once, she agreed with Toranaga's strategy. Theodore Kurita couldn't allow her to usurp too much glory. So, a compromise: Theodore would base his operations on Deneb Algedi and focus on Altair. She could have her own success, but Theodore's star must burn brighter.

No matter what, they would attack in January. Only an idiot would fail to see that Toranaga wanted to make his gift of her victory to the coordinator at Theodore's birthday celebration. That would steal a little of the heir's limelight, of course, but bolstering her would certainly rub off on him.

"And will I ever be free of you, you crocodile?" She scooped a handful of fragrant bubbles, studied how they shimmered in the light. How beautiful and yet how fragile. "Will you always hold me in the palm of your hand, a stone to be placed where you wish?"

Hamada's voice: *Don't fail.*

She blew the bubbles all to pieces.

# 44

Their sex was fierce and passionate. Afterwards, she lay, spent and sweaty, in Shakir's arms. The air smelled of warmed vanilla and cinnamon, and Shakir's skin glowed amber in light thrown by squat ivory candles.

"Can I ask you something?" she said. Shakir's fingers were in her hair, massaging her scalp while her fingers made lazy figure eights over his bronzed skin. "Are you having second thoughts?"

"Second thoughts?" He sounded genuinely bewildered. "Why?"

"Because you have dreams. Nightmares. You talk in your sleep."

"Yes?" His voice was mild, almost amused. "And what do I say?"

"Nothing very intelligible, most of the time. Sometimes you talk about Sakamoto, though. As if you'd been there or known him."

*Now* she felt something: just the slightest tensing of his arms about her. "A lot of soldiers have dreams."

Cautiously, mindful of her bad leg, she pushed up. Shadows inked his face, and his eyes were dark. "But Sakamoto didn't attack Proserpina."

"But I went to Al Na'ir. You don't get over something like that."

"I understand that. It's just that you say things that make no sense."

Now he reached up to caress her breast. "My dreams frequently make no sense. I have to admit that I like the ones *you* give me much more."

She captured his hand. "Come on, I'm serious. You talk

to Sakamoto. You say you don't want to be left behind, and then you tell him to stop, not to kill someone." She bit her lip in thought. "*Liz*. It's strange . . . Sometimes, I don't think you're telling me the truth."

He didn't answer. She sensed his control, as if he were used to dealing with the unexpected, spent his time watching, waiting, evaluating.

Then he said, "Have *you*? Been telling me the truth? Telling all?"

Startled at this sudden turn, she said, "What are you talking about?"

"Stop that." His tone was no sharper than before, but she stung from the lash of command in his voice. Then gently, slowly, he sat up, dropped his hand, and cupped her belly.

Her breath caught. The muscles of her abdomen tensed, and she wanted to pull away. She didn't. Shakir's fingers were gentle, with a familiarity and intimacy so profound. A shudder rippled through her body like a coming wave. His eyes never left hers, and they telegraphed a demand that left her breathless. And she realized something else, too. *She* was the one with doubts.

*Because I've let you touch me in a way that no one has in what feels like forever . . .*

"You loved them," he said. "You still do. But *I'm* here now, Dasha. I share your bed, but there are walls. Right here." He placed a palm over her chest. "Around your heart, one that guards you like"—and now he touched her locket—"the metal of that locket. But you possess the key, and only you can turn it. Let me in, Dasha. Trust me."

She knew what he was asking. For the story of her children. What felt like her whole life. So she told him, finally. Her eyes were dry at first, and she talked a little like a computer, without emotion. Eventually, he gathered her in his arms when she'd begun, at long last, to do something she hadn't allowed for herself in nearly a year. She wept, and Shakir didn't let go. Afterwards, *they* did something *they'd* never done before because she hadn't given either of them the chance.

They made love.

Her eyes were now dry, but they itched. She felt wrung out, exhausted but at peace. She lay on her back, staring into the darkness above their bed, and holding Shakir's hand.

He said, "May I ask you something else?"

She gave a shaky laugh. "What more is there?"

"A lot more," he said quietly. He rolled onto his side, propped his head on his hand. "Dasha . . . what are those cylinders? What are they for?"

She went very still. "I can't tell you that."

"Why not?"

*Because I don't know if I can go through with this.* "Because you don't need to know. Not now, anyway."

"And when do you think will be the right time?"

She reached for his face, and he pressed the palm of her hand to his lips in a kiss. "Soon, but not now, I don't want to spoil this. When the time comes, I'll tell you," she said, pressing her body against his. His skin was warm, and he smelled of musk and sex, and at her touch, she felt him stir.

"Soon," she whispered, as desire knifed her loins. "Soon, but for now . . . love me, Shakir. Just love me."

Dasha slept. One of the candles was already out, but there was enough light to fire the facets of the diamond stud he held in his palm.

*What am I doing? Pumping her for information, you'd think I was doing my job. But I do want to know and be known. I've been running ever since I was a child, that first time I killed anyone, and I'm so tired . . .*

Here was his chance to be responsible to no one but himself, and this woman. He could rest here. He could stay. Maybe they could fake his death, and then he and Dasha could get away. . . .

Maybe. Until Dasha and Yamada took over the nuclear power plant in little more than three weeks, any number of things could go wrong. Dasha and Yamada mercilessly drilled their squad, practicing every step of the takeover, with Yamada throwing in contingencies, the unexpected. But anything could happen between now and then. Most especially, then.

*I can stop this.* The diamond twinkled, like an orphaned star. *I can contact Parks, warn him so they can be waiting. Maybe bargain for Dasha's life but give them the rest, and she and I can go back . . .*

But to where? There was nothing in his old life he wanted or that mattered. There was no one.

But he put the earring back in. Just because.

# 45

*Marauder's Notch, Shaul Khala*
*New Samarkand Military District, Draconis Combine*
*3 November 3136*

Christ, but Miki had to pee so bad his eyeballs were swimming. Hunkering down into his cold-weather gear, Miki did the freezing-man-bladder-about-to-bust two-step. The temp was somewhere around minus sixteen; the night sky was milky with stars hard as diamonds; and the wind blew blades of cold that hacked through his insulated skinsuit like a laser through butter.

There were a lot of things that bothered Miki about living in a cave three thousand meters high, even if there were five other guys sharing the misery. For starters, the food was lousy, cooked by a guy who wouldn't know a frying pan from a Frisbee. Sleeping on a foam mattress spread over bare rock wasn't too fun either, and don't get him started on boredom. Trimming his toenails was the highlight of his week.

But the biggest thing was the cold. Think desert, a guy figured hot, right? But what Miki got instead was snow, bone-cold cave, middle of the night, pulling guard duty for Boss Alzubadai.

The view was pretty boring, too. Through his NVGs and to his right, a twinkle of lights from Alzubadai's compound nestled square in the middle of a valley. You'd think that was a bad place for a compound until you counted the three other mountain bunkers like this one, and the sand.

Lower elevations, there wasn't snow but sere scrub the color and consistency of straw. And rocks everywhere. Big rocks, little rocks, crumbly scree. Stuff that looked like some bad-ass *BattleMaster* had had a temper tantrum.

Miki checked his watch: three AM. That was about right. He always took a whiz round about now. Propping his laser rifle against a rough-hewn rock wall that encircled this observation post, he threw one leg over the wall, then the other. His boots sank up to his ankles in a clot of fresh snow, but that was as bad as it would get. They kept clear a narrow, meandering path along the ridgeline that would be hard to spot from anyplace other than the air. He usually went about fifty meters to where there was a natural kink northeast and, below the edge, a draw. Snow usually gathered in a wide bowl. Great place for a piss because the wind came from behind. Minimized the chance of blowback.

Miki tore off his right glove, clamped it between his teeth, working fast because his fingers were always damp from the glove. After two minutes or so, they'd be numb. His skinsuit had a couple of zippers, one right over his crotch, and he tugged it open, the metal chattering in the frigid silence. An instant later, he felt that wonderful relief as he got going—and then he did something he always did because, hell, he could. He wrote his name in the snow: big black swoops through his NVGs. Never had made it past the upstroke of the *k*, but tonight he was pretty tanked. So he might.

*M . . . I . . .*

He was on the down stroke of the *k* when, all of a sudden, he felt something hard and round press into his neck, right below his left ear. Startled, Miki jerked. His *k* slashed an exclamation in the snow. In his surprise, he also lost his grip. Warm urine splashed onto his boots and around his crotch until his bladder seized, and his dick ducked for cover.

A woman's voice: "Well, would you look at that? Things really *do* contract in the cold."

# 46

The tongue was warm and still drippy. Its hapless owner, gargling blood bubbles, was dragged away to be rendered, bit by bit, into fish food. (His koi positively thrived.) Eddie Alzubadai dropped the pulpy flesh into a massive aquarium that occupied an entire wall of his office. Instantly, the water boiled as razor-mouthed piranhas thrashed in a feeding frenzy.

Ever the perfect host, Alzubadai crossed to the maple sideboard and poured a cup of strong black tea. Alzubadai was lean, with long fingers, a pair of soulful sable-colored eyes, and a full head of hair black as a raven's wing. He took pride in the fact that his nose—aquiline and perfectly proportioned to his angular features—had never been broken, despite his line of work. He turned, and proffered the teapot. "Tea?"

"*Iie.*" Matsuro Kamikuro sat in a wingback upholstered in jade-green silk opposite Alzubadai's desk. The *oyabun*'s eyes were puffy with fatigue, his hair mussed and suit rumpled. "I do not take tea with men of no honor."

"Stop, stop, you're killing me, you and this honor shtick. You've got to learn a different tune." Alzubadai plucked a cube of sugar from a matching canister with a pair of gold tongs. Sliding into a rosewood chair at his desk, Alzubadai sipped tea. The liquid was smoky and sweet. Replacing the cup on its saucer—china touching china with a tiny chime—Alzubadai turned his attention to a bowl of fresh fruit squared on his desk. Succulent fresh figs, luscious pears, fat brown dates . . . He selected a pear and began to skin the fruit with his favorite, wickedly long dagger.

"You keep talking about honor," Alzubadai said. He

carefully sliced skin from the mellow ivory fruit, the length of unbroken peel scrolling like a curlicue. A little game, trying to peel the skin in one go. "Here it's been almost two months, and no word from your people and *nothing* from Tormark's command. What's up with *that*?"

Kamikuro said nothing. Humming, Alzubadai worked the dagger, nipping off the last bit of peel. He sectioned a wedge, delicately grasped the fruit between his thumb and the blade, and popped the morsel into his mouth. The ripe, wine-like flavor of the fruit exploded on his tongue, and he groaned with pleasure. "So," he said, swallowing, "now you need *them*, and where are they, hunh? You're yesterday's news."

"If so, then why am I still alive?" Kamikuro asked. "Clearly, you think I'm still of value. What, you are waiting for Ito to give in, perhaps?"

*Yeah, what about Ito?* Alzubadai popped another bit of pear into his mouth to milk the moment. Yeah, make the old guy wait for it. He shook out a cloth and began cleaning his dagger. "I'm hoping your guy Ito makes contact, and you know why? That little stunt he pulled getting off Ludwig, stealing my DropShip. So now, instead of being a DropShip richer, I'm down two, if you count his. Pretty smart guy, the way he locked out his DropShip's computer. But, you know, win some, lose some." Alzubadai gave a good-natured shrug and replaced the cleaned dagger on his desk. "Can't win you don't take chances."

"And what game of chance are we playing?"

"Life and death aren't enough?"

"I am a realist. There are many more days behind than ahead for me, Alzubadai. I'll not beg, nor is my life for sale." Kamikuro paused, scrutinizing the younger man more carefully. "I think . . . Katana Tormark is *alive*, isn't she? That's why you've kept *me* alive. A swap: me for Tormark. Ah, I begin to see how it is. You're afraid, aren't you? Of your master, I suppose. Did you seize Katana Tormark *first*, or did you steal her from someone else?"

Suddenly, Eddie Alzubadai found his tea less tasty than before. "Pretty fast for an old guy. You got all the answers, you tell me."

"Oh, I don't have to answer to anybody for anything. That's your problem. But you must've had help, only there are layers insulating the prime mover. You'll take the fall, and there will be no way to connect you with Warlord Toranaga." Kamikuro gave a satisfied grin. "What an unpleasant end you shall meet, Alzubadai, because Tormark will not forget."

"Yeah, right, you got all the answers. Well, wanna know why I rousted you from your beauty sleep? Tormark's coming for you, old man. We caught our JumpShip coming in and let it pass, made it all cool. Same for the DropShip. Now, anyone who does night ops, they strike between three and four. So when she comes, I'll be waiting."

"She'll have help from my *waka-gashira*, Ito. You can't win."

*Yeah, you think you're so smart? Suck on* this, *old man.*

"No? Well, Ito and me, we're like *this*," Alzubadai said, crossing his fingers. He enjoyed the way Kamikuro's smile dribbled away. "He's *mine*, old man, and has been for months," Alzubadai said. "He's *mine*."

# 47

## 0315 hours

**H**er hip was killing her, her body felt like a wobbly gelatin mold that hadn't had time to set, and *now* Viki was ticked off beyond all reason.

"*Leaving* me here? That wasn't the plan," she said. They were clustered just inside the cave's entrance. Viki made a sweeping gesture that took in the mountain redoubt and the valley floor that glimmered like a white damask tablecloth below. "You need every experienced troop you can muster, and that's me. I can see leaving *Lance* behind. . . ."

"Hey," Lance said. In his snow camis, he looked like an advertisement for a Terran tire company. "I ain't no virgin, you know."

Viki ignored him. "Lance and Ito's guys, they make sense. But I've got combat experience and . . ."

"And that makes you an asset here," Katana said. Pulling back on her pistol's slide, she jacked a shell into the barrel, clicked on the safety and then holstered the weapon. Reaching around, she withdrew a needler from a concealed carry holster snugged at the small of her back. Checked to make sure the safety was on, the flechette cartridge cube good to go. "With this view, you'll have a greater tactical advantage if things spin out of control."

"But you're changing things. You change things, things screw up. This is our only shot . . ."

"Negative that," Katana said. She reholstered the needler. Like the rest, she wore snow camos: an irregularly patterned white and black parka, and insulated pants. The stretch acrylic of the matching face mask was bunched up like a watch cap, and NVGs perched on her forehead. Ito, clad in a matching suit, stood alongside Katana, the butt of his laser rifle resting on his hip. Katana said, "I watched you on the hike up here. You're better, but that hip isn't anywhere near a hundred percent. When this goes down, it's going to go down fast, and that means we'll have to *move* fast. Your hip can't cut it, and that means you stay here. Lance, too, because however good you are, you also need backup, and Lance is it. Besides, I need someone on site with combat experience, especially if we have to call in a strike, and as you've so nicely pointed out, that's you."

Defeated, Viki pulled in a breath. "Okay. But I don't like it."

Lance came to stand at her elbow. "Cheer up, kid. Think how happy your old man McCain's gonna be to see you again. Me, we walk in with Katana *and* Kamikuro *and* the whole shebang, and that jerk-off Parks, he's gonna have to eat it. Man, that'll be good."

"Yeah, but only if we get out of this," Viki pointed out.

"Hey," Lance said. "Don't jinx it."

*Tormark.* Miki sat cross-legged, fingers laced behind his head, his back pressed against naked rock, and the business end of a laser staring him down. He was dry, but his pants smelled like a latrine. When he thought back to the moment when Tormark caught him out, his cheeks burned. His dislike had been organizational before, something expected. Now it was personal. Just give him an excuse . . .

He went analytical. Like someone threw a switch in his head, and he clicked into observation mode. He was low level in Ghost Clan, kind of a fuck-up, but this was his chance to get a leg up in the organization. He did this right—say, take out Tormark—he'd be golden.

The big guy with the laser looked like *yakuza*. This guy had *tough* and *smart* in his face, big as life as his tatts. Miki watched as Tormark and the *yakuza* came his way. When Tormark stood over him, those dark eyes of hers lasering his skull, he didn't look away.

*Wanna read something loud and clear? Then get this, baby. Give me an excuse, just give me the chance, and I'll splatter your brains to . . .*

"You," Tormark said. With the rifle and snow camos, she looked like some kind of crazy woman out of a bad horror flick. "You got a name? I didn't quite catch it when we sort of interrupted things."

Heat flooded his face. "Miki." She waited for more, but he just stared. Wouldn't give her the satisfaction.

Finally, she said, "Okay, Miki. You're coming along for a little ride. Just in case we need some kind of pass codes to get into the compound."

He perked up. If he could stick close, he might get his chance. "Yeah, there are codes."

"We're going to need those. We're also going to need information on what'll be waiting for us on the other side."

"Yeah? What's in it for me?"

"Living. And maybe I'll remember your name without you having to spell it out. Let me clue you in on something, sport. When you're pulling guard duty and need to take a leak? Bring a bottle. Fresh pee on snow? On infrared? Might as well take out an ad. You copy?"

*Yeah, and when I blow your brains out, you just copy that, toots.*

"Uh-huh," Miki said. "I copy."

The hover bay was a rough cavern of hollowed-out rock just high enough to clear a grown man standing upright on a fully operational sled, and it smelled like rubber from the sleds' skirts. There were two sleds lined up in single file, each with its stand deployed. Neither sled, which essentially looked like a modified Tamerlane, was tricked out with weapons. Miki could see Tormark didn't like that, but she could suck on it.

Tormark waved him onto the lead sled. There were only two seats. The big guy slid into the driver's seat, and Tormark pointed Miki to the second seat. As the big guy cranked the engine, Tormark said, "Good thing about these sleds. Sure beats walking."

Miki was so surprised, he almost gave it away. *Walking.* "Yeah," he said, "sure does." He saw the big guy half-turn as Tormark opened her mouth, probably to say something else really snide. Never got the chance.

The big guy moved fast, real fast. Right arm whipping round, POW. Tormark went down.

The big guy grinned. "Okay, Miki. Change of plans."

## 0355 hours

Eddie Alzubadai looked up as his office door slid to one side. Beaming, he spread his arms wide. "Ito, *buddy!* Come on in!"

Alzubadai got a real charge out of the way Kamikuro sort of crumpled. Lower jaw unhinging as Tormark stumbled through, hands behind her head, a thick sludge of blood smeared over her chin. Her parka was unzipped, the hood bunched along her neck. Ito followed right behind, prodding her along with a pistol between the shoulder blades. Then one of *his* guys, Miki? Bicki? Alzubadai couldn't remember. A lookout, though, meaning that Ito had come over the mountains the way he said he would and had gotten Alzubadai's guy to ease them through into the compound. Alzubadai jerked his head left, and his guy got the message, fading to stand in front of the aquarium. Then Alzubadai said, "Hey, Tormark, you don't look so good. Someone mess you up?"

"Yeah, yeah, Eddie." Ito was brisk. He stepped out from

behind Tormark, his weapon still drawn. "Cut the crap. You wanted her, I got her."

"Not so fast, not so fast," Alzubadai said. He made a gimme motion with his fingers. "Let's have the weapon."

"What the hell? I thought . . ."

"Yeah, yeah, you thought, you thought. Thank Christ, I do the thinking. Gun first, talk later." He watched as Ito struggled with his training. Alzubadai understood. He'd have felt the same way. *Only it's my show now.* He waited, hand outstretched, and saw the moment Ito crossed the line: the way his forehead smoothed.

Ito proffered the weapon, butt first. "Take the damn thing."

"Thanks," Alzubadai said. He hefted the weapon. "Nice piece. A Glock 88. I am *impressed!* Always wanted one of these."

"It's mine," Tormark said. Her voice dripped hate. "Bastard took it."

"Yeah?" Alzubadai gave her one of his best, most winning smiles—and was just plain tickled when she looked mad enough to scratch his eyes out. "Well," he said, turning the gun on Ito, "now it's mine, just like you." He looked at Ito, and his manner turned brisk, all business. "Parka, too. Let's see what you got under there, big guy, and while you're at it, show me your ankles, nice and slow." He waited as Ito shucked his parka, did a three-sixty and then teased up his trousers.

Alzubadai nodded, satisfied. "Okay," he said, turning to deposit the gun on his desk, "let's talk a deal here."

"We already did that. We make an even trade, Tormark for Kamikuro, and then I'm out of here."

From behind, Alzubadai heard Kamikuro struggle to his feet. "Never," the old man said. *"Never!"*

"Kamikuro-*sama.*" Ito moved toward Kamikuro. "Let me help . . ."

*"Buta!"* Kamikuro roared. "How *dare* you shame me like this! Where is your honor?"

Alzubadai rolled his eyes. "This crap about honor . . ."

"Shut up, Eddie," Ito said, his eyes never leaving Kamikuro's face. "Please, forgive me, but Tormark's cause is not worth your life. It is . . ."

"Be *silent!*" Kamikuro slapped Ito hard enough to stagger the big man. The sound cracked like a pistol shot. "Not worth my life? I *have* no life if you steal my honor! How can I face my people knowing my life's been brokered by a traitor willing to betray one we have *sworn* to serve?"

"Yeah, well, I hate to break up this little lovefest," Alzubadai said. He jabbed Ito in the chest with a forefinger. "Now, listen. You just walking away is *not* what we agreed to, man. We *agreed* that you were gonna cut me in on a little action. We swap, and then Kamikuro here *retires*. Then we talk about how you're going to ease us into doing you, ah, a couple favors, right? Run a couple missions, take down some of the competition?"

Ito's mouth was like a fissure in stone. "First, let me get Kamikuro-*san* out of here, and then we can . . ."

"Naw, naw." Alzubadai shut that down but quick. Now he was getting irritated, and you just didn't piss off Eddie Alzubadai. "No can do. Think I'm stupid? Naw, naw, we work out the details now."

"No," Kamikuro said. "No!"

*That does it.* Cursing, Alzubadai pivoted, backhanding a blow to Kamikuro's face that sent the *oyabun* crashing back against Alzubadai's desk. Blood spewed from Kamikuro's mouth, fruit plopped to the floor, and Alzubadai's cup skittered off the desk to explode in a starburst of cold tea and jagged bone china.

"You gonna shut up now, right?" Alzubadai advanced, his right fist cocked. He heard a faint zipping sound that didn't really register. "Right? Because you know, old man, I'm getting really tired of your lip . . ."

He froze as something stabbed his neck. Fist suspended in midair, guts icing with surprise. Dropped the fist. Turned around very, very slowly.

"Yeah." Tormark jammed a compact hand laser against Alzubadai's forehead. A short strip of clear adhesive curled from the barrel, torn free from her neck where she'd taped the weapon out of sight beneath her parka. "My sentiments exactly."

The whole thing went down in less than five seconds, but Miki saw it all happen. Saw Tormark ripping the concealed laser free. Saw Ito's hand start for his holster, and then Miki remembered: *Glock on the desk, get the gun, get the* gun! Turning, he lunged for the desk, saw the old man uncoil from his slouch against the wood. Half-turning, Miki threw out his left arm, aiming for the old man's head. *Out of my way, old man, just get out . . . !*

At the last second, the old man ducked and plowed into him. Winded, Miki staggered back, and that's when he felt the pain: sharp, like a hawk's talon ripping his skin, and now the hawk's beak tearing at his insides. A fresh, spiking agony sheeted his vision red. Now the old man was pushing him, driving him back. Miki tried to swat the old man away, but his arms suddenly went to water. Blood boiled into the back of his throat. Breathe, he couldn't breathe. He had to get air! But the old man was strong; he slammed Miki against the wall. And the old man was grunting now, doing something with his hand, throwing his weight into it.

Miki's knees buckled. His strength fled. His throat closed down and refused to open. He was slithering down along the wall, collapsing. Something hot and wet splashed his hands, and he looked down. Saw blood.

*Knife.* Miki's vision closed down to a single, bright point. *Knife, on the desk, the boss's knife . . .*

And then he was gone.

Breathing hard, Kamikuro backed up then stepped away as Miki crumpled to the floor. Kamikuro's lips were crimson, and his hands slick with fresh blood. Alzubadai's dagger stood buried to its hilt in the center of Miki's belly, protruding from a lake of blood. The hilt ticked in time with the last fitful spasms of Miki's heart. And then, it stopped.

No one moved for a moment. No one spoke. Then Alzubadai said, "Look, okay, we can work with this. I can tell you who gave the orders."

Tormark's stare was ice. "I already know."

"But we can *deal*."

"I don't deal."

"But you can't just kill me," Alzubadai said.

Katana Tormark smiled—and that, too, was ice. "I don't see why not," she said.

And pulled the trigger.

# 48

From their earlier trek from a hover bay, Katana knew only four buildings lay between them and their ride, all unguarded except for the two guards outside. Easing out of Alzubadai's office and into an empty corridor, they moved fast, silently. Katana led with her needler. Kamikuro followed right behind, then Ito, his rifle holstered, laser pistol at the ready. At a T-corridor, they hung a left, and Katana called a halt just shy of the front door.

Looking over at Kamikuro, Katana whispered, "I'm sorry, but you'll have to be a prisoner just a bit longer." She holstered her needler and lifted her hands. "Me, too."

"As long as I am in such good company," he said, putting up his hands. Black seams of dried blood creased his palms. "It is very good to see you, Tormark-*san*."

The guard on her immediate right turned as Kamikuro and then Katana stepped through. The building's front was illuminated, and as Kamikuro moved into a puddle of white light, the guard's head swiveled round. "Hey," he said. "Where's . . . ?"

Katana and Kamikuro ducked as Ito straight-armed the pistol, killing the guard with a single, quick green dart of ionized energy right between the eyes. Pivoting, he caught the other just as the guard's mouth opened to shout. Ito fired. Laser fire spat into the guard's mouth, flash-frying his tongue, then licked air as the bolt drilled through flesh and bone.

The compound was situated on a rocky shelf, like a small mesa, and scalloped all around where rock met sand. Their hover was exactly where they'd left it: slotted in a rectangular metal bay with a bare rock floor behind four Tamerlane strike sleds. For a split second, Katana thought about taking a Tamerlane. That medium laser looked inviting, and a mini-rack of SRMs wouldn't be such a bad thing. Plus, the Tamerlane was faster. Their sled was essentially a flatbed with two seats, little cover, and no weapons. But they'd have to figure a way to bypass the control console's computer lockout. If someone found Alzubadai . . .

As if some malevolent spirit had read her mind, the first growl of an alarm rolled through the compound. "Go," she said to Ito. When they were past, she took out the skirts of one Tamerlane with the needler, the flechettes shredding rubber. Drew the Glock and shredded another skirt. Two down. That should help. Then she sprinted after Ito and Kamikuro.

As Ito cranked their sled, Katana pulled up her sleeve, clicked her microcomm, and shouted: "Viki, you copy? This is Katana. Do you . . . ?"

"Copy that. Out." Viki clicked off. "Time to go. She's calling it." Viki was amazed how calm she sounded. Her insides were jumping like they were wound around pogo sticks.

"Then we are outta here," Lance said. He and Ito's three men had spent the time trussing up Alzubadai's lookout team, figuring that it was better to be safe than sorry. Now Lance scooped up his weapon and jogged after Ito's men and Viki, who was already clattering down the stairs as fast as she could manage while shouting orders into her comm: "You got a fix? . . . Copy that! On my mark . . . Mark! Five minutes to let us get clear, five minutes! Then *fire*, no matter what, do not abort! Do not . . . !"

The wind roared in her ears like something alive, and they were going so fast the mountains scrolled by in a blur. Still, peering back the way they'd come, Katana made out two bullet-shapes rocketing in pursuit.

"Here they come," Katana warned. She'd slung down her rifle locked and loaded to hip fire. To her left, Kamikuro was sighting down Ito's laser rifle. She saw at once that while she had better range with the rifle, they were either going to have to outrun the sleds or slow down to close the distance. She peered through her night-vision scope. The closest of the two sleds was fully loaded with two men, one to pilot, the other to fire. Only it looked like the gunner held something long, like a tube . . . What *was* that?

She watched as the nearest sled gobbled up distance. *Weight's slowing us down.* Katana read the distance her scope flashed in bloodred letters. She was so busy worrying about her distance that what the gunner was pointing in their direction didn't click until the very last second: when the long barrel spat out a tiny puff of white exhaust.

*Oh,* shit! And then she was screaming: "Ito! M-73, incendiary grenades! Right on our tails! Look out!"

Viki could hear the alarm rolling across the sand, echoing into the bay, banging against rock like an ululating chorus of bugles. She saw in an instant that they were too many for one sled, but Viki wasn't leaving anyone behind. "Come on, move, *move!*" she shouted, clambering aboard. "We've got less than three minutes!"

"I'm on it!" Lance was already revving the sled, and as he disengaged the stand, the sudden jolt sent Viki staggering left. Lance's hand flashed for her forearm to reel her in while he tried urging the sled forward with the other hand. "Hang on, kid, hang on!"

Viki grabbed hold of the sled's console as the hover bucked in a fitful, jerky, hesitant lurch that threw Ito's three men against one another like passengers in a packed bus that was standing room only. The sled canted left as the men tumbled and rolled.

If they couldn't shed some weight, they weren't going anywhere. They'd flip right here, right now, and by the time they managed to right the sled, it would be too late. But what to jettison? Viki looked around wildly, but there was nothing. Her thoughts broke apart as the hover tipped like a yacht about to capsize, yawing into a death roll. Crying out, Viki threw up her hands as the rock wall rushed for her face. "Lance!"

"I've got it, I'm on it!" Cursing, Lance wrestled the sled horizontal then cycled up its compressor. A fresh burst of air pummeled the rock beneath the sled's skirts. The cords bulged in Lance's neck as he jammed the throttle, pushing the shuddering vehicle for all it was worth. "Goddamn it, move, you lousy piece of shit, *move!*"

The sled hesitated. Skipped. Jerked forward. And that's when Viki went for broke. Whirling on her heel, she grabbed her rifle and jumped.

"Hey!" one of Ito's men shouted. *"Hey!"*

She fell. The drop wasn't far, maybe a meter and a half, but her bum right hip picked that moment to seize up. She slammed into the rock hard enough to knock the wind out of her lungs.

*"Viki!"* Lance screamed, but the sled was moving away, picking up speed, and he barely turned back in enough time to avoid ramming the sled into rock. As the sled raced for the entrance, Lance spared a look over his shoulder. His face was a mask of anguish and disbelief, and he was shouting. She heard his words even over the tortured whine of the sled's engine and the wild throbbing of her heart: "What the hell are you doing, Viki? *What the hell are you DOING?"*

*Giving you a chance, you idiot!* "Go!" Her lungs burned as she reeled in air. "Lance, you've got two minutes. Go, *go!"*

At Katana's scream, Ito jammed the sled to full throttle. The sled leapt forward, and then, as Ito cut right, Katana caught a glimpse of the grenade eating up air, arcing down . . . "Look out! Ito, look out!" she shrieked. Whipping round, she flung herself at Kamikuro, tackling him, bringing them crashing to the deck.

The grenade hit. The night bloomed with a bright, angry billow of orange flame that seared her retinas. The air cracked, ruptured wide open with a deafening, hellish roar. Hot gases roiled over the sled, heat licking at the exposed skin of her arms, singing her hair. Sand rained, and above the ringing in her ears, Katana heard Ito's scream as gases boiled over his body.

*No parka, he's got more exposed skin, hair . . . Oh, my God . . .*

The same superheated gust of air pitched the sled thirty degrees. Air spilled from beneath its skirt, and for an instant, their speed dropped enough that Katana easily could've rolled right off. For a split second, she considered it, wondered if maybe taking up a firing position to take out the oncoming sleds might not help . . . and then rejected it as the sled slammed back to horizontal. But they were out of control; she could feel it in the wild yaw of the sled slipping from side to side on its long axis. Blinking against purple afterimages, she swung her head toward the pilot's chair.

The *yakuza*'s limp body slumped over the controls. She could make out irregular patches that looked like cooked flesh along his arms. She rolled off Kamikuro, battled her way to her hands and knees and started for Ito. Her skin was tingling. . . . Was she hurt? Then a restraining hand clamped over her wrist.

"I will pilot," the *oyabun* said. Sand glazed his hair and face. "You are a better shot than I."

She didn't argue. As Kamikuro hauled the unconscious Ito from the controls, she scooped up her rifle, sighted down her scope, checked her distance. Her skin burned, and it felt as if maybe she'd been cut.

She focused. The sleds had veered right and left as she expected, but they'd gone *very* far out. They'd lost precious time, let *them* regain a bit of a lead. But why?

As she waited for the sleds to loop back, her mind raced over a puzzle she couldn't resolve. Why incendiary grenades? *They* were easy-enough pickings for a missile. She rubbed absently at her hand. *Burning like hell.* Maybe the question was what was *different* about a grenade than an SRM? She thought back to that roiling billow of superheated gases. Designed to upend the sled. That *might* kill them, but the sand would cushion . . .

She registered in the next half-second that her hand was *wet*. Startled, she looked down, saw that the back of her hand was starting to *ooze*. Her gaze skipped to Ito's body, picked out black patches on his arms: *blood*.

The tumblers clicked into place in her mind even as she saw their pursuers had joined up.

*Oh, my God! It's not* sand!

As they rocketed out of the bay, Lance debated for a half second about turning right around. But turning back was suicide. They were moving because Viki was no longer aboard. She'd bought their lives with her own. In less than two minutes, if she couldn't find shelter that *wasn't* a tunnel, Viki would be dead.

Then that pillar of flame torched the sand ahead, dazzled

his vision. He made out two Tamerlanes peeling away, and then that smaller hover. Lance's determination firmed. Viki stayed behind, gave up her life, and he'd be *damned* if she was going to die for nothing!

"You guys want to save your boss?" Lance roared. He pushed their sled as fast as it would go. The sled's variable thrust propellers bellowed as their speed inched up. "Then let her rip!"

*Got to get out into the open, out of the tunnel!* Viki scrambled over rocks using her hands to pull her along. Then she was out. She was maybe a meter above the sand, and she thought about simply dropping, then sprinting as fast as she could to put down distance. But her leg would slow her down. Besides, all she had to do was take cover—with breathing room.

*Literally: When those thermobaric bombs detonate, the pressure wave'll suck the air right out of everything and everyone in these tunnels.*

Her eyes ticked to her digital readout: thirty seconds and counting.

Kamikuro jammed the sled left, jagging in a wild arc as another grenade flashed past, then detonated on impact: *BOOM!* Screaming, thrown off balance, Katana caromed off the edge of the passenger's seat. Her rifle and the laser went spinning away. She slammed to the deck, slid toward the sled's lip. Ito's body plowed into her but, at the last second, her blood-slicked hand snagged the passenger's seat bolted to the deck. For the moment, she and Ito were safe . . . But only for a moment.

The sand was eating them alive. They were going so fast the mountains whirred in a blur. She couldn't move, couldn't let go of the much heavier and bulkier Ito, not without sacrificing him to the sand. They were almost out of time, and yet it seemed an age since she'd screamed for Viki to call in a strike. And where the hell were the thermobarics? She craned her neck and looked forward. Somehow, miraculously, Kamikuro—bloodied, his clothes in tatters—was still on his feet, still urging the sled into a series of darting, jagged evasive maneuvers to throw off their adversaries.

Then, as the mountains loomed before them, she saw another sled heading their way.

*Viki, Lance, they're out, and that means the thermobarics are . . .*

"Brake!" she screamed. "Kamikuro, *brake*!"

Clinging to her rocky perch, Viki watched the drama playing itself out on the sand even as the seconds bled away. She saw Katana's sled speeding for the mountains and knew instantly what her *tai-shu* hoped would happen. And she cheered her on, she shouted herself hoarse. As much as she feared what would come next, Viki urged the time to pass faster, faster!

Ten seconds, nine . . . *Hang on, Katana, hang on!* . . . six seconds . . . She saw Katana's sled suddenly brake, and her pursuers rush past, veering to avoid a collision, and now *they* were careering toward the rocky slopes!

And then she heard Death coming. Raising her face to the heavens, Viki spied the missiles, like shooting stars, hurtling to earth, screaming through air, arcing to the four points of the compass . . .

Two seconds . . . *one!*

The very air shattered. The night blew apart into a hail of rock and fire. Into the very picture of Hell.

# PART SIX

## *Hamete:* Trick Play

# 49

Loveland sat across from the ME in his basement office. The office was adjacent to the autopsy suite and perfumed with a lemony disinfectant that couldn't quite cover the stink of rotted meat.

"You've got to be kidding." Loveland felt like he'd taken a sucker punch to the gut. "Please tell me this is a mistake."

"No mistake," the ME said. He eyed Thereon who sat to Loveland's right. "I would never have caught this. What tipped *you* off?"

"Our unsub likes playing games. That *K*, for instance. He's familiar with investigative techniques. It just felt obvious. All those cold hits, I started to wonder if there was something about *cold* we'd missed."

Loveland still couldn't believe it. "Why didn't this turn up before now?"

"Because a DNA match doesn't hinge upon intact or fresh specimens. You get blood or skin cells or whatever, and then you *extract* the DNA, which means you bust up the cells. No one would study the cells themselves unless there was some reason to, which I just did on Jane Doe. There's no mistake. All these cold hits from skin and blood?" The ME shook his head. "Every single specimen had been frozen *ahead* of time."

"Meaning that our unsub is planting someone else's blood and skin, and that person's *not* in ISDIS," Thereon said. "And if they're not in the InterSphere DNA Index System, then it's some victim we haven't identified, or a new unsub we've never run across. My money's on the former, but either way, that means—"

"End of the line." Loveland sagged back with a sigh. "Shit."

The restaurant had a pianist playing tinkly jazz. His martini was dry and so icy Loveland's teeth hurt. He sighed. "Fell on our asses."

Thereon nursed a vodka tonic. "We went as far as we could."

"You mean, as far as *he* let us go."

"He's not God, and he's not invincible. Remember, the one cold hit we've got that *doesn't* match the frozen samples came from that prostitute on Proserpina. The one who turned up January, two years ago. I think *that's* our guy. He slipped up. Things got out of control. He'll lose it again."

"Great. Wait around for him to kill someone else so we can catch him." Loveland sipped vodka flavored with a whisper of vermouth. "So, what'll you do now?"

"Same ol', same ol'. Go back to the office, do the paperwork. Wait. You?"

"I'll go back to being a detective-detective. But I'm going to put in for some time first. Maybe go see my kid."

"Must be nice to have a family," Thereon said.

"Not when you got to shuttle between cities, but it could've been worse. Since the HPGs were down, judge wouldn't let my second wife go off-planet. Pissed her off so bad I thought her hair was gonna catch on fire."

They laughed. Loveland tongued an olive off a swizzle stick and figured he'd had his greens for the day. Thereon shook ice into his mouth. "Never been married," Thereon said around ice. "My dad's on Misery, though. Time off wouldn't be a bad thing. He's due a visit."

"Misery? Thought you came from Devil's Rock."

"Six of one, half dozen of the other," Thereon said easily. "Besides, everyone knows: Misery loves company."

Loveland groaned. "Man, that's *so* lame."

# 50

Justin Pierpont drove northwest, easing his hover up a series of bluffs that led to the reactor facility. The heater was going full-blast, but Pierpont was freezing. His stomach was tied in knots. He slipped his right hand into the pocket of his jacket and withdrew a slim, gurgling flask. Steering with his knees, he untwisted the cap and tossed back a mouthful of scotch. The liquor went off in his stomach like napalm: a nice, hot glow.

He shouldn't drink. If his boss smelled booze, he'd be canned in a second. If everything went according to plan, though, this was the last shift he'd ever pull because then he'd get the hell off this rock, and go be with his wife and kid, and then get his ass planted someplace where they didn't have booze or cards or men like Tony Yamada.

He'd taken his one big shot at backing out about four weeks ago when Dasha hadn't shown for work. Normally, she came by his station twice a day. They'd chat, ha-ha, just like friendly coworkers, while the whole time he was slipping her documents on data crystals.

The first day she didn't show, he thought: *Okay, a fluke.* By the third, he worried that maybe something had gone wrong. He'd worked all day in an agony of suspense, expecting that the next people through the door would be carrying laser rifles. No one did. So, he thought maybe Yamada and Dasha had gotten caught. Or maybe they were dead, and he was in the clear.

The fourth day, he'd whistled on the way out the door, past security. The night air was crisp and spicy. Hard stars sparkled in the sky. Nightfall came early these days, and all the sodium vapor lights were on in the parking lot. The asphalt twinkled. As he approached his hover, he dug into his pocket, pointed the remote, popped the lock. He dropped into the driver's side, strapped up, flipped the rocker switch to power up the hover's compressor . . . and then felt cold steel press below his right ear. His eyes flicked to his rearview, and then an icy fist of dread squeezed his lungs.

"Hey, Pierpont," Yamada said, "how ya doing?" Conversational, like he didn't have a pistol jammed against Pierpont's neck.

"Uh." Pierpont swallowed. Yamada's eyes glittered in the low light from the dash. "Where's Dasha?"

"She took a couple days." Yamada's filed incisors were pointier than ever. "Didn't want you to get lonely. So, how're things coming?"

To this day, Pierpont didn't know what got into him. But he said, "I'm not writing one more line of code unless you let me get my wife and kid off-planet."

"Yeah? What for? Ain't nothing going to go wrong, right?"

"Nothing will go wrong. The virus will do what it's supposed to do."

"So, why do they need to get off-planet?"

"I just want them off, okay? I've done everything you've asked. This is the only thing I'm asking for in return."

"The only thing, my ass. I'm canceling your debt, right? You get to keep certain *valuable* pieces of your anatomy, right? Only thing, my ass."

Pierpont felt those certain valuable pieces of his anatomy try to retreat into his abdomen. "You need me. I'm the only one who can do this, and do it right. So, either I'm taking them to the spaceport tomorrow, or you'll have to kill me."

He watched Yamada's eyes, watched the man work the decision tree, ticking off pros and cons, figuring angles. Saw the moment right before he knew that Yamada would agree. In the end, maybe Pierpont's victory was hollow. But it still felt good, and now, at least, his wife and daughter were off-planet and safe.

He spotted the three natural-draft cooling towers from ten klicks out. Each tower was one hundred twenty meters high but seemed much higher because the reactor was set on a bluff by the sea. The complex was entirely surrounded by a perimeter fence, though security had never been much of a concern. (The physics involved with a fission reactor was so archaic that no one seriously considered there was much risk.) There were three entrances: southwest, west and a third gate to the north used exclusively for cargo deliveries and the landtrain.

The complex housed two working reactors called, appropriately, Reactors Two and Three. Pierpont worked in Reactor Two's control room. All control-room personnel worked a six-week cycle, rotating through the various shifts: days, afternoons, nights. Pierpont was on a team currently rotating through days. But he absolutely had to work tonight. So he'd feigned an emergency and switched out of rotation, volunteering for this duty shift. He wouldn't know his coworkers on this shift. That was fine, because they wouldn't know him, either.

Getting in was easy. His change of shift had been duly noted in the complex's computer database, and the guard, after verifying his story against the computer, checked Pierpont via a portable retinal scanner and then waved him through.

Pierpont's office was in a five-story building adjacent to Reactor Two. The adjoining lot was about one-third full, with most of the vehicles clustered in pools of yellow light like gazelles fringing a watering hole. Pierpont skimmed the lot, bypassed the other cars and then nosed his hover to the far right beneath the naked limbs of a maple. He engaged the stand and then killed the compressor. The hover wheezed to silence.

He didn't get out. Instead, Pierpont sat, wondering what the hell he was doing with his life. He listened to the silence outside and the thunder of his heart in his ears. His eyes drifted southeast to the spindly forms of cranes and the blockier outlines of a ConstructionMech highlighted against the illuminated shell of a half-completed parking complex.

At the entrance to his building, he repeated the ID and retinal verification. Satisfied that he was who he said he was, the door sighed open. Once inside the main lobby—a sterile, well-lit space smelling of floor wax and manned by two bored-looking guards—he emptied his pockets and walked through a scanner. The guard gave him back his watch, told him to have a nice night and that was that.

His shoes slapped linoleum. The sound was like that plastic bubble wrap his daughter liked to pop. The overhead office light clicked on as he entered. Once inside, he powered up his computer, entered his passwords and then he was in. He wore laced-up oxfords, and he now reached down, untied his right shoe and slipped it off. He used a fingernail to pry a pin from the heel. Then he swiveled the rubber heel to one side, turned the shoe over and shook a ruby-red data crystal into the palm of his left hand. The facets caught the fluorescents and twinkled like a gem.

*Don't think. Just do it.*

He fitted the crystal into a data port. His computer queried as to which decryption program he wished to use. Tapping the screen, he selected one and waited while his computer worked. In less than twenty seconds, it chimed. He paused, a finger poised, like a symphony maestro about to cue the violins. Then he tapped <Upload>.

The program would not tie into the control room station where he'd be working. *That* system was password-protected by several firewalls. Once he was in the control room, Pierpont would suddenly remember that he needed information stored on his office computer. He would then bring down the internal firewalls, retrieve garbage, and re-erect the firewalls.

Within twenty seconds of retrieval, his virus would begin its silent, deadly work on the Safety Parameter Display System.

His computer chimed again. The upload was complete. Ejecting the data crystal, Pierpont returned it to the false heel, fit in the pin, and then slipped on and laced his shoe.

Thirty seconds later, as he headed down the hall, he passed a bank of windows that faced southeast. He saw a landtrain slowly inching its way toward the construction site. The landtrain must've passed through security without a hitch.

No turning back now. Pierpont pushed into a stairwell, heading for the control room.

In his office, his computer idled. Waiting.

# 51

**D**asha hadn't been there when they geared up, and she didn't show by the time they had to leave camp. When Fusilli asked, Yamada cut him off with a curt assurance that she would meet them two klicks shy of the facility, where they'd hide the hover and hitch a ride into the facility via landtrain. Only she wasn't there either, and none of the others—Conley, Bridgewater, or Abby—knew where she was.

This was a change in plans, and Fusilli didn't like it. Yamada didn't want to hear it. The others kept their mouths shut. And then there was no more time because the landtrain was coming, and Fusilli was either with them, or he wasn't. If he wasn't, and if he didn't stop yapping, Yamada explained *he'd* be happy to put a slug into Fusilli's brain right then and there—something he just might do anyway, on general principle.

Fusilli shut his mouth. Yamada obliged by not shooting him. When the landtrain slowed to a near crawl, Fusilli did as he'd drilled these many weeks. But he felt Yamada's eyes PPCing his back all the way.

By the time the landtrain groaned through the gate, Fusilli's arms were weak as shivery jelly, and pain scythed either side of his spine. His face itched from a slick of green and loam camo paint. When he licked his lips, he tasted salt and grease and track grit. He wore black, padded, fingerless gloves, but his palms were chafed, and his forearms cramped from hanging onto the train's steel axles. A stout leather harness was cinched round his waist, the thick steel clip hooked to the landtrain's undercarriage.

When they rolled to a stop at the cargo gate, there was enough light for him to make out that the laces of one guard's left boot were undone. Above the thrum of the engine, he heard the crackle and pop of gravel as guards circled the landtrain. He was seized with a sudden superstitious dread that if he kept watching those boots, the guards would feel his eyes, bend down, shoot him on sight. So he closed his eyes and focused on melting into the landtrain's grimy, oil-spattered undercarriage.

The crunch of gravel receded. For a long moment, there was nothing but the squeal of a metal hinge. Then the landtrain jerked and shuddered and began its slow progress across the facility's grounds. The light visibly dimmed as the landtrain curled north nearer the sea.

Yamada's voice in his ear: "Okay, people. On my mark . . ."

Fusilli eased his left hand toward his securing clip. Suddenly, the light cut out. Yamada said, *"Now."*

With lightning speed, Fusilli disengaged his clip and pushed off with his left foot, pitching himself clear of the train. The earth rushed at his face, and he twisted, taking the blow with his right shoulder. Rolling once, twice, three times, he skidded to a stop on all fours below the crest of a berm.

Behind him, he heard the far-off *whoosh* of the sea, and above, cargo cars scrolled by. To his immediate left, he spied Conley, tarantula-like in a black skinsuit, awkwardly scuttling for his position. Yamada, Abby and Bridgewater were to his right and also clear of the tracks.

Fusilli's gear was secured to a chest-fitted knapsack that he now snugged to his back. His rifle was a semiauto sniper with a sawed-off barrel. Besides the rifle, he wore a Skye Raptor 50-Mag semiauto in a cross-draw, forward-canted paddle holster riding his left hip. The Raptor was a blocky weapon with punch, muzzle flash and a *BOOM* that advertised. Tonight, sound didn't matter.

He joined up with the others, wading through grass that, on this seaward side of the berm, was wild and lushly overgrown. They skidded downhill as Yamada checked their position against a SatNav.

"Right around . . ." Yamada turned a circle. *"Here."*

They were far enough down the hill that when Fusilli looked back toward the crest, he saw only a green shimmering sliver of the building behind which they'd bailed from the landtrain. When his gaze swept seaward, however, he was startled to see that the perimeter fence on this side of the facility had collapsed in several places. He wondered why they hadn't come in there. Would've saved time and effort. But he held his tongue.

Abby found the access hatch buried in a mat of thick thatch. The hatch was secured with an old-fashioned padlock that Conley easily cut away with a laser torch. As Conley eased open the hatch, Yamada speared the opening with a razor-thin penlight. Fusilli made out ferrocrete walls and a set of stairs that vanished into the darkness. All power facilities featured a network of tunnels that allowed a team easy access to each reactor. The same tunnels also served as evacuation routes if above-ground evac was impossible. These tunnels serviced Reactor One and were sealed.

Shrugging out of his pack, Bridgewater tugged it open, then doled out positive pressure SCBAs. Each self-contained breathing apparatus covered not only the mouth and nose but the eyes as well. The tunnel system had no ventilation. Fusilli fitted his SCBA onto his face and then strapped a tank to his chest. He checked the tank's fill. The SCBA had enough oxygen to last five hours. More than enough time.

The mask's comm circuit fizzled. "Okay," Yamada said. He sounded as if he were talking through a ball of fuzz. "Figure fifteen, twenty minutes to get to the junction, then hour and a half, max two hours to burn our way into the adjacent tunnel. Another twenty minutes, and that puts us in the control room between zero-one-thirty to zero-two-hundred hours. By then, the virus will have shut down the power grid, and we make our move."

"What about Dasha?" Fusilli said. "Could the Dracs have her?"

"The kitchen staff knows everything," Abby said. "I'd've heard."

"Then where is she?" Fusilli asked.

"She's taking care of a couple loose ends," Yamada said.

"What loose ends?" In the next breath, Abby answered her own question. "God, she's doing something *else*, isn't she? She must be running some sort of side operation, probably when the power goes."

"Which won't happen unless we get into that control room. Bridgewater, you're point. Abby, you're next, then

Conley. And Shak?" Yamada's expression would've been coy, except for the teeth. "I'm right behind you every step of the way, buddy. Me and my nice shiny rifle."

# 52

*11 November 3136*
*2300 hours*

**A**bby was right. No one guarded a dump.

The Dracs were lenient when it came to the townspeople scavenging whatever they wanted: lumber, metal, chairs, tires, clothes and the like. It was just trash. The base generated about ten metric tons of trash a week. Waste was hauled in converted J-37s twice a day to a landfill three klicks south of the base. There was a lined landfill for organic materials, and an unlined sanitary landfill for inorganic wastes due south.

Dasha had joined a cluster of women and children around four o'clock at the sanitary landfill. Winter was coming, and sundown came early. By five-thirty, everyone had taken their booty and left. The landfill was deserted—except for Dasha, who crouched inside the kneehole of a metal desk that was missing two legs. The desk was a fresh discard from the noon run and, because of its size and weight, had tumbled from the mound's apex to the very bottom where it canted off kilter at the junction where garbage met dirt hard-packed by heavy transports. The perfect hiding place.

Now she waited, ears primed for the rumble of an approaching transport. Her pack lay at her feet, the clothes she'd been wearing tossed aside to mingle with the other garbage. After tonight, she wouldn't need them anymore. Instead, she wore a black, insulated skinsuit with gloves, a hood to hide her hair and, for the moment, a pair of NVGs.

As she waited, she tried not to think, found she couldn't avoid it. She wasn't worried about herself. Hard to believe that anything would go wrong. She and Yamada had anticipated all eventualities.

Except Shakir. A solitary tear spilled down her cheek, and she angrily smeared it away. What scared her was that with Shakir, when they made love—and it *was* love, not just sex—she saw herself reflected in his eyes, in the way he touched or held her. Then she forgot about who she'd been and started to imagine a future. Started to hope.

Hope was dangerous. Love wasn't allowed. And yet . . .

A far-off rumble shook her mind away from those thoughts. She was relieved. Too late for her. Just . . . too late.

The J-37s came single file, the twin shafts of the lead's headlights punching the darkness. There were two troopers per transport. Neither carried weapons. They were delivering garbage, for God's sake. The soldiers gossiped, their breath pluming in the chill. Meanwhile, squealing, telescoping twin hydraulic cylinders raised the beds. The Dracs' garbage tumbled out in crashes and bangs, and the splintery sound of ruptured glass. Off-loading took ten minutes, and the soldiers clambered back aboard.

Dasha tensed, shifting her weight to the balls of her feet. She wrapped her left arm through and around a strap on her green sack. She'd practiced this maneuver a dozen times over, knew how far she could run before the sack proved such a drag that she would lose her chance.

She let the first transport rumble by in a cloud of dust and diesel fumes. As the second slid past, she pushed herself to her feet, heaving the heavy sack onto her left shoulder in a one-handed carry. She surged for the transport. Her booted feet pounded the hard pack. Her breath came in harsh, jagged hitches, pushed out of her lungs with every step. Reaching deep, she put on a burst of speed, running as hard and fast as she could. The transport loomed. She lunged for its bed, felt hard metal cut through her right glove as she grabbed hold. Then she was torn off her feet. She swung like a heavy pendulum, the sack thudding against her hard enough that she nearly lost her grip. As the transport rattled and bumped over ruts and potholes, she hung on for dear life, braced on a narrow rim of metal just above the transport's rear axle. For a moment, she couldn't focus on anything beyond the wild gallop of her heart. Then the J-37 hit pavement, the ride smoothed.

She had to put the sack on one-handed to keep from being thrown. Now the second test of her strength: Reaching up, she wrapped her hands around the bed's rim and boosted herself. Her shoulders bunched and strained, and her bones tried to pop out of their sockets.

And then she was up, jackknifing at the waist as the sack's weight shifted, pressing her belly into metal. She threw up her right leg and then her left, and she dropped into the bed. She crumpled in a far corner, not to avoid detection—the soldiers couldn't see her—but in relief. The metal let out hollow bangs as the bed shivered on the transport's axles.

For the moment, she was safe. She would rest. Gather her strength and resolve. Change into a purloined DCMS uniform. No going back.

Her only prayer was that when the time came, Shakir's death would be merciful and quick.

# 53

### 0130 hours

Dirt pinged against Abby's face mask, spattering her hair and arms with grit. Startled, she flinched back and banged her head against the tunnel's earthen wall hard enough to see stars. Blowing out, she only succeeded in fogging up her face mask, and that made her grumpier still. That and her nose itched. "Goddammit, watch it!"

"Sorry," Shakir huffed. "Mainly clay . . . harder to dig . . ."

This was true. The dirt fill occupying the nearly nine-meter space between this tunnel and the next was hard-packed and gluey with age and seepage. They'd worked in shifts, chopping out a tunnel with folding shovels. Abby was tired, but Shakir sounded like he was on the near side of exhaustion. "You okay?" she asked.

"It's just . . . hard to breathe in the . . . mask."

Not just winded. *Panting.* That wasn't right. They wore fitted headlamps clamped around their scalps, and Abby played hers over Shakir's face. She was shocked at how bad he looked. Shakir looked close to collapse. He was sweating so much that his camo paint was bleeding. His neck and forearms glistened, and his chest worked like a bellows.

"Hey," she said, suddenly concerned. She touched his chest. His tee was soaked and his heart banged against her palm. "Do you feel okay?"

"Headache. Air's getting . . . thick."

"Thick?" Then: "Oh, Christ." Dropping her tool, she fumbled for the gauge on his air canister. "Holy shit." She thumbed open their comm channel. "Tony, we got a problem here."

Yamada's voice came back. "What?"

"It's Shakir. I just checked his air. Tony, he's almost out!"

"Hell you talking about?"

"I'm talking about his *air*, what the hell do you think I'm talking about? His gauge says he's got another twenty, twenty-five minutes max."

"That's crap. Something's screwy with—"

Bridgewater interrupted. "Abby, does he have a headache?"

"Yes," she replied.

"Shakir, what about your chest?" Bridgewater asked, urgently.

"Hurts," Shakir managed. "Sharp, and I can't . . . get, I can't . . ."

"That's carbon dioxide," Bridgewater said. "Tony, he's running out of air!"

"Can't be," Yamada said. "I checked those fills."

"Tony, no one's blaming you, but he's going to suffocate! We've got to get him out of here. He'll be fine if we can just—"

"Hell with that. I need everyone to work."

"Oh, for God's sake!" In the back of her mind, Abby

wasn't so sure that Yamada hadn't engineered this. "Come on, Shakir, we're getting you out of here."

Yamada cursed as they backed out of the tunnel. As soon as his feet touched ferrocrete, Shakir, wheezing audibly, sagged against the tunnel wall.

"He's faking," Yamada said. "He's faking this shit."

"No, he's not." Bridgewater snagged Jerrar's wrist, counted silently, then said, "Heart rate's really up there, and his nostrils are flaring." Bridgewater tugged up Jerrar's sweat-soaked tee. "He's retracting, too. You can't fake this."

"Hell does that mean?"

"It means that if he isn't out of here soon, he'll die."

"Then that's too bad." Yamada's tone was cool now, detached. "We got a timetable."

Bridgewater stared. "What are you *talking* about? We're nearly through. Maybe, what, another meter? Between you, me and Conley that's plenty. You don't need all five of us, and once we set up the jammer, we won't have to worry about tunnel surveillance."

"No," Yamada said.

"Oh, for Christ's sake." Abby had had enough. Shouldering her rifle, she pushed between Yamada and Bridgewater, and knelt by Jerrar's side. "Come on," she said, looping his right arm around her shoulders and wedging her left shoulder into his right armpit.

"Sorry," Shakir panted. "Abby . . . I . . ."

"Shut up," she said, helping him to his feet. "Save your air."

"Abby," Yamada warned. "Don't make me . . ."

"Don't make you *what?* You going to shoot me, Tony?" She didn't wait for an answer. Instead, she staggered away as fast as she could, Shakir stumbling to keep up. She waited for a bullet or the sting of a laser, but neither came.

Then Yamada's voice seeped, mosquito-thin, through her mask's speaker. "He dies, you get your ass back here, you understand? Otherwise, you *watch* him and both of you keep outta sight."

"Yeah, yeah, yeah," Abby muttered, and clicked off.

She didn't think they would make it. Then she saw the entrance, first as a gray splotch, and as they drew nearer, she caught the *whoosh* of the sea through the open hatch.

She didn't think she was imagining it either, but the air was a little cooler. Shakir must've felt the same thing because suddenly he ripped off his mask and began gulping air.

She half-pushed Shakir up the stairs. Once he was through, he fell onto his back in the tall grass and worked at breathing. Exhausted, she collapsed beside him, took off her own mask, and gave her nose a good, long scratch. Eventually, Shakir's breathing slowed, and then he whispered, haltingly, "Sor-sorry, A-Abby. Sorry."

"No big deal." She looked out at all that black water. "Maybe just as well. We'll get the hover so when they come out . . ."

"No," Shakir interrupted. "I mean . . . I'm *sorry*, Abby. *Really*. But thank you."

"Oh," she said, turning back, "you don't have to thank . . ."

And that's when he hit her.

# 54

*0235 hours*

The high-pitched wail of a trumpet punctuated a jaunty, super-caffeinated, manically energetic swing tune. The control room supervisor was some kind of nutcase who had this thing for old-time jazz, swing and something he called "big band." All the music did for Pierpont was pulp his brain. The music was also loud—not shouting-at-the-top-of-your-lungs loud, but Pierpont wasn't sure which resonant frequency would be reached first: his coffee mug's or his eardrums'. Considering his run of bad luck, probably both.

Pierpont was monitoring reactor coolant levels, the depth of the water that flowed amongst more than thirty-six thousand fuel rods. This kept fission-generated temperatures within tolerance. So long as the flow of feedwater—water heated to steam that powered the plant's steam turbine and, in turn, the electrical generator—was constant, there should be no problems. So far, his system hadn't so much as burped, just as it shouldn't. All the excitement was yet to come: in twenty-five minutes, to be exact.

But Pierpont couldn't shake this really bad feeling. People in books or movies always screwed up, driven either by guilt or just plain dumb bad luck. His gaze nervously skipped from his workstation to a bank of six LCD status boards to his left. The control room was arranged in a horseshoe, with Pierpont and two other operators clustered at a central pod of workstations. Each operator was responsible for a specific system. Directly behind was the supervisor's workstation. The supervisor had both computer access and command override lockout capabilities.

He gulped cold, sour coffee. Damn it, the plan absolutely *hinged* on a precise timetable: commands Pierpont *must* enter that would then translate to a certain chain of events. Everything depended on the supervisor being unable to lock *him* out, and it had to be done *soon* or else . . .

*BANG!*

Pierpont jumped as the control room door flew open. Coffee sloshed on his khakis, but he only stared as three men with dirty green faces and wearing muddy camos burst in. But Pierpont's shift supervisor was already whipping around, right hand shooting for the alarm.

One of the men brought his weapon to bear. "Don't. Hands up where I can see them. You, you're in charge, right?"

The supervisor, his eyes buggy, swallowed. Nodded. "Who the hell are you? What do you want?"

"I'm your worst fucking nightmare." The man grinned: a wolfish, ravenous razor smile Pierpont knew well and which still made the hackles along his neck bristle. "And for starters, I want only one thing," the man added. "Kill the goddamned music."

# 55

Fusilli nearly lost it at the top of a hill. Mashing the accelerator, he crested the rise and then saw, to his horror, that the road took a sharp turn. In another second, the hover would bullet over the edge and into dead air, open space, certain death.

Fusilli jerked the wheel in a fierce, hard right. The hover slewed wildly; the rear bumper lipped the drop-off. Instantly, the hover's computer howled a warning as the ground fell away, leaving the hover nothing to push against. The hover popped, and Fusilli caught a sudden glimpse of a starless sky. Then the hover stabilized, and Fusilli gunned it.

He'd planned to kill Abby. He'd planned to kill her silently, the same way he'd surreptitiously bled his oxygen little by little. But after he'd knocked her cold and bent to break her neck cleanly, swiftly—he couldn't do it. He wasted ten precious seconds staring down at her soot-smeared, war-painted face. Then he'd stood, fished out the keys to their waiting hover—and let her live. Knew it was a mistake, but did it anyway because she'd been kind, compassionate. That counted for something now in a way it hadn't before.

Bleeding his air was a calculated risk, even stupid. Yamada might've let him die or simply killed him outright. Fusilli risked it anyway because he'd run out of options. Even with his rifle, he could never kill them all. And maybe he wanted to atone. For Liz Magruder. For Compton. For a lot of things. So he'd gotten away: climbed over that dilapidated fence, picked his way halfway down to the beach before ducking around and running for the waiting hover two klicks away.

What Abby said as they'd descended those stairs into that dark, awful tunnel must be right: a two-pronged attack.

There was no other explanation for why Dasha wasn't with them. But Abby didn't have it all because Fusilli had been with Dasha that night in the woods, and only *he'd* seen those sacks.

Yes, Yamada would storm the reactor room. Fusilli knew Parks would mobilize a response *quickly*—just as Yamada *knew* he would. *They'd* drilled through the scenario over and over again. So Yamada was *expecting* a response, maybe even set up the means by which Parks would know something was going down. Yamada *needed* this diversion—because the reactor was *not* the primary target.

Ahead, the horizon glowed amber, and Fusilli was close enough to pick out the regimented phalanx of bright lights that demarcated DCMS Biham Command. At the sight, Fusilli felt an unexpected pang of . . . what? Relief? He gripped the wheel, felt his knuckles strain against his skin. Yes, relief, and a crazy kind of hope that he still had time and no one else would have to die.

Because he now knew with blinding clarity what Dasha planned.

He had one shot, one chance.

Those sacks.

The woman he loved. A woman who knew fission and reactors and all things nuclear.

A woman who knew how to make an atomic bomb.

# 56

### 0236 hours

The jazz cut out in mid-blat. The sergeant put a finger to a bud nestled in his left ear, cocked his head, and listened. Then he keyed open a command channel and said, "That's a go, sir."

Parks's voice came back as a whisper. "Wait for it."

\* \* \*

"That's good," Yamada said as the music died. His weapon was still trained on the supervisor. "Now, there a way to bring up the feed from the holocam in that hall out there? I want it right over there." Yamada hooked a thumb over his shoulder. "That center screen up there, okay?"

The supervisor swallowed. "I can do that."

"Good. Just in case. Wouldn't want to have any unexpected visitors. *And*—" Yamada zeroed the bore of his rifle on the supervisor's forehead. "I know which button is the alarm, okay? So, do us both a favor. Don't slip."

Grimly, the supervisor jabbed controls, and the image of the outer corridor shimmered into focus. "Nice," Yamada said, studying the picture. Then he jerked his head at his men, and they took up their positions.

Conley drifted left. Bridgewater flanked Yamada's right, opposite the only point of entry into the control room. He now had a clean shot not only at all three engineers but at anyone who might try to come through. That door was a natural bottleneck, and there was only one hall that led to and from this wing. Their jammers had prevented building security from detecting the trio as they emerged from the tunnel through a false-fronted panel located in the holocam's blind spot. Even if they had been detected, the first security guard to cross that threshold could be cut down in an instant.

Yamada said, "Okay, everyone just do what I say, isn't anyone gonna get hurt. You," he lifted his chin at the supervisor, "step away from that desk where I can see you. Back up against the wall, hands behind your head." As the supervisor complied, Yamada turned to the three engineers still frozen in place at their workstations. "Okay, I need one of you . . ." He looked them over then aimed a forefinger. "You. What's your name?"

"P-Pierpont." The quaver was real. "Justin Pierpont."

"According to the seating chart," the sergeant said, "Pierpont's on the supervisor's left."

"All right, that clinches it," Parks said. "We're a go, people. Remember, contained bursts. We can't fry those circuits. Let's move."

\* \* \*

Yamada nudged Pierpont's neck with his rifle. "Okay, Slick, here's the plan. I want you to cut power to that Drac base."

This was not what Pierpont expected. "Pardon me?"

"You got a problem with your hearing, Slick?"

"Uh," Pierpont said. He was thoroughly confused. This wasn't the plan. In less than ten minutes, that virus would go active. Then he'd be dead meat because *he* wouldn't have done anything to account for why things would start happening. "I . . . it's not that simple. The only way to cut power is to scram the reactor or cut off the water pumps."

*"Pierpont,"* the supervisor said, "what are you—?"

"Shut up," Yamada said, without turning around. To Pierpont: "What happens if you cut the pumps?"

This was more like it. "Cut the pumps, there's no feedwater for steam or coolant, and that's dangerous. Scramming the reactor is safer."

"Okay then, Slick. Here's what I want you—"

Yamada never finished the sentence. A dart of laser fire zipped from above and speared Conley's chest. Screaming, Conley reared back. His rifle spat a tongue of orange flame, discharging with a deafening *boom!* The air was immediately saturated with the stench of spent cordite and burnt pork.

Pierpont just had time to see a trio of men—one of them a grizzled giant with a salt-and-pepper beard—drop from the ceiling screaming: "Down, down, down, everybody *down!*"

The other two engineers hit the deck—but not Pierpont. The next thing *he* saw was the *O* of Yamada's rifle.

At the first shot, Bridgewater dove for cover. He leapt right, dropping into a roll that carried him behind the supervisor's workstation. He came up on his knees, and as he brought his weapon to bear, movement flickered out of the corner of his left eye. He tore his gaze off Yamada just long enough to see that the supervisor gripped the business end of a laser pistol.

Yes! Bridgewater sighted down his rifle at the same moment, and then he and the supervisor shouted, in unison, "Freeze, *freeze*—!"

\*     \*     \*

For Tony Yamada, it was like being in the eye of a hurricane. He understood instantly that he'd been betrayed, had known it as soon as Conley took that first shot and not Bridgewater, who was much closer and an easier target. He had time to comprehend that as perfect as their plan had seemed, they'd forgotten about air ducts. They had not thought of them because with their jammers, security should not have been alerted to their presence. Yet, somehow, they *had* known, and worse. He knew that the men dropping from the ceiling, like spiders on invisible tethers, were DCMS.

In less than a heartbeat, he saw it all, understood exactly what it meant, was conscious of the weight of the rifle in his right hand and the drag of a sidearm at his hip. And yet triumph thrilled through his veins.

Because he *still* knew something they didn't.

"See you in hell, Slick," he said to Pierpont. And then he drew his pistol and jammed the muzzle beneath his chin.

*"Tony!"* Bridgewater screamed, reacting first, understanding the danger, starting up from his shooter's stance. "Tony, for God's sake, *NO!*"

# 57

**0245 hours**

**"W**hat do you mean *Chu-sa* Parks is off base?" Fusilli shouted. *"Where?"*

The MP, a lieutenant, suppressed a sigh. "I'm not at liberty to say, ah, *Tai-i*—" His eyes flicked to a noteputer. "Fusilli? According to our records, sir, you're not even attached to this command and I—"

"My God, man, haven't you been *listening?*" Fusilli looked like he was about to start ripping out fistfuls of hair. "There's a woman on base with a *bomb!*"

"Sir, I don't know you. Your retinal scan matches that

of Captain Wahab Fusilli, but a scan can be faked with an appropriate prosthetic."

Fusilli stared, incredulous. "Faked? For God's sake, I'm trying to save your goddamned life, you moron! What do I have to do, stick a pencil in my eye to convince you that I am who I say I am?"

"I need the appropriate paperwork, sir," the MP persisted. "Or someone who can vouch for your identity. Failing that . . ."

This time, *he* was the one cut off. "Someone to vouch for me?" Fusilli said. "Fine. McCain. Get me Matt McCain."

## 0245 hours

"Oh, Christ," Parks said. Glistening, gelatinous globs of pink brain—Pierpont's—slopped his uniform. His beard felt squishy. He'd been closest to Pierpont when Yamada simultaneously put a rifle slug into Pierpont's head while aerating his *own* skull. In hindsight, Parks was lucky the slug hadn't drilled right through Pierpont and hit *him*.

Yamada didn't look much better than Pierpont. He lay in a slowly expanding pool of blood. A sluice of jelly-like brain, pulverized bone, and singed hair sloshed over linoleum as if his head had been an overripe cantaloupe smashed against the floor.

The control room supervisor—a DCMS sergeant—said, "I'm sorry, sir. He was just too fast."

"Not your fault. No way to know that he was a leftie, *too*," Parks said, though he wished *he'd* known. Two dead men, one of whom he'd hoped to interrogate, had *not* been on the evening's agenda.

"Yes, sir." The sergeant didn't sound convinced. "Sir, the control room operators?" He nodded toward a corner where they stood with a third man, whom Parks recognized as the shift supervisor his sergeant had impersonated. "They want to check their systems, make sure everything's okay."

"Do that." Parks turned to Bridgewater. "What about this woman you mentioned . . . Dasha, right? Her and this guy Shakir Jerrar, where are they?" As soon as Parks had heard the name, he knew Fusilli was still alive. *Shakir Jerrar* wasn't exactly unknown within the Combine.

Bridgewater was ashen. "I don't know. Dasha didn't show."

"Could she have suspected something was up?"

"I don't know. And Shakir, well, don't you have him?"

"Have him?" Parks frowned. "Why should we?"

"Well, I just assumed that you must." Bridgewater explained what had happened in the tunnel.

*Oh, Lord.* Parks listened with growing dread. *No, he can't be dead. Not when we were* this *close to bringing him home.* When Bridgewater finished, Parks said, "So what happened then? To this . . . Abby woman?"

"When she didn't call in one way or the other, I think Tony assumed that she was pissed, and Shakir had made it. Otherwise, she would've hustled back." He told Parks the location of the hatch through which they'd accessed the tunnels, then added, "I guess I assumed your people must have taken them. If not, then they're probably still there."

"Well, let's find out." Singling out two men, Parks rattled off orders and added, "Remember, they're armed, and at least one of them may not be real happy to see you."

Bridgewater's eyebrows crinkled. "One?"

Parks was saved from a reply when he caught sight of a third man clumping into the control room. "Sir Eriksson," he said, and extended his hand. "Thank you for this."

Eriksson merely glanced at Parks's hand, then said, with a revulsion he did not disguise, "You're thanking me?" His face was florid with anger, and his rime of white hair stood out like a gauze bandage wrapped round a wound. "You gave me your assurances that you would use all caution."

*You pompous, self-righteous jackass, you think* we *pulled those damned triggers?* Perhaps this was uncharitable. Had he been in Eriksson's shoes, *he'd* be tempted to lead a few resistance movements himself. But they were not equals, and like it or not, Eriksson would have to live with the fact that he was one of the conquered.

"Sir Eriksson, I know that coming to us after your man Bridgewater here gave you the gist of what Yamada and his cell planned . . . I know that was difficult. For what it's worth, I believe you did the right thing. No one could've predicted Yamada would kill himself *and* his inside man."

Eriksson drew himself up. "On the contrary, it was perfectly predictable for a man like Yamada. He wouldn't want to leave any witnesses behind."

To Parks' surprise, Bridgewater said, "Beg your pardon, but it doesn't make sense for Tony to kill himself *and* a man he'd *already* betrayed. What for? Probably Tony would stand up to interrogation, but I'll bet he figured that Pierpont wouldn't. Tony killed Pierpont so you couldn't talk to him, and Tony killed himself because . . ." Bridgewater paused and then said, as if he'd just now had a revelation, ". . . living didn't *matter*."

Parks and Eriksson traded startled glances. "Say what?" Parks said. "What . . . ?"

*"Colonel!"* A corporal standing alongside the operators' workstation called. "Sir, I think we've got a problem here." As if to punctuate his words, an alarm suddenly whooped, and a bank of lights flashed from green to bloodred.

"What is it?" Parks rasped, but the operator didn't look up. Instead, the man hunched over his computer, his fingers flying over keys. Lines of urgent script scrolled in flashes of amber and blue over the operator's computer screen.

"Status!" the shift supervisor barked. Pushing Parks aside, the man threw himself at an adjacent workstation. "Has the automatic trip engaged? What about the steam turbine?"

"Negative, negative! Turbine has shut down, but that's a negative on the magnetic field!" the control room operator said. His tone ramped up a notch. "Field reads fully operational! She's not scramming!"

"Switching to manual override!" The shift supervisor banged out commands. "What about now? Has the PORV vented?"

"No effect," the operator said. "Pilot-operated relief valve has *not* opened, and magnetic field has *not* disengaged! Control rods are completely exposed! Pressure's spiking! I read two-two-five-five psi and climbing! Fourteen seconds since turbine shutdown!"

"Will somebody *please* explain what's *happening*?" Parks roared.

"It doesn't get any more basic than this, Colonel," the supervisor said grimly. "We're on our way to a meltdown."

"Meltdown?" Parks rapped. The supervisor had cut the

alarm, but both he and the two operators had leapt into action, barking out commands and stats that, to Parks, were gobbledygook. But the way every indicator light was flipping red in an accelerating cascade, he figured a meltdown must be pretty bad. "What the hell's a meltdown?"

"Exactly what it sounds like," the supervisor said without looking up. He rattled off a string of commands, didn't like what the computer said back, swore, spat out more. Waited for the computer to come back at him. "If we can't stop it, that core is going to melt, literally."

"How?"

The supervisor rattled through the basics then said, "The system's designed so that the pilot-operated relief valve can vent steam. Or the reactor scrams: The magnetic field disengages and the fuel rods drop back into the reactor core and stop nuclear fission. But even if you scram, there's still residual heat, and that has to go somewhere. That's where emergency feedwater pumps kick in, but they're not. Nothing's working, and that reactor's still going."

"Meaning what?" Parks asked. "Are we talking a bomb here or what?"

"No. But just as bad. All the remaining water is turning into steam, and there's no way to vent it. Between that and the core literally melting . . . we're talking an explosion. It's going to rip this complex apart, and when it does, it'll spew radioactive contaminants into the atmosphere."

*What Bridgewater said: Yamada killed himself because living didn't matter.* Horror blasted through Parks like a raw wind. "How long?"

"Ten minutes," the supervisor said, "and counting."

# 58

"McCain, we've got to find her before it's too late!" Fusilli said.

"And I'm hearing you. The problem is it's a big damn base." McCain turned to the MP, who'd wisely stepped aside. "How many men can we mobilize and how fast?"

"As many as you need and as fast as you want, sir," the lieutenant said. "But, like you said, it's a big base."

"Then we've got to figure out how she got on the base to begin with and fan out from there. You know her, Fusilli. How would she . . . ?" McCain broke off as his comm shrilled. He tapped open a channel. "McCain, go ahead . . . Parks, yes, I . . ." McCain listened, his features going slack with shock.

"What?" Fusilli demanded.

"I need *numbers!* How bad? How *far?*" Parks grated.

"Bad enough," the supervisor said. "Assume an immediate ten klick radius, enough to contaminate your base and the outlying suburbs south of here. Depending on the wind, the debris could spread for kilometers. But the prevailing winds are south, Colonel, they're *always* to the south. So when this reactor goes, every man and woman on your base will receive a lethal dose. And there is nothing we can do to stop it."

Parks didn't need any more than that. "McCain," Parks said into his comm, "you've got less than nine minutes to get as far west as you can. Evacuate the base, and I mean now, mister, *now!*"

"No, they're *wrong,*" Fusilli said. "Why bring a bomb *here* if you've already set up *another* explosion that will do the same thing?"

"Insurance? Or maybe they just hate us real bad. I don't know, I don't care, and I don't have time to argue. Lieutenant! You heard the order. Get your men and get our people out of here! *Go!*" As the MP dashed out, McCain started after, talking into his microcomm: "Sorrel, this is McCain! Emergency evac! Load up our patients . . . Yes, *all* of them, and right *now!*"

Fusilli grabbed McCain's arm as the doctor swept by. "McCain, please, *listen* to me! Don't you see it? If we're evacuating, there's chaos, confusion. She'll go wherever she wants. *Dasha's* the threat, I *know* she is. You have to stop *her*, or we *will* die."

McCain shook free as the first alarm klaxons wailed. "Sorry, Fusilli, but I can't take the chance that you're wrong." And then he was out the door: "Sorrel, you copy? Five minutes, or we're all *dead!*"

The alarms were like a tidal wave, curling, redoubling, then crashing over the base, saturating the air with a primal force that was brutal, final. Irrevocable. Dasha was the eye of the hurricane, an island of calm in the midst of the storm. She walked amongst and through them all, not a soul challenging her: this woman, in a DCMS uniform, with hair red as a river of blood and Death as her escort.

*Like a ghost.* She felt as if her body were already evaporating like a cloud beneath a hot sun. *I'm gone, a dead woman walking. I was a fool to believe that it could be any different, that this moment isn't what I've been hurtling toward. This is my destiny . . .*

And then she looked up—and Shakir was there.

For Fusilli, everything dropped away: the alarms, the roar of people movers, the swirl of personnel who did not notice this woman or him. Everything. Except. Her.

Her own words had led him, what she'd said one night in his arms: *We're not disposable. We're not garbage.* But if a woman were going to throw her life *away* . . . It was a chance he took, and now here she was.

*Please, God, please, don't make me do this.*

"Dasha." Somehow, he'd drawn his weapon, because the Raptor was in his hand. "Don't make me choose between them and you."

She was very pale and deathly still, her hands at her sides, the pack still on her back. "Why aren't you running, Shakir?" Her voice was flat, a little dead already. "Why aren't you trying to get away?"

"Because I know the reactor's a hoax. It will right itself. It's just a diversion, a way of keeping everyone's attention elsewhere."

"Except yours." Her eyes were liquid and very large. "You're one of them, aren't you?"

"In your heart, you know that's true. But I can't let you kill all these people."

"I don't care about them. I don't care about them any-more than Sakamoto's men cared about unexploded ord-nance in a playground where there were children. *My* children. What I do now, I do for *them.*"

"Dasha, your children are dead," he said. Her eyes flut-tered, as if he'd slapped her face. Tears spilled down her cheeks, and he wanted to weep with her. "But *I'm* here now. Please, give me the pack."

"At least tell me your name." Her voice was watery. "Your *real* name."

"Fusilli," he said, wishing that this were not so. "Wahab Fusilli."

She nodded. Then her thumbs hooked the straps of her knapsack, and she shrugged off the pack. "Thank you for telling me the truth."

"But that's not all the truth I have to tell," he said.

"No?" She smiled faintly, a little sadly. She was on her knees now, her fingers working the straps. "Does it mat-ter now?"

"Yes, it does," he said. His eyes stung with unshed tears. "It matters because *I* matter, and so do you. Dasha, would *love* stop you?"

She stared at him. "No. You forget. I loved my children."

"But they're dead, and I'm here, and I *do* love you. I've waited for a place to call home all my life, and now I've found one with you. Please, Dasha." His eyes filled, and her face wavered and fractured. "Don't take that from me. Don't make me choose."

"*Make* you choose?" she asked. He could see the bomb now, the red smear of a digital readout. Just waiting for the flick of a rocker switch or the press of a button. "Whatever you do now, it will be because *you* do it even if or *because* you love me, and for no other reason." She paused. "I love you, Shakir. But I can still let you go—because this is *my* choice."

She reached inside her pack.

They detected Fusilli's transponder signal two minutes after the reactor didn't melt down. McCain and a trio of MPs found him three minutes after that: on the ground, cross-legged, head bent. A woman's body cradled in his arms, her blood seeping into his clothes and the dry earth. His diamond stud was clenched in his left fist, and there was a pistol, still warm, in his right. An open pack sat to one side, the digits on a readout fixed at *5:00*.

McCain knelt. Gently, he eased the pistol from Fusilli's nerveless fingers. "Fusilli?" He put a hand on the man's shoulder, and he felt a tremor shudder through Fusilli's body. "Wahab?"

Then, slowly, as if waking from a dream, Fusilli raised his head, and McCain was moved with such pity that he felt like crying, too.

"Take me home, McCain," Fusilli said. His face was wet. "Take me home."

# PART SEVEN

## *Uchikomi:* Invasion

# 59

**T**he best part about coming back from the dead is the look on people's faces. The bad thing is you get a pretty good idea of who's really not thrilled to see you. Like the Kitten: She was *not* a very happy camper. On the other hand, seeing as how her patron tried to disappear me? Tough shit.

After I scraped him off the ceiling, Andre wanted to know each and every detail: how those thermobarics took out those caves; how Viki was lucky enough to find that little hollow above the sand. I don't want to think about what would've happened if she'd been out in the open. Probably like those guys in the Tamerlanes, who shot right past us after Kamikuro braked, and who ended up buried under who knows how many kilos of rock. When Ito's DropShip showed up right after, that was the whole shooting match. Pretty much. Kamikuro-*san* will have some scars, just like me. My hands mainly. But that diacetylsilicate sand really did a number on Ito. Still in the hospital on a respirator. His lungs took a beating from all that hot gas.

So, yeah, Toranaga: I'm not forgetting.

Then it was Andre's turn. He filled me in on Biham and the other border worlds. For now, we've essentially shut down these resistance cells, and Sandoval-Groell, if its him . . . we'll deal with him sooner or later.

As for how Fusilli came through, I was surprised. Fusilli never struck me as entirely being with the program. I feel bad now for doubting him. Andre's brought him back, keeping him close for now. That's a good idea. Beyond the medal he'll get, we all owe Fusilli. He saved a lot of our people. But, my God, what this must've cost him.

Of course, I got an earful about the Kitten. (Andre made

me watch that sim twice; he's *still* tickled about killing her ass.) Theodore's on Deneb Algedi, getting ready for an assault on Altair. I'm more than okay with Theodore's part in this. Plus, you have to hand it to the Kitten. She *has* gotten things ready to go, and on time, too. We'll launch on New Year's Eve. As Andre said, it'll be a hell of a New Year.

Ah, and *speaking* of new:

"He's O5P," Andre said. "Emi sent him. He checks out. His ID and authorization codes are legit. I think you need to hear what he has to say."

The weirdest thing, when this man walked into the room . . . I had this strange sense of déjà vu. Like I *knew* him. Something about him, those smoke-gray bedroom eyes. And his body: well-muscled but lean, his movements economical yet graceful, a thick shock of black hair shot through with silver. A thin scar jagged through his left eyebrow and curled like a scimitar along his left cheek. A knife wound, perhaps. And his voice was very . . . well . . . *sensuous*. I know I sound like some infatuated teenager, but he had this *presence*.

He pinned me with those eyes. "My mission was reconnaissance on the Keeper's behalf, monitoring the Nova Cats."

"The Cats?" I sat straight up. Shot a perplexed frown at Andre who only shrugged. "Why?"

"I don't know, *Tai-shu*," he said apologetically.

"Okay." I had to wonder, though, how Emi knew about the Cats. I'd only told Andre. Unless . . . Bhatia? "Go on."

The agent hesitated. "I'm sorry, but . . . two Nova Cat mystics, a man and a woman, have been assassinated."

For a minute, I was so shocked, my mind wouldn't process. *"What? Where?"*

"Athenry and Styx. ISF *investigated*," he said dryly as he extracted a sheet of paper from a slim brown leather satchel. "This is their final report."

One stupid piece of paper and five measly lines that read more like a kindergartener's idea of a detective holodrama: *Nova Cat Mystic Tanaka murdered. Nova Cat Mystic Hisa murdered. Bodies brutalized. Agents(s) unknown. Reasons unknown.*

"That's *it*?" God, I was so angry, I wanted to tear the

stupid thing to shreds. "Two mystics are *butchered*, and that's *it*?"

The agent nodded. "There's been no forensic analysis, nothing. Bhatia hasn't seen that yet, but I don't think he'll take it further."

"Well, that's unacceptable." I needed to move. I pushed back my chair and began to pace. "Do we have *any* idea who gave the orders?"

"Not exactly." The agent dipped into his satchel again and fished out another paper. "But there's something at both scenes the ISF conveniently overlooked."

I took the paper, glanced at it. "Dirt?"

"No, *not* dirt. *Sand,* actually, a very minute amount."

"So?"

"*So,* both mystics died where there *was* no sand. Not only that, but *this* sand . . . ."

It hit me. "Oh, my God." Now I concentrated on the report. I felt suddenly dizzy, sick—and yes, déjà vu all over again. "Diacetylsilicate."

"That's right. Until your experience on Shaul Khala, I would've said there was only one place in the entire Sphere you'd find that."

"The Internal Security College," Andre said. He looked grim. "Except we *do* know about Shaul Khala, and we know that Alzubadai broke off from the Saurimat, an assassin sect. Either way, we're looking at New Samarkand. So, either Bhatia or Toranaga."

"Or maybe both," the agent said. "I'll be happy to help in any way I can. I'm at your disposal."

"We could use the help," Andre said. "Even with Viki back and Fusilli, we can always use another set of eyes and ears."

"Well, I'm grateful for what you've done so far. You can stay with us as long as you want." I extended my hand. "Welcome aboard, Agent . . . ?"

# 60

He took her hand, felt the fresh ribbon of scar marring her flesh, and the frisson that skipped the rungs of his spine was so wonderful, he wanted to cry out the same way he had when he discovered that she was alive. Yes, *she* had drawn him out of his darkness.

*Because I have shed my prison, my own private pain, for you. I am the bearer of your soul; I am the god born of your* kami, *baptized in a mystic's blood.*

"Jonathan Yurei Kamimori. But, please, *Tai-shu* Tormark." He smiled. "Call me Jonathan."

# 61

*Deber City, Benjamin*
*Benjamin Military District, Draconis Combine*
*5 December 3136*

Chomie thought that this time around, at least, the room was nicer: warmer, a little dark, and not as sterile-smelling. As before, Emi—faithful, dependable Emi—was there, holding her hand. Clad only in a thin smock, Chomie lay on an examination table, the kind with a strip of paper over the vinyl.

Makoto Shouriki wore a white doctor's smock, one with his name done in red embroidery over the left breast pocket. "Excuse me, my lady," he said, as he gently drew up Chomie's gown to expose her belly. Then he squirted a cold gel on her skin. She flinched, and he said, "Sorry, but I need to use the gel so we can hear."

"It's all right. Just cold," Chomie said. She'd seen the baby on ultrasound at twenty-two days, had seen that tiny heart beating, but this!

Shouriki maneuvered what looked like a microphone over her belly, squishing through the gel, then pressing down a bit, trying to pick up any sound. As he did so, he closed his eyes and listened. It was a little as if he were trying to detect some faraway music. He moved the device once more, and then she heard it, magnified over a speaker: an almost indescribable sound, like the rapid *shushshush-shush* of water squirting through a tube.

Her child's heart, pumping blood. Chomie almost couldn't breathe; she didn't want anything to interfere. Yes, that was her baby's heartbeat, and so *fast*. "It's so fast," she said, suddenly fearful. "Is he all right?"

"He's fine." Shouriki smiled. "Like his mother."

Chomie was only aware that she was crying when she felt Emi dab tears from her cheeks. She looked up at her sister-in-law and squeezed her hand. "Thank you. I don't know what I'd do without family around, now that Theodore's gone. I'm just a big baby, I guess."

Emi's eyes twinkled. "Well, I hate to disappoint you, but in case you haven't noticed . . . that position's taken."

## *Yamabushi Retreat, Ogano*
## *Benjamin Military District, Draconis Combine*
## *10 December 3136*

The elder monk was perplexed. His face pruned in a frown. "I haven't requested new attendants for the coordinator's son. The Keeper usually advises me well ahead of time, so I may prepare . . ."

"We are most sorry." The shorter of the two monks bowed. "We share in your consternation. Yet we exist only to serve."

The monk harrumphed. He rattled the monks' papers again, but he knew what they contained. Everything was in order. As for *him?* Well, the nobility *would* have their way, and not even prayer could change that.

They found Ryuhiko busily turning a wood bowl blank upon a lathe. The coordinator's son preferred working in the open air, even in winter. Ryuhiko's breath came in white puffs. His two escorts—Jamon and another the elder couldn't call to mind—stood in attendance, bundled in woolen robes. Privately, the elder was most pleased by Ryuhiko's industriousness. After all, every monastery must earn its keep.

But when the elder told Ryuhiko of the change, he couldn't miss the look that Jamon and the other agent gave one another. Jamon said, "I've not been informed. Master, you are quite sure the *paperwork* is in order?"

"Of course." The elder proffered the papers, snapping them for emphasis. Jamon and the other agent turned the papers over in their hands. They murmured together but did not engage the replacements who stood in respectful silence behind the elder.

But then Jamon bowed. "It will be as the Keeper wishes. We with return to Luthien at once."

At that, Ryuhiko said, "But who will stand by as I make my bowl? You know I need help."

*"Tono."* One of the new attendants, older than his fellow and with viper-flat black eyes, stepped forward so smoothly he seemed to glide. "I have done some time with a lathe. Let me help. Then you'll see what a beauty we'll make."

# 62

**Kyusha-*class JumpShip*, Kurita's Pride**
*Deneb Algedi, nadir jump point*
*20 December 3136*

**T**heodore floated in his private quarters before a small portal. Beyond it, there was the eternal night of space. The stars had never looked brighter nor quite as distant. The night had eyes, and they were impersonal spectators to his drama. A final act?

*Stop this.* He braced a hand, his right, against a bulkhead. The metal thrummed against his palm, as if his ship were alive. His ship waited, gathering strength—as *he* should be doing instead of dwelling on mortality.

*The man who can imagine his end is already dead.*

Angry with himself, he said, "Resume play, audio only."

His computer complied, and Katana's voice picked up in mid-sentence: ". . . travel time to Altair is ten days. I wanted to reach you before you made your jump. If everything goes as planned, we'll both strike within an hour of one another on New Year's Eve. As Andre said, that ought to make for a hell of a New Year.

"But none of this would be happening if you hadn't stepped in, Theodore. I owe you more than I can ever repay. You know that you will always have my loyalty."

There was a slight pause, as if Katana were gathering her thoughts. When her voice came again, Theodore heard the emotion: "I am your friend, Theodore. You are the brother I've never had, and a man I will always respect. I will stand with you, Theodore, no matter what. Be well, my friend. Be safe. Good luck and Godspeed."

The computer whirred. Clicked. Went silent.

"Luck." Theodore's eyes fell to his left hand, those jittering fingers. "Luck."

## Chimeisho-*class Warship* East Wind
## *Deneb Algedi, nadir jump point*
## *25 December 3136*

Tormark was so taken aback that her mouth actually fell open. Yori waited her out as the very picture of serenity, of the good little soldier ready to take orders rather than give them—which she had in all but deed and enjoyed immensely.

*Well, too bloody bad. You owe me, and now I've come to collect.*

She'd debated about how and where to press her demands, and decided that Tormark's ready room aboard ship was best. More official that way, and while she knew she could push this through, there was no need to actually humiliate the woman. After all, Tormark had an invasion to launch, and it would not be in Yori's best interests to interfere too much.

She had an ulterior motive for choosing privacy. If things got ugly, she didn't want witnesses. Couldn't risk exposing any weakness or chinks in her armor to anyone who couldn't keep his mouth shut. Tormark wouldn't talk, though she might vent to Crawford. That Yori expected. But Tormark also would go by the book. She didn't have any choice, really.

Tormark closed her mouth with an audible click of teeth. When she spoke, her tone was just shy of deadly. "You want to do *what?*"

*Oooh, temper, temper . . .* "I wish to lead the assault against The Republic's southern base in the Aomori Mountains."

"Uh-huh," Tormark said. The muscles of her jaw worked. "That's what I thought you said. This wouldn't happen to have anything to do with the fact that, to the best of our knowledge, this base is larger and more heavily fortified? Quite a little prize, a nice feather in anyone's cap."

*Leaving you with a bee in your bonnet.* "I believe I'm within my rights. I am a Kurita."

Tormark made a disgusted sound. "Look, you simply don't have the combat experience. I know things are,"

Tormark searched for the word, "*tense* between us, but I've always given you your due. You saved my people's butts on Ronel, and I'm grateful. You updated our sims, you've given us troops . . . I know all that. But you're not qualified to lead that kind of assault, you're just not, and I don't care whose blood you've got where. Can you get that? I don't *care*. What I care about is the safety of my people, and I care about success. You'd be better off taking the northern base."

"I do not agree." Oh, a part of her understood that Tormark was right. Yet there was another voice in her brain that had nothing to do with conscience and everything to do with survival.

*Yes, you want to poke your finger in Toranaga's eye, not just hers. You pull this off, and he'll start worrying because you're young. You're a rising star, and you* are *a Kurita, and Toranaga would do well to treat you with a little more respect. Maybe even a healthy dose of fear because that is the cold hard calculus of war and survival—yours.*

Aloud, she said, "It is my right, and I claim it. Your command authority does not exceed mine in these matters."

Tormark's cheeks flamed copper. For a minute, Yori thought the woman was going to haul off and let her have it. Instead, Tormark floated closer, invading her space, choosing an attitude in microgravity that forced Yori to look up, like a child.

"Very well," Tormark said, looking down her nose. "Then, in exchange, I want *Tai-sho* Crawford back in my lance."

She didn't see how that would hurt. "Of course."

"Then I will take the northern spur of the attack." Then Katana stepped back and executed a stiff bow: subject to master. "*Gokouun o inorimasu, Sho-sho.*"

*And not Godspeed?* Yori didn't smile or return the sentiment. Instead, she said, "I will not require luck, *Tai-shu*. I am a Kurita, and that is sufficient."

The door to her ready room dilated, then swirled shut.

Katana let out a long breath. "And a big fat fracking Merry Christmas to you, too, sweetheart."

# 63

## Parsonage Airspace, Dieron
## 31 December 3136

Her *Union* smashed through the moisture-heavy, towering pillars like a monstrous bolo loosed from the hand of a giant. Gravity fisted Katana's body as the DropShip hurtled for the surface, pulling disintegrating streamers in its wake. Below the clouds, there was snow, but anyone watching would see the great glowing ball of her ship as an eerie, ghoulish second sun, its skin hot with the friction of a passage through a screaming atmosphere that sheeted like lava over heat shields baked into armor.

Yet, instead of the anticipation of the hunt, she felt an unwelcome finger of dread tickle her spine. She was sweating, too. Not a lot, but enough that the bridge's chill air coaxed gooseflesh from her damp skin. She suppressed a shiver. A little déjà vu, like she'd been here before. In part, she knew why. She stood behind the captain's chair, exactly where she'd been the day her *Achilles* had perished, along with all the crew except her.

And their situation was not normal. Under normal circumstances, she'd be in her *Kozo*'s cockpit, ready to charge with her three lancemates the minute the DropShip touched down. Katana had even toyed with the idea of a combat drop. But the weather deterred her—that, and the rather startling fact that *no one* had challenged them. Not outside the system, not when they'd passed Dieron's moon, not when they'd entered Dieron airspace. No one. At. All.

Helm sang out: "Altitude sixteen kilometers, Captain!"

"Maintain present course and speed," the captain said. She craned her head around with some effort, pulling against gravity. "Tactical?"

"That's a negative, Captain. I read no enemy forces on intercept."

"What about land-to-air defenses?" The captain was a little younger than Katana and seeing her first action, but Katana detected nothing but calm and assurance in her voice, with just a hint of steel.

"Checking . . . I read activity, but . . ."

"What is it?"

"Captain, it's weird, but there's no spike, nothing to suggest that anything's really active or trying to acquire." Tactical's eyebrows met in the peak of a frown. "It's like everything's *there* but idling."

"Maybe just waiting," Crawford put in. He stood beside Katana. Like her, he wore only what he'd require in his *Black Knight*: his cooling vest and shorts, his boots. "Could they have fortified in underground bunkers?"

Tactical said, "Before this storm moved in, we got some pretty reliable readings. We didn't pick up any underground pockets other than typical bunkers you'd use for shelters, and those don't look hot."

"Fourteen kilometers, Captain," Helm said.

Katana shook her head. "This doesn't tally. We've used their satellites to monitor their comm chatter! Everything says that they should be *right here*. So where the hell *are* they?"

"*Well,*" Crawford drawled, "there's another alternative."

## Leopard CV-*class DropShip* Singing Star
### *On final orbital approach above Aomori Mountains, Dieron*

"But you're not certain," Yori said. A flash of irritation jagged her gut, and she reeled in a sharp breath that smelled of astringent coolant and cold metal to calm herself before she could let loose with a snide comment or two. Oh, but this was just like Tormark, trying to throw more obstacles in her path! Yori had already been strapped in a full half hour, enough time to power up and begin running through her diagnostics. Her eyes drifted from her weapons console—her DI chugging through its routine—to the view outside her cockpit. Far below, she made out the antlike figures of a trio of their twelve 'Mech techs swarming around the legs of her lancemate's *Panther*.

She said, "Perhaps they're simply entrenched and waiting for *you* to come to them. Unlike you, we *have* met with resistance." *And you know that, too: What, you think the fighters that engaged my two forward DropShips were sims? You just can't stand that I've blasted them to rubble while you've not seen a scrap of action.*

"You're not listening." Tormark's voice was gnat-like and noisome, her frustration popping through Yori's internal speakers. "For the sake of argument, I'll grant that there may be troops waiting, okay? But the energy signatures are inconsistent with a large force, and we're practically on top of them. Could this be an ambush? Sure, but I think Andre's right."

"That they've redeployed here? I would have to agree with you, and we're more than ready for them. We have the more massive force," and she couldn't resist adding, "which we'd *agreed* would be required for this base and which I've already used. Or wouldn't you call a defensive strike force of five aerospace flights enough of a threat? They certainly seemed real enough to the captain of the *Dauntless*. As it is, I've lost the use of twelve foot platoons to the damage done to the ship's transit drive. Lucky for the troops, the hull breach was in the adjacent cargo bay, or else my fighters would be maneuvering around bodies instead of people movers." Leaving her an *Avenger*, a *Triumph* with another battalion's worth of troops and people movers that she'd deploy north and west of the base, and an *Overlord* with its thirty 'Mechs that would sweep a scythe of destruction south and east. With her *Union* punching into the bull's-eye of the base smack dab in the center of that canyon, not only would any fleeing troops be cut off north and south, but The Republic's troops would be caught in a squeeze play. Nowhere to run, no avenue except retreat, and she—*her* fighters, *her* troops, *her* lance—would be right there.

There was a moment's pause that Yori filled with the image of a furious Tormark going thin-lipped.

Then Tormark came back: "Fine. I grant that you've

seen much more resistance than we have." A sigh. "All of it, in fact, and that just proves my point. They've clearly redeployed to protect the base you're after. Now that you've blown through their first defensive perimeter, they're probably regrouping, and you have no idea where they are. You'd be much better off sending the *Avenger* in first. Combine that with three lances of fighters, now you're talking about plowing the road."

*You idiot, don't you think I've thought of that? Why do you think I commandeered a* Leopard?

Yori knew where this was going. Tormark would try to get her to wait. Tormark would join her in a cooperative effort. That's where this was going. Oh, yes. It was plain as a PPC burst on a cloudy day. She thought to grab hold of *her Dragon*'s coattails.

Well, Yori thought not. "It seems to me that you've overlooked three very important points. One is the weather. The weather favors you, not them. They have no 'Mechs—"

"That we know of," Tormark put in.

Yori rolled with it. "And the weather would only hamper an engagement further from base. Their people would be exposed to the elements. If they are forced to retreat, getting back will be twice as hard. They gain nothing by engaging you at a distance. But we have already seen action. We have recorded activity consistent with targeting locks. Our orbital surveillance confirms aerospace fighters in power-up mode on the tarmac of a physically separate facility ten kilometers northwest, and my plan already calls for dispatching aerospace fighters to provide a forward assist to my *Triumph*. We've detected towed artillery bracketing the valley, and I have 'Mechs deployed to the south . . ."

"Beyond the canyon. Beyond help and . . ."

Yori plowed through. "So you see we do know exactly where they are and what they are doing. I have anticipated them by deploying troops north and south to empty out the center where we will make our stand. We have the advantage of mobility, and an *Avenger* capable of both an aggressive assault and cover for my ground troops." She heard her slip almost immediately then decided that there was no need to pretend that these troops were anything but hers. "Our situations could not be more dissimilar."

She fell silent. Tormark said nothing. Yori's DI chirped

that her diagnostics were complete. Now all that remained was for her to communicate with the other members of her lance, a *Shockwave* and a lighter *Firestarter*, determine their readiness and then deploy her remaining forces: fighters first, then her lance, with the *Avenger* close behind.

Tormark said finally, "Let me tell you something. Every time I think about Tony Ito fighting for his life, I know that I'm mostly to blame, and I *did* my recon. Hell, we spent days in recon, figuring out exactly where to hit and why. We had inferior forces, but we had the element of surprise, and we'd figured out where people were hiding. Still, even with all that prep, the one thing that bothered me but which I never resolved was why the compound was where it was. That sand was a trap I didn't foresee even when it stared me in the face. The best way to hide something is in plain sight. This situation doesn't feel right. You're not here, but this is like a ghost base, and I can't believe that they've risked everything just to defend one base. Unless . . . unless the idea is to get you to throw everything in, commit to a full-scale assault."

"Which I've done anyway. Which I've had to do."

"Yes, yes, you've had to fight your way through, I don't have a banged-up DropShip or casualties. But this *isn't* right."

"For you," Yori said, deciding that she'd had enough. "I have all the indicators required to complete my assault, and I will launch. In your situation, yes, I would reconsider, and in that, we are of like mind. But we are not the same, *Taishu* Tormark, we are as different as night and day. I appreciate your concern, but I have an assault to launch, and a base to finish taking."

And then she added, as a one-two sucker punch: "Kurita, out."

"Well?" Crawford said. He'd heard only one side of the exchange. Wisely, Katana had chosen to don a headset. He knew from Katana's face, though, the way her lips had thinned to a gash, that Yori had just blown her off. Stupid: Crawford knew better than anybody the price one paid for assumptions. "What would you like to do?"

Katana slowly massaged her scarred right hand with her

left. "We're going to make sure before we commit. This setup is too perfect."

Crawford wanted to protest. He was spoiling for a fight like everyone else because Dieron had been a long time coming. Could Katana's experience on Shaul Khala have left her gun-shy? Or was that whole thing with the mystics still bothering her?

Then his gaze dropped to her hands, and the hatch marks of scars tattooing her flesh.

*Of course, it bothers her, you idiot. More than anyone, she's ultimately responsible for everything that happens on her watch.*

He looked from her hands to find her eyes on him.

"Not on my watch," she said, in a preternatural echo. "So, here's what we're going to do."

The last time Yori had done a combat drop was in training at Sun Zhang Academy. Then, she'd been terrified. Who wouldn't be? A thousand things could go wrong in transit. Today was different. Today her forces had already known battle, had punched their way through and were now engaged in an action that would loose her into this Republic stronghold just as surely as an arrow piercing a heart.

Her *Dragon* scythed through the air, cutting gravity's hold with two searing blades of superheated plasma. Her jump jets gave a throaty growl as they beat back the death that might claim her, and she felt their overwhelming power in the shudder that surged into her very marrow and made her heart seem to throb in unison.

Her prize unfurled below, a verdant carpet of evergreens intermingled with the jagged gray teeth of bare peaks that bit into a brilliant, azure sky. To her far right, a thin silver ribbon spooled east as a mountain river was diverted well away from the base which occupied the deep, broad well of a valley. She was pleased to see that the terrain was as depicted in Luthien's sim, with one very important difference. The data upon which that simulation had been constructed was old, pre-Republic. That bowl was what remained of the river that had not only been diverted but was diminished in width, speed, and depth by three-quarters.

The reason why was north. A curved, gleaming, bone-white ferrocrete expanse of a gravity dam wedged at a natural chokepoint between thick towering swaths of granite. Behind the dam, a once-modest lake was now a vast reservoir—what they'd estimated from recon as two hundred and thirty-five kilometers long and a maximum of twelve kilometers at its widest point.

Beyond the dam, she spied twinkles of laser fire, the emerald bursts from PPCs, like a million fireflies glittering over the surface in a way that might have been called beautiful. A milling black mass that was her assault force was closing in, flowing over the terrain like a wave of ants bearing down on prey. Even from this distance, she could make out the burning hulks of a Mars assault vehicle and two Demons, looking like discarded toys, with flames scorching their Republic blue to sooty ash. The blocky carapace of a JESII, its right rear track coughing black smoke, was struggling to retreat, and before her eyes, one of her S-7s screamed past the JESII, loosing a quiver of MRMs before hurtling away. An instant later, the missile carrier's racks pillowed in a series of catastrophic fireballs so intense and so searing the light hurt her eyes.

Yes, she had been right to do things this way, and now she was seeing the results.

*Plow the road, my ass. What the hell did you think I was going to do? Simply launch an assault with my one lance and a samurai bellow?*

Oh, there were obstacles. This wasn't going to be a cakewalk. Despite the fact that she had maneuvered her forces to engage The Republic and draw them out from their base, this combat drop was the most dangerous portion of her passage to earth. She and her lancemates—Katanga in his olive green *Panther* to her left, the tongues of fire from his jump jets pulsing in rhythmic bursts to control his descent; and, two kilometers beyond Katanga, the crimson and yellow *Firestarter* keeping pace with its heavier mate, the *Shockwave*—none of them would be as vulnerable to attack from below or encounters in the air than at this moment.

The ground was coming up fast. She was low enough now that the planet had lost its natural curvature and flattened. Below her feet, a new flurry of orange firefly twinkles danced and darted in bizarre, swooping patterns.

Pretty, under other circumstances, but she knew from the comm chatter bleeding through her internal speakers that the Blues had spotted them.

"Dragon Five Seven engaged offensive! Two bandits left two, nine klicks, medium!"

". . . one two tally, visual, press!"

". . . left, left! Dragon One Two, *break* left! Bandit *your* left seven, six klicks, low!"

Her mixed flight of three fast, very well armored *Sholagars* mated to three bullet-shaped *Lucifers* were pitted against two lances of *Tridents* and *Zeros*. The *Sholagars* were fast, twirling on their long axes like platters spun on edge, evading return laser fire from the flat wedges of the *Tridents*. She watched as one *Trident* broke right, rolled until it was nearly inverted and then pulled down sharply, hurtling nearly ninety degrees down and using gravity assist to increase its speed. A good strategy: The maneuver would spoil the *Sholagar*'s target lock as the defender accelerated and rolled, screaming into a tight nose-low spiral.

Ah, but her *Sholagar* did not disappoint. The pilot anticipated the moment that the *Trident* snap-rolled into the spiral. The *Sholagar* delayed his pull-down and then, as the *Trident* began his spiral, the *Sholagar* continued its level turn. The fighter rocketed to a point directly above the *Trident* and then began its own pull-down. The *Trident* lost visual as the *Sholagar* loosed an SRM. The missile dug a trough in the air, bulleting for the *Trident*'s right rear quarter then bursting into a cloud of hot orange and charred debris. Butted from behind, the *Trident* flipped end over end; the *Sholagar* swooped after. Laser fire battered the beleaguered craft, flaying through armor that boiled and bubbled.

A click in her helmet that coincided with the scream of an alarm signaling a target lock: "Yori-*san*! Bandit, bandit to your right! Look out!"

Heart leaping into her mouth, Yori jerked her attention away from the drama below to the sight of a fighter that her squadron had either not seen, or allowed to slip through. Not a *Zero* or *Trident*, but the arrowhead of an *F-94 Stingray*, closing fast. Before she could blink, the fighter let fly with spread of ten LRMs.

Her cockpit erupted in a squall of alarms. Yori had one

choice. Pivoting fast, she throttled back on her jump jets at the same instant that she straight-armed her *Dragon*'s right PPC. Her intention was to loose a molten blue gout that would batter the *Stingray* at its most vulnerable point: the ferroglass cockpit. Take out the pilot and neutralize further threat.

But before she could fire, gravity howled up from the planet's surface. It snatched at her *Dragon*'s sixty tons of endosteel and armor, grasped her 'Mech with greedy hands and yanked. Screaming, she plummeted toward earth, accelerating so fast that the red glow of crosshairs on her HUD's target lock fizzled out. Wind howled over her canopy, and her head ballooned, growing hollow as her vision grayed.

*Pulling gs, got to compensate . . .* She grunted, tried forcing blood into her head, but she felt ill, sick to her stomach, and she was rolling, she thought, her body riding a swell and . . .

A voice, cutting in on her command channel that somehow, miraculously, she heard over the wail of alarms: "Dragon One Two, padlocked, engaged offensive! Tally one, left eleven, one klick high!"

Another voice, in answer, steely calm: "Dragon Seven Three tally, visual, press."

What? Who? Her numbed mind pulled in the information, stitching the words together . . . Then blinding red streaks so bright they hurt her eyes flashed from left to right in her visual field. There was a moment's silence then a *boomboomboom!*

The missiles! In her panic, she'd forgotten, but where were they, who had they hit . . . ?

Katanga now, urgent, tense: "Yori! You're off center! It's your right arm! You've thrown off your center of gravity, your legs are splaying, and you're starting to roll! Do you hear me? Two *Lucifers* have engaged the *Stingray*! They destroyed five of the missiles, but you've got another five still on you, hang on, *hang* on!"

Gasping, she craned her head until she thought she was looking up, but something was wrong; it was like the sky was tilting because she didn't have to look far to catch the glistening streamers released as the missiles detonated harmlessly. Or so she thought. No secondary explosions followed, no scream of debris raining around her cockpit as evidence that the missiles had, in missing her, found their mark in Katanga. In fact, it was as if she were settling into a chaise lounge on a beach, stretching to get a tan . . . an absurd thought, what was wrong with her?

*No, no!* Grunting, bearing down, shaking away stars from her vision to force blood to her head, she blinked away from the edges of unconsciousness. She was off-center, falling fast, too fast. Her body felt as if she'd been poured into a vat of molten endosteel: heavy, gluey, unresponsive. Marshaling her will, using every scrap of concentration, she hauled on her *Dragon*'s right arm, pulling it lower, lower, lower until it had crossed her vertical plane . . .

*God, oh, God, oh, God, make this work, please,* please!

"Clear!" she managed through lips that felt macerated and torn. For the first time, she tasted the rust of her own blood. She didn't know the correct fighter lingo, and it didn't matter. She just had to warn them . . . "Clear, clear, firing!"

More comm chatter bleeding through, the sudden *BOOM* of detonations high above, and now—oh, God, could it get any worse? She spied multiple arcs of tracer fire swarming all around—and knew that the towed artillery they thought might be squirreled away along the canyon's rim were there. But if they were firing, and their distance was no more than a kilometer at best . . . !

"YORI!" Katanga screamed. "You're too *low!* Do you copy? Whatever you're going to do, do it, *do it.* Hit your jets, *hit your jets!*"

*NO!* She didn't bother searching out her altitude because she knew she'd run out of time. Marshaling all her will, she tapped out a single burst from her PPC at the same moment that she battered on her jump jets.

The jets came to life, thundering through the cockpit like the eruption of an angry volcano. The sensation was like being simultaneously slapped on the back while getting kicked in the gut. Bile, hot and sour and foul, roared into the back of her throat, and she gagged, coughing out air and a mouthful of blood. Her visual field suddenly swung drunkenly, like the slow righting of a bobbing yacht, and suddenly she caught a glimpse of green earth and gray rock.

Katanga: "That's got it, I'm with you! Hit it again, hit it!"

Banging out another rush of ionized energy from her PPC she jammed her jets to full power. This time she righted fast, almost too fast, and she barely had time to cut back as the view in her cockpit swirled. She saw green and gray and very little sky because she was that close to the ground. The gray rushed at her face, and then she realized that this was the western rim of the canyon. She recognized all those ledges, the ones in the Luthien sim, but she was too close to the rocks, her DI shrieking a proximity alarm as she angled her jets, trying to blast herself wide of the rock. As she passed, she glimpsed multiple flashes, like single fireworks going off one after the other, but then she felt the *bam-bam-bam-bam-bam* pummeling her armor, battering at her *Dragon's* right leg.

*Gauss rifle!*

Slugs shattered her armor plating, ripped at myomer bundles. Something gave with a metallic groan she heard in her cockpit, and then there was another, much bigger spark and flash—but from above. Crying out in exultation, she raised her sweat-stained and bloodied face and saw her *Avenger*, with a lance of fighters flanking right and left, release another blistering torrent of autocannons. The armor-piercing, high-velocity explosive shells hammered her attacker's position, pulverizing rock to rubble.

And then she was past, the battle still raging above. There was the sun at twelve o'clock high, spraying beams of light upon the stone canyon bottom, flattening her perspective, killing the shadows. And she was coming down fast, perhaps too fast, but no choice, no choice! She was only dimly aware that Katanga must be right above and to her left, but her frantic eyes searched out the altitude on her HUD. Those glowing digits whirring down, ticking out the seconds of her life, she remembered the foolish, seven-meter drop that had doomed her in a sim. She would *not* let that happen here, not here, not in the arena where she *must* win!

"NOW!" Grimacing in fear and fury, she throttled back, cutting her jets, praying they would cut out at the right . . . !

Her *Dragon* hit. She bounced against her harness then banged back into her command couch. Explosive bolts ignited beneath her undercarriage, jettisoning the now-useless jump jets. The chassis shook with the impact, and she could feel the heat practically bleeding through the deckplates of her cockpit. Sweat ran freely down her neck and arms, and soaked into the waistband of her shorts, but her cooling vest responded with a blast that made her gasp at the chill. And she saw the worst on her internal damage status screen. Those Gauss slugs had mangled her right lower leg actuator.

Then a blur of green to her left as Katanga touched down, his jets cutting out. Swinging right, she spied the *Firestarter* and *Shockwave* already down and moving in, and above were the *Avenger* and her fighters—blessedly, all six, including the two who'd bought her time and saved her life, transforming the canyon's rim to a cratered waste.

She was down.

## Parsonage Airspace, Dieron

"Pipe that back up to us again," Katana said into the ship's comm. She'd taken up position next to Tactical, her gaze intent upon the screen. Her flights of *Zeros* were neutral yellow icons against a green-grid schematic of the Blue's base. They'd broken the kilometer barrier above the base, and yet nothing had changed. No challenge. Nothing.

The lead pilot said, "Akira Five One cleared, float."

"Akira Five Two confirm, visual," his wingman replied, and Katana watched as the yellow blips spread laterally. With so much snow and no gradation in light, shadows were nonexistent, the horizon taken as a leap of faith in one's telemetry. What the pilots would do next—a low-altitude flyover of an enemy base—required a similar faith in the vigilance of the DropShip's captain.

Although she didn't doubt the woman's ability to provide air cover—indeed, she was the one who suggested the idea in the first place—Katana looked the question her way. The captain caught her eye, and nodded.

"We're ready," the captain said. "They so much as sneeze and they'll be picking autocannon slugs out of their teeth."

The next set of images flashed in a compartmentalized display on the bridge's main viewscreen. To the untrained eye, the images were a total whiteout. With her experience, though, Katana could now identify that they were looking down and then skimming over structures. Katana spied a row of low, long metal containers; she saw a flash of green. She pointed. "Trash bins. So that big rectangle's got to be the mess." She turned back to Tactical. "Ask them to go back and shoot those bins again."

"What are you looking for?" Crawford asked.

"See the way the snow's piled on the bins? This storm's coming in from the west. You can see snowdrifts behind the bins."

"So?"

She shrugged. "Let's see." They waited until the flight passed over the base again and the pictures flashed back up on the viewscreen. Katana peered at the ones of the trash bins. "Okay, what's wrong with this picture?"

Both Crawford and the captain inspected the picture, looked at another, and then the captain hunched her shoulders. "I don't see it."

"The drift in back. It's higher than the bin's cover. That means . . ."

"It can't be opened," Crawford said.

"Correction," Katana said. "It hasn't been opened in *weeks*. The one constant on a base: People gotta eat, and even if they eat nothing but ration bars, there's still garbage. If those bins had been in use, someone would've had to remove the snow. Otherwise, the lid's too heavy. And *that* usually translates into shoveling the snow to either side. But that snow is uniform throughout, with only the front that hasn't been hit by snow visible."

"So no one's been taking out the trash," Crawford said.

"Nobody's there," the captain said wonderingly. "No one's been on this base for weeks, maybe *months*."

"That's right," Katana said. "Nobody."


## Aomori Mountains, Dieron

She was wrung out and exhausted, and she hadn't even engaged in true battle yet. She'd slapped her DI to silence, just to save her sanity. She was so hot that it felt as if the waste heat from her reactor was bleeding into the cockpit. Her controls were smeary from a combination of sweat and her blood. She'd wiped her mouth with the back of her hand several times, and while the bleeding hadn't stopped, it had slowed. Her heart was still battering her chest, the sound thudding into the space between her temples. So she didn't catch it right away.

Katanga said, "The rest of those fighters bugged out. Those artillery batteries have stopped firing."

"Either they're out of ammo, or they're subatomic particles," Yori said. She faced east. The dam was to her left, and she saw now what she hadn't before: a high retaining wall added to redirect east the much-diminished flow of the river.

To her right, she saw that the *Avenger* had touched down, blocking a natural wide draw that was the only egress out of the canyon and from the base. Its troop bay doors were open, and men spilled out, scurrying to take up assault positions. As she watched, the *Firestarter* pivoted left, away from her troops, leveled its left arm and belched a fusillade of flame back and forth in a sweeping motion. There was a massive boom, followed by a fireball that merged with secondary explosions as munitions detonated. Debris flew on a pillar of combusted gases to rain in smoking bits of char and mangled, fizzing metal.

She swiftly reviewed her plan of attack. *She* would be slow, but the plan was still intact. With the combination of troops, the *Avenger*, and her 'Mechs, she would bracket the base north and south while her troops already down scourged the perimeter. Positioning her *Avenger* at the draw meant that any enemy troops left on base who tried to flee would have to get around the DropShip.

Translation: No way out.

Then Katanga again: "Would you double-check me on something? I think my thermal imaging is on the fritz. I don't pick up anything."

"What?" Her gaze skipped to her HUD . . . and then she frowned. Cursing softly, she initiated a short-range sensor sweep, her eyes snapping to her secondary viewing screen. She registered their 'Mechs as neutral icons; read their ID via IFF, but she waited in vain to catch even a glimmer of a reactor signature, motion . . . Yori swore again. "How can this be? For God's sake, we were fired on. We were *attacked*."

"Unless," the pilot of the *Shockwave* put in, "that was

all of them. They've thrown the kitchen sink to the north and south, which is what we wanted. Maybe that's why the fighters bugged out."

"Because there's nothing left to defend?" Yori didn't want to believe it. Why make it so hard to get down if there's nothing on the base of value? Even more bizarre: Why mount such a fierce resistance beyond the base? There had to be something here to justify the loss of life. No general stained the ground with the blood of her troops if there was nothing to gain.

*Oh, but I can understand that: When the fighter has nothing left, she becomes an engine of death, a kamikaze, destroying the enemy and herself.*

She knew she had that in her. She'd done it, even if only in a sim. Yet even a fighter as able as Julian had not understood why.

She waved a hand, and her *Dragon* followed suit, a sweeping gesture that encompassed the base. "There are buildings, there are *vehicles,* tanks, sleds, there are . . ." She broke off because that's when she finally noticed it.

The quiet.

Yes, she still heard the far-off rumbles and booms of the fight that was going on beyond this base, but that was dying as well, the frequency of explosions and the report of weapons more sporadic.

*As if The Republic's troops were all dead or out of firepower. Or gone.*

She jerked right, peering down that wide bowl toward the *Avenger.* The conflagration started by the *Firestarter* was still burning. She saw her troops, broken into squads, scurrying between buildings. But she saw no ruby lancets of laser fire, heard no battering of autocannon fire.

Then the *chu-i* in command of her infantry cut in: "*Shosho,* the base appears to be, well . . . *deserted.* They're like props on a stage. The buildings, they're *empty.*"

Yori closed her eyes. *This can't be happening. I've been tricked into chasing phantoms.* "What about those SM1s, and those sleds?"

A pause. "They're . . . *mock-ups.* They're hollow, like cut-outs."

"What the hell?" said the pilot of the *Firestarter.* His

cockpit swiveled, and though she couldn't see his face, Yori heard the scowl. "What's going on?"

His words had barely penetrated before Yori felt the shocks of three terrific explosions, one right after the other, their echoes overlapping, building and gathering. The vibrations and shockwaves shuddered up the legs of her *Dragon,* rattled her consoles. She looked back toward the *Firestarter,* thinking that the fire had spread, that another dump had gone up. But she saw only the one fire . . . and then she saw the *Firestarter* start back, its arms flung wide open in an imitation of the pilot's surprise.

And then his voice, hitching now with awe and then maybe understanding: "The dam, the *dam!*"

Yori spun left, her damaged right leg chunking a wide furrow from the rock. Then she could only gape in horror—

At the dam that no longer was. At the ferrocrete barrier between this valley and at all her men, who seemed to melt before her eyes. At the water barreling with the full-throated roar of something only heard in nightmares.

Yori screamed, "*Chu-i!* Get your men out, get them out, get them *out!*"

Bedlam broke out on the comm channel, voices and shouts and screams overlapping as her men swarmed for the *Avenger.* What must be trillions of liters of pent-up water and energy roared in an immense cataract, and because she and Katanga were closer, they were hit first.

Katanga gave a shout, and then Yori lost him as the water whammed her left side. A massive chunk of the dam battered her left leg. Her weight shifted, came down on her damaged right leg, and then she was flung off her feet, as if the *Dragon*'s sixty tons were nothing more substantial than tumbleweed in a tornado. Gasping, she jammed out her right arm to break her fall, but then a fresh gout of water smashed into her back, shoving her completely under the swirling tide. Instinctively, Yori threw her hands up to protect her face even though she could no longer see anything except the foamy, raging water. Her *Dragon*'s ferroglass crashed against something very hard, and then she was hanging from her couch, saved from falling into her canopy by her harness. Her breath caught in her throat as she waited for the canopy to shatter, the water to rush in and drown her.

Then her heart slammed back to life, and time started up again. The canopy was intact, and her systems still operational. Alarms wailed in her cockpit, and her helmet was filled with the dying screams of her men. The *Avenger* might have a few seconds grace, but that water was moving fast, and the ship's low-slung design meant the troop bay was open. They'd take on water, be submerged within minutes, if they didn't close up right now and get away! And *she* had to get upright, she had to get *out*, and she only had seconds to do it!

*All that water, it's going to rise fast, that's what the Blues counted on, drowning us before we can get out!*

Pushing back her fear, trying to block out the roar of the water *hooshing* over and all around, she wrestled her 'Mech to a kneeling position, and then she got a knee up, the left. "Come on," she urged, jamming her throttle forward. "Come on, come . . ."

The water pounded, tried to drive her down, and the titanium-steel bones of her *Dragon* groaned, strained as she fought to push to her feet. Another wallop smacked against her right side, and she gasped, heart in her throat as she lurched forward in an awkward stumble. Her cockpit *BAMMED* against something unyielding—and then she realized that the water had been so powerful, she'd been thrown against the base of the canyon's western wall. And that's when she remembered.

*Ledges! If I can just get my head above the water, even for a second . . .*

She couldn't see much other than rocks and water, but if she could get a handhold! She wrestled her joystick, and her intentions were transformed into movement as her *Dragon*'s right arm rose, the hand open, reaching, reaching . . . She felt a jolt as the metal came in contact with something solid, and she jammed the hand controls down, locking the *Dragon*'s hand actuators in place. The hand closed over something solid—and held.

No more time, go, go! Grimacing, she pulled herself up. She felt the *Dragon* push back the water even as the water shoved it left, trying to force her off her feet. She knew if she fell again, she would not get up.

"Please, please, *please!*" By now, she'd screened out everything, all the alarms—but there were no more shouts, none, they were all dead—and focused on hauling her 'Mech as upright as she could. She had no idea if she were succeeding, no way of judging which way was up except that there was rock beneath her 'Mech, rock in her hand, debris pummeling her *Dragon,* and water trying to sweep her. from her feet, trying to destroy her.

And then she broke the surface. It happened so fast, so unexpectedly that she was stunned. Water, roiling and black with churned earth and rock, swirled and broke over her canopy, and then she saw that she was looking up. There was open sky, and yes! There they were, those ledges. Maybe . . . !

Then, before she could think about it anymore, she reached down with both hands and yanked back on her ejection handlebar as hard as she could. Her canopy blew away with a sharp series of bangs as the explosive bolts detonated. She felt the jolt as the connections to her neuro-helmet instantly detached, the tug at her vest as her coolant lines separated, and then everything blurred as her couch shot up and away.

She looked back only once and for a brief instant at the water pouring into the open cockpit of her 'Mech that was still, miraculously, clutching rock and on its feet. The other 'Mechs and the *Avenger* were gone.

And then she jerked back, saw the ledge rushing at her face, wondered—too late—at its depth. In the next few seconds, her parachute would deploy, and she would either be able to guide herself to the ledge . . .

Or her body would burst like a blood balloon. Or she'd bounce back into the water and drown.

Or . . .

## 64

**Chimeisho-*class JumpShip* East Wind**
***Dieron nadir jump point***
***1 January 3137***
***Just past midnight***

"**T**hat EM pulse is ten minutes old, and I'm still not getting the correct identification code," Comm warned. She was young, just the far side of twenty-four. Yet when she twisted to look down at her captain, standing behind his command chair some ten meters below her station, she backed her warning with a firm and unwavering gaze. "I'd say from the pulse's rate of decay, they'll be through in two more minutes, max."

The captain nodded up at her. "Then let them come." He craned his head around his right shoulder toward Tactical, who sat strapped into a seat level with the command chair. "Weapons status?"

"Lasers show ready, *Tai-sa*," Tactical replied. When he snapped his gaze from the console to his captain, the movement sent tiny shimmering orbs of sweat expanding in a slow-motion halo. "Delta Squadron reports they are at optimum distance to intercept."

"No one twitches until I say so," the captain said. "Understood?"

Tactical wet his lips. "All stations report battle ready and . . ." He broke off at the warble of an alarm. "Here they come, Captain, here it comes!"

"Ready to fire on my mark!" The captain turned his fierce gaze toward his viewscreen. At the first EM burp, they'd immediately retracted their solar sail and repositioned the ship to face the jump point head-on, bringing their forward ER lasers to bear. Now he saw the point where the unknown JumpShip was winking into existence:

how the space gathered, bunched, puckered, then reddened to a bloody smear . . .

*Here it comes.* Without realizing it, the captain held his breath. He raised his right hand, ready to give the order, and convention be damned! If these were Blues, and they fired on him, well, he'd show them some heat! *Here it comes . . .*

Space twisted, convulsed and then ripped a seam from which rocketed out . . .

The captain's breath left his lungs in an exhalation of horror and disbelief. Someone somewhere let out a muffled cry, something between a moan and a scream. But the captain didn't turn around. Couldn't tear his eyes away.

"Oh, dear God," he said. "It can't be."

## January 3137

Theodore's WarShip was barely recognizable. The gnarled hulk was twisted along its axis, like the business end of a corkscrew, but then telescoped back upon and within itself, as if the ship had accelerated, passing through some kind of wringer before striking an inflexible barrier head-on. Portions of the ship's armor were simply gone, as if the ship had been skinned, and places where chunks of the hull had blown out revealed a tangle of bulkheads and structural supports. No portion of the ship had escaped unscathed, and what remained of its decks was gutted, riddled and pockmarked with scorched blast craters like the irregular holes in a slice of Swiss cheese. Others looked as if they'd been transformed into runny, molten red-hot lava that, once cooled, solidified into a congealed, amorphous lump.

Astonishingly, the only portion of the ship Katana did recognize was the thimble-shaped field-initiator that looked remarkably intact—as if whatever had mangled the ship intentionally spared that section.

*And sent the ship back here to make sure we saw it.*

"And the computer-activated jump drive was the only functional system?" Katana asked. It had taken her eight days to reach the jump point, even pulling max gs. When the news first crackled over her command channel, her immediate impulse was to launch a rescue mission. She hadn't, though squelching the impulse had taken all her will. Instead, she'd mentally prepared herself for the worst. Now, looking at the wreck that had hurtled through ten days ago, the worst she'd imagined wasn't bad enough. "I can't even tell where the bridge is."

"It's been pushed to the opposite side. You can't see it from this angle," the captain said. He looked gray, as if he hadn't slept in years. "Frankly, I'm amazed that the drive functioned at all. With all this damage, you'd think that would knock out the drive core altogether. As it was, the core developed a helium leak within fifteen minutes after the ship reappeared. It's dead now, and the fusion drive's completely hydrogen-depleted. I had repair crews rig external thrusters to keep her from drifting, then got my people working her around the clock."

"Escape pods?"

The captain's chief engineer, a reedy man in a rumpled green jumpsuit said, "I thought they'd been jettisoned, but then I found two still in their bays. Their condition . . ." He faltered and then cleared his throat. "That's when I began to suspect. The pods weren't really intact. They'd fused to their ejection bays. No way to get in, so we had to torch our way through. Same thing inside as out . . . it's as if the ship liquefied or stretched for a few seconds then quickly solidified. So then I started to get the idea that the ship hadn't been blown apart so much as . . . well, rearranged. The ship's all here, *Taishu*, most of it anyway."

*All* there? Katana's lips were numb. Her head felt like the inside of a helium balloon. *What kind of weapon could generate that amount of power?* "What about the 'Mechs? What about the crew? Did they . . . ?" Katana caught the quick glance the engineer shot at his captain, and her dread blossomed like a black rose. "Where's the *crew*?"

The engineer was ashen. "The 'Mechs are all there, still tethered to their umbilicals, but they're in the same shape as the rest of the ship. It's like whatever happened was all at once and went through all sections and desks like some sort of, I don't know, propagation wave. Waves pick up debris, churn the sand as depth decreases. The shallower the water, the more the underlying seabed is disturbed, so that what was four meters from shore moves to within half a meter or is carried out in suspension when the wave recedes. That's what this is like."

"But that doesn't answer my question," Katana said. "Where's the *crew?*"

The engineer cleared his throat. "I've been over enough sections of the ship and gotten the same readings every time. And just to be sure, I had our ship's doctor recheck the same data. There's no mistake. Intermingled with the metal, the armor, the bulkheads, plastics, in what's left of the armor, even the 'Mechs . . . there are degraded nucleotides, proteins, even inorganic elements like zinc and calcium that have no business being there."

"But what does that mean? Where's *Tai-sho* Kurita?"

"I can't tell you exactly where the *tai-sho is,*" the engineer said. "That is, I can't tell you precisely *where*. But the crew, including *Tai-sho* Kurita . . . they're *all* there."

For an instant, she thought time had jumped over some sort of gap, that she'd missed something or blacked out. "What are you saying?"

"*Tai-shu,* somehow . . . the crew and the ship? They are one and the same."

# 65

*Deber City, Benjamin*
*Benjamin Military District, Draconis Combine*
*21 January 3137*

One look at the utter devastation on Emi's face, and Chomie knew. Then she shrieked her grief: loud piercing wails that split the air with a violence that was matched only by the half-mad frenzy with which she tore at her hair, scratched her face, and ripped her clothes. Finally, a physician—not Shouriki, who'd departed for Luthien three weeks after the procedure—gave Chomie a sedative. Between him, two servants, and Emi, they put Chomie to bed.

Emi slumped on a low stool next to Chomie's bed. Her sister-in-law's sleep was fretful, broken by small sighs and whimpers that even a sedative could not stop. The physician had departed after giving her assurances that the fetus, now nearly three months old, was safe.

*Oh, Theodore, how will I go on without you?*

She hoped Theodore's death had been swift. That, at least, would've been a mercy.

Murmuring, Chomie flung an arm over her head and shifted. She moaned, like a child having a bad dream. But this was no dream, and the nightmare still would be there when she awoke. Worse, Emi knew that her nightmare was just beginning. She would have to leave for Luthien within the next day or so. Her father would hear the news within the week. Ten days on the outside, at the rate the news was crackling through space: first from Katana's command via black box and then from a line of JumpShips she and Theodore had specifically put into position well before the assault. Then, they'd been confident of victory and so wanted the news to reach Benjamin and Luthien as quickly as possible.

No one could have foreseen this. By now, the news must be rippling throughout the Combine like the expanding wave fronts of a stone shattering the surface of a pond.

*And there are still others we must not forget.* She ran the back of her fingers along Chomie's feverish cheek. Chomie's hair was damp through with sweat. *Even this news must pierce the veil of my mother's dementia and my brother's insanity, and then I will bring them back to Luthien, for Theodore's funeral. Surely, Father cannot begrudge them this shared grief.*

She also knew that Chomie could not be left alone. *Can't bring her with me, though . . .* Surely, Chomie would see the wisdom of leaving for Luthien at once. Shouriki was there, and Chomie should be with family, not here on Benjamin, surrounded by veritable strangers.

Chomie moaned again. Turning aside, Emi wrung cool water from a cloth and sponged sweat from her sister-in-law's ravaged face. Her heart swelled with fresh grief and pity.

"Be strong, Sister," Emi whispered, her tears falling unchecked. "You are our future."

## Unity Palace, Imperial City, Luthien
## Pesht Military District, Draconis Combine
## 9 February 3137

The sake was steaming hot, the temperature perfectly suiting his mood. He'd downed two cups straightaway, the liquor exploding like a small bomb in his gut. He'd thought of a woman, but considering his frame of mind, he'd likely have beaten her senseless. Or worse. Wisely, he'd refrained. The palace *was* in mourning, after all.

He again stared with bleary eyes at the very end of the field report that had begun with such promise before tripping into disaster. No matter how many times he read the thing, the words seemed unreal. Theodore's death had outpaced *this* particular bit of news, and now it seemed that Fate was playing a bad practical joke.

Katana Tormark, that little bitch geisha, alive. *Alive.*

He replaced his cup upon the table and closed his eyes. The lamp at his elbow was too bright. His eyes ached from the liquor, and the inside of his eyelids were red from his blood.

*Calm down. There is still much to do, and plans I dare not derail, things that Toranaga and I . . .*

And then, all of a sudden, his mind snagged: *Saurimat.* The report mentioned the Saurimat. Why was that important? Eyes still closed, he frowned. What did he know of them? An ancient mercenary sect, more feted for their colorful assassinations than anything else. Based on . . . was it Valmiera? No, no, it was Shaul Khala, yes. Just inside the New Samar—

*My gods.* Bhatia was so stunned he flinched. His eyes flew open. *Operating out of New Samarkand . . . Toranaga arranged this!*

All those months ago, when his intuition had nagged him that Toranaga had some hand in that whore's death, he'd dismissed the idea. Now he had to wonder. Why hadn't Toranaga just had the geisha killed? Well, it was possible that Toranaga had somehow lost control of the situation, the Saurimat, or this . . . what were they? He scanned the report again. Ghost Clan, yes, and *that* had given Tormark the chance to make an escape.

Then another more disturbing thought: If Toranaga was this cunning, what *else* had the warlord arranged?

His gaze fell to the report once more. Bad news heaped upon bad news, and more was the pity. Even those Cats of hers had stabilized Styx, Athenry and Saffel. What a waste! Here, he made sure Kev Rosse could not aid the geisha, and Tormark still did an end run, gathered her damn felines, and they triumphed! And yet that bit about the mystics' murders . . . Wasn't this *exactly* what he'd contemplated months and months ago? So how had this happened? Simply by his wishing it so? He'd told no one. And . . . the report mentioned that the bodies were *brutalized*. Now *that* was interesting. His first thought had been: Kappa. *(And curse the man, jamming the secret holos, and then vaporizing the complex!)* These killings bore his stamp.

Unless.

If Toranaga could scheme to rid the Inner Sphere of a warlord, just how formidable would two puny mystics be? Answer: not very. If true, it was yet another masterstroke and a worthy risk, because if the mystics' deaths *had* derailed the Spirit Cats, then Tormark or her Dieron command would've been that much weaker.

And this gave Bhatia pause. Not only might the ploy have worked, but if *he* had managed to connect the dots to Toranaga, perhaps this smoking gun was pointed squarely between *his* eyes as well.

*Oh, my dear Toranaga, whose star is rising, which of us grasps the coattails of the other? What other surprises do you have up your sleeve?*

He picked up his cup once more and sipped. The sake was cold.

*JumpShip* **Shouri,** *recharging Midway jump point*
**New Samarkand Military District, Draconis Combine**
**9 February 3137**

Hatsuwe drifted, asleep, his features slack. Toranaga had
very gently teased free a tangle of sheets twined round
Hatsuwe's legs, and now Toranaga's eyes feasted on the
samurai's back, his thighs, that river of black hair freed
from its topknot and on end, like a fan of seaweed. Just
the sight of all this luscious muscle and flesh made Toranaga's mouth water and his loins flame. Ah, Hatsuwe was a
superb catch: skilled lover and devoted acolyte and able
pupil rolled into one.

When the Saurimat botched things with Tormark, they'd
groveled, though not much. They'd offered to right their
failure with a, well, what else could he call it? A freebie?
Because that's what the offer was: an assassination at no
extra charge. Toranaga had been *soooo* tempted. If he
hadn't been plotting for just this turn of events—though
that Tormark was blessed somehow—he might have accepted. But he had declined with both threats and regrets.
He had his own assassin, and he wouldn't think of giving
the work to anyone else. Not if he wanted to keep his head
on his shoulders.

No one suspected, not even Bhatia. Toranaga wanted to
laugh. The director fancied himself so deep and so cunning,
but Toranaga could envision this Igo board playing itself
out. What a beautiful shape he'd created, such perfect eyes
for breath and still many liberties at his disposal. Yes, this
was *amashi* at its finest, allowing his opponent to play out
his strategy while staking out enough of his own territory
to win. And win Toranaga would because he had his plans,
his stones yet to play.

Floating, Toranaga drew Hatsuwe to him, only gently, so
gently, his tongue and fingers already busy until, still asleep,
Hatsuwe stirred and moaned.

"Wake up, my young blood," Toranaga whispered into
the perfect shell of Hatsuwe's ear. At the hitch in the samurai's breathing, Toranaga's lips parted in his silent dog's
laugh. "Time to sharpen your blade."

# 66

*Imperial City, Luthien*
*Pesht Military District, Draconis Combine*
*15 March 3137*

**M**akoto Shouriki brought the news before three weeks had passed. Vincent Kurita had wept, alone, until he was limp, depleted. Empty, like someone had taken a spoon and scooped out his guts.

Then yet another blow: news of his wife, suddenly taken by a fatal heart attack. Despite the fact that they'd not lived as husband and wife for more than two decades, he had loved her once and had been faithful in his way, taking no lovers and giving her this measure of dignity at least. And so, now a widower, he grieved.

Then, a week ago, and just when he thought he might bear up after all, news arrived that Emi's DropShip had exploded in transit from Ogano to its JumpShip. There were no survivors.

First Theodore, then Ramiko, and now *Emi* . . . His old heart hurt. At least, Chomie was safe on Luthien now, guarded in his house. And growing in her, there was hope for their dynasty's future, a gift from the ashes. He clung to that.

Vincent now stood, motionless as a mannequin, as his silent attendants scurried on soundless feet, readying their coordinator for the afternoon's ceremony: Theodore's birthday celebration. He had all eternity to grieve for his lost children and his wife, but today Theodore *would* have his moment, his triumph, and he was certain his son's *yurei* would hear.

*Ah, you demons, you ghosts . . . You think you've broken me, but you have not. I created you and I will destroy you as surely as my blood rained my curses.*

\*　　　\*　　　\*

The audience was packed: nobles and lords and the war-lords, all dressed in finery so bright and glittery that his eyes burned—because he would have no mourning, none, not on this day. Or were those tears? No, he would not succumb, though he noted Chomie's absence. Understandable, given the toll Theodore's death had taken on her.

Silent, he faced his people. Saw the eyes staring, some measuring, others calculating, all waiting.

*My son is dead. But, by the Dragon, we will celebrate his* life.

"We would . . ." His throat clenched, and he stopped, cleared it and began again. "*I* would tell you," he said. "I would tell you of my son."

The far eastern wing of the palace was so still, Jonathan barely breathed as he wound his way through corridors lined with intricate silk tapestries and jade baubles on black pedestals. The light was dim, given the hour, and though he knew that this was a risk, so far Bhatia had kept his end of the bargain. Months ago, the ISF director had obliged him with detailed plans, including secret passages accessed from points well away from the palace proper. In the end, he hadn't needed them. He'd come out of the darkness and into Katana's light on his own.

Ah, and *he* had done it! Nurtured Katana's *kami* all this time, and then to be rewarded with her in the flesh . . . A tiny laugh escaped his lips. So tantalizingly close, and still so far. He now saw Katana in his dreams: saw what he would do, how she would look, what she would say. How she would moan and shudder with pleasure in his arms, and then when his tongue teased that first drop of her blood . . . He would have his satisfaction. A long time coming, considering those damned little cats.

His buoyant mood soured. The woman had been the worst of all: completely silent and denying him even as he cut deeper and deeper, making her last and last. He'd felt the spasm and death flutters of her heart through the pommel of his blade: like a bird's wings, beating, beating . . . faltering. For a time, he'd been enraptured, watching the life bleed from her eyes, her mouth. So close and yet . . . she made no sound. He read the suffering in her eyes, but she had a will of titanium, and she did not break. He remembered how, so very impatient, the tension unbearable, his body ready to explode with ecstasy, he'd covered her mouth with his, savoring the brackish taste of her blood filling his mouth, drinking her down, taking her soul. Surely *that* would break her, she would *beg*.

But, no, not a word. Not a syllable. Not even a sigh—not even when he'd reached in and tore her heart from its roots with his bare hands. In the end, she had been so white, so depleted of blood that had saturated the ground upon which she slept. What had remained of her face looked like wax. Everything else was just meat.

He'd felt empty afterward. Not satisfied or even victorious.

He was so immersed in his thoughts, he didn't watch where he was going. A sudden, small jolt made him gasp, and he whipped round, saw an ornate jade vase slowly topple. He sprang to catch it, but he was too late. The heavy stone banged against the marble floor. The vase did not shatter; jade was a hard stone. But the damage had been done. Quickly, he crouched, scuttled back into a shadow of drapery. His right hand snaked for the wood-handled wire garrote in his trouser pocket.

*Guards on their way any second.* His pulse thudded in his temples, and his breathing grew shallow, a little ragged, as he waited, all his nerves tingling, his weight centered on the balls of his feet, ready to spring.

But no one came. He waited a full twenty seconds, then ten more before slowly, cautiously, pushing himself to his feet. Something wrong . . .

*Yes, there's something wrong, you fool!* You! *Can't afford to lose your edge, not now, not ever. Not if you want to survive and claim what's yours!*

But where were the guards? Although he imagined that Bhatia had put great care into selecting the guards for this particular post on this very particular day, even lobotomized *idiots* would've investigated.

When no guards came, Jonathan . . . hesitated, and that was also unlike him. He was usually so sure, so in control. And now, see what happened when he allowed others to dictate his path! Never again. He would dispatch of the guards and Chomie . . . well, he might spend just a few moments on her. After all, all work and no play . . .

Eventually, he found them. The guards first: sprawled in pools of cooling blood that coated the hardwood floor and soaked the tatami mats. Their throats had been cut, releasing crimson founts that had painted arcs on the walls. He saw the knife the assassin had used as well: a half-serrated, black blade twelve centimeters long and clotted with gore.

And Chomie . . . on her back, head twisted at a weird angle because the killer had cut so deeply, he'd nearly decapitated her. Jonathan saw hacked flesh, pink bone, shiny knobs of cartilage. Her sightless eyes bulged, her mouth gaped, and her abdomen . . .

Shock blasted through Jonathan. Chomie, *already dead*, how could this be? Someone there before him? *Who?*

He wasn't sure how long he stood there. Perhaps no more than ten seconds before his brain kicked into gear again, though haltingly, like a faulty timepiece. My God, he should have seen this coming. *This* was how Bhatia was planning to trap him, ensnare him in a web from which there was no escape. And he was *standing* here, precious seconds ticking away, and guards probably swarming in at any minute! Think, *think!* If Bhatia had arranged for Chomie's execution, then he'd have arranged a sort of signal so he'd know when the deed was done and when it was safe to trigger an alarm. But, if so, where were the guards? Why weren't they here by now?

*No time, got to move!*

Then his eyes fell on the gored dagger.

*Blood. They'll believe blood.*

Swiftly, without hesitating, he plucked up the knife. Blood slicked its handle and was already tacky with clot. With a single, swift stroke, he slashed hard and deep through the left sleeve of his uniform jacket. The fabric caught, and he jerked the knife, forcing it through. He hissed as his flesh parted beneath the blade like butter, and then his jaws clenched against the pain, he cleavered his flesh from wrist to elbow.

*Not too deep, watch the ulnar nerve, no use risking paralysis, and the artery, go easy . . . !*

Working fast now, he swabbed the handle clean on a guard's pantaloons and dropped the dagger back where he'd found it. Then, blood streaming behind, he bolted from the room, heading for the audience hall at a dead run.

# 67

When the coordinator began to speak, she couldn't concentrate. Instead, Katana's mind chased round and round. She'd tried telling herself that death was part of war, and that all samurai accepted this. How one died was as important as how one lived. Pretty words, even noble, but scant comfort, because her brain snagged on one thing: those black boxes.

*Fool, she was a fool!* Her hands fisted around air, though she wasn't conscious of that until her nails bit into her scarred palms. How stupid, *this* was something she *should've* foreseen! As soon as their advance scouts had reported the lack of an organized defense around Dieron, she should have suspected. Of all people, Katana knew that if *she* had the black boxes—an advanced bit of technology whose origins were misted by time—then logic *demanded* that even more ancient technology, the stuff of legends, must still be safeguarded somewhere. Clearly, The Republic had withdrawn, knowing the Combine would follow like a slavering pack of dogs on the heels of a fox, *already knowing* The Republic could defend its perimeter. That line wasn't a dare. It was a warning: *This far, and no farther.*

After all these months of planning and what her people had endured, Dieron was hollow and meaningless, a planet that fell with scarcely a shot. The Republic had *given* it to them, discarding the planet the way you threw out an apple core. And then The Republic had crushed Theodore and his men and their ship.

There was only one bit of irony. If Theodore had been as ill as she suspected, maybe a warrior's death was a merciful swift end.

Her eyes drifted over the assembled crowd, divided into their many camps: Bhatia, of course, to the coordinator's right and just a shade closer to the dais than anyone else. Saito and Toranaga were next, each with his command staff. Toranaga stood ramrod straight, his attention unwavering . . . but she'd wager his mind was running circles, too, wondering how to turn this to his advantage. After all, Yori Kurita was his protégée, and he her patron. Toranaga must be ecstatic, even *though* the Kitten was absent, very pointedly left behind, and to hell with Yori's pedigree. After that disaster, Katana would never trust her again. Oh, Yori had resisted, but Katana had been firm. "I am *tai-shu,* and it is my place to be there." She'd spiked Yori with a look that flung daggers. "You might have right by blood, but Theodore was *my* friend. My grief is *personal,* and it trumps you and whatever you want to call yourself every damn time." Yori hadn't spoken or argued. Her battered and bruised face had been stony, but Katana had seen that creeping flush staining her neck.

*One thing is sure: She is a cat, always landing on her feet. But watch your back, little Kitten. These dragons, including your patron, have teeth.*

And what about her people? Surely, they felt the loss most keenly. Some, like Andre Crawford, her anchor and good right hand, had fought alongside Theodore, not only out of duty but for honor. She knew that Parks would've wished to be here along with all her commanders, but there was still much to do in her fledgling district, and so only Crawford and a contingent of O5P—including Fusilli and that new agent, Jonathan—had preceded her the day before, as had all the security personnel attached to the different warlords, to check out the various venues to their satisfaction.

Of the rest, Fusilli worried her. She now studied him, noted his posture, the way his shoulders sagged a bit and how the corners of his mouth were grimmer. Fusilli was . . . *sad,* as if he'd passed through some trial by fire of the soul, and she felt a new prickle of sympathy for him. Maybe that was good.

Then she frowned. Leaning toward Crawford, she murmured, "Where is Jonathan?"

"Jonathan?" A wrinkle creased the space above Crawford's nose. "He ought to be . . ." Crawford broke off, turning to look behind them. Katana now heard it, too: some sort of scuffle and commotion to their rear. Crawford stared, mouth agape. "What the hell?"

Vincent *saw* that something was wrong before he *heard* anything. From the dais, he had an excellent view of a pair of massive burnished walnut doors with brass hinges. These now swung open, and a palace guard began bullying his way through the crowd. In his grief, Vincent wasn't astonished so much as outraged. How dare *anyone* interrupt? Anger, something he rarely acknowledged, fired his gut. If he'd a katana in hand, he'd have gladly lopped off the guard's head with a single stroke.

Furious, his blood boiling, Vincent did the unthinkable. He left the dais. He strode forward, ignoring Bhatia who scrambled after, and he shouted, "*What* is the meaning of this outrage? How *dare* you . . . ?"

"*Tono!*" The guard flung himself to the floor in a bow. "Forgive me, but your son, *Tono*, your *son!*"

The words hammered his brain. He reeled, his rage evaporating to be replaced by stunned amazement. *Theodore, alive? How can this be, how can . . . ?* His thoughts staggered to a halt as he spied a tangled knot of guards advancing through the crowd. The guards hustled some people forward, and that brief flicker of hope guttered, for Vincent now saw them clearly: a trio of monks in glossy black robes—and one he recognized instantly.

*Ryuhiko, here . . .*

"Father! *Tono!*" Ryuhiko cried. He was sobbing, and his face gleamed with tears. Breaking free of the escort, he half-shuffled, half-stumbled toward his father. "Father, I've brought you something, I've . . ." He broke off as the guard who'd prostrated himself leapt to his feet, his hand moving to the butt of a laser pistol.

"*STOP!*" Vincent roared. "Who *dares* draw a weapon against my son?" He swept forward through a crowd now stunned to silence. "My son," Vincent said, catching Ryuhiko by the elbows. His son towered over him, and how much he had changed! How strong he was, and how bronzed his skin, like a god! "My son, I am so glad you have come."

"I brought you a gift," Ryuhiko said, his voice hitching

between sobs. He proffered the box. "I worked on it very hard. I made it especially for Theodore, for his birthday."

His son's face blurred in his vision, broke apart. "My son," he said, "how I have mistreated you, how I've let you down, and yet I pledge this from my heart. *Anata-wa kuso desu.*"

Something he'd never have imagined he would own: his love for his son. Clasping the man who was his child to his breast, Vincent bowed his head and wept.

Watching the spectacle unfold, Wahab Fusilli was stunned. Ever since his return, he'd felt unreal and strangely adrift. Not in the sense of being in between camps so much as wondering where he fit in at all. Katana's gratitude had been genuine, and he thought he saw that she understood exactly what he'd lost. Absurd, of course; Katana was not a mind reader. Coming here, he also knew that Bhatia might task him. Yet, for the very first time, Fusilli thought he might not obey.

Now, looking at the embrace of a father and son— hearing the coordinator's avowal of love—pain's claw ripped Fusilli's heart, and his throat convulsed in a sob he struggled to suppress. Only one person had loved him that much, and he had killed her: not because anyone made him or even because he thought that death was what Dasha really had wanted all along, but because he knew that it was the right thing to do.

*This could be home.* His eyes burned, and he blinked back tears. *This could be what it feels like to belong.*

Without realizing it, he moved a little closer to Crawford and Katana.

As if jerking awake from a long sleep, the crowd came alive. The hall filled with the buzz of voices and muffled exclamations. Bhatia had followed the coordinator from his dais and stood now barely a meter away from father and son. Yet Katana saw that, for once, Bhatia looked absolutely stunned, his mouth gaping like that of a beached fish.

So, clearly, Bhatia hadn't known Ryuhiko was coming. Someone else arranged for him to appear here, now, taking everyone—including Bhatia—by surprise. But who?

For whatever reason, or perhaps because her subconscious knew before her conscious mind, her eyes drifted . . . and came to rest on Toranaga. And she saw him do a most peculiar thing. As Ryuhiko and Vincent fell into each other's arms, Toranaga edged *back*. Not just a respectful step or two as they all had done, but several paces, fading back into the crowd—and then she saw his head turn toward the entrance. She followed his gaze and saw that the monks had allowed themselves to be pushed back by the guards. Indeed, they were *backing* for the door.

*Oh, God, no . . . Ryuhiko, that box!*

"*Tono!*" Katana surged forward. "*Tono*, look out!"

Bhatia was not a man easily startled. Indeed, he could count the number of times on the fingers of one hand and not run out of fingers. But this was like a punch to the solar plexus, and he was winded, rooted to the spot and gasping, as his mind spun: *I didn't send for him, no one knows where he's been kept. Emi's DropShip exploded . . .*

This was not what he'd planned, this was not going according to plan at all. Kappa should have finished Chomie by now. What was one paltry pregnant woman and two inexperienced guards? So why wasn't that alarm being raised? Where were the other guards, where—

Maybe it was intuition, or maybe he'd known all along. Whatever the reason, Bhatia's eyes jerked away from the coordinator and Ryuhiko. He spun on his heel, searching . . . and saw Toranaga edging away.

In a flash, he heard his own words, tolling his death knell: *No witnesses.*

Lungs screaming for air, Jonathan dashed headlong through the halls trailing blood. He knew something was wrong, yet he couldn't see it clearly. What could it be? Then, at a cross corridor just ahead, he saw guards. Relief washed over him and for an instant, he imagined that things were going as planned after all. But then he realized that this knot of guards was hurrying the *other* way. He spied that trio of black robes but recognized only one.

He skidded to a halt. *What is he doing here? Emi's dead, but Ryuhiko is here, and that means he was gone before she got there. And now he's here, and those monks—how could they know ahead of time, how could the news . . . ?*

And then it hit him, all the facts clicking into place with swift and deadly precision because he was, whatever else, first and always a killer and a professional, and the answer was absurdly simple: *No witnesses.*

*Toranaga. No!*

Heart thundering in his chest, Jonathan pounded down the hall, eating up distance, knowing that if he went around to the main entrance he would be too late. *They're in there, they're all in there, and Katana . . . !* Veering left, he darted through a separate entrance, the one usually reserved for the warlords, and in a second, he was through, blurring past a clutch of astonished guards, breaking through—

He saw Ryuhiko hulking over Vincent, who held a carved teak box. He saw Bhatia backing up, and then his frantic eyes found Toranaga already well away and moving ever farther . . .

And then there was his Katana, struggling forward, squeezing from the crowd, with Crawford right behind and Wahab Fusilli jolted into action and trying to beat her a path.

Katana was shouting, fighting her way to the coordinator's side: "*Tono! Tono,* look out, don't open the box, *don't open the box!*"

"*KATANA!*" Jonathan screamed. He surged forward, knowing he was out of time, he was too late, no time, no *time!* With a wild cry, he launched himself with everything he had left. "Katana, Katana, *no!*"

And then the bomb went off.

# EPILOGUE

## *Yose:* Endgame

# 68

## *Somewhere on Itabaiana*
## *30 April 3137*

**T**he cottage perched along a mountain pass in a remote wilderness surrounded by thick evergreens that smelled sharply of resin. It was night, and there was no moon. Outside, the wind moaned. Through an open window, Emi caught the faraway cry of some animal, then the closer, soft creak of a floorboard as her guard and protector, Joji Ashido, shifted his weight.

She tried very hard to pray as she knelt upon a plain tatami mat, her eyes squeezed tight. Instead, the bamboo bit her knees. Her incense—jasmine, and her favorite—smelled cloying and too sweet. She'd also discovered that the space before her eyes was not black but red as blood.

So much blood: her father's, Chomie's. Her mother, lying in that pool of congealed blood, her mouth open and eyes bulging . . . At the final instant, when the assassin's blade sliced her throat, had her mother come to herself, finally?

*And Theodore, brother of my heart, what did you see? Were you frightened? In those last moments, did you even know you were dying?*

She would never know. In a perverse way, Fate's hand may have dealt kindly with Theodore. He couldn't have saved Chomie or his unborn heir. He'd have gone mad then, and welcomed death. So, perhaps, in the end, it was the same thing.

Joji had made her flee after they discovered her mother's murder, and Khan Jacali Nostra had granted her sanctuary for as long as she wished or needed, the special bond between the Mystic Caste and the O5P never more in evidence than now. The fiction of her death was necessary, for the moment. But what kind of future could she have? And what to do now?

*Don't be a fool.* She let out her breath very slowly and opened her eyes. Her candles still flickered; the wind still moaned. *You know exactly what must be done.*

Her way was clear. She was fated to live.

She pushed to her feet. Her knees crackled, and the folds of her white mourning robe rustled in the stillness. The room was thick with shadows that danced and shifted.

*Now,* I'm *the only one left. The only one left who* can.

Her fingers found the loop of cloth binding her robe about her slim body, and as she turned toward Joji Ashido, she worked the knot. Her robe fell open, and she made no effort to hide her nakedness.

Joji was very still. His dark eyes never left her face. She read much meaning there and knew that he understood at once what she wished and what she must do. Even when she stood before him and felt how the air quickened over her breasts, her thighs, her belly, Joji did not move.

He said, "I am pledged to you, my lady. I am yours to command. But are you sure, my lady? Are you very sure?"

"Yes," she whispered. Her eyes filled, and her lips trembled. She closed her eyes as his fingers cupped her cheeks. He smelled of strength and that slight tang that reminded her of the sea. "I'm the only one who can," she said, her voice breaking, "the only one left."

"Sshh, my lady, ssshh," Joji said, as he gathered her in his arms—but slowly and with such exquisite care that it seemed he was afraid she might break. "I am here, my lady, and I will never leave you. So don't cry, my lady," he said, as he kissed her wet cheeks and then the hollow of her throat. "Don't cry."

# 69

## Borealis Glacier, Misery
## 15 May 3137

Icy snow blasted the Kat's windscreen, sluicing across the ferroglass with a hiss like sand scouring rock. The wind snatched at the lightweight steel cab, and the Kat bobbed, like a cork on a turbulent ocean.

In so many ways, the landscape had not changed, and would not for centuries to come as the glacier proceeded in its deliberate, suicidal run for the sea. Thereon barely glanced at the dancing green blip of his SatNav as the computer guidance system patiently drew him on to a past that was etched in his heart and soul, preserved in the amber of memory.

Seven years ago, this glacier was a ruin: pocked with craters from autocannons and missiles, and the larger concavities left by the passage of a *Legionnaire*. There had been bodies, too. And there'd been blood: startling, staining the snow a deep, nearly obscene crimson.

Still, Death was white. Fitting, then, that white was the color of mourning because here, in this blasted wilderness, Death had final dominion.

Clearly, his investigations had triggered something because, several months ago, he'd received an encrypted data crystal. When he finally broke the code, he'd listened with a sort of horrified fascination to a voice that, even electronically altered, he recognized as bubbling up from a nightmare.

*"If you're listening to this, Richard, then we will assume that you've finally caught on to my little joke. You will forgive me this indulgence, but you, being a trained investigator in—dare I say it—another life . . . well, I thought your mind might be up to a bit of challenge. So congratulations are in order.*

*"But if you want to truly understand, remember: The*

*mind is the great poem of winter, just as one man's misery is another's triumph. You can be sure I'm enjoying mine. Sketching my way through the Inner Sphere. Well, our paths might cross since we all proceed from whence we began. If so, then your misery may keep company with mine."*

On the glacier now, the thickening snow whipping round in gauzy veils. He was encased in cold-weather gear, his furred parka hood drawn tight around his face, a protective mask over his chin, mouth and nose, and goggles so he could see. He bent to his task, sonic drill in hand.

*It's got to be here.* His shoulders and hands hummed from the drill's vibrations as sound waves pummeled through compressed ice and snow. The work went fast, and that surprised him. When his depth gauge told him that he was no more than four centimeters from his prize, he knelt upon the ice and switched to a sharp-edged ice trowel. *Because this is where I began, in earnest.*

The trowel struck something harder than ice with a perceptible *clank.* A metallic wedge protruded from the ice. When he'd unearthed the steel container and scraped away ice from the lock, he hesitated.

*Not entirely unlike Pandora, except Evil was let out long before I happened along, and where is Hope now?*

He hit the lock with a burst of laser fire set at minimum intensity then fitted in a key that was still warm from his body heat. The lock popped open, and he lifted the lid. His breath plumed as he released a sigh.

The silver *tsuke* was still pristine, untouched by time or the elements. The care and precision the silversmith had lavished upon the silver was reflected in an intricately rendered dragon's head, complete with horns and toothy snarl. The silver was worn smooth in places from long use and the oils of a man's hand—the same hand that had cut down Thereon's father so long ago.

An icy lump of old grief lodged in Thereon's heart. He'd sworn over his father's grave to avenge his death, and he'd done that: blasting men into ruins of pulped flesh and splintered bone. On this very spot and in this desolate waste. High in a stolen *Legionnaire,* he'd massacred an entire lance and savored their dying screams. He didn't regret one moment because that was only the beginning of vengeance.

Snow silted over the silver dragon's face. He'd returned

to his origins in a place that was forever winter in his mind, on a planet called Misery. But something nagged him.

*He said our miseries may keep company.* And then: *The ice wasn't as hard as I thought it'd be, as if someone's already been here.*

He found it within ten minutes. First, a dark hummock of something. Abandoning the trowel, he dug with his gloved hands, scooping out fistfuls of snow, uncovering what lay beneath. And then he just sat there, stupefied.

A bright green helmet. A very *distinctive* bright green helmet.

With shaking hands, he prized the helmet free. The helmet was heavy, as if it had been weighted down with snow and ice. Tugging off his right glove, his fingers crawled over frigid metal, searching for the catch to raise the visor. A minute click, a sense of something giving—and then, as the visor scrolled back, Thereon gave a guttural, muted cry of horror.

The man's face was perfectly preserved: lean and wolfish, with high cheekbones, thin lips. The wind snatched at a fringe of camel-colored hair, and snow blew into eyes that were sable-colored and unblinking.

Later, he would find every single scrap of that disarticulated armor, and the jigsaw of this man's body—his every limb and joint, his torso. Everything. Much later, forensic analysis would reveal that the body had been preserved through plastination, a process whereby the body was impregnated with acetone, then cured in gas and infused with silicone rubber. The work of an expert.

But, for now, he could only stare into those dead eyes. And in his mind, he heard his faceless nemesis: *"Next time, Michi dear, choose a name with a little more imagination."*

## 70

### Imperial City, Luthien
### Pesht Military District, Draconis Combine
### 15 May 3137

The criers, the *naki-onna*, wailed: high, eerie, keening shrieks that were the stuff of bad nightmares and dark nights to come. These were professional mourners, but Yori knew they weren't acting. Maybe they didn't mourn Vincent Kurita the man, but this near-fatal blow dealt to the Combine? Yes.

The antechamber was small, and just off the Throne Room. In principle, the room served the way a sacristy did a priest. She now studied herself in a full-length mirror provided for that purpose. Her face still bore the traces of her disastrous campaign. The bruises were gone as were the stitches, but the scars remained, including a too-pink slash along her right cheek. A reminder she'd decided to keep because men had died—her lancemates, her troops— for no other reason than her feckless, selfish pride.

She would never make that mistake again. Never.

She plucked a pure white silken cloth from a small side table. Her garments were snow-white, the color of mourning and of Death, and she carefully draped the cloth over her hair. She was a small woman and in the mirror, she looked fragile, her dark eyes huge and rimmed with purple hollows. A little like a ghost.

That, too, was fitting. In a few moments, she would begin the rite of *tama-yobei*, soul-calling. Legend said that if the souls of the dead were not ready to depart, then they would reanimate their bodies and rise once more. That, she knew, would not happen. She doubted, though, that Vincent Kurita and the souls of his family—Emi and Ryuhiko, Theodore and Chomie and their unborn child—would ever leave this place.

*I will hear them in my dreams, the same way I relive that awful moment when Toranaga met my DropShip, and I looked into his eyes—and I saw and knew what he had done, and why. I know everything.*

What awaited her when this official mourning ended and she'd passed through the Rites of Ascension to take her place as the Combine's new coordinator—and what could be done about Toranaga—was for later.

And yet, there was one thing she now knew that she would never have suspected. Before all this bloodshed, and longer ago than that—when Toranaga had left her behind with Julian and the others—she had only focused on survival. Just that. Staying alive had been her imperative.

But now there was more. Yes, she was alive, and Toranaga would have to be dealt with. Yet her destiny unfurled in a path too brilliant, too awful, too important to ignore.

*She* was the hope of the Combine. This wasn't about her life anymore. This was about leading the Combine and her people not only to glory but to safety, security. To *life*. This was the heritage she now must honor and before which she was utterly humbled.

For the moment, though, she would honor the dead.

As she turned to go, her eyes fell on an ink painting left here, on a stand, deliberately. The painting was strange and eerie, filled with ghosts and demons twining through a landscape she recognized because she'd walked its paths. And with the painting, a note, in a strong, bold hand:

*Hell paints the canvas of the lonely mind. You will lose nothing if you open yourself to trust.*

"Perhaps, Physician," she murmured. "But Vincent Kurita was killed because he trusted, and then he loved, and that destroyed him. Rest assured, Makoto Shouriki: *I* will never make the same mistake with you."

Even so, the demons' whispers trailed in her wake, and she could not decide if there wasn't just a bit of laughter, too.

## 71

Thank the Dragon, the *naki-onna* had ceased their infernal wailing, and not a moment too soon. His headache was blinding, and so intense, his brain was practically leaking out of his ears. It didn't help that the room was crowded, all this maddening and unbroken bone-white glare, and thick with the too-sweet aroma of lotus and jasmine. Although the easternmost shoji had been pushed aside to allow the souls of the dead to reenter if they chose, the Throne Room was stuffy and too warm.

But, wrapped in mourning robes, Ramadeep Bhatia was cold. He was scarred as well. Only good fortune and blind luck that he'd put it all together, the pieces snapping into place in time for him to dart behind a thick pillar just as the bomb went off. His memory of the event was jagged as glass, bits and pieces he couldn't quite fit together. A blinding flash, a deafening roar, and then a hot, thick wind that rained blood and flesh and bone.

But cold is what he remembered most, that icy premonitory frisson the moment he saw Toranaga's face on that awful day—and realized that Death had painted Bhatia with the same bloody brush. And he was cold now, but with rage that was hard and as glittery as the most flawless diamond formed by millennia of pressure and heat.

*Dare you imagine to have gotten rid of me as well? Well, relax. For you are safe for now,* Tai-shu. *But if your protégée makes a misstep, I will make sure that her skirts pull you down after, and I will not be there to catch you.*

He had other problems, all of them named Kappa. Yes, of course, he fulfilled *some* of what he'd promised. Chomie was successfully dispatched, and her child with her. But Kappa had not arranged for so spectacular an end to Vincent Kurita's life; that was Toranaga. Unless . . . Kappa was in *league* with the warlord.

The more he thought about it, the less he liked it. Well—Bhatia ground his teeth so hard his jaw ached—that put a new complexion on things. Would Toranaga dispose of such an asset? Probably not, and Bhatia would bet good money that Kappa was alive and well and waiting in the wings somewhere. His black eyes clicked over the sea of faces: most of them anonymous and a few too many, like the geisha and her contingent, familiar in the extreme. Kappa could be here, standing right next to him, and Bhatia would never know, never understand until a blade slid between his ribs or a garrote tightened round his neck.

*He knows all my security protocols now. I'll have to change everything, even the back doors into secured systems.*

His only advantage, a microscopic one at that: As per protocol, he'd had Chomie's body autopsied, her death thoroughly investigated, and he knew something that he wagered Kappa did not. Chomie had not died easily. There was skin and blood beneath her nails, and several strands of hair that were not hers mired in blood. So they had DNA; they were, in fact, running it at this very moment. All they now had to do was wait for the day when Bhatia might make a match—and hit it cold.

# 72

**W**arlord Matsuhari Toranaga arranged his face into an appropriate mask for mourning, but his heart was jubilant. His unwavering gaze tracked Yori Kurita, all in white, as she ascended the dais upon which the Dragon Throne rested—and then the perfect symmetry of it all struck him. This was *yose,* and Yori Kurita his white stone, and the very last he would place upon this particular Igo board. He'd won. Oh, there were other games yet to play. For the moment, however, he allowed himself this satisfaction, basking in the reflected rays of Yori Kurita's glory.

They were all gone, and he was still standing. Well, he and Bhatia . . . and too bad about that, but no matter. Bhatia and he were bound by snake's coils, and they would see which was the stronger. Actually, he already knew the answer.

As for Yori? She'd disappointed. Dieron had been a disaster, but what a stunning reversal of fortunes! Still, he had no illusions about her. There was no love between them and never would be, but she would not be where she was without him. Yes, he knew that *she* knew all.

*But she will remain silent because she understands that she cannot bring me down without toppling herself. No one will ever believe that we did not plot this together. Ah, Yori. One of us is the fly snared in a web spun by an exceedingly clever spider. And believe me, my dear, whatever you think of yourself—you are no spider.*

A whisper now at his ear, so faint it faded almost before it could form: "Something amuses you, *Tono*?"

Toranaga's eyes slid round. Hatsuwe was close, close enough to touch. So close that the warlord saw the flutter of the samurai's pulse beneath the smooth skin of his neck. Hatsuwe was dressed for mourning, and that was a good thing because those sleeves hid the scars left from those scratches very nicely. And who knew the woman would have nails like knives?

"No," Toranaga murmured. "I am just thinking of the pleasures I shall take in my bed this evening." It gave him a thrill to watch the color march up Hatsuwe's neck, the way the young samurai dipped his head to hide that quick, sly smile.

*And what a pity for you, Hatsuwe, that you'll be standing just a little too close to that airlock when the seal fails— because I know what you've failed to learn. There can be no witnesses.*

Still, it would be a loss. So, maybe bed first. Pleasure before duty . . . just this once.

# 73

**N**othing was the same anymore. They were all dead, and there was nothing she could do about it. Nothing to take back, and only regrets she could not wish away. She'd been trying all day to remember what it was that she and Andre Crawford had been talking about right before the disaster— only she couldn't dredge up the memory. It was gone, like her voice. She'd wanted to journal but couldn't find the words. The microrecorder's light winked its readiness—and she was struck dumb. As if some bottomless chasm had opened up beneath her feet, and she'd fallen through, lost in a darkness that swallowed her whole.

The sky beyond her balcony was black. There was no moon, and the stars looked broken, like pieces of glass embedded in obsidian. The day had been unusually warm, still and humid, and now the night air was cloying and uncomfortable, like a heavy swag. There was no wind, but the air was alive anyway, prickly with spirits.

She wore a short kimono with nothing beneath, and her feet were bare. Her skin still tingled from a scalding hot bath, her third that day—yet, try as she might, she could not scrub out the thoughts that stained her mind.

*Because I should've died. I should have taken my place with the dead, and I would gladly trade places with the coordinator, with Theodore.*

She blinked back sudden, hot tears even as her throat convulsed with a bitter, choking laugh. Yes, she hadn't died, so she'd better learn to live with that, right? She was alive only because she'd been knocked back and out of the kill radius. The blast was directed and contained, meant to kill those in the immediate vicinity: the coordinator,

Ryuhiko—and Bhatia. Yes, Bhatia was *supposed* to die. Only he hadn't—and maybe that was because he had recognized the danger, seen the same thing she had at the very last second: that moment when Toranaga took that fatal step *back*.

And she had seen much else this afternoon, standing there before the Dragon Throne. The throne was new; the other was splinters. The Dragon Mural had taken some damage but had been repaired, all the jewels replaced and new ones added: Biham, Al Na'ir, Athenry, Styx. Bloody, ruby-red Dieron.

Their contingents had been arranged in an arc, sweeping from left to right: Toranaga, then Saito, followed by Katana and what remained of her command staff. The far right position of the arc had been empty, save for a single, white silk pillow upon which replicas of Theodore's double swords lay, the originals having been destroyed with their owner.

Yori had begun the ritual, calling the names of the dead, and although Katana's heart bled with grief, one thing she knew. She would never forgive Yori or forget. Yori Kurita was a pretender, the Kitten who landed on her feet.

Dry-eyed with rage, Katana had watched as Toranaga, his face appropriately arranged into sorrow, faced the assembled mourners and witnesses, and took up the call—and that's when *she* had heard it: that little thrumming note of Toranaga's triumph.

*Ah, you had a hand in this, Jackal, didn't you?*

Then it had been her turn. Katana and her retinue had executed a crisp about-face. She remembered taking that deep breath and holding it, not wishing to let go. But she had let go. Had no choice. So Katana had called for Vincent Kurita's soul and all the rest: Emi, Theodore, Chomie. Their heir who would never be. Tears had spilled down her cheeks, but she was not ashamed, and her voice had been strong and only faltered once: when she'd invoked Theodore's name. And although she could not say their names aloud, her mind also had cried out for her friends. For Toni, so long dead now, a wound of the heart that never quite healed, as perhaps it shouldn't.

And then, at the very last, her soul had called out for Andre Crawford. Two steps behind, at her right hand as he had always been, so that when she was thrown clear—when Fate had intervened—Death had sidestepped her and claimed Andre instead.

At the memory, a fresh pang of grief stabbed her heart. She closed her eyes against the night and this pain, and saw only more blackness.

*Oh, Andre, I will miss you most of all. There are all these souls crowding round, waiting on me, watching—and I am so very alone.*

Yet even as she thought this, she knew it wasn't quite true. There was another: the one Fate had thrust her way. The man to whom she owed her life was just down the hall. Her good right hand now, as he'd stood by her side that afternoon, his presence solid and reassuring. When she *had* faltered, he'd brushed the back of her scarred hand with his. Just a touch, very fleeting, but the contact was electric. She felt his strength, and when their eyes met, she saw his devotion. But there was something else in those gray eyes—shaded now silver, now a light blue—that plucked a responsive cord.

She was not alone, so long as she had her memories, and him.

"So, do not be restless, my friends," she whispered now. Her voice was husky and cut her throat as if she hadn't spoken in centuries. "*Ten no Sabaki,* Judgment Day, will come, and then he and I will avenge you. I swear it."

Even so, she wept, and her tears were bitter.

## 74

*She is just down the hall, near enough to touch, close enough to feel, tethered to my soul, the memory of her flesh against mine burning like a hot coal. I wanted her then. I want her now, and more than I've ever desired anything in my life.*

*It's dark in my quarters. So still. So quiet. Times like these, I wish I were weightless, defying gravity, soaring through the air like a god. As it is, lying here now upon this bed, naked, every nerve in my skin alive to the slow, sensuous slide of silk whispering over my body . . . well, it's no substitute. For now, it will have to do. I will enjoy this moment, my triumph. I've earned the right. And wanting is so very sweet. Wanting is the hunt.*

*They say that everything comes to those who wait. Still, I make my own luck. Like Chomie: With all the mayhem and madness, everyone accepted my story about grappling with an intruder, too late to save Theodore's wife or child, or the hapless, nameless guards about whom no one gives a damn. I'll be the first to admit it, though. That little slash to the arm? A nice bit of theater, that. Blood adds such an air of authenticity that no one questions. Because no one in his right mind cuts himself, right? (Although I will have to watch that: Between last year on Biham and this, I'll end up a mass of scars.) And lucky for me, all I took away from the explosion were burns, and bits and pieces of, well, several people. You really can't quite appreciate how much mess a bomb makes until you've washed someone's brains out of your hair.*

*There is nothing to stop me now. I've stared Bhatia in the face, watched those eyes bounce away to think about other things—and, oh, the wheels and gears turning in that brain; I can practically hear his thoughts chittering round and round like a computer caught in a recursive algorithm. Yet he's looked his nemesis full in the face and does not recognize me. Excellent. Even if, by some fluke, he eventually does, I have more than enough to bring him down. All those wonderful words from that night on New Samarkand when he hatched his little plot with Toranaga. If that became public, if I happened to do a bit of investigation, say, and turned up a data crystal . . . Well, it would be Bhatia's head on a pike.*

*And as for Toranaga: Well, let's just say that his comeuppance may come sooner rather than later. A process I've already set in motion with a little DNA. A simple data crystal strategically placed. Ah, Toranaga, I wish you'd been there when I was baptized in a mystic's blood. To be fair, it was Bhatia's idea, but I'm sure you'll appreciate taking credit. Maybe not my best performance, but I think I made, well, quite a splash. Certainly created some buzz, hmm?*

*So sleep now, Tai-shu Toranaga, while you can. I am the nightmare you haven't even dreamt yet.*

*All the rest—the ones who would stand in my way—are gone . . . well, all except two. (I regret Crawford, a little, though the bomb wasn't my fault. Crawford, I actually liked. He was a man who understood expedience.) These last two, they think they're safe. Doddering old fools. They think they've found sanctuary. Perhaps they live in that mist of age and encroaching senility that many mistake for peace. Well, they will not know peace much longer, and for them, there is no sanctuary. I'm certain that when Bhatia learns of it, he'll appreciate the gesture because it reinforces one of the first lessons I learned so very long ago from my oldest master: No witnesses.*

*Like dear old Marcus was. Oh, I'd pay good money to see Michi's face when he finally figures out the codes and discovers those little tokens of my esteem. To tell the truth, though, I'm a little disappointed. Michi's not nearly as imaginative or resourceful as I remember. You'd expect better from a trained investigator and, certainly, when we worked together, he was the most perceptive of the bunch, always the first to see the connections. That part of his cover story is, at least, no lie—though his name isn't Michi, either. Or Fraser. Ah, but what's in a name? Well, I'll tell you.*

*Richard: meaning rich or bountiful. Or Bounty.*

*Thereon, derived from Theron, meaning . . . Hunter.*

*You do the math.*

*Yet he and I are of a kind, kindred spirits down deep, that green armor the egg from which we've hatched. Only he's quite distressed. He wants to crawl back inside.*

*Not me. I don't need a shell anymore. I don't have to hide. Oh, I lurk in the shadows. I'm at home in the dark. I'm the flicker you see out of the corner of your eye. Turn your head, try to look at me—I'm gone.*

*But I have changed. Utterly. Completely. Like a butterfly emerging from a chrysalis. A process begun when Katana's kami poured into my body, in the instant I cried out for her soul. In a way, I've been born and in the birthing, willed Katana back to life.*

*I am the alpha and the omega: the beginning and the end. I am like Zeus from whom Athena sprung, fully formed. No, that's not right. I am a god. I am.*

*And perhaps, very soon, skin to hot blood, pounding heart to feverish desire, Katana shall know passion, that fiery ecstasy that only I can give. Soon, perhaps. Soon.*

*Because the Bounty Hunter is dead. And I am here, Katana. I am here.*

# About the Author

**Ilsa J. Bick** is a writer as well as a recovering psychiatrist. She is the author of prize-winning stories and novellas, including tales set in the Classic BattleTech universe (Battlecorps.com), including "Memories of Fire and Ice at the Edge of the World," "Break-Away" (the first installment of the *Proliferation Anthology*), and her most recent work, *The Gauntlet, Books I and II,* set in the weeks before the Steiner-Davion wedding.

Other work has appeared in *SCIFICTION, Challenging Destiny, Talebones, Beyond the Last Star, Subterranean* (with coauthor Tobias Buckell), *Paradox, Star Trek: New Frontier: No Limits,* and *Star Trek: Voyager: Distant Shores,* among many others. She has several *Star Trek: Starfleet Corps of Engineers* e-books to her credit; her next *SCE* e-book, *Ghost,* is forthcoming. Her first published novel, *Star Trek: The Lost Era: Well of Souls,* cracked the 2003 Barnes & Noble Bestseller List.

She is the author of *Daughter of the Dragon* and *Blood Avatar,* a MechWarrior murder mystery. *Dragon Rising* marks her third outing in the *MWDA* universe.

When she isn't working, she frets about when she'll find time to work again which, her long-suffering husband points out, is counterproductive. (Clearly, he's learned a thing or two, hanging around a shrink.) Then she usually has a martini—Belvedere, straight up, very dry, three olives—lies down, and waits for the feeling to go away.

# MECHWARRIOR: DARK AGE

## A BATTLETECH® SERIES

**AVAILABLE WHEREVER BOOKS ARE SOLD OR AT
PENGUIN.COM**

R020

# Classic Science Fiction & Fantasy
## from
# ROC

**2001: A Space Odyssey** by Arthur C. Clarke
Based on the screenplay written with Stanley Kubrick, this
novel represents a milestone in the genre.
"The greatest science fiction novel of all time." —*Time*

0-451-45799-4

**Robot Visions** by Isaac Asimov
Here are 36 magnificent stories and essays about Asimov's
most beloved creations—Robots. This collection includes
some of his best known and best loved robot stories.

0-451-45064-7

**The Forest House** by Marion Zimmer Bradley
The stunning prequel to *The Mists of Avalon*, this is
the story of Druidic priestesses who guard their ancient
rites from the encroaching might of Imperial Rome.

0-451-45424-3

**Bored of the Rings** by The Harvard Lampoon
This hilarious spoof lambastes all the favorite
characters from Tolkien's fantasy trilogy. An instant
cult classic, this is a must read for anyone who has ever
wished to wander the green hills of the shire—and after
almost sixty years in print, it has become a classic itself.

0-451-45261-5

S527